Madness of Flowers

A NOVEL OF THE CITY IMPERISHABLE

Other books by Jay Lake include:

Novels
Rocket Science
Trial of Flowers
Mainspring
Escapement
Green (forthcoming)

Collections
Greetings from Lake Wu
Green Grow the Rushes-Oh
American Sorrows
Dogs in the Moonlight
The River Knows Its Own

Edited Works
Polyphony, Volumes 1-6 (with Deborah Layne)
All-Star Zeppelin Adventure Stories (with David Moles)
TEL : Stories
Spicy Slipstream Stories (with Nick Mamatas)

MADNESS OF FLOWERS

A NOVEL OF THE CITY IMPERISHABLE

JAY LAKE

NIGHT SHADE BOOKS
SAN FRANCISCO

First Edition

Printed in Canada

ISBN-13   978-1-59780-098-3

Night Shade Books
Please visit us on the web at
http://www.nightshadebooks.com

This is for everyone who loved Bijaz,
and all the more for the people who found him dreadful.

Acknowledgment:
This book only exists because of the kind assistance of many people too numerous to fully list here. With apologies to whomever I manage to omit from my thank yous, I would like to offer gratitude to Kelly Buehler and Daniel Spector, Sarah Bryant, Michael Curry, Anna Hawley, Shannon Page, Ken Scholes, Jeremy Tolbert, Amber Eyes, and of course my entire blogging community in all their fractured magnificence. There are many others I have neglected to name: the fault is my memory, not your contributions.

I also want to recognize the Brooklyn Post Office here in Portland, Oregon, as well as the Fireside Coffee Lodge and Lowell's Print-Inn for all their help and support. Special thanks go to Jennifer Jackson, Night Shade Books, and Marty Halpern. As ever, errors and omissions are entirely my own responsibility.

The City Imperishable

I
POLLINATION

BIJAZ

He had quickly tired of divinity. There was a soul-satisfying warmth in opening his empty hand to find a flax seed or gaming chip. The trick never failed to amuse at dinners. But he had not been prepared for the expectation of spiritual purpose that accrued around him like flies on a street drunk.

Bijaz had always taken pride in being his own dwarf. Now he seemed to belong to everyone in the City Imperishable. Especially the Numbers Men, those strange gods who had gifted him with these powers and since remained obstinately absent from his life and his dreams.

"It's not so bad," he told his drinking glass. Bijaz sat in a café on the lower slopes of Heliograph Hill. The place smelled of steam and the mild spices of Rose Downs cooking. The chair was comfortable, perhaps too much so. The vintage, a straw-colored wine from beyond the Sunward Sea, tasted of dusk and romance and the warmth of distant shores.

Idly, he opened his left hand to dribble pale sand to the floor. The flow sparkled as it fell, catching the late afternoon sunlight.

"Building castles, are we?"

Kalliope. Tokhari war mistress, with spirals tattooed upon her cheeks and teeth stained blue from some ritual drug. Once she had been a child in the household he had managed. Sister to Jason the Factor, the dead man of winter who was now in hiding. Kalliope was a sandwalker, a desert mage, more than a month's ride from the edge of her domain.

And a friend to him, of sorts.

These days they were both strange, in a stranger land. Her camel riders had gone home, save for a lingering rearguard and a few would-be immigrants.

She, like Bijaz, had been touched by the noumenal. Also like him, she had been left wanting.

"Is this your desert I have grasped?" he asked politely.

She sat in the velvet chair next to his, reached to draw her fingers across the pale spray on the polished wooden floor. "No. Our sand is yellow as a coward's

1

liver, harder than the flat of a sword. This was made for dancing or lovemaking, not fighting."

"I should hope." He signaled for more wine. He had paid for nothing in months. Somehow that was bothersome, too. "Drink?" he asked, as the waiter approached, stiff in his formal whites.

"Water," Kalliope said. "Filtered through cork and silk. Nothing from the river." She looked back at Bijaz. "No wine. It brings dreams."

He let that pass. Far too many people asked him to interpret their dreams. *Will my number be lucky now?*

Why does the elephant stalk my sleep?

My grandmother won't quit shrieking.

The answers were always too easy. He had no idea if they were true, but people seemed satisfied. Then, once or twice a week, someone brought him a dream which lit white fire in his head.

That was when he cursed the Numbers Men. He might have died peacefully if not for their meddling.

Another wine was set before him, a tall blue goblet in front of Kalliope. The latening sun made the entire table glow. Drops beading off her glass were tiny diamonds, each a swelling reflection of the room. His wine swirled with motes from a distant harvest. Dampened, the table wood discharged the memory of forests.

"Trees," said Kalliope, stepping into his thoughts. "They walk. Not two-legged, like bark-clad men, but scrabbling on a thousand woody toes. Masts sliding with purpose through the soil."

"You dream of the timber harvest," Bijaz said almost automatically. He stared at the water-spattered tabletop. "The wealth of softwood come down the river from the Pilean Hills, the hardwoods carved out of the swamps along the Jade Coast."

"No." Palms flat on the table, disturbing the tiny droplet worlds, she leaned forward. "I am a sandwalker. My dreams are borne on the wind. I do not spend my sleeping hours considering economics, or the petty anxieties of foresters."

He looked up. Kalliope's eyes were storm gray, exactly the shade her brother Jason's had been before she'd killed him and brought him back. The same as their father, torn apart by a mob so many years before. Lenses, doors, opening in succession across the years. If he just stared hard enough into the black pool at the center of her gaze, he could see—

"You're glowing," she said.

Bijaz gripped the table's edge so hard his fingers ached. "I hate this."

"You would have died, otherwise."

"That was the idea. I only lacked the courage to do it all at once."

Her fingers brushed his, desert brown on city pale. "It takes more courage to live."

"Perhaps." He looked at the water droplets. Forests stood in each tiny lens, rippling like wheat in a summer field. "I know your dreams are real."

"You know too much."

"Yes." He released his hold on the past and took up the wine. The vintage seemed sour now. "We all gave too much."

They followed little streets and alleys toward the Limerock Palace. With the Imperator Restored cast down, being a wanderer was more-or-less safe again. No more monsters in the dark, sniffers or water fetches—the noumenal world had returned to the interplay of night and shadow.

The City Imperishable's usual run of beggars, pickpockets, footpads, and drunks abounded. They were as inevitable as head lice on a dockside whore.

"I've been wondering," Bijaz said. White rose petals fluttered from his fingertips toward the cobblestones, so many pale butterflies in evening's encroaching shade.

"Yes?"

Kalliope still moved with the bandy lope of an old Tokhari. She wasn't tall, for a full-woman, but Bijaz was still very conscious that his head barely came to the level of her breasts.

Almost six decades a dwarf in the City Imperishable and he still measured himself against those around him. *Enough*, he thought, though his gaze lingered on her body a moment longer.

"The last of your camel riders left the Sunrise Gate this past week. Yet you remain in the City Imperishable."

"My rearguard abides." He could hear the smile bending her voice. "I am not convinced they will ever leave."

It was a small force, but Bijaz knew that Lord Mayor Imago had his concerns. For example, the possibility of a more substantial Tokhari force lurking in the Rose Downs so long as their sandwalker remained in the City Imperishable. "And yourself?"

"The sand calls me back," she admitted.

They found themselves on Roncelvas Way. Downhill, the pale bulk of the Limerock Palace shone almost orange with the last of the daylight. Wind off the River Saltus carried the scent of spring from the Pilean Gardens within the palace walls.

"Do you wait for Jason?" asked Bijaz.

Kalliope had wrought a terrible sandwalker rite on her brother during the abortive Tokhari invasion of the City Imperishable, at the time of the Trial of Flowers. Between her death magick and the power of the Numbers Men, Jason had become *sula ma-jieni na-dja*, the dead man of winter. Since the overthrow of the Imperator Restored, he had gone into hiding.

"No, not him. I would see Jason again, but that is not need enough to keep me away from the sand."

"What then?" They passed two men pinned to the trunk of a linden tree in passionate embrace.

"We are not an order. Not like the philosophick doctors with their sworn convocations and bone-swallowing. Each sandwalker answers only to the spirits of her desert."

"Mmm?" A fig dropped from Bijaz's fingers. It glistened with dew from some distant morning. He snatched the fruit before it hit the ground, and sniffed. Rich, almost meaty. Riper than anything ever come in an oil-packed barrel.

He offered the fruit to Kalliope, who took it with an absent-minded murmur of thanks. She had become accustomed to his strange little miracles, unwanted and uncontrolled.

"The City Imperishable…" Her voice trailed off.

"She eats her children," said Bijaz softly, "this city of ours; eats them and spits them out again."

"I am Tokhari, skin and sweat." Kalliope sighed. "I have ridden the seven trials. I have seen three buried sunrises. I have prayed in each of the Red Cities. The sand took my spirit, and the sand gave it back to me."

She broke her stride. "I can do *this*." Kalliope closed her eyes and tightened her fist around the fig. She swayed slightly, focusing on some inward point. With a sizzling, crackling noise, a green tendril shot from each side of her hand.

The fig was sprouting. The cobbles at her feet smoked.

Bijaz was surprised. The magicks of the priests and petty arbogasters had always seemed mere sleights. His own experience of the Numbers Men had convinced Bijaz of the deep and abiding power of the noumenal, but that power did not lie in the hands of men. Or women.

He took the sprouted fig from her trembling grip. "I'd always thought sand-walkers a sort of tribal elder."

"And so we are." Kalliope resumed walking, with only a slight stumble. "But our deserts stretch a greater distance than a man can ride in a lifetime. Some are interrupted by oceans or forests or blackland farms, but there is always more desert. Between sky and sand, there is little room to mistake what one sees for what one wishes."

Bijaz laughed. "A man who walks far enough will find anything." That proverb was chiseled above the entrance to the old Messengers' Guild Hall.

She gave him a sidelong glance, her face almost puckish in the guttering of a corner gas light. "You of all people should understand the price and purpose of power."

"I maintain a firm hope in the segregation of the noumenal from the ordinary."

Kalliope laid a hand on his muscled forearm. He felt a crackle where she touched him, though her fingers were cool. Bijaz wondered when the tiny hairs curling across his skin had silvered.

"Power follows its own paths, my friend," she said. "The sand bids me stay awhile."

How long had it been since he'd simply made love? Perversions and miseries loomed in recent memory, but years had passed since Bijaz had laid his head upon his wife's breasts.

This woman could have been his granddaughter.

"I feel it, too," she told him. "I need it, too." She dropped her hand away. "But I fear the power more than I feel the need."

Bijaz felt regret mixed with relief. "I fear your dreams of trees, sandwalker."

"You should."

They walked on, sharing nothing more than each other's company.

ONESIPHOROUS

Big Sister paced his office. The floor creaked with her step. Onesiphorous had barely gotten used to the space himself—a wooden structure slung from the bottom of an arched stone bridge connecting two of the myriad islands that made up Port Defiance. Axos and Lentas, in this case. The interior plastering and door-high coastal-style windows made the room seem normal until a strong wind or a heavy step disturbed the balance. Then it felt like a giant cradle.

His cradle was being rocked by a woman as iron-gray as any senior Tribade, but rather more plump than normal for the sisterhood. Not so much maternal, which would have been strange enough, but matronly. Yet it was she who Biggest Sister had sent with him to Port Defiance.

Bells rang outside, a complex code concerning the harbor traffic. She stopped, cocked her head. "Sails sighted, inbound from the Sunward Sea, not a local flag."

The dwarf was amazed that Big Sister had picked it up so quickly. They'd arrived on the same riverboat nine days ago. He'd brought gold and commissions and official seals. She had brought a knife. Each of them was sent to step into the dissent fermenting beneath a thin crust of despatches wending up and down the Saltus.

To a dwarf from the City Imperishable, Port Defiance was as alien as the moon. To the south the sea climbed toward a horizon which could never quite be discerned for haze and the long slope of the world. North across the muddy waters of the Saltus delta lay the jungles of the Jade Coast, a viridian wall where moss-green monkeys and parrots brighter than the tears of demons shrieked.

East and west, the coast was an endless maze of swamps and jungles occasionally punctuated by the weathered stone outcrops on which the Jade Rush had been founded. Plantations rotted there as well, in water meadows or on cleared land.

Port Defiance was quite strange, with its close-crowded islands and rope bridges and stands of swamp-bound hardwoods. Too many city dwarfs lived here, most sent by Onesiphorous himself when things had been different in the City Imperishable. Too many disaffected scions of fallen houses, younger sons of Burgesses and trade factors brought by the Jade Rush half a generation past and now settled into louche disarray. Too many local families, stiff with contempt for the naïve parvenus disrupting their ancient prerogatives.

Worst of all were the fights. Not between settlers and locals, but amongst the dwarfs themselves. Demagoguery and sheer incitement mixed dangerously with the hardest question to come to his people in half a thousand years.

"You have a better ear than I," Onesiphorous admitted.

She quirked him a smile as she spun on her heel for another pass across his office. "Men never learn to listen."

"I'm listening now."

"No you're not. You're thinking. You're wondering, *What's she want today? Why has she come into my office with that look in her eye?* That's not listening, little man, that's looking ahead."

"And what would listening be?"

She stopped, the smile lingering a bit this time. "A listener might use his eyes as well as his ears. Have you ever seen me walk with a limp? Where is the copper butterfly I wear in my hair? Why is my right boot stained brown? What would bring me here in such haste, yet be so difficult to discuss that I would comment on the bells rather than simply arrive at the point?"

"You and I listen differently."

"We learned in different schools," she said. "You'd best lesson yourself in my ways if you plan to survive here."

"As I am a fool, please do me the courtesy of enlightenment."

"I came to report one thing, but on the way found cause for my loss of courage. There are two dwarfs floating out to sea right now who tried to permanently interrupt my trip."

"You were attacked." He managed to make it a statement rather than a question.

"Indeed."

"By singularly stupid dwarfs, I would think." Onesiphorous marveled at the foolhardiness of anyone attempting assault against a senior Tribade sister.

"I would also think." She stopped in front of his desk. "Lord Mayor Imago sent you here to act as his deputy. Neither of you understood what that would mean. Today it meant two dwarfs tried to kill me. Tomorrow they could be after you."

"Slashed or Sewn?"

Big Sister leaned forward. "*Both*. One of each."

Onesiphorous' heart skipped a cold, slow beat. "You jest."

"Would that I did."

Back in the City Imperishable, Slashed and Sewn had been implacable opponents, albeit through debate rather than murder. The Slashed were in a sense his. Onesiphorous had led the movement of discontented dwarfs who cut away their traditional lip stitches, abandoned fingertalk, and struggled for social and legal recognition. The Sewn clung to old ways, fighting to preserve the quiet power their kind had always weilded in the City Imperishable.

The two groups had come together only in the autumn of the past year, as the politics of the City Imperishable had for a while turned fatal. Onesiphorous and Bijaz, a leader of the Sewn, reluctantly cooperated to evacuate dwarf families from danger. Rather to his surprise, many of those then sent downriver to Port Defiance had since been in no hurry to return.

Now the dwarfs had found a new passion to divide them in novel and terrible ways.

"Do you know why they tried to kill you?"

She shrugged. "A message, perhaps. They shouted no slogans when they attacked, and had no dying words when I was finished with them."

"Will you exact further vengeance?" The Tribade was known for slow and thorough punishment.

"I would be forced to chastise half the dwarfs in this miserable place," Big Sister said. "I scarcely see the point. It should be enough that they do not return to their plotting. Let their fellows wonder."

"Wonder, indeed. My thanks for your restraint. What errand were you about before your interruption?"

She tapped her lips with an index finger. "There is a citizens' council forming. I was asked to participate."

"Ah." Port Defiance had been under the control of the City Imperishable since before the days of the long-vanished empire. Local lore held that the port had once been the seat of a mighty thalassocracy—something Onesiphorous found doubtful.

Various forms of governance had pertained over the centuries, ranging from a Judge-Intendant to a Board of Visitors to a Commissioner. In recent years, one local syndic or another had served by appointment as Harbormaster, who also stood as chief executive on behalf of the City Imperishable's Assemblage of Burgesses. That post was currently held by Borold Sevenships.

More to the point, administration of Port Defiance was *not* part of the Lord

Mayor's responsibilities. Onesiphorous was here purely as a representative. He had no power over the affairs of this city. The Assemblage of Burgesses being in continued disarray, as a practical matter there was no higher authority attending to affairs here.

Hence, someone had dreamt up a citizens' council. "They intend treason?"

"They would scarcely name it that."

"Are dwarfs involved in this idiocy?"

"Yes. Slashed and Sewn alike."

Affairs in Port Defiance definitely needed tending to. He asked the next logical question. "Boxers?"

She nodded.

And there hung the crux of the thing. Should the traditional growing boxes be reduced to kindling and burned for a sacrifice? Or was there significance in being a dwarf of the City Imperishable once beyond those ancient, crumbling walls?

That was the crucial temptation here in Port Defiance: In a single generation, dwarfs could end their kind's time under the sun. Let the children grow freely. Once they were all full-men, no one would ever think to box a child again. Without the customs of the City Imperishable to constrain them, why would anyone subject their children to that terrible pain?

So said the Openers.

The Boxers decried the death of their race, the loss of their power, the melting of the dwarf families into the sea of full-men which covered the endless length of the world.

It was not a question of Slashed and Sewn, of politics and tradition. People would kill for tradition, but they would die for their children.

"Boxers." Onesiphorous drummed his fingers. He'd always detested the practice of boxing. Given all that business with the Old Gods after the Trial of Flowers, the purpose of dwarfs was so much more important: harbingers of the power and fortune of the City Imperishable.

Even though he'd spent years promoting the Slashed cause, he found himself in sympathy with the Boxers. He didn't want to imagine a world without dwarfs. The pain of the box was a price. What they gained for it could be debated endlessly, but his people *did* gain. Their home, the center of all things dwarf, was the City Imperishable.

And the City gained all the more. *Civitas est.*

"Why break away?" Onesiphorous let his line of thought drift loose.

"Control? Perhaps they fear reform at home." Big Sister leaned close. It was like being leered at by a homicidal grandmother. "I told them I'd meet with the council."

"Perhaps that was why someone sought to kill you."

One last smile. "See? You can listen if you put your mind to it."

With that, she was gone.

Onesiphorous let himself feel the gentle sway of the room a while as he watched the windows for the inbound vessel. Port Defiance was like a ship filled with unknown cargo, every crate a volatile surprise. He had no authority here, but neither did any council which might form.

And it galled him to trust the Tribade in this matter. Onesiphorous barely understood their ambitions, and he could imagine any number of advantages they might see in an independent Port Defiance.

He watched awhile, until even his untrained eyes could espy the sail visible beyond the curve of Barlowe's Finger.

IMAGO

"You are to be having an army as I am to be having a parade of washerwomen," said Captain Enero of the Winter Boys.

They were in Lord Mayor Imago's wedge-shaped office on the topmost level of the Rugmaker's Cupola. He'd moved two floors up from the tower's third level after the fall of the Imperator Restored to better his view and make a point about his oversight of the City Imperishable.

The floor was covered with hand-woven rugs, the walls papered over with maps, charts, and great running lists. Morning sunlight made a bright glare of his view south and west toward the river. He had not yet found time, or sufficient commitment, to relocate to the Limerock Palace. Besides, here he was under no one's control but his own.

Imago growled, a wordless mumble of frustration. He turned his remade chain of office over in his fingers, feeling the cool solidity of the new-cut gems. Finally: "I am well aware of that problem, my friend."

To say the training of the City Men had gone poorly would have been a kindness. The bailiffs had to a man refused transfer into the new force. Green Kelly's so-called Restorationists were disbanded, and no one sane wanted them under arms again. Most of Imago's early recruits had returned home to their jobs and families.

As a result, the walls of the City Imperishable continued to be guarded by the Winter Boys, a company of southern freeriders originally hired by the twice-late Imperator Restored prior to his accession to the Bladed Throne. Technically mutineers, Enero's men had acquitted themselves well opposing that brief, bloody reign.

Now they wanted to go home.

"I am to be receiving ever more pointed letters from the south," the mercenary commander added. "Higher authority is to be calling me home."

"Though the Tokhari have mostly departed, there are still several hundred Yellow Mountain tribesmen camped outside the River Gate." Imago rubbed his eyes—he was still troubled by the newly odd proportions of his body. "They seem in no hurry to return to their peaks."

"Men from the upper valleys. Until the high passes are clearing, there is being no point in their departure."

"I suppose they'd just fight if they rode home with the others."

"To be taking their women and horses, yes. This is being sport for them while awaiting the thaw."

A diffident knock echoed gently. Imago nodded and Enero tugged the handle.

It was Marelle, a pale dwarfess and one of the endless round of people seemingly needed to accomplish anything. "There is an incident in the street," she said. "At Little Loach Close, near the Spice Market."

"Fighting?" Imago and Enero shared a startled look.

"Not exactly. Arguing, I think." She glanced at a piece of paper clutched in her hand. "A runner came, from the Water Captain's office. They're worried."

Imago stumped across the room, each shortened footfall still a bit of a surprise, and took the despatch. The note was simple enough, written in a swift copperplate hand.

I urgently wish to inform the Lord Mayor of a disturbance in the Spice Market, requiring his full and immediate attention. Respectfully, Moraine Simpkins, Associate Water Captain, Northern Districts.

"No detail?"

"How would I know?" she asked with asperity. "A boy brought it in. He wanted two orichalks for his trouble. A runner, nothing more."

"I trust you tipped him?" Imago turned the note over. An ordinary piece of foolscap. The City bought the stuff by the wagonload from the Paper and Card Cooperative. Nothing to be learned from that.

"Boys are a city's best friend," she said.

Enero leaned over Imago's shoulder to look more closely at the letter. "You are to be going to the Spice Market now?"

"I've had a hankering for ginger all morning."

The curtained carriage rolled to a stop amid the racket of a crowd—not the full-throated roar of riot, but more like a festival out of place. Enero placed a finger on his lips and slipped a pistol from his belt. "Being a moment," he whispered, then pushed open the door and rolled out in a smooth, rapid motion.

Imago waited, bouncing impatiently on the leather bench. It would be beneath his dignity to draw the curtains and peer out.

How things have changed, he thought. During the desperate days of the Trial of Flowers, he would have been with Enero, sword in hand. But the Old Gods had made him over—now he was only four feet tall, with stumpy legs that pained every step. The wealth of the City Imperishable had been gleaned on the backs of the City's dwarfs, almost all of them specially grown so in their boxes. Being *made* short, on the other hand, galled him.

The pain was another matter. Jason might have reveled in it, but Jason had his own troubles now, grave-deep. Imago could hardly complain in the face of that.

The noise outside dissolved to raucous laughter. Enero opened the carriage door. "To be coming, then?"

"Of course," Imago said smoothly. He allowed the freerider to help him down.

There were hundreds here, if not more, spilling into the streets around the Spice Market. Someone was performing from the sound of it—another wave of laughter flowed across the crowd.

"To be following." Enero found his way to a wall.

They walked along the slimed brick, behind a series of stalls which reeked of roots and soil and dark things beneath the earth, before reaching a rickety wooden stair. Enero led the way up to a landing.

There Imago could see.

The Spice Market had ceased operation. At this hour there should have been buyers from the restaurants and chophouses, not to mention guildhalls, temples, and every other place with a kitchen. A great many people were going to be disappointed tonight if this gathering did not soon disperse.

From here he could see people crowded in around the market tables and standing amid the racks and barrels of peppers, herbs, and powders. Everyone watched a stage set up atop a large wagon, parked on the far side of the market from the landing Imago occupied. A white bear danced upon planks, wearing a harness of silver bells and blue silken cords. Three dark men with bone flutes played its tune. The only rhythm was the pounding of the bear's feet upon the wood.

Imago could not decide whether to be amused or irritated. "I was called out to see a dancing bear?"

"To be taking note of the men with flutes."

"I see," said Imago.

"From the north, I am to be thinking."

"You figure north because of the white bear?"

"I am thinking north because the Spice Market is being close to the River Gate."

The music came to a close in a skirling disharmony foreign to Imago's ears. The bear thumped its right foot three times on the planks and bowed. A shower of coins rose from the crowd to rattle onto the stage. The bear plucked a single bell from its harness and threw the bauble in a high overhand toss that seemed very human.

Imago watched hundreds of faces lift as the glittering bit flew in a great arc. He held out his hands. With the inevitability of prophecy, the bell landed there.

Enero grunted.

When the Lord Mayor looked back at the stage, the bear was gone, as were its pipers. A woman stood there now. She was of middling height, pale as any native of the City Imperishable, with chestnut hair. Not of Northern blood, despite Enero's assertion, though she wore Northern garb—a blue silk cloak matching the bear's harness, richly trimmed with pale fur. She did not appear to have any weapons about her. What she did have was the crowd's undivided attention.

"You have seen a spectacle." Her voice was ordinary, yet it carried across the expanse of the market square as firmly as if she were standing beside Imago. She turned and began to pace. The motion threw her cloak out in a billowing cloud the color of the sky. "Did it please you?"

The crowd roared their approval.

She stopped, the noise stopping with her. "Your city is nothing but spectacle. Your lives are a diversion. Madness came and went in your streets, and they called it *flowers*. I come to bring you a true spectacle. Worthy of your great City Imperishable and its timeless history. Worthy even of *empire*."

Her voice made that last word a spell and a curse at the same time, raising Imago's hackles.

The crowd roared once more. This time she waited them out. Impassive. Radiating cool power.

"She missed her calling," Imago said quietly. "The Burgesses could never stand before her."

"Your Burgesses are never being women, I am thinking."

"There is that. Thank the Old Gods she doesn't make her home here, or I'd be out of a job."

"I know something." The woman leaned forward slightly. The entire crowd leaned toward her in response. "I know where your secrets are buried." She straightened, threw her arms wide. "I know where your Imperator Terminus fell, to be entombed with his jeweled gods and his gold and silver treasures and coin enough to fund an army marching across half the world."

This brought a ragged cheer. "With your help, I can bring the power and the glory back to the City Imperishable." Her gaze locked with Imago's.

"By Dorgau's syphilitic paps," said the Lord Mayor.

Enero nodded. "You are being in great trouble, my friend."

BIJAZ

He set out from the Temple of Inordinate Vice in search of lunch. Bijaz found two of Enero's Winter Boys astride their horses on the temple steps. Both smiled to see him.

"To be having the time for coming now, little dwarf?" asked Malvo, a grinning ape of a man with whom Bijaz had spent time drinking. He had three wives and four children, or perhaps the reverse, in ports along the Sunward Sea.

"To be having a choice, polygamist?"

"Ah, he is gaming." Malvo added something rapid in a Sunward language Bijaz did not speak. The Winter Boy hauled the dwarf bodily onto the cantle of his saddle. A spray of orange butterflies erupted like so much bright fire. "We are being off now."

It was not a pleasant ride. The only virtue of the trip was brevity. The midday streets were crowded, with a strange rhythm to the traffic which reminded Bijaz of the unrest of the past autumn. The ride along Cork Street was especially annoying due to a right-of-way dispute with the tram. Soon enough they were across the Bridge of Chances and hieing up Nannyback Hill, deep into the territory of the Numbers Men—a locale Bijaz avoided of late.

He preferred to stay south of the Little Bull as much as possible. The Numbers Men had been his patrons, saviors even, yet he felt a profound discomfort whenever his thoughts turned to them.

The rapid pace was a favor, he realized. Bijaz's divinity was well known in the City Imperishable—hence the open doors and welcome tables at every turn. He was widely considered a dwarfen symbol of the City's luck. As such he found it difficult to wander freely without being accosted time and again.

They soon arrived at the vast edifice of the Rugmaker's Cupola. The distinctive spiral-striped tower had been built long ago of red and yellow desert sandstone as an outpost of the Tokhari when they came to render tribute to the Imperators of the City Imperishable. The Worshipful Guild of Rugmakers who now controlled it had given their tower over to Imago when the Lord Mayor's accession had been in dispute.

Malvo unceremoniously dumped Bijaz at the entrance. "Not to be climbing too fast," he said with a laugh.

Bijaz flicked a handful of flax seed at the freerider. "Give my regards to your wives."

He turned to make the long ascent to Imago's office, only to find the Lord Mayor standing in the doorway with a grim expression on his face.

Imago eschewed the winding stairs and instead headed down a back hall Bijaz had never before used. He realized that it must connect to the larger complex next door. The smells were different, too, dominated by the spicy pungency of Tokhari cooking.

Then they were in a room with an enormous rectangular table topped by wooden panels. The chamber had the air of long disuse—threadbare wall hangings, cobwebs in the chair legs. Three narrow windows let in a bit of light. Enero waited, along with the pale, crook-backed little dwarfess who worked for Imago. Marelle, that was her name.

"Why here?" Bijaz asked.

"Rumor control." Imago's tone was clipped. "And a map, if we need one."

"You have maps in your office."

"There are being maps and there are being maps," said Enero, with a glance at the table.

It was a very big table, Bijaz realized. "If you want to start a rumor, having me dragged through the streets is a good way to do it. Besides, I'm hungry." He slapped the wood, leaving a tracery of dark, glistening fluid in the pattern of his palm.

"Marelle," said Imago.

She slipped out the door. Enero sniffed at the handprint. "Lamp oil," he said. "That is being a useful trick if you are controlling it."

"Hardly."

Marelle swiftly returned with a bowl of mashed chickpeas, a small plate of olives, and several fingers of a strong, salty cheese the color of a drowned man's belly. The food was accompanied by four warm rounds of Tokhari flatbread. "Thank you," Bijaz said before he popped an olive in his mouth.

He realized the three of them were staring at him.

"Talk," he mumbled as he chewed. "My ears are not eating."

"A woman has come to town," Imago began.

"Marvelous." Bijaz broke off a piece of the cheese. "I understand there has been a shortage lately."

"Not—" The Lord Mayor broke off. "We have a problem. She claims to have found the tomb of the Imperator Terminus. With much of his treasure still within."

Bijaz choked on a sliver of flatbread. "That's insane."

"If it is being true, it is being bad for your city," Enero said.

"We just got rid of one Imperator," Marelle added. "We don't want another. Even if he has been dead for centuries."

"The last one was dead, too," Bijaz said, "and he didn't work out so well. Imperator Terminus marched over the horizon six hundred years ago and never came back. Took a rotting lot of gods and priests and bureaucrats with him, I believe." *Archer would have known*, he thought, then put the godmonger's memory right out of his head. Archer's kind had virtually vanished from the streets since the battle of Terminus Plaza, another minor mystery in the ongoing existence of the City Imperishable.

A pity, too. How much that poor dwarf could have helped him now. Bijaz flexed a fist, willing that no raisins or pebbles dribble out of it.

"It doesn't matter whether it's *true*," Imago said. "It matters whether people believe her."

Enero nodded. "She was to be making speeches in the Spice Market. With a dancing bear. The people of the City Imperishable were to be cheering."

"She's a mountebank. The Temple District is full of them. I should know, I *am* a god."

Silence followed that statement.

"And…?" he finally said.

"Her dancing bear threw me *this*." Imago tossed something small and bright onto the table. It jangled as it rolled.

Bijaz picked the thing up. Round, like a little harness bell. There was a slit at the bottom, and a smaller bit of metal within. Something stamped along the edge, the words too worn for him to read.

"*Civitas est*," said Marelle. "The city is. Our words. That's a bell from a herald's cloak, six or seven centuries old. There's several on display down at the Limerock Palace."

"We checked," Imago added.

Bijaz rang it next to his ear. "A dancing bear threw you a six-hundred-year-old bell from one of our own uniforms. And you think that it doesn't matter if her claim is true."

"It *doesn't* matter." Imago began to walk the boundaries of the great table. "True or not, she's a liar and a cheat, out for gain very much at our expense. A sensible explorer would have come to me." He paused, a sour look on his face. "Me or the Assemblage of Burgesses. Not made a public show of it, like some traveling fair."

Bijaz laughed. "And a sensible Lord Mayor might well have shipped that explorer off to the Sunward Sea at the bottom of a crate of pickled melons. There are truths too dangerous to set into the world."

"Perhaps." At that moment Imago looked capable of sending a full dozen explorers to their untimely deaths.

"The people are scarcely over their disarray from the recent unpleasantness," Marelle said. "This sort of thing will only incite new unrest."

"Absolutely," said Bijaz. "And if she produces the very body of the late Imperator Terminus, whose face is on every coin, we have a crisis of government. I believe we just resolved one of those."

"A problem for the Burgesses." Imago snorted. "I am Lord Mayor. A parade of Imperators will not change that. No, if she produces the very body of the late Imperator Terminus, we will have disruption on a grand scale. Almost half the City dwarfs are still hiding down in Port Defiance. Many may never come home. Do you know what wages for a skilled clerk are these days? Factors and trading houses are cutting back for a lack of them. That puts laborers on the street without pay. We thought the end of the Ignatius business would set things to rights, but the dwarfs had been pushed too far.

"Worse, there are almost no families with children in boxes. In five years' time, a skilled clerk will command tenfold even today's inflated wage. If there is anyone left to hire him."

"Or her," said Marelle.

Imago glared sidelong at the dwarfess.

"You don't want people haring off after some tomb," said Bijaz. "Fair enough."

"Not just that." Imago's voice was quiet, now drained of its frustrated passion. "I don't want people *believing* in that tomb. The dwarfs need to come home. I've sent Onesiphorous down to the Jade Coast to try to bring that about. Without them, our city will see such change as to bankrupt us all. With them, we can resume trading half the goods in this corner of the world."

"Yet you cannot kill her now, or run her out in dark of night. If she has raised a crowd in the Spice Market, too many already know of her."

"And she did excellently well." Imago sat down in one of the chairs. "There are few who could speak against her and be believed."

"No," said Bijaz, as understanding dawned. "I'm not taking to the streets against this mountebank. Let her raise some money, leave town. It's nothing to do with me."

Enero stepped to the table, collected Bijaz's plate and bowl. "You are being the City's little god." He set them on a chair. "You are being loved by many. Listened to, even. Other gods are being dead, or freaks. You are being special." He grabbed the edge of the table and began to pick up the first of the panels.

It was map beneath, Bijaz realized. The tabletop was little more than a thin wooden screen covering a map twenty feet long and half as tall.

"Even if I go shout her down in the market," he said, "so what?"

"So this." Imago looked at the map. "Somewhere in the North lies the Imperator Terminus' remains. This woman may have found the tomb. She had the bell, after all. We need to know where."

"You just told me it doesn't matter if it's true."

"You cannot be affording to think otherwise," Enero answered.

Bijaz shrugged. A crust of snow clung to each open palm. "North, you say?"

ONESIPHOROUS

He paid a boy to row him out to Barlowe's Finger. The tide was slack, which meant two or three hours before he would be forced to head back. Even then, they'd be moving with the water, not against it.

Barlowe's Finger was more a rock than an island. It struck skyward sixty feet at low tide, rising stark from the foaming sea and making no compromise for its waterline. The Finger crooked slightly as if to beckon. A tiny stone dock jutted from the base. Generations of visitors had worn an upward path.

He hadn't been out here before, though various locals and City dwarfs had commended a visit to him. "You'll never get the spirit of Port Defiance 'til you've climbed the Finger," he was told over and over.

With rebellion in the air, Onesiphorous very much wished he did have the spirit of the place in the palm of his hand.

"Putting in," said the boy. A full-man youth, his name was Boudin. Pretty boy, too. Onesiphorous would wager on some beautiful sisters. "Mind the step," Boudin added.

Onesiphorous stood unsteady in the front of the little boat. The dock towered above him at this turn of the tide. An iron ladder was slimed with seaweed and moss. He timed the rise and fall of the boat to lean forward and grasp the rungs. As he put his weight on the ladder, barnacles cut sorely into his palms, but there was no helping it. The boat had already slipped away.

Resolving not to curse, he climbed.

The path followed vagaries of rock and weather, with no accounting for the shortness of dwarfs. As he inched his way around the Finger, Onesiphorous wondered whether any of his helpful recommenders had made this climb themselves.

The path was sometimes no wider than one of his feet. There was very little vegetation. Onesiphorous had a selection of slick rock and tiny vines with which to brace himself. Everything smelled of gulls and the sea.

Sixty feet didn't sound like so much until one had to climb it in an erratic, rising spiral. Three times around the Finger he stretched himself, reaching and pulling and stepping, before he found the top: a roughly flat area that covered fissured stone, gravel, and scraggly grass. Some helpful soul had affixed a brass marker in the middle.

The plate was small and round, with an arrow pointing inland, the words PORT DEFIANCE around the edge.

Onesiphorous lowered himself to a tailor's seat, legs folded together. The sea seemed so very close all around him, patterns of foam racing over the bottle-green swells. It made him feel as if Barlowe's Finger were moving.

He looked up instead at Port Defiance.

From the ocean side it was a different city.

Barlowe's Finger was the rock most distant from shore. A few jags further out came and went with the tide, but they scarcely counted. This was the beginning of Port Defiance, and the end of the City Imperishable's writ.

The Sunward Sea stretched southward behind him. The Southern Ocean lay beyond it. Port Defiance occupied the mouth of the River Saltus, an indifferent river delta blending with the forested swamps of the Jade Coast. Due to the lack of stable land along the shoreline, the city had been built on a collection of islets, rocks, and gravel bars standing off from the river's debouchment, wherever buildings could be raised high enough to withstand the occasional storm surges. These rocky outcroppings were part of the same irregular scattering of stone which dotted the Jade Coast for a hundred miles, some hosting the rich veins which had given the region its name. Bridges connected close-standing portions of the city, along with a network of ferries for wider channels.

Nearest to him, just north of Barlowe's Finger, were the Gaterocks—curved pillars facing one another, each tall as his current perch. They were bare of construction. He had been told they'd once supported a great arch. Onesiphorous fancied he could see the lines of caryatids weathered into the curves of stone.

He tried to imagine standing above the tide for half a lifetime to carve your goddess—or perhaps your queen—in the face of storm and sun and sea.

The city spread out past the Gaterocks. Clusters and groupings of the outcroppings were analogous to districts back in the City Imperishable. To the west he could see the low, blocky warehouses of Loska. Almost directly north, through the Gaterocks, were the Fairwinds. Beyond them loomed the Ivories, including his own Axos and Lentas. Borold Sevenships held court in the Ivories, too, in the Flag Towers, a keep that leapt across five or six foundation rocks with the sea ever churning beneath its arches.

The city ran on, marbled mansions side by side with the meanest driftwood shacks. Height meant wealth—further from the rage of the waters, when the worst came.

So many flags, so many boats bobbing, so many people toiling at the marge of the ocean.

So many dwarfs unwilling to go home. Here was an entire city unboxed, opened to the sea and the land, riding the tongue of the river. Port Defiance was so different from the City Imperishable crouched behind its walls, a withered shadow of what had once been a great empire. The City was a dwarf. This place was so many stone ships already on the ocean.

He might not have seen it so, had he not made the trip out here.

Boudin would be another hour coming back to fetch him. Onesiphorous spent his time watching the play of light on water, and trying to frame a letter to Imago which would make sense of what was happening here. Boxers and Openers. Dwarfs, changing as they had not in half a thousand years. The legacy of the Trial of Flowers stretched onward in unexpected ways.

Watching Boudin pull in from the city, Onesiphorous was startled by a shadow passing overhead. It was large enough to block the late sun. An Alate spilled air from its wings and dropped to share his pillar.

The flyers had circled the City Imperishable during the past autumn, eventually fighting on behalf of Enero in the winter battle that had overthrown the Imperator Restored. Onesiphorous had never understood their loyalties. Or indeed, whether they were a strange species of men or just creatures with intelligent faces and sharp weapons.

Up close the Alate seemed less human than from a distance. It was unclothed but for a harness which held three darts and a slim-bladed sword close to its body, exposing its slate-gray skin to the elements. The face was sculpted for wind. The features were almost manlike, except the yellow eyes with no dot of a pupil. The body was less familiar—the Alate had an enormous chest through which very narrow ribs showed, a thin waist, exaggerated hips with a featureless groin, arms and legs that seemed permanently bent. The wings were spread wide, balancing the Alate on the wind—feathered, with long, bright pinions contrasting with the skin. It smelled like a bird's nest.

Though he did not suppose his life was at risk, Onesiphorous lost several breaths to the racing of his heart. Why was the creature here? What did it want?

It opened one fist and extended a hand, palm upward.

Onesiphorous took what the Alate offered.

A silver bell. Something from a dog's harness, or a child's toy. He jingled it, feeling foolish as he wondered if some snow demon or Tokhari jinn would appear. "Thank you."

"Some debts are never forgiven," the Alate replied in a voice that piped like a child's.

He had not known they could talk.

The Alate nodded once, stepped back, and fell from the top of the rock. Its wings snapped to catch the wind before it skimmed off close to the surface of the water.

Onesiphorous tucked the bell into an inner pocket of his tunic and began the laborious process of climbing down. He had to focus on the footholds and handholds, but still he wondered what the encounter had meant.

A bell.

Why?

Even if it was pure silver, the thing was too small to hold much value. And the creatures had never come near him during the struggle. Jason had believed they might have been Ignatius' kidnappers, spiriting the Second Counselor away before he had returned to such disastrous effect as the Imperator Restored.

These Alates were no one's friends, in other words. Except possibly Enero's. The freerider gave good counsel but kept his own thoughts close as his skin.

Perhaps the southern mercenary would understand the bell.

Onesiphorous raised his eyes from the rock to see if Boudin was close. In doing so he lost his balance and tumbled into open air.

Where was that damned dock? *Too late*, he thought, arms and legs flailing though there was nothing to catch except the chilly water below.

He hit the ocean hard enough to knock his wind, breaking the surface amid a cloud of bright bubbles. The chill more than the impact robbed his will. Onesiphorous struggled for the light—he was no waterman, but panic had not yet trapped him.

Gasping, he found the surface in time for a rope to hit him on the head.

"Grab the line!" shouted Boudin.

Onesiphorous grabbed. He was then offered the blunt end of a boathook. With help from the boy, the soaked dwarf tumbled into the boat. He felt wretched.

"Here, sir," the boy said with a grin. "I have a blanket and some hot tea."

"Real tea, or some swamp swill?" Onesiphorous immediately regretted his words. "I'm sorry, Boudin."

"S'ok." The boy pulled at the oars, not meeting the dwarf's eyes. Then: "Don't make mock, sir."

Snake eaters, he'd been told in the port city. Jungle rats with no more sense than monkeys, not living in real houses nor doing honest labor. Onesiphorous understood prejudice, but his work here was among the dwarf refugees, not the local underclass. Still, he knew nothing more than the dismissive rumors.

"I didn't mean to." He huddled under the blanket. "I'm just…" He patted for the bell. It was still in the inner pocket.

"Everywhere's got its magick," Boudin went on, stubbornly. "Herblore and whatnot. Jungle's no different."

Onesiphorous shivered. "And it makes no matter to me, boy. Just take me home and I'll pay you double in thanks for the kindness of the blanket."

"A lizard told me you was going to fall," said Boudin with a shy smile.

"I see."

All the way back to the jetty at Lentas, Onesiphorous could hear the bell faintly jingling with the movements of the boat.

The day bells rang the trade exchanges closed just before Onesiphorous climbed the winding stair from the jetty. A group of clerks clattered by, the young full-men shouting as they pushed past him.

They barely knew he was there.

His joints ached. He made the first walkway, the tier known on most islands as the Tidewatch. There he paused a moment to let his legs tremble.

A young dwarf approached. Sandy-haired, pale-skinned, eyes brown as a polished nut, wearing the traditional muslin wrappings of their kind. Perneto, that was the name. A runner and aspiring clerk to the Stone House Factoring Cooperative—one of the local businesses that some of the City dwarfs had bought into after fleeing south.

Onesiphorous had been something of a rabble-rouser, to put it mildly, before he'd become a bureaucrat. In both lines of work, a good memory for names and faces was nigh essential. "Hello, Perneto."

"S-s-s-sir." The young dwarf blushed. A distinct reek of sudden perspiration washed outward.

By Dorgau's ruby testicle, thought Onesiphorous with a flood of pity, here's one not suited for a commercial life. He smiled, trying to breathe through his mouth without being obvious. "Yes?"

"Master B-b-brace s-s-sent me."

Surely the lad was used to how he affected people. Onesiphorous took a great gasp. "My best regards to Master Brace."

Perneto looked confused. "B-b-but I have not d-d-d-delivered the m-m-message yet."

"Of course." He waved a hand. "Please, carry on." It took an act of will not to echo the poor dwarf's stammer.

"I am ch-ch-charged to t-t-tell you that B-b-b-orold S-s-s-even-sh-sh-sh—"

"Sevenships," Onesiphorous said quickly, not waiting for Perneto to find his way out of the other end of the name.

"Yes." The younger dwarf glared. "He is t-t-t-treating with c-c-corsairs. F-f-from the S-s-sunward Sea."

"Ah." Onesiphorous didn't know what to make of this news. Corsairs and trade factors were natural enemies as much as wolves and shepherds. "Was there m-more?" Thunder and ruin, he'd gone and slipped into the boy's stammer.

"I don't kn-n-n-ow." Perneto looked miserable.

"My thanks."

The young dwarf stood, shifting his weight. Did he want a tip? "Are you hungry, lad?"

Perneto nodded.

Onesiphorous fished into his pocket and found a silver obol. Far more than a few minutes of a messenger's time was worth, but he'd given the last of his chalkies to Boudin the boat boy. "Here," he said, "go eat well."

As Perneto scuttled away, Onesiphorous walked slowly along the Tidewatch, jingling the Alate's bell. He wasn't certain this had anything to do with him, really, but Sevenships talking to corsairs didn't bode well. He wished he knew who he could trust here in Port Defiance.

It was time to talk to Big Sister again. And add this news to his next letter to Imago.

IMAGO

They spent the next several hours looking over the map table. Not even the redoubtable Enero had been further north than Sourapple Roads, less than a day's ride past the River Gate.

The map itself was an ancient masterpiece. It depicted the lands of the old empire, ranging from the Silver Ridges in the north to the Yellow Mountains in the west, and the great extent of plains and hills southeast along the Sunward Sea to the old tributary ports and the Tokhari deserts beyond. Cities and garrisons were marked with dusty pockholes which might once have contained gems. The boundaries of provinces lost to history were marked as well, painted borders crossing what were now wildlands or tribal strongholds or young nations with no memory of the Bladed Throne. Bright bars from the narrow windows marched across the map as the day went on.

What interested Imago the most was the northern boundary. Where had this mountebank come from? What could she possibly have found that would have given up the little silver bell from the time of Imperator Terminus?

"There are being only five good passes beyond the Silver Ridges," Enero said, pacing the north edge of the table—one of the longer sides. "To be seeing the marks? All of them were having a fortress at one time."

Bijaz ran his finger along a border, leaving behind a trail of grime. "Presuming she didn't rob a museum or dig up some grave in the Rose Downs, she still could have found Terminus anywhere between here and there."

"It is being your history."

"No," said Imago. "If the Imperator Terminus had died within the borders of the old empire, he wouldn't be a mystery. He marched *out* of history, remember."

"Or into it," said Bijaz.

Marelle studied the map. "The Whitetowers archives are in the old Footsoldiers' Guild Hall. We should look there, see what they said about that."

"What are the Whitetowers archives being?" asked Enero.

Imago looked up. "I'm afraid I don't know."

"The old universities," said Bijaz. Marelle nodded. "Abandoned, what, four, five hundred years ago?"

The dwarfess pointed to a bend in the Saltus far to the north and west of the City Imperishable, where the river made its closest approach to the Silver Ridges. "Here. There were four of them in the old days. Imperatorial University, now over in the Wine District, is the only surviving school. They moved it down the river after the Grain Rebellion, *anno* 202 Imperator Terminus. When the empire was collapsing. The Saltus School was founded about the same time by refugee faculty from two of the other universities."

Imago was fascinated. "The empire lost three universities? But kept their archives?"

She looked up. "A dwarfess named Marja-Louisa saved them. She was a Whitetowers dwarf, boxed and raised there, but she could not stand to see the libraries burned. She held off the Bloody Scythes single-handedly, then rousted those who couldn't flee the siege to load the books onto the last of the grain barges."

"What happened to her?"

"Hanged from Lame Burgess Bridge here in the City Imperishable less than a year later," Marelle said in a distant voice. "By a mob of students." Her eyes met Imago's. "Marja-Louisa was only a housemistress, you see. A dwarf and a female, twice over forbidden to touch the books."

"An ancestress of yours?" Imago asked, sympathetic.

"No. Merely a woman. Just like me."

"When we are done here, I would be pleased if you would show me the archives. I'm afraid I don't even know where the old Footsoldiers' Guild Hall is."

"It is being east of the Green Market," said Enero. "Along Heliograph Hill."

Imago had spent plenty of time on Heliograph Hill. A great deal of money lived in the fine houses on the crescents and closes up on that height, money which had firm opinions about how the City Imperishable should conduct its affairs. Still, he couldn't bring the building to mind.

"We will look, then, and see where the Imperator Terminus is said to have met his end," the Lord Mayor announced. "I can recall a dozen stories told to me as a child, each stranger than the next. Maybe the archives hold the truth."

"Or reliable rumor," Marelle said.

Bijaz bent slightly to achieve a spider's eye view of the table. "You're assuming north, though."

Imago nodded. "She came through the River Gate. She has Northmen in her train, and an ice bear."

Bijaz looked up at the Lord Mayor. "It might be an albino."

"Not that big."

"I am agreeing," said Enero. "There are being great bear skins in the market, from hills to the north, but an albino would not be having black eyes."

"North." Imago tossed the bell onto the table. "I want to know where she found this thing. I don't believe it was the tomb of the Imperator Terminus, but others will. At the same time, I want her gone from the City. In disgrace, or mockery. Something that will keep the people from following her." He looked at Bijaz.

"I know," the dwarf said. "I will not contest her directly, but I understand your need."

Enero rolled the bell idly in his hand. "It would be helping if we were to be knowing which pass she was using."

They all stared at the map, willing there to be some epiphany in the ancient lines of pigment. None came.

Imago and Marelle passed through town in an enclosed fiacre. Blue velvet curtains were drawn over the glass windows. A necessary subterfuge of his position, he was told time and again. Travel in closed carriages, keep armed riders close by. Sometimes carriages ran empty.

No one had tried to kill him since the battle at Terminus Plaza. Not even a close call. Nonetheless, Marelle, Biggest Sister, old Ducôte, and his other counselors would not let him walk the streets, nor ride. He no longer had the length of leg to control a horse, sadly, and the pain of that day had never quite left him, so Imago supposed he must be a passenger in any event.

"You said Marja-Louisa was a Whitetowers dwarf?"

She nodded. "Boxed and raised."

"I thought the boxes were peculiar to the City Imperishable."

Marelle gave Imago a puzzled look. "In the days of the empire, Whitetowers was part of the City Imperishable."

"They never boxed dwarfs down along the Sunward Sea," he pointed out.

"Those were tributary cities, not vassals."

He worked that out a moment. While the minutiae of urban governance had become all too familiar to Imago of late, the logic of empire was considerably more obscure. "Meaning they paid tribute to the City Imperishable but were not under its rule?"

"Exactly." She gave him another puzzled look. "How can you rule this place and know so little of its history?"

"I rule nothing." Imago laid his head back against the buttoned upholstery, took a deep breath of the musty, oily air. "I have limited authority over the affairs of some two hundred thousand people and several hundred trading houses, corporations, guilds, and great families. My powers are only persuasive. Even then, I only influence the City Imperishable, not the old empire. Such as it remains, the empire is the domain of the Assemblage of Burgesses. They rule over the River Saltus, the Rose Downs, and Port Defiance. As well as having the courts. What cities once paid tribute and what cities once paid vassalage, or whatever vassal cities do, is scarcely relevant to my concerns."

"You used to be a barrator, right?"

"Yes." Imago grinned. It had been an interesting life, though chronically underfunded. "Old statutes were my stock in trade. That's how I came to revive the office of Lord Mayor, after all."

And in the bargain, diffusing the power which had concentrated sufficiently within the Inner Chamber to draw the Old Gods up from their stony tombs beneath the streets.

"History is nothing but old statutes." She leaned close, grasping tight to his arm. "Consider this, Lord Mayor. A tributary city, or any tributary territory, would have been the concern of the Imperator and the Burgesses. The Tokhari, for example. But a clever man could argue that a vassal city was part and parcel of the City Imperishable. Should you feel the need to exert your influence."

"Still history," said Imago. "We have no vassal cities anymore. The old empire is either empty lands or in other hands. Besides which, the very last thing I want to do is further undermine the Burgesses. Keeping the powers in our city spread out is far safer."

"Port Defiance is a vassal city," she said.

The fiacre lurched to halt. The Winter Boy atop the driver's bench banged on the passenger box.

Imago found Marelle's remark about Port Defiance to be a curious thought as he lurched down to the cobbles. He still had sufficient pride to be annoyed by the little iron step provided for his convenience in making the descent.

Marelle had brought him to the Whitetowers archives. They were in a winding alley that sloped uphill, though he didn't recognize it. He could *smell* the Green Market—that many tons of vegetables and grain carried its own odor in the spring warmth.

The Footsoldiers' Guild Hall rose before them, a building in the late stages of terminal distress. It had a grand frontage for something that faced an alley—portico with six pillars in a classical style, though the plastering had long since shattered away to show the rotting laths beneath. Cheap construction. One would not have expected wealth from such a guild as this, even in its heyday. The location told the same story—far from the Limerock Palace and the seats of power, built in the days before Heliograph Hill became a posh address. Today the place was further from wealth than ever. The stoa was jammed with junk—everything from fruit baskets to velocipedes to old chaises longues rotting beneath the weight of birds' nests. Much of the mass was wired into place.

The guildhall looked like a madwoman's attic turned inside out. Smelled like it, too, Imago realized as he waddled up the steps after Marelle. "This is an archive?"

"No, it's a dump. The Whitetowers archives are inside because there was nowhere else for them to go."

Imago imagined the endless halls of the Sudgate, layer on layer of vast chambers and tiny closets, so many of them containing only dust and mice. "I see."

The entrance was certainly a footsoldier's door. It was higher than normal, to admit men carrying spears, and wider as well, for armored men who swaggered. Each pillar was carved as a soldier deep out of history—the right side carried a club and wore skins, the left side baroque armor and a short, wide sword. Under the portico roof, surrounded by junk, these carvings had survived centuries of weather. The building would have been unused four hundred years ago, he realized, for the archives to be deposited then. Land was available for the asking along the eastern wall, but it was hard to imagine that the wealth of Heliograph Hill hadn't since found better use for this building, or its location.

The things a mayor never knew about his own city.

Marelle tugged at the door. It slid partway open with a horrendous squeal, startling rats out of the porch junk piles. She squeezed into the darkness beyond. Glancing back at his man on the fiacre, Imago followed. Once he had entered the shadows, Marelle heaved the door to.

"No one is here?" he whispered, waiting for his eyes to adjust.

"This is a vacant guild." Marelle's voice was normal. "Charter still stands, and there's money in trust to pay the fees every year. Hasn't been a guildmaster in centuries."

Imago forced himself to a normal voice as well. "How do you *know* all this?"

"I'm a City employee. You wouldn't believe the paperwork we handle." He could hear her grinning, even in the dark.

"But the archives? And whatever else is in here."

"Think of this as a rent-free warehouse," she said. "It won't be torn down until the guild charter lapses, which won't happen until the trust runs out."

They stood a few moments, taking in the tangled, quiet space.

If the Sudgate is the attic of the City Imperishable, this is its midden, Imago thought. The mess on the portico had been a mere hint of the waste within. The bulking masses around him had an organic quality that spoke of long neglect.

"A person could make a career out of mining this place." Marelle began following a path that wound through the clutter. He trailed behind her, ducking clusters of old dining chairs, stepping past barrels of metal rods, across ankle-deep fuzz.

This had been the great hall once. The junk above him had layers, a sort of informal scaffolding. Imago devoutly hoped he did not have to climb.

Marelle's winding path led to a cleared area before a door. "One of the old *certamentaria*," she said. "Where they fought."

"Surely they had a sward to drill on?"

"The Green Market, now."

Of course. Everyone knew it was an old parade ground.

The door was padded. Several judas holes were scattered at various heights, each covered with tiny steel flaps. His fingers brushed one. Imago could feel the shouts and blows from half a millennium past still captured in the battered, rusted roundels. "They fought with what weapons in there?"

"Everything, I think." She grabbed the door and yanked it open. Imago's retrospective moment vanished.

The past was safely gone. He was just a man—a dwarf, now—standing amid an enormous junk heap with a very strange woman. The bell in his pocket jingled as he stepped into the next room amid the scents of leather and dry rot.

BIJAZ

He stomped through the streets playing the angry god. That came too easily to him.

He was the City's luck, after all. The Numbers Men had told him so, that fateful day when he'd been dragged to the white room with the blank gaming table. But this mountebank with her tales of Imperator Terminus' wealth would be ill luck indeed for the City Imperishable.

So he stalked down the middle of the road. Instead of confining his powers to flights of feathers and drabbles of sand, Bijaz allowed free rein. A faint coruscating nimbus enveloped him, an antishadow which stood out even in the afternoon sunlight. Tiny lightnings played among his fingertips. His glare set puddles steaming.

More to the point, he drew a crowd. They trailed in from the pothouses, the alleyways, the carts and platforms that did business on the roadway, gathering like the skein of a fishing net being drawn tight in a sailor's hand.

His hand.

City people loved a show.

Bijaz had no idea where to find the mountebank. He couldn't say where she'd gone since leaving the Spice Market. Enero might know. He trusted the City's weird to find her.

The Card King waited at the intersection of Filigree Avenue and Orogene Avenue. The krewe leader was in full regalia, red and gold robes, mounted on a horse the color of bleached straw. He might have been just a fat man in a tasteless suit with hair the color of tarnished brass, but for the stillness with which he met Bijaz's advance.

Bijaz and the Card King had helped save the City. Imago's rush to power would have stumbled but for their bright distractions that winter's day.

"Hello, friend," the Card King said softly.

Bijaz stopped, arms akimbo. "The powers of the City are taking note." His voice boomed oddly loud.

"As they do." A meaty hand reached down. "Will you ride with me?"

"Where are you bound?"

The crowd had gathered around. Bijaz knew this feeling of power, and feared it. Where crowds gathered and men grew large, the Old Gods began to direct their dreams of wakefulness. This hour had acquired that focused sense of inevitability.

"I go to hear a mystery play about the uttermost North, from a woman with a bear and bells."

"Then I am your dwarf." Bijaz clasped the Card King's hand and leapt weightless to a saddle which was set higher than his head.

Power, indeed, he thought, leaving a trail of smoldering flowers in his wake. They formed their own processional heading toward the River Saltus.

People followed, gathering the stinking blossoms as they came.

The Card King reined in his horse on Water Street before the Softwood Quay. They were opposite Ducôte's scriptorium, amid rambling stacks of lumber both green and cured. The air was filled with the reek of murdered forest. Beyond the docks, the Saltus steamed thick as blood though it ran the color of old oil. Ships and barges rode at anchor, while carts and drays stood about, but work had ceased.

The air itself was noumenal. Bijaz willed the magick to stop, but the City was having none of his petty wishes.

A stage was in the process of hasty assembly. Workmen scuttled about with slightly dazed expressions. A high-wheeled wagon with a leather tent atop the bed stood nearby.

"Is that her?" he asked, pointing.

"Wait." The Card King turned to look at Bijaz, a plain man's eyes panicked in his broad-beaming face.

So they both played a role today. It seemed to Bijaz that a krewe king must be ever ready for his part. They were priests, of a sort, with their strange rituals to keep the Old Gods dreaming. Now one of *them* was present in this man's body.

He'd never understood which krewes served which of the Old Gods, and had been reluctant to reason it out. Some things were better left asleep.

Until they woke up, and then understanding might come too late.

Enough, he thought. This battle had already been fought and won. *We have a new chapter before us now.*

Bijaz spent his waiting time imagining how large a bird he might conjure, *something* to carry this troublesome woman away and sharpen its beak upon her bones in a distant aerie. When he realized that flights of shocked curlews were speeding away from him with screams tearing from their mouths, he stopped. "I will abide."

The Card King grunted.

The stage was quickly built. Workmen dropped their tools and slipped away as a drumbeat began. The air stilled. Traffic stopped on Water Street, and the crowd began to breathe as one animal.

It was a summoning, whether of god or spirit or just people massed in panicked awe did not matter. *He* could break a summoning.

Balancing against the fat man's back, Bijaz stood on the Card King's saddle to scatter silver coins from his fingers. He laughed in the booming voice that the Numbers Men had granted him.

He shattered building momentum like a thrown mug.

The woman stepped up on to the stage, a sour look on her face so fleeting as to be almost unnoticeable. The crowd's attention was divided among her and Bijaz as the noumenal world slipped back into the spaces between the air. She gave Bijaz a short, sharp nod, then spread her arms wide to speak.

"The City Imperishable—" she began, her tones sonorous and pitched for oratory.

Still using the great voice, Bijaz interrupted her. "She knows our name." He grinned so wide his lips hurt. "My congratulations on your scholarship, girl."

This time her gaze brimmed with rage. "Indeed. I see you are a rare man."

"Hardly." Grasping the Card King's shoulder, Bijaz bowed. The hand that swept wide spread gleaming confetti cut from cloth-of-gold. There was a scrambling at the horse's feet as people grabbed for the stuff. "Half a man at best. I'm sure you can see that I am the *better* half."

This time the crowd roared with laughter. By Dorgau's sweet fig, he preferred music hall comedy to the kind of shadowed power that she had been gathering for herself. Did this rabble-rouser even understand what forces she played with?

Bijaz had come to appreciate the horror in which old Ignatius had held the raw use of magick. Jason had explained to him why the Inner Chamber had been such a danger to the City Imperishable, and indeed, even the world as a whole.

"Half me no halves," the mountebank called out. "I am *dwarfed* by your demi-measure of wit."

At least she was playing the game, though her sally was not so well received. People at the edges began to drift away to their errands.

"Forward," Bijaz hissed. The Card King's horse eased through the crowd at his host's barest urging. Then, loudly: "I am told you come from the North, girl. There's nothing up there but ice and lice. Got any frost on you?" He flicked his wrists and a spray of snow settled on the people close around the horse.

They were hooting now.

"Hardly." His words had her temper up now. Or perhaps it was his casual displays of magick. Half-miracles for a half-god, but by the brass hells if he could use his powers to peacefully shame her away, so much the better. "I—"

"You had best get a permit for your circus," Bijaz said. "These good people have work, and you are blocking a dock." The Card King sidled the horse close to the stage. Bijaz climbed up to look into the mountebank's eyes. They were blue-white, and very angry. "Give it up," he said quietly.

"Another time," she muttered, then looked around. Losing her audience, she simply stepped back. Her shoulders settled as her hands rested at her side. Suddenly she was just an ordinary woman, pale with brown hair, overdressed for the spring weather in blue silk and pale fur.

Bijaz felt an unaccountable surge of pity. "I would advise you take your business elsewhere."

"You don't know my business, little man," she snapped.

"Actually, I do." He forced a smile. "Enough to know what is and isn't needful. Those tricks I was doing, to distract your audience?"

He could see she was interested despite herself. "They were well done. I could not spot the take-in." Now her tone was mellower. The kind of voice to make man or dwarf dream.

Bijaz shook off that thought. She'd said "take-in." "You are a mountebank. You see me as another sharp." Bijaz held out his hands, palm up, then closed his fists. When his fingers flexed open again, two silver fish wriggled, one on each palm. "There is no sleight, my lady."

"Miracles." This time she laughed. "Any fool can pray down a miracle from a willing god. It takes a true artist to create the *illusion* of a miracle and be believed." She turned to climb down off the stage. "Come drink with me and tell me why I am sadly mistaken."

Bijaz looked back at the Card King, but the fat man was gone. With a shrug, he followed, glorying in the touch of her hand as she helped him to the cobbles.

They didn't bother with her wagon, but repaired instead to the Ripsaw, a potshop just off the Softwood Quay. It was a lumberman's place. That didn't seem to bother his hostess. Bijaz had no fear anymore.

Inside, the place stank of sawdust, sap, and burly men. The lumbermen hunched over their tankards and stew in knots of four and five—crews off the barges and log rafts floated down the Saltus basin from the broad country below the Silver Ridges.

The woman didn't even glance at the rough trade, instead heading straight for the bar. *Used to their company*, Bijaz thought. More evidence she had in fact come from the North.

The mountebank turned with two tankards of ale and nodded Bijaz toward a rickety table by the unlit fireplace. He sat, glancing at generations of initials and obscene carvings of the impossible. Bijaz was all too familiar with the confluence between the obscene and the possible.

"I will not drink with a stranger." She pushed a tankard toward him. "I am called Ashkoliiz."

"Bijaz." He sniffed the ale. It was dark, foamy, all but liquid bread. "The dwarf," he added.

"Truly?" She took a deep draught of her tankard. Bijaz followed suit.

He was more of a wine man, but if ale could talk her past the gates, that was even better than laughing her out of town. Anything to avoid a duel of powers.

She studied him over the rim of her tankard. "I would not have marked you for a priest, but you have the touch of *mana*." Those pale, pale eyes held him a moment, glinting like distant ice. He was reminded of the forests embedded in the water droplets at Kalliope's fingertips.

This woman was so unlike his old master's daughter, except for her age. When had the world grown so young?

"Your accent is flawless," Bijaz said. "Nicely done, given your desire to bend the good citizens of the City Imperishable to your will."

"Presuming there are any good citizens here." She quirked an eyebrow. "You seem to believe I am not one of your own."

"No one here would use that term… *Mana?* We are very aware of the noumenal world."

Ashkoliiz smiled again. He found himself warming to her. "You are a little old man come to ruin my drama, throwing birds and coins with abandon, touched by the noumenal. It is as if the City itself has risen to greet me."

"Think of me as a warning. With two feet and a hand for the take-in."

"You were not doing parlor tricks."

"Nor stage magick, either." He set his ale down again—was he already feeling the drink? "You are being straight enough with me. I shall be straight with you.

"You brought a bear and dark-skinned men with strange flutes, and tossed a bell to the Lord Mayor himself. Were you a company of mummers, I'd pay my obol to pass within your tent, for it is a wondrous show you promise.

"This city, though, has barely recovered from the Trial of Flowers and the ugly rule of the Imperator Restored. We cannot withstand another pass through the hands of royalty so soon. Your dumb show aims to raise a rabble and erupt through the River Gate with flags flying and the promise of hope. Our people need to stay home and rebuild the City's trade. Not send their sons and their money haring after old rumors."

She traced signs for a moment in the water pooling on the splintered table, before meeting Bijaz's eyes once more. Something in that pale gaze made him shiver. He was reminded once more of how long it had been since he'd lain with a woman. "I trade in dreams of history, friend dwarf," she said.

Another push of a tiny puddle.

"I've sold maps and bought ancient diaries. Forged a few of both. People love to know what came before, love the wealth and wisdom of history." The smile came back. "We both know the past is tired men and women with baby-chewed breasts cowering in huts, fearing winter wolves. There is no wealthier era than today's. But people always long for a golden age when their nation was strong and their language was pure and everyone knew their place. You were right to call me a mummer. I am. I act out history, and take my fee where I find it."

He released a stag beetle from his cupped hands. The ale was definitely going to his head. "We have more history here in the City Imperishable than any people ought to be cursed with. Take your history and… and…" The room closed in, the clatter of the beetle's wings far too loud.

Ashkoliiz rose to her feet, her smile broad as a cat's. "Take my history and what, little man?" She stepped to his side of the table and pushed his face into the tabletop. She leaned over to whisper in his ear, "No one calls me *girl*."

Girl.

Girl.

Drowning in the foamy residue of brewer's bread, he wondered where he'd ever known a girl. Someone's footfalls melded into the buzzing of wings, then the lumbermen began to laugh in chorus.

ONESIPHOROUS

Returning to his office late in the afternoon, still damp from his tumble into the sea, Onesiphorous found a dwarf huddled before his door. He didn't recognize the visitor. The man was of middle years, dressed in traditional wrappings. His clothing was stained and torn. Onesiphorous sourly noted a few stitches at each corner of the dwarf's mouth—a compromise that nodded at Sewn tradition while being more suited to everyday life.

The dwarf was crying.

A small gathering shouted insults and advice. They seemed mostly concerned with the best way to achieve a fatal dive into the channel below.

Onesiphorous was horrified. He stepped close to grab the dwarf's shoulder. "Inside, man. And pull yourself together."

The dwarf's eyes were red with tears—and drink, Onesiphorous realized, with a stout whiff of the other's breath. "You're the City's man," he said, his words slurred.

"We're all the City's men." Onesiphorous unlatched his office and dragged the unwelcome visitor within, casting a final glare at the hecklers.

He'd planned to change into some old clothes he kept in the office—his apartment was several islets further and required a ferry ride to cross a channel too wide to be conveniently bridged—but not with this visitor to hand. Instead Onesiphorous poured cold black tea from a stone crock. It seemed best to place a prop between him and the crying dwarf.

"Here," he said, voice more rough than he'd intended. "What brings you to my door?"

"I'm asking the City for help." The dwarf ignored the tea. "I've a right to petition the Lord Mayor."

"You've a right to petition the head of the Ropemakers' Guild, too. For all the good it will do. The Lord Mayor's writ doesn't run in Port Defiance. You'll want to speak to the Harbormaster if there's a legal issue at stake, or take your case to the Burgesses back home."

"No." His visitor's face pinched in pain. "This is a *dwarf* thing. Lord Mayor's a dwarf. One of us. Port Defiance is no city for honest dwarfs, and there's been none in the Burgesses ever. They'll not care at all."

Imago was no more a dwarf than he was an Alate. Certainly the Lord Mayor had been made over to resemble a dwarf, but a few passes of the knife by some moldering god was hardly sufficient to claim Imago as one of their own.

Still, this problem was all too obvious. "Are you a Boxer or an Opener?"

"Boxer."

A traditional dwarf then, Bijaz thought, *trimming his stitches to move with the times*. "And what has brought you to my door?"

"M-m-my wife." The dwarf's chest shuddered as he stifled a sob. "She—she's taken our girls out of their boxes."

"By Dorgau's left testicle! How old?" Boxing was not a process that lent itself to interruption. Dwarfs were created by clamping healthy children into boxes to constrict body size. Growing frames limited development of the protruding legs. Onesiphorous had been raised in a box, from ages six to fifteen. He'd spent the first year out of the box learning how to walk again, rebuilding his muscles. This exquisite torture of children was an ancient art, but very well understood.

To release a child *during* the process was even more damaging than boxing them in the first place.

"Six and eight."

"So the youngest just went in?"

"Two weeks ago. We were all so proud." His chest shuddered again. "At least that's what I thought. The houseman-attendant placed her within, and we have—had—a private nurse come twice a day."

Onesiphorous had not thought upon his own houseman in years. Doctors, usually dwarfs, who specialized in the medical and developmental problems of children still in their boxes.

Away from the City Imperishable, the life of dwarfs seemed ever more like perversion and less like civilization.

"What about the eight-year-old?" he asked.

"I don't know." The dwarf sobbed again. "B-b-berra came last night with two dwarfs I didn't recognize." He tried to collect his breath. "One struck me with an axe handle. While I lay stunned, they broke open the boxes and took my girls." Another body-wracking shudder. "I could hear them shrieking."

"Berra is your wife?"

"Yes."

Onesiphorous stared at his desk. He hadn't been here long enough to accrue layers of documents. There was a brass compass left behind by the previous tenant, a large baize blotter, a sheaf of blank letters signed by Imago, four days' worth of Port Defiance's local broadsheets, and a scratched-over draft of a letter to the Lord Mayor.

Though so much had already changed since he'd begun to write it.

The argument which had dominated the exiles' society here in Port Defiance, creeping into the politics of the Harbormaster and the trade factors of the Loska District, was now erupting into the destruction of families.

So it begins, he thought. The end of who we have been for a thousand years. He'd realized the problem as soon as he'd arrived in Port Defiance, but this poor buggerer's children were the first real victims.

The older girl was in a great deal of trouble.

"What do you wish me to do?" he finally asked. "I have no legal authority. I am just a dwarf among other dwarfs."

Red eyes stared at him, face shivering. "Can you get them back?"

"I wouldn't know how to begin," Onesiphorous said softly. "We have no laws to protect children in their boxes. Only the chains of custom. Which your wife has broken. Do you have any idea who the dwarfs with her might have been?"

"I'm not sure." The visitor's voice had broken completely now. The sound of defeat. "They both wore blue jackets. Like the inspectors. But there's no dwarfs in the Harbormaster's service."

"Uniforms?" Dwarfs had never worn uniforms. Styles, yes, most notably the traditional muslin wrappings, but not *uniforms*. His kind were forbidden from being sworn into high office, and a dwarf was never forced to draw a weapon under orders. Each limitation had a privilege hidden somewhere within.

"Could be."

"Look, ah…" He stopped. "What is your name?"

The dwarf stood. "I sign my bank drafts as Trefethen the Spice Factor. Not that it matters now."

"Trefethen. I'll talk to some friends. I can't think what I can do personally, but I'll try. Officially, it's not my purpose here."

"If you're not here to help the dwarfs," Trefethen asked bitterly, "what is your purpose?"

With that he left, his tea still untouched.

"A good question, sir," Onesiphorous told the empty room.

It had all been much simpler when he'd been fighting the Burgesses to make a new way for dwarfs. Children broken from their boxes wasn't the way he'd meant to create.

Onesiphorous watched the late sunlight slant across his window as birds circled low over the water, feasting on something drowned. The Alate's bell clinked slightly as he rolled it in his hand.

Big Sister entered without knocking just as Onesiphorous finally pulled off his sodden trousers. His linen knickers clung to his thighs, but his state of dress was her lookout if she was going to go barging about.

"What do you want?" he snapped.

"I thought we ought to talk again."

"Learned anything new since yesterday?"

"Port Defiance deserves to be free. Port Defiance should be grateful for what it already has. Openers are taking on the Boxers. Openers and Boxers are plotting together. The plantations hate the miners. The miners hate the plantations."

"Scarcely news, any of that." His thoughts were on Trefethen, and the dwarf's poor daughters.

"Scarcely." She leaned against the wall and regarded him with cool amusement. "The warehousemen and the factors over in Loska have a cozy little klatch going. No room for an honest businesswomen to buy her way in."

"They matching you bribe for bribe?"

"Yes. With a sinking fund. Tribade business would be a lot tougher if more people were both clever and consistent."

"Most business would be tougher." Lord Mayor Imago had a close relationship with the Tribade. Onesiphorous himself had cooperated with them in the days when sending dwarfs downriver had been illegal. Even so, he wasn't certain they ought to be the future of the City Imperishable.

Or Port Defiance, for that matter.

"Funny place, this world," said Big Sister. "Also, a dwarf in a small boat set himself on fire outside the Blunt Scupper."

"What did they do?"

"Cut the painter line and let it drift with the tide. He never screamed."

Onesiphorous had a sick feeling he knew the unfortunate dwarf. "Did he say anything?"

"No. But the Blunt Scupper is over on Curlew Eyot. Lot of Openers drink there. Used to be a plantation man's bar. Still is, some. Odd choice of drinking companions, if you take my meaning."

The plantations along the Jade Coast raised indigo, cotton, ground nuts, and other crops on land cleared from the swampy jungles. There was money in that, but also generations of backbreaking labor ruled over by rotting aristocracy. Lord Mayor Imago's family had retreated to a plantation after some financial disgrace in his youth, Onesiphorous knew, though he was vague about the details.

The plantation men had no love for the Harbormaster, or any of the rest of Port Defiance's officialdom. This city hosted the only bourses where they could market their crops—it was that or sell them over the rail to free traders at a steep discount—but exchange fees were a permanent point of contention.

"Poor bastard," Onesiphorous said. "If it's who I think, I know why he did it." *And I sent him to his death.* "As for his choice of venue, Dorgau take me if I can explain. I have enough trouble with politics in the City Imperishable, and I was born there. People here are crazed by too much sun and saltwater. It's like trying to sort out a dogfight."

"Indeed," she said. "And the dogs are growling on the citizens' council."

Onesiphorous tried to put Trefethen the Spice Factor out of his mind. His imagination would not let go of the proud, broken dwarf sitting still as death as flames blackened his skin and his eyes boiled. He had to think. "Is the Harbormaster in on that?"

"Not that I can tell, but old Sevenships is cannier than most. He's likely involved in every little two-bit movement around here."

"And you're back because you thought I needed the meeting minutes?" He stood, tugging on dry, ragged pants.

"The Boxers are angry. It's dwarf business. You're a dwarf. I thought you might want to know they're ready to start knifing Openers."

"Over…?" Onesiphorous asked.

"Some kids were taken, their boxes broken."

"I know." All he could see was Trefethen drifting aflame into the sunset.

"Good. Let's just say there's encouragement from some of the local types. The sort who drink confusion to the City Imperishable with their morning wine."

"And they'd rather live beneath a corsair flag, or answer to some master down the Sunward Sea?"

Big Sister snorted with amusement. "When do you think the last warship of the City Imperishable passed this way?"

Onesiphorous was surprised. "We have warships?"

She cocked a finger at him. "My point exactly. May I see the bell, by the way?"

"Bell?" He felt stupid, missing some twist in the conversation. "What bell?"

"That the bird-man brought you."

Onesiphorous swallowed a growl. That bastard boy Boudin was spreading rumor about him. "Your sources are curious."

"No, just observant."

He couldn't think of a reason not to, so he tossed it to her.

She rolled it between her fingers. The little clink seemed loud in the flickering light of his oil lamps. "This is old," she said. "City-made, from a long time back. Silver's heavier than a modern smith would make it, unless he was working a fake. Don't know why anyone would forge something this trivial."

"Delightful. The Alates are handing out party favors from summers past."

She shrugged. "Maybe he found it sewn to a corpse floating somewhere. You never can tell." The bell gleamed in the lamplight as she set it down on his desk with a curiously dainty motion. "I think you're in trouble here, friend dwarf."

"So you told me yesterday."

"Not personal danger. That, too. In this case I mean the City Imperishable. Your precious Lord Mayor needs to start watching Port Defiance carefully. The Burgesses aren't likely to look this way during our lifetimes. Not until the tax assessments stop flowing, which will be too late. If Sevenships strikes the City's colors over the Flag Towers, there'll be no way to run them up again."

The loss of trade and the flow of goods would be crippling. Worse, though, was what might happen to the dwarfs once the contentious forces which had broken Trefethen's family made their way upriver. If Imago didn't find a way to focus the City dwarfs on their own future, that would be the end of them all.

And what ill would come of such an ending? asked a little voice deep inside his head. The wealth of centuries had been built on the suffering of children, that the full-men of the City Imperishable might have their captive accountants and business managers.

He looked down at his short, twisted legs and teakettle body. Perhaps it was time for something new.

"You think life as a dwarf is hard," said Big Sister, "try being born a woman."

IMAGO

Marelle used a hard-strike match to light the storm lamp by the door. The *certamentarium* was a reflection in paper of the guildhall's chaos. A fire waiting to happen, feeding on the words of centuries. After a belated moment, it occurred to Imago to wonder why there was a lamp here in the first place.

She adjusted the wicking screw. His nose was flooded with the scent of rock oil for a moment.

This room had a ceiling about fifteen feet high, but he could not gauge the size because of the mountains of books, scrolls and loose paper. Imago had spent quite a bit of time in libraries and filing rooms, back when he was a barrator. The sheer number of pages here beggared his imagination.

"This should have all rotted over the centuries."

"Left unattended, it would have." She picked her way down a canyon within the tottering cliffed walls of books.

Imago followed, wondering who cared for this place. Someone had passed their secrets on to Marelle, obviously enough. He would need to have her background inquired after.

A dozen paces in was a little clearing. Rough lumber provided shoring to keep the archives at bay. Wires were strung between the vertical beams. Hanging from the wires were thousands of earrings, gleaming in hundreds of colors as they reflected the lamp's flickering light.

"Jewelry?" he asked.

Marelle gave him a sour look. "Don't be a fool, sir. You're smarter than that." She handed one to him.

Not an earring, he realized. The resemblance was obvious—wire-strung baubles with a hook at the top. A beaded drop, as it were. Too long to be worn from an ear, though. When Imago looked where she'd taken it down, he realized all the drops in that section of wire were similar.

"It's a code," he said slowly. "A filing system." His fingers moved over the individual pieces of the drop. A flat piece of drilled slate no bigger than a coin. There were scratches on it, deliberate hashmarks. Below that, two glasswork beads gleaming violet in the lamplight. Then a tiny wooden spacer, followed by a pale cowrie shell, and three more irregular stones: two dark green, one either red or brown.

"Indeed."

He looked at her. Marelle's eyes were shadowed in the lamplight. Imago continued: "So though this is chaos to the eye, entombed within more rot and chaos, these archives have been maintained over the centuries since your Marja-Louise brought them down the River Saltus."

"Marja-Louis*a*," she corrected. "There is too much here to let it be burned for soap ash. Treatises, journals, dissertations, maps, herbaria…"

He rolled the beaded drop in his hand. *Clever*, he thought, *very clever.* Even in complete darkness it could be read by someone who knew the code. And if one wandered the streets with this thing, it was not an obvious message of any sort—just an eccentric piece of jewelry. Still, something bothered him. "What good is a library if no one knows it is there?"

The fierceness of her reply startled him. "What good is a library if it is left for dead? Burned? Banned?"

"So what has this place been awaiting?"

"Need." She set the lantern on a rickety table and stepped close to him. "There are books and scrolls here lost to rot, to rats, to the sheer pressure of being buried too deep. There was never another choice. If these had come out in the early years, the masters at Imperatorial University would have reclaimed everything and put it under ban. If the Saltus School had not got there first. Over the years since, things have changed. To whom do these belong now?"

"The shadows, apparently." He continued to finger the beads. "And whoever does all this beadwork." Imago dangled the drop between them. "This coding can be read in the dark, which reduces the risk of fire. What good does darkness do among the archives themselves?"

"There has been blindness among the caretakers," she said. "The archives have become a thing of their own, the reading incidental."

"And how do you know so much?"

She stared at him, eyes glittering. Imago saw that Marelle shivered. Fear? Chill, in the heart of this damp, dark building? "Trust that I will tell you in time."

"Show me what I need to know, and I will trust."

"It is not so simple." She took the drop from him and returned it to its proper place on the wire. "But we can find the histories. They will need to be removed." She shuddered again.

He wondered how often recovery ever happened in this crowded place. "My thanks to you, then; in hopes that we learn."

"Mmm." Marelle ran her fingers over the drops, whispering some mnemonic until she found what she sought. She plucked three off a wire, then stepped between two of the frames. The dwarfess did not take the lamp with her as she began to scale stacks of paper.

Her voice echoed back from the flickering shadows: "Wait."

What else was he to do?

After the first two trips beyond the wired walls, perhaps ten minutes each, Marelle allowed Imago to follow her. "Mind your step."

He minded. It was difficult. Where the path in from the door had used the old floor of the *certamentarium* as a walkway, here they scrambled up the shoals of paper and leather bindings. Imago wondered what had been sacrificed for the footpath. Histories of agriculture? Scrolls in incomprehensible languages?

There was a system here, however eccentric.

She stopped without warning, so that he bumped into her back. "Careful," she hissed before taking his hand and guiding it to a wire. Strung from ceiling to floor was a pattern of beads. It must match the drops she'd pulled. Imago could barely see anything, even though the lamp was only paces behind them.

"So we are among the histories of the empire?"

"Keep your voice low. Your words can cause problems."

"Fair enough," he whispered. "But I do not hold sway here."

"Your office does." Then, digging down. "And no, this is not the histories. The archives are not organized that way." She began shifting a drift of scrolls aside, marking the pile with a wire. "Much of what is here is lost. Rot, like I said. Or simply passed beyond relevance. We mark what matters, and keep it where it lies most comfortably."

"Are the books and papers noumenal?"

She shifted deeper, digging herself a hole. He thought she was following a wire downward. After a moment, she answered: "Not exactly, no. But you've argued before judges. You know words have power."

"The power of argument is not magick."

"Tell that to someone untrained in logic or the law." She handed him a thick book bound in greasy leather. It stank, the smell a mere ghost of something old and powerful. "Hold this, please, sir."

He held it, considering what she'd told him.

"This city is built on blood," she continued. "Ancient, bloody sacrifice, the blood of dwarfs, the blood of our vanished empire. Consider this room we're in."

"A *certamentarium*."

"In a soldier's hall. How much blood do you suppose has been spilled right here? Enough to seal this place in souls and pain."

"So you hid the power of the words inside a box of old struggle."

"Yes." She scrambled back up, handing him a smaller volume, then began to refill the hole.

So it went for several hours, until they had accumulated a barrow's worth of books, scrolls, and maps. Some were in dreadful condition, shedding silverfish and roaches, edges laced to dust. Others had fared better. Imago spent his time following Marelle and thinking on the power of words.

The world was not built on the utterances of some god. Words were carts that carried ideas from mind to mind. If they had power—legal, noumenal, or otherwise—it came from the knowledge those words contained. And the venue. A child could recount the doctrine of adverse possession while walking through Delator Square, but there the words had no force of legal argument. A solicitor elucidating an argument before the Estate Court could recount the doctrine of adverse possession to great effect, moving property worth thousands of gold obols with the power of their words.

But the words here are not law, he thought. Nor the framework of some noumenal magick. These words were just knowledge. The first cliché of every student was that knowledge is power.

Finally the dwarfess hung up the last of her drops. "We should carry these out."

"Does material normally leave the archives?"

"No." Marelle looked sour again. "But the Lord Mayor has never had need before."

"I'm the first, aren't I? To come asking for knowledge. Though I would not have known had you not brought me."

Her sourness slipped into hurt. "The first in centuries. Still, this archive has abided."

"Much like the City Imperishable."

When they reached the hideous porch, dusk still streaked the sky with pale pink. Nighthawks peeped overhead. The first stars were out. The alley was dead quiet. He looked for Enero's man but saw no one. Imago felt a brief flash of annoyance at the absence of his driver, then guilt about his presumption of privilege.

How he'd always hated the wealthy and powerful for that.

There was nothing for it but to continue their errand. He and Marelle took four trips each to bring her treasures out.

"Wait here," she said after their last load. "I must go shut the *certamentarium.*"

"It wasn't locked when we came in."

"It will be now."

Imago stood on the porch, watching moonlight touch the alleys to the west and listening to the night. Heliograph Hill was a quiet neighborhood. Wealth favored silence. Still, there should have been the clattering of coaches on nearby streets, even the wheezing clangor of a steam cart or two. All he could hear was gas lamps hissing on the next street over, and a distant murmur like water running.

He cocked his head and listened more carefully.

The murmur was the sound of riot, or at least a rowdy crowd. *That* was a noise he should have known.

By Dorgau's sweet fig, not again. Not in his city. Where was his fiacre? Why hadn't his staff been out to find him?

Marelle tugged the front doors shut. "Ready?"

"No. We have problems." He mimed listening, a hand cupped to his ear. "Hear that? Big trouble."

Imago would bet a week of dinners Bijaz and that mountebank were in the middle of it.

"Where's your driver?"

"I don't know."

She whirled on him. "We can't leave these books here."

"I can't stand around waiting, either." He was frustrated, angry-frustrated.

A dwarf came up the alley, whistling. Imago turned to stare. The whistler was young, dressed in a leather smock and thigh-high boots, his hair tucked under a tight, slick cap with a little metal lantern.

A dunny diver.

"You," said Imago. "My good dwarf."

"Evening, your worship." The dunny diver touched a finger to his forehead. "Wet Hernan, at your service."

"I am in need of help."

"So old Saltfingers said. He set us to walk above the streets for a change." The dwarf giggled. "Air's different up here. 'Tis easier to lose my way."

Imago didn't even want to speculate on how Saltfingers had known. "I need to get to the riot, but there's a load here that wants carrying away. I cannot leave it behind."

"Valuable loot, I'm expecting." Wet Hernan nodded toward the Footsoldiers' Guild Hall.

Great flaming hells, this one is as annoying as his master. "I'm the Lord Mayor, and I tell you it's not looting."

"I expect it never is looting when you're a toff, eh?" The dunny diver smiled. "What swag have you got, your worship?"

"Books and papers." Imago tried to keep the irritation from his voice. "Four dwarfs could carry it all easily enough."

"Books and papers indeed. And here's me, wondering where to find a life of the mind." Wet Hernan grinned. "I'll be back in a nip, your worship, if you'll excuse me to fetch some help." The dunny diver scuttled over to a hatch set against the stone footing of a building across the alley. He threw the timbered panel open and dropped into the darker shadows below.

"You continue to surprise me, sir," said Marelle.

"That wasn't my surprise," muttered Imago darkly, still straining to parse the noise of riot.

The dunny diver was back in less than ten minutes with three of his fellows. They emerged grinning from the passage like so many rats from a hole. Though he'd expected to see Saltfingers, they were more of the younger divers.

Imago quickly handed out the books and papers. "Please take these to my office in the Rugmaker's Cupola." The newcomers accepted their burdens and dropped back out of sight, leaving Wet Hernan in the alley with the last armload.

"Will you be taking the low road with me then, your worship?"

The very idea made Imago shudder with remembered pain. "I believe I can find my way back. But my thanks to you and your master."

"Not a good night for the streets, I'm thinking, but who is Wet Hernan to tell a toff what he should be about?" The dunny diver nodded, then disappeared, closing the hatch after himself.

"I shouldn't think you would be in any hurry to go back down there," Marelle said after they were alone again.

"Never in life." Imago eyed the cobbles at his feet. "Not if the black dogs themselves return to chase me through the streets."

"Take my arm then, and let us walk with decorum toward the riot."

"Dwarf and dwarfess," Imago said.

Marelle laughed sadly. "You are not what you appear, who once grew to be a full-man. In my own way, neither am I."

He did not often think on the curve of her back, or her sickly pallor. "You are a woman fine enough for me to take pride in being seen with."

She gave him a look which he could not interpret. "And everyone knows the Lord Mayor to be a dandy."

Together they strode down the streets of Heliograph Hill, watching for a cab. The surrounding quiet reminded him of the hardest days during the brief reign of the Imperator Restored. The noise ahead continued as they walked.

He wasn't certain if he'd prefer to reach the riot before or after its conclusion.

Bijaz

He flew over a landscape of white cliffs and strange, narrow valleys. Great golden towers rose in the distance. His flight was effortless.

Water dripped from his fingertips. No, it poured. With a scent like attar of roses.

Ah, roses. He was above a rose. Bijaz wondered if he were a bee. The flower shrieked in a voice much deeper than he might have expected from a blossom.

He opened his eyes to see a big man staring in horror at his own hands. Lumberman, by his clothing. His hands were tendrils of green. Rose canes grew from the wrists of the man's shirt.

More large, angry men closed in on Bijaz. Memories of his back alley rape erupted.

"What you done to Will?" one shouted.

Another wielded a stick. "Going to beat you bloody and roll you out for the dogs."

"Don't," said Bijaz. "Please." He didn't know if he was begging or warning them, but then a boot caught him in the ribs.

Moving faster than he'd ever imagined he could, Bijaz grabbed the foot. He was not so much taking action as watching himself refuse to be abused yet again by larger men. He folded the boot into a nubbin of leather while the owner screamed like a wounded rabbit. Then he grabbed a swung stick. Bijaz pulled himself to his feet as his attacker's arms turned to wood.

The others stood back, gasping, cursing. One began to throw up. The stick wielder sobbed.

"Not so much fun to beat the little man now, is it?" Bijaz's anger was as hot as his bloom of fear had been. "You're from upriver." No one local would have tried to hurt him. To these apes, he'd just been a drunken dwarf, passed out under a table after being cheated by a woman.

"M-m-make them whole," said one man. Smaller, younger than the other lumbermen, in a red flannel shirt and canvas trousers worn to shininess.

"Put down your damned fists!" Bijaz's voice shattered every mug and bottle in the room. People covered their ears and fled, even the barkeep. In a moment, he was alone in the Ripsaw.

"Oh by all the hells, what have I done?" Bijaz tried to hold in a sob. He'd played the amiable fool, for fear of the power of the Numbers Men. Already he could imagine the hatred that rumor would bring to what had just happened. The truth was hideous enough.

And if they were sufficiently angry, his powers would not save him from being crushed beneath a load of rock, or drowning while strapped to a cannon. He would have been happier dying of the violet smoke.

Bijaz rubbed his eyes and stepped out the shattered door, hoping to heal, fearing to fight again.

Outside the lumbermen were trying to raise a mob, distracting once more from

Ashkoliiz's show. An ice bear—white with a harness of bells—stood on stage, surrounded by torches on high poles. Three hard-eyed men played instruments as if they were weapons.

People turned, caught between Bijaz and the stage, not quite understanding the fuss.

Bijaz advanced on his erstwhile tormentors. The five still standing bristled with knives, defending the three he'd changed. The locals knew what weapons meant.

"You!" shouted Ashkoliiz from the stage. She whirled to her musicians and spoke in a rapid, clicking language. They dropped their flutes and slipped off the back. The ice bear lumbered over the front edge, dropping into the crowd to set off a shoving, screaming panic.

The animal locked eyes with Bijaz. So it had come to this. He'd tried another way to stop Ashkoliiz. He flexed his fists, feeling the buzzy, metallic taste of the noumenal.

Wait, said a voice inside his head.

Bijaz recalled the white room, where the Numbers Men had spoken to him, changed him, made him something other than a broken, dying dwarf. He had come outside to heal, not to fight again.

Not even with that woman.

He turned away from Ashkoliiz and went to the lumbermen. He wanted to repair his mistake. But the dockside crowd ran before the ice bear, the ones closest to the lumbermen grabbing staves and hooks to fight the armed strangers.

Bijaz knew panic when he saw it. He took a deep breath and used the shattering voice again to shout, "*Stop!*"

The ice bear roared into the silence which followed. Then the screaming began in earnest.

He was buffeted by people who were neither friends nor enemies in the moment. Bijaz threw out his hands as a cloak of light streamed from them. Using the white fire to push his way forward, he advanced on the lumbermen. Two more were down, one with a bent hook embedded in his bloody face. The younger lumberman, still weaponless, continued to stand protectively over the men Bijaz had changed.

He pushed on toward them, intent on trying to fix what he had done. The crowd shifted to trample the men on the ground, as well as their youthful defender. Bijaz watched with horror as boots, sandals, bare feet passed over chests and faces.

They were dead in moments.

He turned. The ice bear stalked toward him, so tall that even Bijaz could spot it. He cupped his hands, ready to hurl a killing blow at the animal, when Ashkoliiz's hard, dark men slid up to his bubble of light and fire.

"Stop," one said in a curious, soft accent. "Do not," the second added. "Please," begged the third.

He paused, glancing toward the stage. Ashkoliiz spread her arms, bowed, then stepped into shadows.

The bear loomed close. The hard, dark men were gone again. People avoided Bijaz and the bear. He looked up as it leaned down, indifferent to his light.

Bijaz saw the gleam of forests in the ice bear's eyes. One great, black claw slipped through his fiery nimbus, too slow to be an assault, and touched the front of his robes. He smelled the raw meat stink of the animal's breath. Black lips wrinkled back over yellowed teeth, then the bear stepped away.

He backed up until he was against a wall. There Bijaz folded his arms and let his fire go out. In a moment he was just a dwarf in pale, grubby robes, crouched by a water barrel, waiting for a dockside brawl to die away.

It took the combined efforts of Enero's Winter Boys and a troop of bailiffs an hour to settle the fighting. The temporary stage had collapsed. Now several Winter Boys worked with two doctors to sort through the victims, searching for wounded lying among the dead.

Bijaz counted fourteen bodies at the head of the Softwood Quay. They'd dragged in several from further down Water Street, but most had died here.

Because of him.

Three-Widows slid down the wall next to him to sit on the stones. Bijaz had not seen the Cork Street enforcer, sometime avatar of the Numbers Men, since the day Three-Widows had taken him into the white room and made him wager his life at the gods' table.

"Gaming's a rough business, guv."

"So's life." Bijaz's voice was dull.

"Yes. Man places his stake. More often than not, he loses it. Nature of the play, you might say. Does a child go hungry that night? Does a landlord throw him out, come end of the week? Can't say. Not the house's affair."

"This…" Bijaz nodded at the bodies. "This isn't luck."

"No? Man loses his stake, doesn't get knifed for his obols walking home. Everyone knows winners ride in style. Sometimes the luck's in the losing."

"Suppose she'd raised her crowds," Bijaz said slowly. "Suppose they'd passed the hat. Suppose they'd marched from the River Gate with banners flying, dogs barking, a hundred men and boys carrying the burdens of the train." He waved his hand. "They'd still be alive."

"Luck is luck, good or ill," Three-Widows answered. When Bijaz looked, the man was gone. Had never really been there, he realized, though a pale gaming chip gleamed on the cobbles.

He picked it up. The chip was broken in two. When he fitted the halves together, even by the fitful torchlight and the silver moon, Bijaz could see a harlequin painted on one side, a towering tree on the other.

Closing his fist, Bijaz crushed the chip until his hand began to glow and smoke. When he opened his fingers, there was nothing but a twisted lump, like glass which had been in a great fire.

"You are being alive." Enero bent down before him.

Bijaz looked up. His heart was hollow, but he did draw breath. "That is nothing to take pride in."

The freerider extended his hand, helped Bijaz to his feet. "Men are to be dying now, men are to be dying later. It is being sad, but her message was being too dangerous to your city."

"The mountebank is gone?"

"I am being told she passed the Sudgate an hour gone now."

"I wouldn't like to take a wagon down the river road." Bijaz's brother had been a factor, before being seduced by the Jade Rush. He knew perfectly well how goods moved up and down the Saltus.

"To being sure, but I am thinking she can be taking care of herself."

He thought of ice-blue eyes and some foul drug in ale so strong no one would notice. Oddly, he missed her. "Ashkoliiz," Bijaz said. "Her name is Ashkoliiz."

"The Lord Mayor comes," someone shouted from further down Water Street.

"We are to be explaining ourselves now." Enero began walking.

"There were no monsters this time." Bijaz trotted after him. "Nothing evil from the noumenal world."

Except for himself, of course. Except himself.

The inside of Ducôte's scriptorium was silent. Even the great steam engine at the back barely grumbled, its fires banked while the press it drove was quiet for the night. The old dwarf sat wrapped in a dressing gown, grumpy as ever. Biggest Sister had arrived as well, representing the Tribade. Otherwise they were Enero, Imago, Bijaz himself, and Marelle.

Just like the dark days of winter, Bijaz thought. They lacked only Jason.

"I wish Onesiphorous was here." Imago looked around. "I will need to send him a letter by fast packet, warning him of the mountebank. Her game should mean little in Port Defiance—they have no great love for our history there."

"Nor here, I am thinking," grumbled Ducôte. "Fifteen dead, I heard."

What Ducôte heard made the morning broadsheets.

Imago looked around, catching their eyes one by one. "A terrible brawl, lamentable deaths, brought on by that scheming con woman and her dancing bear."

"It was not—" Bijaz began.

Biggest Sister interrupted. "You did not go unnoticed."

A shadow stirred, then the Card King stepped into the light. Without his suit and wig he was just a fat man in a grubby tunic. "Some of us had our plans."

"Some of us might have known that," Imago snapped. "There are powers and powers here, and Dorgau knows I make respect my business, but I *am* the Lord Mayor."

"You're missing the point!" Bijaz shouted. "I killed them! All of them!"

"You were not to be trampling men," Enero said gently.

"I started the damned riot."

"Stop," said Imago. "Go pray if you need to. Or drink. Or cry. But I asked you to turn back the mountebank because you are the only one of us who can call those powers to defend the City Imperishable."

"I didn't defend the City. I killed some lumbermen."

"Self-pity doesn't become you." Biggest Sister's foot tapped, impatience flickering. "There has been death. I expect there will be compensation. But what could have been was far worse. As it happens, I know you first tried a simpler tack. That the woman did not let you succeed. She raised the stakes."

"Stakes." What Three-Widows had reminded Bijaz of.

"Stakes," said Imago, his voice gentle. "You have turned away the greatest threat since the Imperator Restored. How many died in Terminus Plaza that day? You had no more blame then than now."

"I…" He stopped trying to convince them of the horror he'd wrought on those men. There were witnesses—everyone else in the bar, to begin with. But who knew what was true after a riot? Especially in the City Imperishable, with recent, raw memories of the noumenal.

"My good Ducôte," Imago went on. "I would never dream of asking an honest printer such as yourself to carry my words in your broadsheets, but if the public were to understand the true role this despicable mountebank played in creating this sad riot, they might realize that brighter days will only return with honest toil and long patience."

By Dorgau's brazen nipple, he is arguing before a court again, Bijaz thought. Imago hadn't been in such rare form in quite some time. The Lord Mayor's afternoon must have gone well.

Ducôte hawked and spat, making the brass pot by his desk ring. "I'll not bend for you, but the truth will out. I want trouble no more than you do. I do live by this riverfront, after all."

"Fair enough." Imago looked around. "Dwarfess Marelle, meanwhile, has shown unexpected talents. We've recovered some documents which may help us ascertain whatever truth lies behind the mountebank's assertions—"

"Ashkoliiz," said Bijaz stubbornly. He was going to get one thing right tonight.

"Ashkoliiz." Imago gave Bijaz a narrow-eyed look. "They will be in the Hall of Maps, at the Rugmaker's Cupola. I have reached an understanding with the

Worshipful Guild, which will keep casual visitors out until we determine what it is we have. Should any of you feel a sudden rush of insight, please lend us your wisdom. No one else will be aware of what we're about."

He plays the City's stakes again. The Lord Mayor was not made for administration, he was made for the great games of state. They would need Onesiphorous back from Port Defiance soon, or find someone else capable of filling that role of chamberlain and major-of-the-palace.

"I would go pray," Bijaz announced. In truth was the last thing he wished. But he needed to be alone with his thoughts. "I will find my own way to the Temple District," he added, as Enero and Imago exchanged glances.

He slipped out into the night, wishing for some footpad with a cosh to take him unawares. It seemed unlikely he was unguarded, but a dwarf could always hope.

Ashkoliiz, he thought. *Her name is Ashkoliiz.*

Onesiphorous

He awoke from hot dreams of drowning. Someone was knocking on his door. Onesiphorous had been granted a dwelling near the bottom tier of a narrow, tall building which clung to the west face of The Boot. He occupied a level and half, an open space like an artist's studio with a high ceiling and a balcony built within. He enjoyed a view of the western sky over the jungles of the Jade Coast, currently brightening with the morning.

It was scarcely a mark of the Harbormaster's respect to set him so low to the water.

The door again, he realized. It was not the knock of an angry mob, accompanied by hinges breaking. This was almost diffident.

Not Big Sister then. She would have simply slipped the lock and entered.

He groaned, rolled out of the niggardly rope bed, and tugged on a dressing gown. It was after dawn, he might as well be awake.

Negotiating the ladder down to the floor, Onesiphorous was glad that he'd carried so little with him through life. This apartment held nothing but clothes and a few books. That made for a bare floor, safe for stumbling unshod and half-awake.

At the door, he realized the spy hole was placed for a full-man. Nothing for it but to open up. He tugged.

The boy Boudin stood outside. Today he was dressed oddly—a fur vest, homespun trousers, bare feet, and a small, soft cap which he currently twisted between his hands.

"You've been paid," Onesiphorous said roughly. He was still irked that the boy had told Big Sister of the Alate's bell.

"Nah, she ta'k different this day, ah." Even the boy's accent had changed.

It dawned on Onesiphorous that he was seeing a swamp rat—though surely they called themselves something else. Boudin had come from the people who'd lived here when this was the South Coast, long before the Jade Rush or even the slow spread of exiled money which had built the plantations.

Curiosity battled irritation. "What do you want?"

"This day a benny day you come, ah."

Hah, thought Onesiphorous. Someone, somewhere in the local hierarchy was getting worried. That the touch came from people at the bottom of the ladder didn't worry him. Years of being a Slashed activist in the City Imperishable had made Onesiphorous quite familiar with the breadth of that rung. Still, he had to play this right. "Come with you where?"

"See she, ah. Come up the blackwater." Boudin stopped twisting his cap and straightened, shifting his voice to the more ordinary accent of Port Defiance. "It will be worth your ride, sir. I promise."

"Right. I'll meet you at the tie-up in ten minutes."

Boudin nodded enthusiastically. Onesiphorous shut the door and went looking for clean knickers.

He was down quickly enough, a mug of tea in one hand. Onesiphorous had also tucked some money in an inner pocket. He was wary of giving insult, but he was equally wary of going without resources. Boudin waited in his little boat.

The Boot was a northerly island in Port Defiance's constellation of points of land. It actually lay in the Saltus delta proper, where the water ran muddy and slow when the tide was out, but gray and fast when the tide was in. Shoreline spread east and west. The ragged jungle made a tracery of the bottom of the heavens.

He stepped into Boudin's boat, hoping that there would be no saltwater tumbles today.

The boy's hat was back on his head. It was a cone of orange felt in morning daylight.

"Show me the way," he said.

"She benny this day, ah." Boudin smiled and set to his oars.

They crabbed across the current, in effect rowing upstream to drift down. Boudin seemed to know where the boat was headed without ever turning to look. Onesiphorous simply watched the shore.

He'd only recently come south from the City Imperishable aboard a steam packet. The captain had been a City man, though most of his crew were sailors from the cities of the Sunward Sea. They were deepwater boys working the river a season or two to avoid summer storms on the ocean. The packet had stayed mid-current to avoid snags as the captain muttered darkly about brigand apes and raiding birds along the shore.

Onesiphorous had received the clear impression that only a lunatic would go ashore in these foetid, fevered jungles.

At the time that had suited him just fine. He was a City dwarf, after all—pavers beneath his feet were his natural estate. So far as he was concerned, trees existed largely to give dogs a place to piss.

The politics of this port city were maddening, though. And no one would talk to him but Big Sister, who'd shipped down as a deckhand on the same steam packet.

So he went ashore. Great, tall trees with a cluster of knees stood right at the water's edge, apparently without benefit of beach. Vines tangled between their glossy dark green leaves, some thick as the trunks of the lindens back home. Sharp-nosed creatures with striped tails ran along their extents, disturbing birds and drawing mournful hoots from the deeper shadows. Beneath it all the water disappeared into shadow as well, only pale green bushes showing the way. Too pale, too green.

"She say no draw you hands down in her water, ah."

Onesiphorous looked down. Something longer than the boat paced them, a sinuous crest barely breaking the muddy surface.

He looked up again as Boudin shipped the oars and they passed into shadow.

He didn't miss the roll of the ocean until it vanished with the sunlight. The jungle swallowed that sound, along with the wheel and cry of the sea birds and the distant bells from Port Defiance. In the course of a few boat lengths, that world was gone.

Here within the shadows of the great trees, the air was thicker, heavier. Birds cawed by ones and twos. Smaller sounds echoed, bubbles and squeaks and slow burps which might have been the water itself roiling, or the steam of muddy life beneath the knob-kneed trunks.

Boudin laid his oars in the bottom of the boat and drew out a short, broad-bladed paddle. "Slow now, ah," he said with a grin. The boy's tan looked walnut-dark in here. His teeth gleamed to match his eyes. The pacing crest still followed them, but it gave the paddle some distance.

"Your people live here?" Onesiphorous asked.

"Ah."

Slow dips of the paddle. The air continued to move fitfully, as if it lacked ambition.

"Not plantation men, not jade miners."

"Slugs, she call 'em."

"Slugs?"

"Pale, slow, and full of juice, ah." Boudin laughed. He didn't seem so young now. In the shadows that conical hat was pale and indistinct, blurring the shape of the boy's head.

Onesiphorous wanted to ask who "she" was, but he held his tongue. Boudin was different here, under the trees. Time for a smart City dwarf to listen with eyes and ears.

Boudin paddled for more than an hour. The boy wasn't marking his way—there was no possibility that Onesiphorous could pick a return path through the trees. So he just watched.

Land began to appear after a while. Little hummocks at first, nothing more than rotting deadfalls. Soon he could see soil on them, sprouting plants, vines, even grassy mounds.

The long fin dropped away, whatever it had been. A whole troop of animals crashed through the trees, pacing the boat with whistles and calls.

Flowers, too—big, fleshy blossoms resting in shallow water. They were the color of marbled fat and smelled like a dead dog. Insects the size of his hand buzzed the blossoms, dark and indistinct. Onesiphorous had no ambition to meet them up close.

The water became channels, the hummocks became islands. Boudin finally beached the boat on a little mud bank no different from a dozen others they'd passed.

"Go with respect now, ah." The boy climbed over the bow. "Benny dwarf do benny well."

"Respect." Onesiphorous clambered after. "Always."

Boudin clapped a hand on his shoulder. "She know you, ah. Else you no come."

They walked a few dozen yards through blossoming bushes to reach a little clearing. Seven of the great-kneed trees surrounded it, these growing out of dirt rather than water. An old woman sat on a misshapen chair. Her skin was dusky.

She was knitting.

Onesiphorous realized that Boudin had not stepped out of the bushes with him. He slowly approached the woman. The air felt strange, almost like taffy.

"Hello," he said. "I was called here."

She knitted a few strokes more before looking up at him. Her eyes were filmy. "Welcome, holy City man."

"I'm not holy." He looked around for a place to sit, then felt foolish. There was nothing in this clearing but her.

"You expecting maybe a hut, with chickens and lizards?"

"I don't know, ma'am. I don't know anything about your people."

The needles clicked again. "You thinking Boudin he maybe tell your secrets, but you come anyway."

"An invitation, ma'am." He paused, then plunged onward. "I'm here to find things out. Port Defiance is not what I thought it might be."

"What you see, when the boy row you out to the Old Tower?"

Barlowe's Finger? "I saw the city. I saw the Sunward Sea. I saw the shore."

"Ah." She continued to knit.

The invitation was clear. "People, spread out from rock to island, from island to rock. They don't face the City Imperishable anymore. If they ever did. They face south, and east, toward the cities of the Sunward Sea."

This time he got a hard look as the needles paused. "What you think Port Defiance be defying, ah?"

He'd wondered that. "The ocean. They cling to those rocks and weather what the sea brings them."

"My people, we got a story." The needles clicked again. "Everything a story for my people, but this story different. Long time there was a city here, different city than now. Twin city to the big stone house upriver where you come from. Like twins, they fight. Like twins, they stand together. One hand and other hand, anyone come upon them, they join. World, she bigger than a man's life. Ocean, *she* bigger than a man's life. City, she just a town got too much money. World never die, ocean never die, city, she die.

"So this one time, the twins they fighting. It don't matter what, every story tell that different, but they fighting. Sea King, he come out of water looking for boys and girls and bright gold to lie cold on the ocean bottom. This twin here, she say, 'ah, Sea King come, be helping us now.' T'other twin, stone house upriver, she say, 'no be no Sea King, you must of eat bad oysters.'

"So the Sea King, he pull the city down. Your Port Defiance, they disobey the Sea King. Them islands? They the towers of the old city. You go down, look inside rocks, you see."

Onesiphorous watched her knit awhile. This didn't sound like any history he knew. Port Defiance was on the verge of defying the City Imperishable—it didn't matter who they'd challenged in mythic depths of history. "What does this mean today?"

"Ah." The needles flashed. "You ask question longtime enough, you find answer. Stone twin got its hatred too. Land have powers just like sea. When trees come walking to you stone house walls, what you going do, ah? Remember history, or become history."

"Our problems are more, well, immediate."

"Got problems here, too." The needles stopped again. The old woman glared at him. "That fool Sevenships make too many deals south, new people come with big swords, bigger ideas. They cut down our trees, our forest become big plantation, what we got?

"You come down river, you solve problems, bring the little people home to the stone house city. Good, maybe you solve our problem, too. She no like slugs in their farms and their holes-in-the-ground, but they twin people, ah? Corsairs, Sunward sailors, no twins at all. People of the Sea King maybe. She no want no more change."

"You don't want change." Onesiphorous was on more familiar ground. "Neither do I. Not completely. I want my people to come home, not to tear themselves apart."

"Not set themselves on fire, ah." She laughed, a reedy whispering cackle.

He winced. "Right. We need the City Imperishable, the City Imperishable needs us. If dwarf money and dwarf discontent go back up the river, things here might be more normal. I can't replace Borold Sevenships, I don't have that power. But I can take away some of the fuel that drives the engine of his ambitions."

"You talk pretty, little man. Benny dwarf, ah. I tell you this thing, no argue. The river, she bring bad, bad news now. Maybe you make it good news. She no say, I no say. But them corsairs, you no want them, we no want them, she no want them. Take you troubles home to the stone house, little man, and leave us ours. We know how to live with our own worries."

"Believe me, I'd love nothing more." He wondered what news the river was bringing. Had someone important died, setting the City Imperishable into disarray? Was Imago safe?

At that thought, the old woman sank into her chair, which folded like a fist and slithered into the muddy ground.

Chilled to the bone, Onesiphorous stared at the dimple in the soil for a moment. He backed toward the bushes. What in Dorgau's ninth hell had that *been?*

"Come." Boudin tugged at his elbow.

They lurched back to the boat. She'd just *collapsed*, like the rubbery crust from a wine vat being sucked through an enormous pair of lips.

He sat shivering as Boudin poled them back out into the channels leading to the open swamps.

"Who was that?" Onesiphorous finally asked.

"She us."

"What?"

Boudin paddled, looked thoughtful. "Not every monkey fall out of same tree, ah? Not every people spring from same mother. She *us*. Swamp people mother."

"Mother to you *all?*" He couldn't figure whether to be horrified or amazed.

"Yea. Wife to Sea King, one time back in the long ago. All the swamp her house, all the animals and people her children."

Her pets, maybe. Onesiphorous sat in silence, thinking about drowned cities and what kind of news could come down the river to worry an old swamp goddess with green lungs a hundred miles across.

He was never so glad to see sunlight as when Boudin finally broke out from under the trees.

IMAGO

The Lord Mayor and Biggest Sister were alone in the map room. Morning reflected in through the narrow windows, but the lamps were lit as well, in order to banish shadows from the table. The harvest from Whitetowers archives was spread out along the map's southern edge, carelessly stretching across the Sunward Sea and the pocks of the tributary cities.

He'd flipped through a few pages, but lacked the inclination to buckle down yet. Imago knew how to do that work—for years his livelihood had depended on clever readings of obscurities in the law, a pursuit available only to a dedicated researcher. Today, even after a rough night's sleep, he was still taken up with a sense of what could or should have been.

Something threatened his city. *This* was his work—riot and marching armies, not sewers and acreage under till.

"The Tokhari woman has been behaving strangely." Biggest Sister trailed her hand across his shoulders.

They'd spent a memorable night together, back before the Trial of Flowers when he was still a full-man. He'd been told he might service other members of the Tribade. They'd never come his way since.

"How so?" Imago suppressed a shiver.

"Inquiring in the markets and taverns after Northerners. From the real North, not just farm boys and lumbermen down from the foothills of the Silver Ridges. People who came over the passes."

"The North." They both stared at the map. "Why would a Tokhari, even an adoptive one from the City Imperishable, care about the North?"

She shrugged. "Why would a foreigner come through town claiming to know the secrets of the North?"

"Kalliope is a sandwalker. The real thing. Not a confidence woman like that Ashkoliiz. As for Bijaz, I am worried."

"He committed deep noumenal violence on three men."

"Yes." Imago chewed on that thought some more. "I did not want him to confess last night. He seemed to require unburdening at a moment when moving on was the best counsel."

"He becomes dangerous," she warned.

When the *Tribade* thought you were dangerous, you were either becoming a great deal of trouble, or already in a great deal of trouble. Both, Imago imagined. "He is the City's luck."

Another shrug, another pass of the hand across his shoulder. "Luck is good or bad, you know."

"She is gone. And we do have Bijaz to thank."

"Thank away. Nonetheless, he is your problem. If he *becomes* our problem, we will solve him."

"I appreciate your honesty." Imago circled the table, poking at the books. "Have you looked at these?"

She followed. "No. I can deliver a few pliant clerks to sort through them if you find that needful."

"Thank you. However, I am pleased to report that I already have an abundance of clerks, both pliant and otherwise." He opened a leather-bound volume entitled *Beyond the Passes: An History of the Civic Empire in the True North*. Maps were bound in the front, but he would need a knife to slit them open. Imago idly thumbed through the pages.

"What will you do if that Ashkoliiz returns?" asked Biggest Sister.

"Have her killed if I can. If that's not practical, have her run out again. She can go peddle her stories down along the Sunward Sea."

"The bear concerns us."

He recalled the creature tossing him the bell. "It's an ice bear. Extremely well-trained, I'll give you, but I doubt anyone else could manage the bear in her absence."

"Hmm. I'll leave you with this. Does she seem the sort who would trouble to raise and train a bear cub?"

Imago searched Biggest Sister's eyes for some hint. "No, I suppose not. Perhaps one of those Northmen brought the bear."

"There is more behind those eyes than a beast, my friend." She stroked his hair. "I should send one of my sisters to you soon. It would be a shame to lose your blood."

At that, she left him with his book.

He spent more time leafing through the material while considering the enormous map. The most popular story about the Imperator Terminus, the one believed by people who'd never thought it through, was that he'd marched downriver with his armies and his priests, searching for the limits of empire.

Imago knew Terminus had left to draw off the bloodiest of the Old Gods. That had given the City Imperishable back to itself, granting a chance to grow and prosper. In that sense, his direction and stated purpose were irrelevant. But obviously he hadn't *marched* downriver. That road became impassable somewhere between the Sudgate and the Jade Coast, and had been so for many centuries.

The simple response was that he'd taken the water road, but that didn't make much sense either. Where would he go? West along the coast was a hundred leagues of empty jungle. Beyond that loomed the ironbound cliffs where the Yellow Mountains met the sea. Then, well, who knew? The world was broad, and wide.

East and south were the cities of the Sunward Sea, tributaries in Terminus' time. Why invade again? Overland beyond them lay the Tokhari deserts. South of the Sunward Sea was a limitless ocean. Again, who knew what was beyond that?

That was the way of the world. Each man knew his neighbor; every city knew its neighbor. No one could see past every horizon.

So north made sense, as did east. Neither of which jibed with the popular imagination. If Terminus had really wanted to bury his troublesome gods and their priests in great, deep holes, the Imperator could hardly have done better than some ice crevasse past the Rimerock Range. No one would come back from there until time itself had wound down.

East would have taken him across the Rose Downs and into a country of high plains and hills which had long since lain fallow. Nothing to conquer there, and too easy to return from.

It had to be north. The so-called True North, to be precise.

He also learned, in flipping through the books, that there had been garrison towns in the upland deserts beyond the Silver Ridges. They provided supply lines and support for the fortresses defending high passes in the Rimerocks. Imago tried to imagine some City-born full-man enlisting in the Imperatorial army, marching a thousand leagues north, and living out his life inside some frozen rockpile far past the edge of the world.

Then he tried to imagine what force could push through passes a thousand leagues distant and harry forward in sufficient strength to threaten the City Imperishable at the height of its imperial power.

If Terminus were anywhere to be found again, it had to be the upland desert country between the Silver Ridges and the Rimerocks. Imago wasn't so sure the legendary Imperator hadn't simply set sail with his money and his women and found a villa off the coast of a decadent city far to the south.

There were days when he had no trouble understanding that choice.

He closed the book and went looking for whatever trouble this new day had brought him.

"If you do not by Friday present a viable solution which represents the interests of my clients, I shall carry the suit before the Burgesses."

Imago stared at the lawyer—Roncelvas Fidelo. The bastard was a full-man, scion of some great family judging by his schooled accent, though still young. *Young enough to have his arse warmed by the flat of a sword*, Imago thought.

Marelle hovered behind the lawyer with a worried expression. She should be worried, he realized, as he found himself considering the distance from his open window to the pavement below.

Old habits. Refute the case, counterargue, keep the momentum going.

"First of all…" Imago held up one finger. "By your own admission the decedents assaulted Bijaz prior to his taking action. Any reasonable observer would conclude this releases Bijaz from his culpability. A simple case of self-defense." Another finger. "Second, he was unconscious at the time the assault began, and was forced to respond to attack as he was gaining consciousness. Here your charges against him fail a test-of-reasonableness." A third finger. "Finally, he is not employed by the City Imperishable or the office of the Lord Mayor in any capacity. He is a private citizen, and I cannot answer for his actions."

Fidelo smiled. "One does not strip a man of his hands, then of his life, simply for cocking a fist. This Bijaz now presents a clear danger. He disrupts public order and creates a climate of fear through his extreme actions."

"I myself can do nothing for you." Imago's eyes narrowed as his voice tightened. "And I can scarcely keep you from laying a complaint before the Burgesses. But better that you let this matter lie quietly. There are affairs of state close to these issues. If those are opened up for public examination, you and your clients will be placed in a very bad position."

Marelle bobbed behind the attorney again, miming hands closing across her throat. Imago nodded slightly. "Good day to you, Counselor."

"Indeed." Fidelo stepped around Marelle as if she were something distasteful.

"If you can do something," Imago said after his door had shut, "do it quickly and discreetly."

Marelle nodded. "Yes, sir."

"*And* non-fatally," he added reluctantly.

She slipped out.

How in the brass hells was he going to keep this whole Northern business from becoming a nine days' wonder? Especially if it went before the Burgesses. Anger and mockery had sloughed off Ashkoliiz's efforts to rally support for her little game, but if this became a matter of writ and testimony and endless witness lists—which he had no doubt young Counselor Fidelo was capable of generating—then the Terminus scam would come out regardless.

And who was really paying for Fidelo? Surely not the aggrieved families of a few dead lumbermen. It was possible, barely possible, that the syndics who controlled the northern lumber trade were sufficiently outraged.

More was afoot.

Marelle slipped back in the door. "Onesiphorous was a thorough dwarf. You lost much when you sent him south."

"How so?" asked Imago. "Or do I want to know?"

"Let's just say he was master of both contingency planning and the unsavory connection. Counselor Fidelo is going to arrive home to find a paternity complaint against him being dumped upon his mother. A trap Onesiphorous had arranged in the event of you being bothered by any young highborns. He won't be before the Burgesses in the immediate future." She almost giggled.

It was a shame that his taste had never run to dwarfesses. This was a woman he could admire, but she did not move his blood. "Whoever is behind him can always hire another attorney." Lawyers in the City Imperishable were thick on the ground as linden leaves.

"One problem at a time," she said.

"Still, this points to something else. People have taken note of what Bijaz did at the Ripsaw. Enero is there today, inspecting the place. It was one thing when Bijaz wandered around town farting butterflies, being a hero of the recent revolution. It's another thing if he spits fire and turns people into rosebushes."

Theogeny was a distinctly uncomfortable process for all concerned.

"Perhaps you should send him south to aid Onesiphorous."

"Is Onesiphorous in need of aid?"

"Bijaz may soon be in need of some air outside the City."

"There are more problems in the City dwarf community down there," Imago said. "Recent reports are not encouraging. If Slashed and Sewn were seen working together, that might be to the good."

"I do not think it is a matter of Slashed and Sewn, sir." Marelle frowned. "There are rumors of boxes being broken in Port Defiance."

"Broken boxes." Imago sighed and rubbed his eyes. "I need them to come home. That's why I sent Onesiphorous. By the ninth hell, he was the one piling them on southbound ships last year. Surely they can settle their affairs and make their way back?"

"Perhaps." She pulled a sheaf of memoranda. "On the good side, the last of the tribal encampments outside the River Gate appear to be saddling their ponies for a long journey."

"Hardly that good. Their presence was all that has kept Enero and his Winter Boys here. Once they ride west, he departs for the south. Then we're back to bailiffs and what few City Men we've been able to piece together." *Damn* the old Inner Chamber for the hash they'd made of his city.

"You'll have to speak with Fallen Arch about the bailiffs," Marelle said. "His debt is strong enough that he should be moved to aid you."

Zaharias of Fallen Arch was now First Counselor of the Inner Chamber. The new Provost was a backbencher from the Assemblage of Burgesses, a chair warmer named Jarrod Selsmark. Imago still wasn't sure where Selsmark took his orders from. Zaharias, on the other hand, was a known quantity.

"I lack for a chamberlain in Onesiphorous' absence," Imago said with a sudden urge. "Not that his job was ever official. Will you take that role?" Marelle was secretary to the Lord Mayor's office, but had not been a part of the executive.

"There has never been a woman sworn to office in the City Imperishable," she said. "Let alone a dwarfess."

"Be sure and mention that to Biggest Sister. The Tribade will be thrilled to hear it. Besides, I wasn't going to cry your accession through the streets. Just accord you the dignity of the post you already fill."

"I—I cannot, sir." She stared down at the floor.

"Why not?"

"I should never have ever…" She looked up at him. "I have other responsibilities."

Imago felt a cold stab of betrayal in his heart, until he realized what she must mean. "The archives?"

"Yes. I never should have come to work here, but during this past winter when the situation was so bleak, I thought I might help the City."

"You can still help. That's what I'm telling you. You're capable, and I need someone who can see to all that detail."

"You don't know anything about me."

"I'm asking you to work for me, not marry me!"

She shook her head. "I'm not what you think I am, I'm not who you see me to be. I'm no traitor, just not the woman you know."

"Who is?" he asked bitterly. "I was neither born nor raised a dwarf. Onesiphorous is a man without a mission now that his Slashed are no longer persecuted by law. Bijaz has been touched by the divine and wears it most poorly. Jason is *dead*, by Dorgau's sweet fig, yet skulks somewhere in the City wallowing in his sorrow. How are you different?"

"Have you ever wondered why my back is crooked?" she asked softly.

Imago suddenly wished he hadn't started this conversation. "I had always assumed a defect in your boxing."

"No. I came out of the box as proud a dwarfess as a father might have hoped for." She rubbed her neck.

"Then I must presume disease or accident." He was afraid of her answer.

"I was hanged from Lame Burgess Bridge by a mob of students," Marelle said. "I have never fully recovered."

Silence stretched. Finally he asked, "Are you dead?"

"Deathless would be closer to the truth. And now, having given away my secret for the first time in more years than I wish to count, I believe I should depart." She reached into her robes and pulled out a set of keys. "The offices and cabinets, sir. It has been a pleasure to serve the City alongside you."

"Wait," he said.

"For what?" She pulled the door shut behind her.

BIJAZ

He sat in the tiny watchtower atop the Rhodamine Abbey and stared across the City Imperishable. Morning mists still coiled around the low-lying areas. The gilded domes of the Temple District spread around him. He could see the hulking pile of the Sudgate far to the south, Heliograph Hill to his left, and the New Hill to his right.

Smokestacks and factories and mansions and commercial buildings stood all across the City Imperishable, pointing the way toward the future. A future the City would only see if they did not fail now, with the dwarfs scarce and recalcitrant.

Ashkoliiz would be the death of them all.

This little watchtower was only a folly, but still the builder had half-walled it and finished the underside of the roof with slatting to keep the pigeons out. Bijaz had been forced to climb across tiles, but that suited him. He enjoyed the run of the Temple District, being the only deity of any sort to wander the City openly these days—though Three-Widows certainly got about—but that freedom came with the price of nearly constant attention. Sometimes he wanted to be alone.

"I've got no room for prayer," he told the sky. "And the Numbers Men don't heed prayer anyway. But I've killed some men because of who I am. If they'd lived, that might have been worse. I would have healed them if I could."

The sky had no answer, but someone else did. "Must you hide in these ridiculous places?"

Bijaz looked around. Kalliope balanced on the ridge just behind him. She was dressed very traditionally, in the manner of her adoptive people—a rawhide vest, laced leggings, low riding boots.

"Apparently not sufficiently ridiculous." He offered her a hand in.

The watchtower was barely big enough for both of them. So close, he studied her. She had Jason's same storm-gray eyes and pale straw hair, but she was weathered. Her brother had still looked like something of a child to Bijaz, right up until his injuries. Kalliope had become one of those timeless women who'd left youth behind before arriving at age.

"To whom does a godling pray?" she asked.

"I don't listen to myself, but there's no one else to hear me."

Kalliope ran her hand through Bijaz's thinning white hair, scratching his scalp in a way that made him want to sag to the floor. "It's not so different from being a sandwalker, you know."

"Mmm?" He slumped against the half-wall.

"What the power does to you, I mean."

Bijaz gave a long, rattling sigh. "I turned a man's hand into a rosebush. Had he lived, he would have been a horror."

"I have given life and I have taken life, more times than I can count without careful effort. Sometimes in error, or for reasons so trivial as to seem meaningless. Power subtracts something essential from us, and gives something else in return." She tugged him into the crook of her arm. "It is usually a poor bargain, my friend."

"I didn't want this." He opened his free hand and a bat scuttled out of his fist, squeaking as it found its way into the daylight sky. "I am not safe, for myself or anyone else."

"Safe?" Her voice grew tight and hard. "I killed my *brother*. Then he became a miserable revenant. Don't speak to me of safe."

"No." Bijaz settled into Kalliope's chest, acutely conscious of his cheek just above her left breast. Her heartbeat echoed in his temple. "It scares me."

"You never sought it," she said distantly. "You never planned the trade the power takes, or worked for it, or remade your life around it as I did. Your power was thrust upon you one day in the confusion of the City."

He slipped his arm around her back and returned her hug. It felt good to lie so close. "Was it easier for you?"

"No," she said shortly. "Just more expected." She kissed his balding scalp. "It is never easy for us."

He turned his face toward her to meet her lips. "Ah," said Bijaz, who had not touched another human being in tenderness since being gang raped.

Kalliope's hands slipped down his tunic, finding his chest. He pressed his face harder into her, lips mouthing across her breast beneath her Tokhari vest. She tugged at her lacings with her free hand, until he found the sense to help her. When they spilled free, her small breasts were as sun-browned and hard-used as the rest of her.

He did not care. He closed his mouth around her nipple and began to suckle. When she tugged at his hair and asked him to bite, he bit.

Later, Kalliope pressed up against the half-wall of the watchtower as he rode her from behind like a dog. She called him "father." Bijaz was far past minding as he spilled his seed into her, coming fountains as light streamed from his fingertips and he made flowers grow wrapped within her hair.

They lay curled together. He tried to make wine appear, but it spilled in a sticky red mess. So instead Bijaz caused water to pour from his fingertips to rinse them both, to fill their mouths and wet their hair.

She laughed at him. "Finally I see a use for gods."

He smiled, though the pain was at the back of his thoughts. "It's a small benefit, to be sure."

Kalliope stroked his cheek. "You're afraid of the power."

"Yes."

"Good. When I first asked to follow the sandwalker's trail, the master I approached beat me senseless."

Bijaz stiffened, his arms sliding around her.

"Heed me," she said. "I tell you this for a reason." She laid a finger across his lips.

"When I recovered sufficiently, I asked my owner why this was. He said I was to ask the master. So I approached the master again. Again he beat me senseless.

"This time it took me longer to recover. I resolved not to be beaten a third time, so I stole into his tent and waited behind a tapestry with a stout club in my hand."

Bijaz giggled at the thought.

She poked him before continuing. "He slit his own tent wall and grabbed me from behind. When I tried to hit him, the master took my club away. Then, instead of beating me, he asked me what I had learned. I told him I'd learned not to try to sneak up on him. He laughed and said he would take me in. I was the first aspirant in years not to prattle on about the many paths to power or something of the sort."

"But there are many paths to power," Bijaz said.

"Of course. That wasn't his point. My master wanted a student who understood that power is a path, not a goal."

"It has been neither for me. More like a curse."

She shifted to curl around him and pull him close to her breast once more. "A curse is an end, old friend. If you let it be. If your power is a path, then find its direction."

He nuzzled. Though the morning was growing warm, and they were crowded tight in the little tower, her nipple swelled again beneath his questing tongue.

Later they climbed off the roof. Once down the ladder through the attic, Bijaz and Kalliope were in the halls of the Rhodamine Abbey. The building was all but empty at this hour, monks and nuns out ministering to the needy. The floors were stained with age and generations of oil, the walls papered with castoff silk from the great houses of the city. It smelled of wealth gone to seed.

They didn't speak now, just passed from room to room and down the stairs. Two old men scrubbed the flagstones in the receiving room as Bijaz and Kalliope entered. They pressed their faces flat.

"I tire of that," Bijaz said. "Once I was a dwarf."

"They do not bow to you in the streets."

The two of them clattered out the great door and onto Upper Melisande Avenue right where it met Bentpin Alley. His old offices were just down the way, burned down and now being rebuilt. Bijaz had no desire to go look.

"A few do," he admitted. "I meant to die, you know."

"I know. Your tale is hardly the stuff of secrets here in the City Imperishable."

"So if you know my circumstances, is there some special sandwalker wisdom you wish to impart?"

"I already have."

"What, don't try to get the drop on your master?"

They both laughed. He stopped, took her hands, looked up into her gray eyes. "You have given me back something of myself today. My thanks."

"Take more than I give," she said. "And be more than you are."

"Be more than a godling?"

She released her grip and spread her arms, eyebrows raised. "Be more than Bijaz." Kalliope turned into the traffic and walked away from him.

Bijaz headed for the Rugmaker's Cupola. He wanted to apologize to Imago for his surliness of the night before, and see what could be set to rights. As Kalliope had said, he was in need of a direction. He'd been bereft of purpose since the fall of the Imperator Restored. It was time to find his way once more.

The walk tired him, so at the New Hill terminus he caught the Cork Street car. That would take him across the Bridge of Chances all the way to the Hilltop terminus. From there it was just a few blocks to the Rugmaker's Cupola.

The streetcars were a curiosity, for the most part. The two lines which had been completed were both paid for by the gaming houses of Cork Street. They didn't quite meet, with a gap on the north side of Nannyback Hill.

He rode the car, paying little attention except to note the Winter Boy following ahorse. Eyes were never far away from him, especially after what happened in the Ripsaw. The Tribade probably had people watching as well, though children or the old were more their way.

"It's you," said a big man in a heavy cambric shirt, with the canvas pants and high-laced boots of a lumberman. He sat on the bench next to Bijaz.

"Excuse me?" Bijaz kept his hands close to his side. He glanced back to see where the Winter Boy was, but a beer cart was blocking traffic.

"There's money on your head, dwarf." The man was of middle years, unshaven, drunk. "I aim to claim the price."

"Please, I do not want to argue."

"Them's as are little always want to *reason*."

"If you know why people are angry with me, then you know why reasoning might be best for both of us."

Bijaz's fists clenched, a rippling feeling within him. He stood to get off when the lumberman grabbed at his arm.

"Let me go," Bijaz said in rumbling voice. The lumberman's fingernails bled as his eyes popped open, unnaturally wide.

The dwarf jumped to the pavement as the man slumped on the bench.

"Murder," someone shouted from the streetcar.

People moved to look. He tried to slip through the crowd. A voice bellowed, "Where's that short-arsed bastard!?"

Not again, he thought. Not another riot.

The freerider picked him up with no ceremony at all and dumped him over the saddle. "To be going now," his rescuer said, tucking into the horse's gait as shouts rose behind them.

Bijaz sat in Imago's office, feeling miserable. Enero was there, too.

"Is there a better time," Bijaz began to ask, but Imago waved him to silence. The Lord Mayor was looking out his window. Finally he turned.

"My pardons, gentlemen. Something I don't understand happened this morning, and it worries me. I may decide to be frightened later."

Bijaz mostly thought that the Lord Mayor looked sad. Nonetheless, here he was. "I came close to another brawl today. Minding my own business, I might add."

"There are being people to pay a price on his head," Enero said. "Friends of the dead, I am thinking." He looked unhappily at Bijaz. "The Ripsaw is having evidence of there being some great magicks."

"I blew all the glass and ceramic in the place."

"What I am seeing there anyone else can be seeing, too."

Imago slapped his desk. "Then shut it down, or burn it out." He then stared at Bijaz. "I realize we said you were not to blame, but surely you know more than this about the art of subtlety?"

"I do not control this power. It controls me." Bijaz felt ashamed. "I aim to change that," he added.

"Then stay the hells away from people in the meantime," said Imago. "A strong case has been made for sending you out of the City awhile. Perhaps you could abide in the map room? And pick no fights with us?"

Bijaz could think of worse things than being sent away. And Imago had moved some of that woman's archives to the map room. "I will go quietly. I ask you one favor."

"Which is?" The Lord Mayor's voice was acquiring a dangerous edge.

"Will you send Jason to see me?"

"I am thinking the former Second Counselor is not wishing to be disturbed," Enero said.

"I am thinking the former Second Counselor is not wishing to be dead," Bijaz snarled. "I have known him longer than anyone else. We are like family. Not close, happy family, but family. And I wish to see him. I will obey you regardless, but the favor will ease my mind. And quite possibly Jason's."

"Go," said Imago. "And for the sake of all the brass hells, stay *away* from people. I need you."

Bijaz went. He picked his way down to the map room without meeting anyone's eye. *No matter*, he thought. He needed time to contemplate the purpose of his power. A map and some histories should do nicely.

He did wonder if he should have asked for Kalliope instead, but Ashkoliiz still hovered at the edge of his memory.

ONESIPHOROUS

Out in the river delta, away from the shadows where a thousand ears listened, Onesiphorous asked Boudin the question which had troubled him all through the slow slide through green darkness. "You said she was you. All of you, the swamp people. Is she your ancestress?"

Boudin pulled on his oars and looked thoughtful. Finally: "Hard to say."

Onesiphorous noticed the boy had lost most of his swamp accent again. "She is not a person, in the usual sense."

"People are who they are, ah. Some got feathers, some got scales, some got hands and feet."

The boy was ducking the question.

"I don't know too many people who fold up and slide underground."

"She is she. Queen of Angoulême."

Despite his initial impression, he was now fairly certain that the woman-thing hadn't been a goddess. He hadn't experienced that rubbery tang of the noumenal. He'd never felt in danger. "You said not everybody climbed down the same tree."

Boudin smiled. "She is she, she is us."

A creature of the swamps, with a woman's face when it was needed. He had seen stranger things.

He looked past Boudin toward the tie-up at The Boot. Three of Borold Sevenships' men waited in their blue uniforms, carrying boathooks. They were burly and out of sorts, reminding Onesiphorous of bailiffs back in the City Imperishable.

"The Harbormaster wishes to speak with you," one said as he climbed up to the dock.

"I shall attend his convenience soon." Onesiphorous knew better than to try to step between them. Behind him Boudin backed water but remained close.

"His convenience is now."

"I see. Then lead on." Onesiphorous smiled brightly and cast one last glance at Boudin. The boy was already setting to his oars to scull away.

They climbed three flights of wooden stairs bolted to the rock. Onesiphorous looked for evidence of an older structure beneath, but it was definitely a rock. At the third level, they crossed a rope bridge to Little Aneh, then back down to a cable ferry to cross the Aneh Race and join the main walkways leading to the Flag Towers.

Everyone in Port Defiance certainly got their exercise.

Like bailiffs, this lot wasn't much for talking. He still had plenty to consider from his trip to the swamps, especially the thought of that bad, bad news. Which in turn was quite possibly what this little jaunt was about.

The bluecoats took him through a little postern gate and into one of the many structures comprising the Flag Towers. It was a series of small keeps linked by bridges, with the river and the tides coursing beneath the foundation pillars. They went up a flight then across an open gallery over one of the channels. The tide slopped thirty feet below them, smelling of fish and seaweed.

The halls and bridges they crossed were quiet, devoid of people and ripe for dark deeds. He wasn't particularly concerned for his safety, despite Big Sister's warnings. That sort of trouble wasn't likely to come from the Harbormaster. Sevenships had much better ways to make his life difficult.

Up another winding stair, and into a small audience chamber. In other circumstances it might have been a conference room, but most conference rooms did not feature a throne at one end of the table.

If it wasn't a throne, it was a very oversized chair. Borold Sevenships sat before a spread of papers, looking grim. He was a broad-faced man with bulging eyes and pasty skin sheened with sweat. This lent him the appearance of a confused fish. He was flanked by several local dignitaries. They appeared to be spoiling for an argument. No one else was present except a slim, light-skinned full-woman in blue silks. She had chestnut hair and pale eyes.

"Ah, the dwarf," said the Harbormaster.

As if Onesiphorous were the only dwarf in Port Defiance. "At your service, sir."

"Hardly." Sevenships turned to the woman. "Here is your man. So to speak. He represents the City Imperishable."

As do you, thought Onesiphorous. He was mindful of Big Sister's warnings about the political currents. "In my own *small* way, you might say."

He hated the pointless jest, but it deflected some of the hostility. Several people smirked.

"Indeed." Sevenships stared blankly. "You have come to speak for the dwarfs here, and hurry them home. Strangely enough, this young woman has come with a message for your dwarfs. One which she was summarily expelled from the City Imperishable for daring to utter."

That didn't sound good.

The Harbormaster went on: "Your home's unceremonious inhospitality to such a talented and lovely stranger does not speak well of the continued decline in the civility and political support we have noted of late. This good lady Ashkoliiz has approached me for assistance. As this is a matter for you City folk, I thought you might aid her in taking up her cause among your fellow half-men."

Onesiphorous swept the woman a bow. "And what is this news not fit to speak on the streets of the City?"

"Glad tidings." Her voice was filled with anger. "I have a found a great and difficult truth which was rejected by a mad dwarf wizard who holds unholy sway in the City Imperishable."

"I… a mad dwarf wizard, you say?" He'd left the city less than a fortnight ago. This was an astonishing political development, if true.

"Bijaz by name."

Onesiphorous burst out laughing. "You cannot be serious."

Ashkoliiz's eyes darkened. "He is crazed with overweening power. Your Lord Mayor stands in his thrall."

"And so I had the right of it," said the Harbormaster. "I was certain you two would have much to discuss. This is not the business of Port Defiance. Perhaps you should take yourselves among your own people and work out your differences there?"

Onesiphorous could see the wisdom of that. The less said within Sevenships' hearing about the City's current troubles, the better. And whatever Bijaz his old friend and older enemy had gotten up to, this woman had a most peculiar interpretation of it. "Come," he told her, "we will repair to my offices and you can elucidate what became of you back in the City Imperishable."

"I must bring my bear."

Onesiphorous wondered what she could possibly mean by that. "Of course," he told her, anxious to move things along.

The bear was thirteen feet tall, white, and wearing a harness of bells. It was so massive that his office swayed when the creature stepped within. Onesiphorous experienced the most piercing look he had ever received from an animal.

Ashkoliiz smiled sweetly. "She is everything to me. The sea seems to make her ill, and so I wish to have her near." She looked Onesiphorous up and down. "Besides, she will defend me should anything untoward emerge."

A small, dark full-man with features unlike any Onesiphorous had ever before seen had followed the bear in. He settled next to the creature at the far end of the office and began to idly finger an ivory flute. His black eyes focused steadily on Onesiphorous.

"I see you are well protected," the dwarf said.

"After my experiences in your city, I must needs be."

It was an act, pure and simple. Onesiphorous was certain he was being played, but he didn't yet know what for. It was up to him to work the problem through. On the whole, he was just as glad this situation had fallen to him. At least this way he knew where the next eruption would be coming from.

Onesiphorous donned a bright smile. "Pray tell me what tidings you brought, and how it was this Bijaz caused you to be expelled in disarray?"

"A simple enough matter." Ashkoliiz smiled and smoothed her skirts across her thighs. "I have found evidence of the resting place of the Imperator Terminus.

I only thought to bring the news of that wealth of history and treasure to the people of your city, as a boon."

"I see." This was a confidence game of epic proportions. No wonder she'd been run out. The political situation was far too unstable for the City Imperishable to afford a return to playing the game of Imperators. The last round had been a disaster, after all. "And this Bijaz fell upon you like Tokhari on a sheepfold?"

"Yes." Her eyes met his. Onesiphorous could see another kind of danger there. "He came to hear a speech I made. There he picked fights and performed magicks. Later he assaulted some blameless lumbermen, perhaps mistaking them for my associates. He transformed the unfortunates into plants. Their lungs choked on their growth. A riot ensued, with deaths. We were run out of the City under threat of more of the same." She shuddered artfully. "I meant bring your people a new future. Instead they treated me like a rabid dog."

Not so much, or they'd have shot her down in the street. "I have known this Bijaz a long time," Onesiphorous said, reflexively picking at the old scars upon his lips. "It is sadly true he has not been himself recently. Still, it is with great sorrow that I hear of your troubles." He wondered why in the brass hells Imago had not sent a letter warning him of this woman.

"And now I am barred from bringing my joyous news to those who would most wish to hear it." She smiled—a wan expression that proclaimed hope's last thread. "How shall I ever find the support to open the tomb and bring forth whatever great treasures which lie within? The glory of your City Imperishable would be restored, and all made wealthy."

Behind her the bear yawned. It showed a mouthful of teeth which could handily have closed over Onesiphorous' head. He found the view distracting, which saved him the effort of shrugging off her honeyed words.

"My good lady Ashkoliiz. I regret the inhospitality of my native city. But this is not a time when history is foremost in the minds of men. I take it you have a map? Or expedition notes? It might be best to sell those further down the coast, to wealthy collectors along the Sunward Sea."

Her smile grew harder. He recognized the expression—the game was on now, and she was playing for stakes. "Oh, Master Onesiphorous. If you read a map with the same perspicacity that you bring to understanding those around you, you would surely know that Port Defiance is itself the first of the cities of the Sunward Sea. It comes to my mind that there are many dwarfs here hungering for a renewed purpose which they have found absent in their distant home."

This woman *had* to be fresh into Port Defiance—otherwise he'd have heard about the bear before this. But she had good informants.

"As it may be, *mistress*. Nonetheless, the hunting is thin here." Onesiphorous let his smile grow lean and toothy. "You might best pursue your efforts elsewhere."

The ingénue was gone now. "You make one error in your reckonings." Ashkoliiz snapped her fingers.

The bear gathered itself to a sitting position, setting Onesiphorous' office to swaying once again. It tugged a bell from its harness and tossed the thing with a hard overhand throw so that the silver bauble rocketed across the room and bounced off the dwarf's chest. He grabbed the bell before it clattered to the floor.

This one was identical to the round, silver bell which the Alate had given him out upon Barlowe's Finger.

"You think I play a scam, fishing with a false lure." She leaned close to him. "What none of you seem to have considered is that I might be telling the truth."

"The truth, madam," Onesiphorous said slowly, rolling the bell in his hand, "is sometimes far more costly than any pretty lie." His curiosity overcame his good sense. "So long as we are being direct with one another, will you tell me what you have actually found? I promise no conjuring tricks or sudden riots."

She sighed. Considering odds, he could see. Thinking whether it helped or hurt her to tell him more.

Onesiphorous was able to be quite patient. Working under the old regime in the City Imperishable had taught him *that* particular virtue.

Ashkoliiz surprised him. "What I have found is the Imperator's last camp, on the slopes of the Rimerock Range. There is evidence there of a long stay by a large body of men, clearly from the City Imperishable. There were old papers in a chest, telling of the Imperator's death and how his party carried him away to a hidden tomb. They carried themselves away too, priests, gods, and treasure, to await his return in a cold cave beneath the hills.

"I came south to raise money and men in order to follow their line of march and open the tomb. I do not imagine an actual army in fighting array sleeps with their gods in some cavern, but they surely buried much around the Imperator Terminus." Her tone shifted from recall to supplication. "Think what lies beneath those stones—wealth, secrets. Your Terminus carried off the heart of the old empire with him, and he never brought it back. Together we might find it."

Despite himself, Onesiphorous was almost convinced. "You tell a story to make a grandmother cry," he said. "And I applaud you for delving into history. Curiosity is an emotion all men feel when they have the luxury of looking past tomorrow's meal. You may even have solved one of the great mysteries of the City's past. All the same, I implore you to take your story southward. The beys and doges of the Sunward Sea will be pleased by your tale, and might even grant you a lifetime pension simply for the pleasure of hearing you embroider upon it. Surely that is better than struggling to some frozen, northern hell in search of a lost cavern which might never have existed at all?"

The bear growled at his words. Ashkoliiz stiffened briefly, as if she heeded a distant voice. Then she gave Onesiphorous a look which approached pity. "So you forbid me to go among the City dwarfs here in Port Defiance?"

"I forbid you nothing." He spread his hands. "I have no power here. I merely offer counsel. The City dwarfs are in disarray, divided by troubles which have little to do with history and everything to do with the present. I doubt your message will find friendly ears."

He prayed that, actually.

"Fair enough. I have listened to your words." She stood. "I hope you have listened to mine. A thoughtful dwarf such as yourself might profit greatly from a part in the Northern Expedition."

"A thoughtful dwarf such as myself might profit greatly by not freezing off any of my appendages, either," he said. "I wish you luck, lady, and hope the sea bears you to better fortune."

"Fortune is where you find it, Master Onesiphorous."

She left, the bear lurching after her. Once again its weight made the office sway. The dark, little man was last. He paused on the doorstep to give Onesiphorous a long, slow stare.

"I don't know about you, friend," the dwarf said, "but I'm much too far from home. In my case that's only a few leagues up the river."

The man nodded, then was gone.

Onesiphorous waited a while at his desk, figuring that Big Sister would reappear soon. He suspected she had no one else to talk to, and was cursed with something of a social nature. He spent the time comparing the two bells. They might have been snapped from the same length of harness, they were so alike. He noticed faint engraving which read *Civitas est.*

"The city is"—the words of the City Imperishable.

He had no way to tell if the bells were genuine artifacts of the past, but it seemed reasonable. If these were fake, someone had gone to a fair amount of trouble. And to what end?

To what end the Alates, as well? Why bring him a bell?

He wondered if the bird-men were people who had climbed down a different tree, much as Boudin had suggested about the people of the old swamp woman's demesne. *Something* drew the Alates to the City Imperishable. They had attended the recent violence, possibly on both sides, even before one had tried to give him a clue as to what was coming.

Now he had to wonder how Ashkoliiz would bend the fate of the City. Could he stop her from gaining foothold among the dwarfs? On the other hand, her engaging the energy and financial support of the dwarf community might distract from the bloody passions running so high between Boxers and Openers.

He could argue this thought in circles all evening, Onesiphorous realized. And

Big Sister was apparently not coming. He looked out to sea, wondering where she was. Three lean ships tacked in toward the city.

They flew no flag. No bells rang to welcome them to Port Defiance and call out the factors and syndics.

His heart felt cold. Corsairs? Perhaps this was the deal the Harbormaster had been making.

Onesiphorous realized that he had been safer back in the swamps, even amid his fear, than he was here. That feeling was underscored when three dwarfs burst through his door with axes and boathooks. They wore blue coats.

"You, City man!" one of them shouted. The other two brandished their weapons.

In that moment he knew what might have happened to Big Sister. A purge was a purge. Old instincts died hard. Onesiphorous scooped the bells off his desk and jumped out the window, windmilling his arms as the running water thirty feet below rushed up to slap him half-senseless.

IMAGO

Enero was back, looking worried. When Enero worried, Imago worried.

"One of the Northmen who was being with Ashkoliiz is to be sneaking into the City Imperishable," the freerider said.

"I thought she was gone."

"I am not knowing what is to be happening in the south, but she is being gone from here. Her servant is not."

"Has he done anything wrong?" There had been no writ of exile against Ash-koliiz—Imago hadn't wanted to draw so much attention to her cause.

"He is being down in the Sudgate districts. He is not to be making trouble so far."

Which only meant he was passing time in quiet basements or the back rooms of taverns. "Do we have Northmen living here in the City Imperishable? I'd never seen their like before."

Enero shrugged. "Again, I am not knowing. People are coming, people are going. The North is usually to be keeping to itself."

Imago supposed he could simply have the man arrested on suspicion. He didn't control the courts or the jails, though, which meant he'd either have to stash the Northman somewhere illegal, or turn him over to the Burgesses. Who would then likely ask inconvenient questions. "Let's keep an eye on him."

"I am not having so many eyes now," Enero said. "Soon enough the last of the tribes is to be leaving, and so my Winter Boys are to be leaving as well."

They'd had *this* argument before. No price could keep Enero here perma-nently—the freerider simply wasn't interested. He was almost certainly a high officer in the army of one of the cities of the Sunward Sea—sent here the previous autumn to keep tabs on what had been a very dangerous situation. Enero and his men had been essential in the Trial of Flowers and the subsequent battle of Terminus Plaza, but now they wanted to go home.

It was scarcely the mercenary's fault that Imago couldn't raise a decent militia of his own.

He would have to apply to the First Counselor, and soon, about extending the bailiff's writ and having them resume policing the City. Imago was certain that Zaharias of Fallen Arch would be pleased to extend his aid, for a small financial consideration to offset the Burgesses' expense in the matter.

Not yet. He would postpone the old buggerer's moment of satisfaction as long as possible. "So we've found someone we'd prefer stay lost. What of Jason? Has he been located?"

"I am not finding *sula ma-jieni na-dja*. He is being nowhere in the City these last two months."

"He could scarcely have gone somewhere else," Imago said.

"I am not knowing."

If they found Jason, Imago could keep Bijaz occupied a few more days, let the fear and hatred die down. Assuming that arse Fidelo was distracted from bringing suit before the Burgesses by Marelle's efforts at entrapment. And with *her* gone, what would he do next? The Lord Mayor had clerks aplenty, but few who knew the ins and outs of governing as Marelle had, and Onesiphorous before her.

He knew where she was. He could send for her. Even go beg her to come back. Ageless or crazed, it didn't matter. She was still valuable to him. She hadn't wanted to come any further into the light, to be named to a post where the broadsheets and the letter-writing crazies and the Burgesses themselves might take note of her. Fine, he would let her be a shadow member of his government.

But Imago knew enough of human nature to realize that Marelle had to return on her own. If she was hiding in the Whitetowers archives, he was best advised to just let her hide.

Jason, on the other hand, was hiding somewhere else. And probably not emerging except under strong persuasion. But where was he?

Imago was tired of sitting in his office, being frustrated by news. At the least he could go out on the street and be frustrated first-hand.

No enclosed coach, no horsemen, just a begging dwarf, someone at the margin of holy orders, walking by the docks.

Jason had spent most of his adult life down by Sturgeon Quay. Perhaps his trail was warm there even now.

Tomb's Shipping and Storage had seen better days. The doors stood open, folded back on each side to gape cavernously toward Water Street. Most of the windows had been broken out. Broken crates, old netting, and cargo tackle were spread before the place like spindrift from ancient wrecks.

Imago studied the warehouse. Eyes gleamed from the shadows where feral dogs had taken up residence. A few stacks of goods remained within. There seemed to be little here.

He turned away, intending to try the Teakwood Scow next. A burly full-man stood glaring at him. "What is this place to you?"

"An empty building." Imago tried to step around the man. "I am sorry to have troubled you."

The man stepped with him, blocking his path. "You're not here to chase out the haint?"

Ah, thought Imago. Something was taking place down here. "I know nothing of a haint. I had a friend here once, that is all."

"Some of us had a friend here once. Others thought he was a right bastard. Last winter ate him up either way."

That was as close as Imago figured he'd hear to an admission of anything. "The dead man of winter?"

The big man relaxed a little. "Can you fix him?"

"What if I can't?"

"Then I'll throw you into the river, and kick you back down the ladder when you try to climb out."

"I am Archer," Imago said, taking the name of the late dwarfen godmonger who was an unsung hero of last winter's fighting.

"Two-Thumbs," the big man growled. "Stevedore, shift foreman, and friend once to himself."

"Where is he now? What is he now? A haint?" That didn't quite sound like Jason, even dead.

"You already know, I'm thinking."

"I have an idea." Imago looked around until he found a broken spool, then waddled over to use it for a seat. He wished he'd thought to bring a stick. Didn't mendicant monks always carry staffs? He peered up at Two-Thumbs. "If I stay long enough, will I see him?"

"Depends on whether you can sit a week or two."

"But he does come here?"

"Yes."

"I can't fix him," Imago said, "but I know someone who might be able to." Visions of Bijaz setting men's hands to blooming flooded his imagination. It must be some use, knowing a budding god. "But I need to take him elsewhere to make the effort."

Two-Thumbs spoke meditatively. "They say his sister did this to him. They say it were the bad Imperator what came back. They say it was the magick of the hour, the Lord Mayor's banner touching him. Me, I don't know about any of that. I know his coin was good and he kept his word, and the warehouse has failed these months without him."

"So where is he?"

"You wait, in time you'll see him. If you can bring him back, so much to the good. Or maybe he's better off dead."

"I can wait, but not a week or more."

"Even an old barker like me knows himself a secret or two." Two-Thumbs headed into the shadows of the warehouse, picking up a length of cable with which to fend off the dogs.

Imago watched him go, wondering.

Perhaps ten minutes later, the dogs began howling. Several raced out of the front of the building, while loud splashes suggested that others were going directly into the river. Two-Thumbs appeared from the shadows and waved at Imago.

Once inside, he could see that the warehouse had an office built into one corner, with a second floor above it. Jason's old apartment, before the poor bastard had been forced onto the Inner Chamber and moved into the Limerock Palace.

"This place belonged to Tomb, right? Bijaz's brother?"

"Aye," said Two-Thumbs. "The full-man son of the family. Went south years ago now, left himself in charge."

The man was not going to say Jason's name. "Do you really believe he's a haint?"

Two-Thumbs paused at the door to the office. "I got no way to tell." His voice caught. "No one cares what happened to himself, who gave all for the City. If'n he's a haint, I reckon he should be rested down. If'n he's not no haint, I reckon he should be helped back up into the light. It just ain't me to be the one who does it." Another pause, then: "I figured who you are, Your Right Honorableness. And you were a friend to him awhile. God-shot besides. You got power coming and going."

"I just want to see him, man. Talk if he'll listen. Maybe I can help. Like I said, I know someone."

The stevedore nodded. "That other one, not just god-shot but god-riven he is. Brother to Tomb." He stepped into the office. "Now come and see what set the dogs to fleeing."

Imago followed him into the little office. It wasn't old and rotten—the place had only been abandoned for a season—but it was heroically messy, with papers scattered everywhere. A closet door at the back wall stood propped open. A cold draft blew from it, carrying the stink of old barns.

"He thought it a secret," Two-Thumbs said. "Those of us who knew just figured him for a fallen toff. They got different taste, up in the high houses."

"What?" asked Imago, stepping forward.

"You just go down there and you'll see."

Imago glanced over his shoulder. The big full-man was between him and the room's only exit, herding him toward the closet. Had this been a mistake?

If you're driven, run 'til you're ahead of the herd. It was a maxim he'd learned the hard way in the last year, trying to maintain a hold on the reins of power.

He stepped into the darkness and promptly rammed his knee on something metal.

Behind him, Two-Thumbs stifled a laugh. "'S a boiler, Your Right Honorableness."

The moment of menace was gone. Perhaps if he'd tried to turn back.

"You steps around it," the stevedore added.

Imago stepped around, feeling with his hands. He found a second door propped open. It was no more than a false panel. The barn stench was stronger, the draft decidedly rising up from below.

How was that possible? This warehouse stood on Sturgeon Quay. Nothing but Saltus water should lie beneath the floor. He headed slowly down the stairs in near blackness, one hand firmly braced upon the wooden wall.

It took several minutes of agonized creeping, but Imago reached the bottom. He smelled straw again, and old meat. The draft was stronger, the scent now mixed with the familiar stench of the Saltus.

"Jason? Are you here?"

He stopped to listen.

Nothing, of course. But he was looking for *sula ma-jieni na-dja*, the dead man of winter. Jason had been stripped of his heart by his sister. His lungs were now little more than leather sacks serving as bellows to drive his voice.

It had been sandwalker magick, a different noumenon than what crawled the night streets of the City Imperishable. Imperator Ignatius had commanded his walking dead, too, but they were weapons with feet. Jason had been forged into something holy to the Tokhari but incomprehensible to his own people.

"*Sula ma-jieni na-dja*," Imago said. His Tokhari accent was horrid, he knew, but Jason's wouldn't be any better. What would Bijaz tell the man? "Spring is on the land, Jason. It is time for you to walk into the light once more."

A scrape echoed, followed by a rustle of straw. It could have been some beam in the building's frame settling. Imago knew better.

"Bijaz asks for you now. His power has grown. He may be able to help you."

A muffled thump. The barnyard smell grew stronger. Imago felt a swell of panic. Wouldn't he hear Jason moving around in the dark? What of the rustle of clothes, the swish of straw? Perhaps Jason's mind had rotted and he was nothing more than a vengeful revenant.

"Jason." Imago could not keep the squeak of fear from his voice. "Come up with me. Please. We need you. The City needs you."

A leather claw closed on Imago's throat, startling a terrified shriek from him, but he was imprisoned in an iron grip. Cold air gusted. Then, words: "Need?" The voice seemed to come from a tunnel, long, dusty, and disused. "What is need?"

Imago tried to draw breath to answer, to plead, but he was trapped. Another leather claw found his neck from the other side.

"No one needed me."

"J-j-jason." He spit the words out, past the closure in his throat. "Come back to us. We will help."

"I never wanted to leave."

Imago fought for air. He could breathe, barely, but speaking was torture. "It, it, it doesn't matter n-n-now."

Then the hands were gone. "Send her to me, at moonrise tonight."

"Who?" Imago asked, rubbing his neck.

"My sister. My lover. My killer." The voice seemed to fade, then paused. "Send her with a closed coach. Send her down to me. Then I will come."

Imago found the stairs and began pulling himself up. "I will find her. I will send her. Kalliope." Around the corner, into the faint light. "I promise," he shouted down the stairs. Then he was out, stumbling in the shadowed safety of the warehouse.

"You seen him," said Two-Thumbs.

"Yes." Imago shivered. "He asked for a guide, t-tonight."

The stevedore grimaced. "Don't betray him again."

"No. I will do what must be done."

Imago walked quickly out the warehouse door, down the quay, and on to Water Street. He *would* do what must be done. Right now he wasn't sure that would amount to any more than an enormous fire.

The Lord Mayor put that thought out of his mind as unworthy, albeit more than a little sane. Two-Thumbs had been right. Jason could not be betrayed again.

Bijaz

He was deep into an old scroll recounting the provisioning and equipage of expeditions beyond the Silver Ridges. A tumult abruptly erupted in the hall outside the map room. Bijaz placed a cup over the rush light and dropped beneath the table. The scroll rattled on the floor as the door banged open, while a flight of wasps tumbled out of the path of his fall to buzz angrily toward the ceiling.

"In, *now*," said a woman's voice. Kalliope, he realized. Feeling foolish, he crawled back out.

A loud argument in the hall was being conducted in Tokhari. She supported someone else as the door slammed behind them, cutting off the racket. Bijaz came around the end of the table to help.

Even with only the moonlight in the windows, he could see she supported her brother Jason.

"Where—?"

Kalliope waved him to silence with a chop of her hand. "Sit," she told her brother, lowering him to a chair.

With an audible creak, he folded at the waist and knees. His head lolled on his shoulders, held on only by his skin. Bijaz felt his flesh crawl. Surely he had seen Jason walking when he entered on Kalliope's arm.

Kalliope touched Jason's forehead. "Hold." A swirl of hot, sere air came from nowhere. She straightened up to stretch her back. "That was not… simple."

A wasp circled close to her. She waved a hand and it crackled, expelling a puff of mist before floating to the floor as a husk. Bijaz hoped his other apports found the windows before they found Kalliope.

"Where was he?"

"Imago located him. In that little dungeon beneath the warehouse on Sturgeon Quay." She sounded disgusted. "I had no idea it was there. If I'd known, I could have told them where he would be hiding."

"Jason was not a kind man," Bijaz said reflectively. "He carried an indifferent violence within him as a youth. I think maybe that had begun to fade with age." He circled Jason, who was now still as his chair. The man was a brittle stick that seemed to glow in the moonlight. Unsurprisingly, the tang of the noumenal hung about him. "Is he held long?"

"Until I release him." She sighed. "Which will happen if I fall asleep, or have my concentration broken."

"Is this power as a means or an end?"

"Don't be nasty." Then, unexpectedly, "Please."

"Of course," Bijaz said. "You had to bind him to bring him in, I presume."

"Yes." She hoisted herself up on the map table, her arse somewhere far out in the Sunward Sea. "I don't know what Jason's plan was, or if he even had one. He scared the hells out of Imago. He asked me to come at moonrise with a closed coach. I suppose he intended to leave." She glanced at Bijaz. "Imago promised to bring him to you."

"Yes." Bijaz began to feel guilty. "I asked for Jason."

"What, to ease your exile to the map room?"

"*No.* I was worried."

Kalliope snorted. "You've become too dangerous for a lot of people. This would be a very good time to find a path for that power. I think Imago has hope of you curing Jason, and thus showing that you are more than just a danger."

"Cure him? From being dead?"

"I know, I know. *I* killed him."

"And then he came back. But he's still dead." Bijaz realized that the argument outside the door had died down.

Kalliope watched him glance toward the hallway. "They're frightened."

"He's frightening."

"To be sure. Where's the light in here, anyway? See if you can do something for him."

Matches stood in a bowl on a sideboard where their hosts had been leaving food. Not meals so much as a never-ending buffet of tangy, salty dishes, and more ways to prepare chickpeas than he would ever have thought possible.

Bijaz picked up the little clay lamp, struck a match, and nursed the flame to brightness. Then he looked up at Jason and nearly dropped the lamp.

At the battle of Terminus Plaza, Jason had been pallid but reasonably human. Somehow Bijaz had assumed his old ward would continue that way—of strange coloration but still recognizably Jason.

The Jason-shaped thing in the chair looked as if it had been dragged out of a peat bog.

He had no hair. His scalp was almost black, with a texture like shiny leather. The eyes were pulled wide open, the balls within shriveled gray pits. His lips were drawn so widely around his mouth that most of the jaw was exposed. The rest of Jason's body was mercifully concealed beneath a ragged layer of clothing, though one clawed hand protruded. The fingers seemed to have fused. Every visible tendon was stretched tight as if in extreme struggle.

"By the stars, what has become of him?" Bijaz whispered.

"He's dead."

"But your sandwalker magicks…"

"He's stuffed with *straw*." She practically growled at Bijaz. "I didn't have the right herbs and weeds. He was brought back, not restored to life. His body wants to rot, but the bindings on his soul will not allow it."

"And yet he was strong enough to contest with you when you came for him."

"Contest and nearly prevail, I am ashamed to say." She shook her head. "That big stevedore had to intervene while my brother was strapping me to a whipping frame. I believe Jason broke his leg. Imago has the man with that Tribade doctor now."

Bijaz paced back and forth behind Jason's chair. "So what do we do?"

"*We* do nothing. You do something."

He squatted next to Jason and poked at the shiny skin. It was like touching a crab shell. "I have no idea what."

"You're the miracle man. That path to power you asked about? I believe it passes through Jason."

Bijaz ran his hand over the stretched face. The expression frozen there was not anger, or even agony. It was despair.

Bijaz had been steward of Jason's father's wealth until his employer had lost everything in the affair of the soul bottles. The father had been broken for debt, then torn apart by a crowd of paupers. Kalliope sold herself to a Tokhari for a concubine, while their mother left Jason standing in the street. Their other sister Ariadne simply vanished, into the dwarf pits perhaps.

There had been nothing else to do, so Bijaz took the boy home. He'd had the raising of Jason from the time the lad was twelve.

In all honesty, Jason had been a vicious, spiteful boy. Still, he was a full-man, and had been willing to fill some of Bijaz's more personal needs in exchange for a bit of freedom of his own. Even now, that memory brought a hot blush of shame. The education Bijaz tried to deliver had stuck sufficiently for the boy to grow to a young man who could read a contract and balance an account.

Bijaz had set Jason to work for his brother shortly before Tomb had decamped for the South Coast amid the Jade Rush. Jason had stayed on the docks in Tomb's employ, growing older if not wiser until he'd made the acquaintance of Ignatius of Redtower. Bijaz avoided his former ward in those years. They had little enough to say to one another, and Jason had spoiled Bijaz's daughters besides.

It all seemed to matter so much less now. The girls were long since launched into their own lives, Empyrea married to a wool factor, Beaulise working on the Jade Coast. Jason had given everything for Ignatius and the City, becoming the first successful regicide in modern history. This even though both killer and victim were already in a sense dead before the act.

They'd let him slip away afterward. There had been a tide of confusion and shame after the death of the Imperator Restored. Some questions were easier not to ask in those hurried days. Bijaz owed Jason a better reckoning: for the sake of his father, for the sake of the boy he'd used and abused, for the sake of the man he'd shamefully neglected.

With that thought in mind, he reached to shut Jason's eyelids.

The skin there was rough, dried, and crackling rather than shiny and smooth. Bijaz closed his own eyes and sought the white place the Numbers Men had left within him. He thought of water and cream and the smooth flow of the river after the spring spate. His fingers brushed across the wrinkled terrain of Jason's face, trying to ease and settle what remained there.

Something flowed. When Bijaz looked again, Jason's eyes were closed, but the desiccated skin of his face was suffused with something dark.

Blood? Tears?

Bijaz sniffed his fingertips.

Oil.

"Careful, my friend," Kalliope whispered as she moved to put the rushlight out once again.

She was right. They did not need flame now. Bijaz let his nimbus flicker into being. It was little more than a glow, not the bright flare with which he had contested Ashkoliiz.

Thinking of her pale blue eyes, he stroked Jason's lids. "Come, grow, prosper," he whispered. "Your soul has clung to this body beyond all reason or measure. Return to yourself and find a better existence."

He rubbed the oil into Jason's face with smooth, circular motions, pushing it into the skin of the cheeks, wetting the backdrawn lips. He opened his other hand to a bundle of sage and rue, and stroked the herbs across Jason's skin.

"The body is too dry," said Kalliope.

"I know," Bijaz replied. "I am trying to restore his dignity, not his first life. My powers do not extend that far."

He slipped Jason's ragged coat free and began to open the shirt. It had been misbuttoned, one buttonhole off all the way down as a small child might have done. Bijaz's hand strayed across Jason's chest, spreading more oil in an echo of the touching he had once forced upon this man when he was a boy.

Kalliope reached to cut her brother's clothing away. "I do not know if you will truly help him, but it eases my heart to see him less withered."

The oil still seeped from Jason's face. Bijaz continued to spread it. He and Kalliope worked it into the dead man's gut, his legs, his arms, his hands and feet. Then they picked Jason up and laid him on the map table, heedless of the oil staining the surface.

Jason weighed no more than a bundle of sticks encased in leather.

His back was raddled too, protruding ribs separated by the knobs of spine. Bijaz oiled there, covered Jason's buttocks, then steeled himself to reach below to the scrotum and the cock.

In time, Kalliope laid a hand on Bijaz's arm. "Enough. You have done all there is of this to do."

They looked at their handiwork. Jason was spread out flat now, once more on his back. His limbs were not twisted or strained. His skin was almost supple. His eyes and lips were shut. It was as if he were sleeping.

"He is still stuffed with straw," she said after a time.

"What would the stuffing have been, back in the desert?"

"Sage. Verbena. Rat's nettle. Nightrose. Wound together with the yellow watervine."

"But here you used straw?"

"Stabling looted from some farm at the edge of the Rose Downs. It was deep winter. I had no green to work with. In summer I might have made him a man of your woods, with ivy and honeysuckle and wild onion and rushes from the streambeds."

"Stabling. So you brought him back as a creature to be ridden, to draw loads, to serve and be whipped and driven to his knees."

"There was need." Her voice blossomed with shame. "We came upon the Stonesource thinking to find the end of all things at hand. And besides, I had cause for vengeance."

"Upon him?"

She skipped a beat, a silent sob. "He stayed and grew fat. I was dragged along on the back of a camel to be a toy for old men."

"It was not his doing," Bijaz said.

"I know."

"Straw. I can make something of straw, perhaps."

He laid his hands on Jason's gut, on the raw stitches where Kalliope had taken out the sweetmeats in ancient ritual. *Straw was bedding*, Bijaz thought. But it was also the corpse of grain, the golden heads which bowed to the wind and sun before being cut and threshed and made into beer and bread. The stuff of life, grain.

Bijaz imagined the stirring of the yeast within a bowl of flour. He called to mind the golden sunlight pouring onto a bright field. A man clad in the leather and linen of a Rose Downs farmer walked there, scythe swinging, cutting down the proud grass to make another generation. Bijaz, intent on his own errands, nodded to the reaper man, who nodded politely in return.

Gather these heads, he thought, *thresh the seeds, make something more out of what was brought before me.*

It could be no more difficult than farting butterflies.

His hands played across the furrows of the soil, which lifted in the pattern of Jason's ribs above his sunken belly. Chips fell onto a table as a wheel clicked somewhere. Bijaz did not allow himself a distraction. If the Numbers Men wished his attention, they could seek audience. He was at work, smiling brightly down upon the fields beneath his care.

Water flowed, pumped by the bellows of air which draw it up from river and ocean to scatter rain across the land. So Jason needed to flow. He needed to keep from being too dry to live, to irrigate the yeast building their tiny empires in the straw of his gut.

A man might never have his liver and lights, and still walk beneath the sun. Could he not then walk in beauty, with light in his hair and eyes the color of winter sky?

Bijaz sank further into the dream. He watched the reaper man cross the hilltop with the scythe upon his shoulder. The water ran now as a wheel turned, mill grinding grain, the ball of chance dancing atop it to find another slot even as the baker turned the loaves and the mother turned her breast to the newborn and life was drawn through the watery lungs of the sky.

He let go of all that was green and gold and opened his eyes to the pink leap of dawn reflected in those blind windows.

"I was afraid," Kalliope whispered.

Bijaz looked down. Jason seemed whole. Sleeping or dead, that was harder to say.

"How long?"

"You have been lost to me five hours and more. I knew better than to call for help. I have sat with others who walked the night desert, but you followed paths I could not take."

"It was not a desert," Bijaz said. "A field of grain beneath a summer sky. There was a reaper man, and a baker, and people laying wager just beyond my sight."

"My path to power is a desert, bone dry and lit by no moon that ever rode our sky. Your path is through the grain of your city's blackland farms."

"Straw." He laughed softly. "You sent me through the stables, because winter had bound you over with nothing more to work your magicks. I have passed again through the white room of the Numbers Men, but this time I chose my own path. Or let you choose it for me." Bijaz wondered what the price would be for walking that route. At the moment he did not care overmuch.

"So was he a means or an end?" Kalliope looked down at her brother.

Jason began to snore.

Bijaz's heart could have leapt with wings to meet the dawn. "All his life he has been used. First by me, then by Ignatius, then by you. Perhaps it is time for him to decide."

"I will send for food," she said. "He will be hungry when he wakes, and I am famished now."

"Yes. But please… no bread nor beer. I do not think I could take grain this morning."

He reached down and picked a curling sprout of green from Jason's lips. Jason moaned, stirring until his eyes flickered open.

They were blue-white, not the storm gray they had been in life. Bijaz's satisfaction at his private miracle was tempered by a quick stab of fear. He had given Jason the eyes of Ashkoliiz.

"I think they're pretty," said Kalliope, looking over his shoulder.

"Hello, sister." A butterfly darted out of Jason's mouth to make its staggering way toward the windows.

ONESIPHOROUS

Boudin fished him out of the water yet again. This time, the boy was not laughing. The incoming tide had pushed Onesiphorous through the race beneath the bridge, but his assailants could climb to the railings and spot their position at any moment.

"My thanks," he gasped. "Now row, boy."

"Tell your mother, ah!" Boudin was already pulling, the swamp rich in his voice again. "She say you got trouble, I think to watch for you. Trouble come soon, I say myself."

Onesiphorous slumped in the bow. "I don't suppose you know where Big Sister might be."

"I not know *who* Big Sister might be."

"Do not worry."

They pulled around another islet. Boudin backed water to drive the boat into a calm pool, then braced them against a rock with an oar. "You're not drowning now," he said, losing his accent as the stress of the moment subsided. "Where you want to go?"

Onesiphorous considered that. His next decisions were probably a matter of life and death. "I don't know where to find Big Sister. The Boxers likely blame me for Trefethen's death. The Openers are the ones in blue who came for me." He very much did not want to throw himself on the mercy of the Harbormaster.

A thought came unbidden: *Ashkoliiz.*

Would the mountebank take him in? *Could* she? Otherwise he would have to head for the swamps, or seek a friendly plantation somewhere along the coast.

No, he told himself. Not her. She'd sell him to the highest bidder.

"What about the Flag Towers?" he asked. "They're largely empty. I can hide there awhile, see what happens next. The Openers won't be searching for me under the Harbormaster's floorboards, not at first."

"There is a place for you in the green shadows," said Boudin. He shoved off and began to pull at the oars. "Best you lay down in the bottom of the boat and pretend to be a bale, ah?"

Onesiphorous huddled as low as he could get, showing only his wet back to the cold wind. He'd likely catch his death of pneumonia. The thought brought a tired smile to his lips—that wouldn't serve Imago's interests in the least.

Boudin let him off by a ladder well underneath the Flag Towers.

"Get back to the swamp and stay there," Onesiphorous said. "It won't take someone long to work out that asking you where I am is a good idea."

"I do what she tell me," Boudin answered. "Right now she tell me to go home."

Onesiphorous reached out to shake the boy's hand, his left fist gripping the slimy iron rung. "Then she and I agree."

"Ah." They clasped a moment before Boudin pulled away.

The dwarf climbed toward the underside of the keep, passing barnacles and mussels and clumps of sodden plant life. The tide was rising. Onesiphorous watched the rock, trying to see the towers of some ancient city.

It was just rock, fractured by wind and wave, slimed from the permanent shadow of the keep above. The stonework was just pillars extending downward to spread the load of the building above.

He paused to study that underbelly. The structure was wooden. Scattered catwalks dangled, and a few stouter bridges including the one he'd been led along before.

No one was visible down below. It wasn't a place a sensible person would linger—chilly, too easy to fall unnoticed into the water below until you were missed somewhere in daylight.

Onesiphorous climbed a few more feet and pulled himself onto a catwalk. He was cold and wet, likely to take a chill or worse. He could *not* stay down here. Going up presented its own problems. He was fairly certain the Harbormaster had no dwarf servitors, so he could not reasonably hope to pass for a palace servant.

He would have to rely on his eyes and ears, and stay to the quiet passages. With luck he'd be fine. He went to find a way in.

A closet full of place settings was the best he could do. The hallways were packed with people running back and forth. This was nothing like the deserted calm when he'd been brought in before meeting Ashkoliiz. Had she already set Port Defiance to riot?

It was a near thing finding an unlocked door that didn't lead to an open space. Inside Onesiphorous was able to skin out of his soaked clothing and wrap himself in a tablecloth—inelegant, but dry.

Outside, voices and more voices. They were not speaking Civitas, the language of the City Imperishable. He recalled the dark ships sailing unheralded into port.

The Flag Towers were full of corsairs.

No wonder the Openers had come for him. They had not wanted the one authoritative voice of the City Imperishable present for their little plays of betrayal and counterbetrayal. Big Sister had said the Boxers were on the so-called citizens' council. The Openers must be aligning with the Harbormaster in his pursuit of rebellion.

Selling oneself to corsairs to escape the City Imperishable struck Onesiphorous as an especially poor bargain—trading chains of money for the flat of a sword. But he was not the Harbormaster.

The citizens' council would likely come to an understanding soon enough if the flow of funds from the City's banks were cut off. He doubted corsairs cared for the business of money transfers. Their reputation was far more direct.

Onesiphorous waited for the voices to die down without. He would need to move soon, to find a more permanent place with a fire to dry his clothes, and food. He might be a spy in the house of rebellion, but he couldn't work cold and hungry.

When he estimated it to be late evening, Onesiphorous stole out to the halls again. He'd wrapped the tablecloth into a sort of very old-fashioned tunic. Things were quieter now, though he could hear distant singing. He tried to move away from the sound, but that was difficult to judge. The floors of Flag Towers served as a series of gigantic drumheads, carrying noises in strange directions.

He kept trying the dustiest halls and doorways he could find, until he came across a caretaker's apartment. It had a firebox and a rope-strung cot, as well as two racks full of tools. There were hammers and saws and vises. He could improvise weapons if need be, though he had never been more than a casual street brawler.

Onesiphorous realized he should have asked Boudin to take him upriver, at least far enough to hail a packet coming downstream and commandeer a ride back to the City Imperishable. He now had no way to communicate with Imago.

It didn't matter at the moment. He built a little fire and lay down. He needed to sleep off his chill. A clear head to think with on the morrow was a priority as well.

Onesiphorous woke to find two children staring at him. One had her finger far up her nose. The other was a boy who was a little older. He also appeared quite suspicious.

"What are you doing in Old Bendlin's cot?"

"Um… Old Bendlin told me I could use it." He tried to swallow a coughing fit.

"Nah," said the little girl. "Bendy's dead."

The boy nodded. "You ain't one of them."

This time he didn't beat the cough. His chest hurt, with a broad, hot ache. "One of whom?" Onesiphorous asked cautiously when he'd got his breathing back.

"Ship men. They come into the quarters last night, drug off Mama and all the other women."

Onesiphorous winced. He wondered how the Harbormaster had felt about that. Certainly the women here had cause to hate rather than serve now. "No, I'm not one of them."

"Can you find her?" the boy asked. "Mama," the girl added.

"I don't know." Another round of coughing. "I'm not the rescuing sort." He tried to smile. "I can send for help."

"You got message birds?"

"No. I need to find my way upriver." Now he truly wished he hadn't sent Boudin away. "Can you bring me dry clothes? Something to make me look different. Something for my cough, too."

The girl nodded. The boy glanced at her, then they both slunk out.

Onesiphorous stretched and rose from the cot. He figured there was a good chance they simply wouldn't come back, but it was also unlikely they'd bring the Harbormaster's men. They certainly wouldn't fetch corsairs.

Not after last night.

He was stiff. His breath didn't come right, either. The chill had settled on him after all. He stayed wrapped in the tablecloth, sitting close to the stove for a long time.

When the children did return, they brought a pinch-faced woman whose eyes were puffy and red. She walked with a limp and wore the gray-stained dress of kitchen drab, with a ratty shawl drawn over.

"He's not a big child, you fools." She slapped the boy. "Run on, I'll take care of this."

They scampered into the hall, giggling.

"I'm afraid you have the advantage of me, madam," sniffled Onesiphorous. His nose had become something of a fountain.

She peered close. "You're that City dwarf. The new one, who wanted to stop their fighting."

"Yes. I am Onesiphorous. And you?"

"It don't matter who I am. We're all invisible here, 'til them blackheart bastards want a woman to turn up her skirts. But that crazy woman come down with you, the Sister. You her friend?"

That was a loaded question. He didn't know which way the bullet was pointing. He plumped for honesty. "Not precisely friends. I don't suppose she had much use for me." A long, burbling sniffle. "But we worked together, and sought many of the same things."

At least he wasn't coughing.

"She's dead, I hear tell." A stab of fearful sadness shot through Onesiphorous. "Shame, that." The woman didn't appear distressed. "They's upstairs tearing things down around our ears. Turned all us women over last night to use us hard, and killed Einette this morning for moving too fast with the tea tray. Himself made a bad mistake, but he's not one to admit that. Not ever. "

"All the City did was tax you."

"Taxes? Me?" She laughed, a bitter sound like sliding stones. "Got to have money to pay taxes. I live here, I'll die here. It don't make me no never mind whose flag is on the towers. I just don't wish to be any man's dog, you get me, mister City dwarf?"

"Oh, believe me, I do," said Onesiphorous with a fervor which surprised even himself.

"Fair enough. I reckon you took a dunking and then some. Stay here awhile, I'll send Padraig and Shanny back with clean clothes. In a bad light you might pass for an ugly girl, we get a wig on you. Ugly's good these days, believe me." She wound down, smoothing her skirt. He noticed she winced as she did so. "Not good enough, maybe," she added quietly.

"Madame, I will do what I can. But I need to send a letter to the City Imperishable." He needed to go there himself, but that didn't seem likely. "If Big Sister is still alive, I'd very much like to speak to her. And if you hear or see anything of the Northern woman Ashkoliiz, I'd appreciate that news as well."

"I'll see what I can do," she said sourly, "me being himself's private secretary and all. You best rest that chest or we'll all be weeping over your shroud in a week's time."

"Thank you."

She favored him with one last glare before stomping out. "You'd be more use if you was a strapping lad with a great sword and a magick shield."

He wouldn't mind being a strapping lad himself at the moment, but that would probably just get him killed faster.

When he lay down to sleep, the coughing returned. He pulled Old Bendlin's rickety chair by the little firebox and tried to rest sitting up. It seemed a lost cause, but after a while he realized his fevered dreams of panic were no different from his memories of the recent day. He ran on and on into them until he forgot himself.

IMAGO

He hadn't even made it to the stairs when a big Tokhari emerged from the door leading to the rest of the rugmakers' complex. The full-man was dressed traditionally, right down to the swords. "Lord Mayor," he growled in an accent fresh off the sand.

One of Kalliope's, then—the personal guard who was still bagging about the City. They fought in potshops, haggled in the markets, and swaggered in the streets; in general acting like big men from every corner of the world acted when they reached the City Imperishable.

Imago wasn't certain whether he should find fault with that. "*Il-mezzi manit,*" he said politely in Tokhari.

"Sandwalker says for you to come."

He glanced about, but saw only two clerks, a messenger boy, and several of Enero's men. The latter watched the Tokhari carefully, hands on their own weapons.

"I'm coming." Imago shrugged out of his canvas car coat—heavy enough for the pre-dawn mists—and followed.

He was led quickly to the hallway outside the map room. It was thick with Tokhari prostrate on the floor. All their heads faced the map room door.

He tried to convince himself that this was a good sign.

Imago picked his way past outflung arms. No one seemed to notice him except for his erstwhile escort who stood back and glowered.

The door wasn't even locked. He took a deep breath and pushed it open.

Bijaz, Kalliope, and Jason stood around the north side of the map table, studying the country beyond the Silver Ridges. Jason looked almost normal. His skin had a faintly luminous cast.

"Hello…" Imago had hoped against hope for success. This was far better than the strange, shadowed terror he'd glimpsed the day before.

"Lord Mayor." Bijaz was almost formal.

The old dwarf's hand was on Kalliope's hip. They both looked exhausted, Bijaz run down enough to seem somehow normal. No farting of butterflies this morning, either. Raising the dead must take a lot out of a man.

Imago swept a bow. "I see things have changed."

"Imago," Jason said.

His voice stopped the Lord Mayor's breath. It was as if a tree had spoken, spring shouted upward from the buds in the soil. A green scent like a laden haywain came on the words. Imago's hair stirred, his skin warmed. Jason was the sun and he the blooming flower.

The Lord Mayor shook that feeling off. He'd been god-touched before. This wasn't the same thing, not exactly. More elemental than noumenal.

The dead man of winter had become the Green Man of spring.

"Jason. It's so good to see you."

"Mmm." Jason didn't smile, exactly, but the warmth of his gaze flared a moment in some indefinable way before he returned the focus of his attention to the map table. "I know no more than you, but there are conclusions to be drawn," he said. "If this map was correct at the time of the Imperator, would he have taken an entire army through the forests? Or would he have chosen a road through open land? How big were his bivouacs?"

Bijaz eyed the stack of books, scrolls, and maps at the east end of the table. "Might be in there somewhere, though we've found no direct account of his departure."

"Odd, that," said Kalliope.

Imago cleared his throat. "If I might ask a question?"

All three gazed brightly at him.

"Why is the hallway outside full of Tokhari in the depths of religious transport?"

Not that he didn't know the answer, in the sense of the proximate cause. One godling around the place was bad enough. If Bijaz had forged himself a twin, Imago was going to ship them both down to the coast in exchange for Onesiphorous. And he wanted to know what to expect when he let this cozy little trio leave this room.

Kalliope smiled. "The *sula ma-jieni na-dja* walks. Would you not be stricken with awe if the lamb rose from the ashes of the altar to bleat for its mother?"

Imago wasn't sure what he'd think. Not these days. "Will they do that in the streets?"

"I cannot say."

"We shall see, I suppose."

Their heads bent to the map once more. Imago felt obscurely betrayed. He had been left out of whatever these three now shared, even though they were precisely doing his bidding. "When you reach a stopping point," he said, "please come to my office. Discreetly."

Kalliope looked up at him once more with a nod.

He turned to leave. It would be interesting to see if they could make it up the stairs without causing a riot.

One of the full-man clerks met Imago in his office. Robert Stockwell, Imago recalled. The man was tall, and favored black suits of the trim found in the more conservative gentlemen's clubs.

"The steam packet *Riverfall* came in to dock this morning, sir," Stockwell announced.

"So soon?" He'd sent Onesiphorous word of the misadventures of Ashkoliiz in a despatch by the same ship two days earlier. It took five days to make the round trip—two down, and at least three back depending on the current.

"They were attacked at the Gravel Bend."

"By whom?"

Steam packets were not fighting ships—they sailed the River Saltus with minimal crews. Trading scows, barges, and ships of all sorts off the Sunward Sea each moved cargo at their own pace. The packets carried messages, money, and people whose time was valuable.

What they did not carry was armament. River piracy hadn't been an issue in a very long time—he couldn't bring to mind any recent record of it. Few people lived on the river between the City Imperishable and Port Defiance. The land was too mucky and overgrown for farming, while there were far better places for grazing or timber, all free for the taking in the empty lands of the old empire.

"The captain could not say who made the assault. They took rifle fire from a wooded copse on the shore. As he put on steam to outrun the attackers, the bow watch spotted cables in the river. The captain felt backing off and returning to be a better choice than sailing unarmed into further ambush."

"Brilliant." Imago slapped his desk. "We have no marines, and no fighting navy. The armed ships in port are all merchants who won't take a commission from us. There is simply no way to respond. *And* my letters to Onesiphorous have not been delivered."

"No, sir. They were sent back to your office with the report of the attack."

Ashkoliiz. He knew the mountebank was behind this somehow. Where had she gotten guns? That was not so hard to imagine. But blocking the river channel? "What sort of cables?" he asked.

"Sir?"

"Go down to the docks. Find the captain of *Riverfall*. Ask him what sort of cables they were. Get details. Make him turn out his crew, and speak to whoever actually spotted them."

"What am I looking for, sir? What will it mean?"

"I have no idea, Robert. Only a hunch that it will signify something, once we hear the answer."

"Yes, sir."

Robert left.

Cables in the river. Onesiphorous out of touch. Jason back from the dead.

Well, first off, he'd best warn the Portmaster before anyone set sail on the morning current. In case this chicanery was something broader than mere interference in his own plans. Imago found a sheet of writing paper and began a memorandum.

The Burgesses would become involved in this. Anything that impeded shipping grasped the attention of a syndic faster than a whore's fingernails clamped upon his scrotum.

Jason was back, he told himself. *Have joy.*

Still, he couldn't forget the panicked dogs down at the warehouse on Sturgeon Quay.

Three arguments later, including a threatening ring from the Limerock Palace via the telelocutor, Bijaz opened Imago's door. "He's here," the dwarf said.

Imago realized that nothing had slipped or flown from Bijaz's fingers the last two times he'd seen the old dwarf. *Interesting.* "Come."

Jason walked in, still slightly luminous, still smiling. A crowd gathered outside.

Kalliope slipped in after and shut the door behind her. "He's hard to hide."

"I do not require concealment." Jason sat in one of Imago's chairs. A faint crackling noise erupted, then quickly subsided.

Something wrong with Jason's eyes, Imago realized. Color… they were the wrong color. How had that happened? He shook away the distraction to focus on the business at hand. "What have you found?"

"We're not sure," Bijaz admitted. "That Terminus went north is as good a theory as anything else. No one seems to have kept records of the Imperator's departure. That can only have been deliberate, as if they wished to put it out of their collective minds."

"There was the razing of the temples," Imago said. "That little bit of history's somewhat more complicated than most people imagine."

Bijaz nodded. "We can't tell much from what we have. Are you considering sending someone northward to have a look?"

Imago didn't want to know where this tomb might be. "The last thing this city needs is for the Imperator's final resting place to actually be found."

He continued to wish fervently that Ashkoliiz might be just another confidence trickster, but there was too much to her. The ice bear, the Northmen, and those damned bells. It was far too elaborate for an everyday con—that would have involved a map and some conveniently discovered old diaries.

Maybe those would have come next, if Bijaz hadn't ensured her departure for points south.

"Am I still to remain concealed?" Bijaz asked with a glance at Jason.

"Another day or two, please. There's been no new riot. I still await a lawsuit over your activities. And now there's trouble on the river. I suspect Ashkoliiz, but we need to know if it was anything more serious, or just violent spite directed at the City."

"You want something else from me." Jason's smile was small and perfect.

Imago nodded. "I want you to take a ride. Will you come, just the two of us?"

"Of course," Jason said as Kalliope and Bijaz both opened their mouths to protest.

"The pair of you can do me a favor," Imago told them. "Get yourselves into Onesiphorous' office and see that it's in order. Then set your heads to recommending someone who might be able to fill his place. Possibly including one or both of you. I have a feeling that getting him back up the River Saltus is going to prove quite difficult."

He rose to leave. As Jason stood, Imago realized that fresh leaves were budding through the lacquer of the chair where his guest had been sitting.

The Green Man of spring, indeed. It seemed Bijaz was contagious. Or perhaps the City was in dire need of more champions.

"Come with me, please," he said to Jason, glad this time for the irritation of the enclosed fiacre.

Through the entire ride, Jason continued to exude a musky scent of sap that made Imago's scalp itch with every breath. He was relieved when the horses clattered to a halt outside the Footsoldiers' Guild Hall. Imago hopped down to the pavement, followed by Jason.

They had not spoken along the way, but the silence had been like that of an empty temple—pluripotent, laden with promise. There was no strain between them.

"A woman is here," Imago said once they were both standing in the alley.

"Hiding within. She needs someone who can tell her that she is fit to live."

"She is dead?"

"Not so much dead as deathless, I believe. She was done a great violence long ago. It has turned her within, forcing her back on herself like an ingrown nail which rots the finger."

"I am not a healer," Jason said.

"No. But you live as she is afraid to. She has spent long years pretending to ordinariness. You might show her another path. I only ask that you go within and talk to her."

They both looked at the looming, crowded mess of the old guildhall. "Perhaps you could show me the way?"

Imago laughed. "So you are not all powerful."

"I have no power at all. I am merely growing once again."

He led Jason up the steps. Together they pulled open the great, ancient door, and followed the winding path through the wall of debris within.

Jason radiated warmth and a faint light in the darkness. "You are like a little sun," Imago said. "Hardly powerless."

"Perhaps I am growing fast."

"Perhaps."

The door to the *certamentarium* was shut. Imago tried the latch, but it was made fast from the inside.

She was there. Or at any rate someone was.

"Her name is Marelle." Imago wondered whether to knock.

Jason set his hand upon the latch. It remained obdurate. He ran the fingers of his other hand over the surface of the door, skimming the little spy holes. Back and forth. *Like listening,* Imago thought, *but with his skin.*

"I do not know what lies within," Jason said. "Too many whispering words, too many old wounds." His hand stilled a moment. "My father was right, you know. About the soul bottles."

"Really?" Imago vaguely recalled that tale, told one late night over wine and oysters.

"It's more than that, and less. The soul can flee the body through any cut or rupture. As breath, as blood, as tears. The trick is keeping it in place." His hand began sweeping again. "My sister bound my soul. Bijaz freed it again, but it still inhabits me. I am my own bottle, containing myself."

Imago didn't know what to say. Instead he laid his hand on the door next to Jason's, ashamed that he was afraid to touch his friend.

"This is a room five times the size of my office," the Lord Mayor said. "Filled with the archives of four great universities, piled higher than ladders. They sit upon a floor where soldiers once trained to kill."

"A woman cries in the darkness at the center." Jason's voice was distant again.

"Power resides within those things which are encoded. When we arrange the world, we make it something it had not been before our minds touched upon it. She is trapped in a web of arrangement."

Imago realized he meant the library beads in their dangling catalogs. "What of the door," he asked softly. Surely there were battering implements aplenty about this place.

"Wood, like any other wood." Jason grinned, his old self briefly surfacing. "There are advantages to being the Green Man."

At that he pulled the door open easily. The bar slithered out, nothing but a collection of leafy twigs smelling of spring's deepest bloom. Even in the dim light of the abandoned guildhall, Imago could see tiny pale flowers, so many eyes peering up from viridian shadows.

"Leave me," Jason said. "I shall find my own way back."

"And Marelle?"

"Only she can choose what she will be."

"Help her choose well." He found the courage once more to shake Jason's hand, but the moment was gone.

Imago picked his way out. He wondered what he might discover if he set a team to clean this place out. Somewhere within, springtime might come to a woman who dwelled inside the desperation of centuries.

BIJAZ

Jason did not return that day from whatever errand Imago had set him on. Which might have explained the Lord Mayor's irritation. It certainly hadn't done much for Kalliope's mood.

She glared at Bijaz over a small meal of poached fish and plump, purple olives. Tokhari food always contained olives, somewhere, somehow. Living in the map room had not widened the culinary options he shared with Kalliope.

They'd made love on his cot when Jason went with Imago, confident of the future for the first time in months. Then Imago had returned alone, tight-lipped and distant. The mood between Bijaz and Kalliope had rapidly disintegrated to something much akin to despair. That Two-Thumbs had been coming to the Rugmaker's Cupola every day seeking audience with Bijaz was only making things worse.

Still, the uncertain bond kept him and Kalliope close. Waiting for news together seemed better than waiting alone.

Kalliope put down her fork. "He should never have stayed in this world," she said bitterly. "Hiding in that filthy hole, sucking the meat off the bones of dogs. The *sula ma-jieni na-dja* is a sending, not a whole new creation."

Bijaz felt his heart shift. "You and I have known him longer than anyone. He was an angry child, then an angry man. Being dead did not improve him. But when we brought him back, he bloomed." He'd seized on that memory of Jason's eerie calm, the detached intensity, the tiny bits of green which had sprung from him.

"So for a day he was better than he'd ever been alive? Then Imago dropped him down some secret hole somewhere. He was my brother. He deserved more from me."

"He might as well have been my son." Bijaz recalled hot, sweating nights where he'd caressed Jason while rejoicing in the boy's pain. "He deserved far more from me."

"So if—when!—he returns, let us give him more."

Bijaz picked at an olive. "We already have, I'm afraid."

That afternoon he sat in Onesiphorous' office and studied the latest writ from the Assemblage. Despite Marelle's efforts, that idiot attorney Fidelo had been busy. Cases were open before three separate benches.

The money seemed to be flowing from syndics intent on undermining the Lord Mayor's regime, which they blamed for the current crisis in skilled labor. The old guard conveniently ignored the fact that the trouble had been created by the Burgesses themselves, and that the Lord Mayor was the only person who stood a candle's chance of bringing the dwarfs back from Port Defiance in any numbers.

Bijaz definitely couldn't leave the Rugmaker's Cupola now. Bailiffs were posted outside at all hours. "For protection," they'd been told by Provost Selsmark. The First Counselor had apologized privately to the Lord Mayor, but he could only affect events, not direct them. The fate of a single annoying dwarf was not high on Zaharias' list of priorities.

The good news was that since the recent episode of raising Jason, Bijaz hadn't gone back to farting butterflies or dripping sand from his fingertips. He still felt the power of the Numbers Men coursing in his veins, but that had settled to something manageable. Kalliope assured him this was because he'd found a path. The wheat field, it seemed, lay within him now.

He had no idea where that path would lead, but he carefully minded her admonishment that power was means rather than an end. Bijaz wished he could have used some of it on Roncelvas Fidelo and this damned writ.

Sworn before the judges of the bench dolus malus, *having jurisdiction over fraud and usury, this day twenty Mars, anno 618 Imperator Terminus, a complaint against one Bijaz, a dwarf formerly of Fireside Street, now residing as an apparent ward of the Lord Mayor in his temporary chambers at the Rugmaker's Cupola on Cork Street, for the cause of misrepresenting himself as a figure of divinity and worship and thereby gaining divers valuable considerations in a fraudulent manner from the religious persons of the City Imperishable. In detail—*

He balled the writ up and tossed it toward the window. The paper bounced off the glass. Where the Lord Mayor's view looked south and west, his faced north of sunset. Bijaz could only see the Sudgate by opening the casement and leaning out far enough to stir incipient vertigo. On the other hand he could readily overlook the River Gate and the road which led north.

All roads seemed to lead north of late. Or North. The place, rather than the direction.

Cannon echoed down on the water. A frequent sound, since the Portmaster had required ships' captains to engage in gunnery practice. Imago had several times revisited the idea of appropriating some of the vessels in port, but had not managed to convince anyone of the plan's sensibility.

Meanwhile, corsairs lay at anchor in Port Defiance, while little word came back up the river. So far they were still letting some vessels through, after an inspection and a markedly dubious fee assessment. No one in the City Imperishable doubted the fragility of that arrangement.

Another thing the syndics blamed on the Lord Mayor. As if centuries of mismanagement by the Burgesses were somehow the fault of Imago, in office a mere half-year.

The worst was not hearing from Onesiphorous. "He is captured or dead," Bijaz had told Imago.

"I will not hear of it," the Lord Mayor said. "Enero must mount a rescue."

"With horsemen?" Bijaz had been incredulous. "He's to swim against corsairs and whatever forces that idiot Sevenships still commands?"

"No, no, I know." Imago had begun to cry then, tears leaking out tight-shut eyes. "I had no notion I would be the death of him."

Slashed, Sewn—what had once been a matter of nearly fatal interest now seemed to pale.

Bijaz drew his fingers across the little map he'd been making on his desk. No triumph of cartography, it was more a diagram of forces than anything.

Like all rivers, the River Saltus flowed to the sea. Port Defiance, having lowered the flag of the City Imperishable, now controlled the outlet. Imago and the Burgesses were forced to treat with the new rulers of the port, or see the syndics of the City lose all foreign trade.

The bankers were in a panic, as were the manufacturers. First they'd lost their managers and accountants, now they'd lost access to their natural markets. The City Imperishable could sell only so much to itself, and there was no one upstream to sell to. Commodities were collapsing as well. The lumbermen brawled over the short wages they were paid when their log loads sold poorly at auctions. No one had the courage, or ready cash, to buy up the wood at full price, nor ores nor any other feedstocks of industry.

In consideration of these forces acting on the City Imperishable, his map was arrows pointing south, with a tiny horseman for Enero, crossed out as the freerider prepared to leave overland via the Rose Downs and roads east—avoiding whatever fighting might break out along the river. Another tiny man for the bailiffs, of questionable loyalty at best. Kalliope could perhaps field a hundred Tokhari, but they had no reason to ride at the City's behest. Besides which, mounted Tokhari could no more assault the rebels at Port Defiance than could Enero's men.

The only consolation was that neither the corsairs nor the old guard within Port Defiance had any means to conduct their own assault upriver. This was almost certainly a game of starvation rather than swords.

Bijaz wished he were still sleeping in the doorways of the Temple District. That had been a simpler life, even with meaningless miracles trailing behind him.

Kalliope leaned through his door. "Can you come to the rooftop?"

"Only if we're down again before the evening bells." The great iron carillon atop the Rugmaker's Cupola that rang the morning and evening hour was loud enough to wake the dead.

"Come on, it's only the middle of the afternoon. Imago wants us for something important."

"Everything's important now." What else could he do? If he left the tower, there'd be a royal brawl trying to keep him from being arrested.

He followed Kalliope up the ladder to the roof hatch. It was already flung back. They climbed out onto the flat top of the tower—slate tiles over wooden flooring and beams, nearly sixty feet across. The carillon was an impressive tower in its own right, almost three stories tall.

Imago faced southwest, watching the river where it flowed toward Port Defiance and the Jade Coast. He was slightly slumped, his linen shirt gathered in sweaty folds about his back.

Bijaz approached and touched his elbow. "Something will change."

"I know," said the Lord Mayor. "I think it already has. I just don't know what that means." He pointed.

The River Saltus flowed almost due south as it passed the City Imperishable, which sat on the east bank. The water made a gentle bend to the west at Dragoman Point just beyond the winch tower on the Sudgate jetty. There it entered the scrubby softwood forest, which in turn eventually gave way to the glossy-leaved hardwood jungles of the Jade Coast.

This high up, atop the tallest tower atop the tallest hill in town, the horizon was a distant blur. The river disappeared among the trees, but made occasional showings of silver light further south as it coiled through that low, wooded country.

A large steamer worked its way upstream. The plume was visible even over the treetops. It was one of the wide-beamed, shallow-draft vessels that ordinarily plied their way high up the Saltus, trading at farming towns and markets amid the ruins of greater cities. Those trade routes stretched almost all the way to the Yellow Mountains.

"We've seen no inland river traffic in almost twenty days," said Bijaz. "Not since they struck the colors down in Port Defiance. Only the few ocean-going ships the corsairs allowed through."

"Right," said Imago. "Whether this ship will be full of angry corsairs, dead dwarfs, or just a sharply worded letter remains to be seen."

Kalliope laughed sourly. "We might hope for better."

"We might," Imago said. "However, I'm not sure why we would trouble to do so."

The steamer fired her signal gun when she passed the marker buoy a mile downstream from Dragoman Point. Three sharp reports, for important news. It meant clear the channel and open a berth immediately.

Imago turned. "We're going to the docks."

Bijaz shook his head. "Not me. The bailiffs will take me the instant I walk out the door."

"No," the Lord Mayor said darkly, "they won't."

Enero waited at the base of the tower, already kitted for his long ride south. "We are to be leaving at dawn," he told them. "I am riding you to the waterfront for my own curiosity. It is being one last courtesy."

"Thank you," said Imago. Bijaz nodded. Kalliope, having fought both against and beside Enero's Winter Boys, appeared more ambivalent.

Freeriders walked the horses in from the street so they could mount up within the flagged hallway at the base of the tower. "For the confounding of bailiffs, yes?" one of the southerners said with a grin.

They slipped oilskins over both Imago and Bijaz, making them small, shapeless figures. Each was seated before a freerider. Kalliope was given her own mount—the Winter Boys had a healthy respect for her horsewomanship. They formed up with Enero and four escorts. The doors were thrown back and the column charged outward.

Bijaz would have loved to spit on the waiting bailiffs, but the redcoats wisely scrambled back across Cork Street. They did not even bother to raise a hue and cry.

"What's the point of a grand gesture," he demanded, "if they won't play the game?"

"To being patient," said the freerider behind him. "The redbacks will be having time to try to be taking you at the docks."

They clattered down Filigree Avenue, heading for Water Street. Unless the Portmaster had an unusual plan in mind, an urgent ship would be landing at

Old Lighter Quay, just south of the Water Street Bridge.

The horsemen arrived before the steamer, though judging from the activity on the docks they were ahead by only minutes. At Enero's signal they all remained mounted.

The incoming ship hove to around the winch tower moments later. The vessel was strung with banners, streamers, and bunting fit to celebrate a coronation. Most of the colors were an unfortunately familiar ice blue. A great, white paper bear's head hung between the twin smokestacks. Its eyes glowed even in daylight, some tricks of lanterns and lenses.

The steamer reached the docks. With a shriek of her whistle, she backed water. The center-mounted paddles threw great plumes of spray. She was making for the Old Lighter Quay.

Standing on the hurricane deck was Ashkoliiz's ice bear. Twice the height of a man, it stared down at the docks of the City Imperishable as if waiting to be crowned. The mountebank waited next to the ice bear, dressed in a shift and cloak of her same blue silk. She waved to the people on Water Street and along the docks. A band played somewhere below her, festival tunes which set an air of merriment that spread quickly.

"By Dorgau's infected nostril," Imago shouted, "this woman will not cease deviling us. Did she arrange the coup in Port Defiance just so she could return?"

Bijaz tried to reach toward Imago. Their horses were too far apart, spaced for battle. "Lord Mayor. I beg of you, use tact."

The whistle wailed again.

"People of the City Imperishable!" Ashkoliiz's voice boomed out over the water with a squeal that meant electricks were being used. *A voice projector*, Bijaz thought, as a round of riotous cheering broke out. The City was ready for something engaging, uplifting. That she used the magick of artifice to make her great as the power of any god only made her all the more a welcome change.

She had a confidence artist's command of human behavior.

When the cheering died down, Ashkoliiz continued. "I bring you most excellent news!"

Another round of cheering.

"Your friends among the émigré dwarfs of Port Defiance have sponsored me on an expedition. I now journey to recover the remains and treasures of the Imperator Terminus. Great days will soon come again!"

Imago began cursing furiously. Bijaz just stared at the ship, decks lined with full-men, and wondered how many corsairs one could persuade onto a steamer.

The crowd, of course, loved her. The people of the City Imperishable streamed toward the berth as if meeting their new queen.

ONESIPHOROUS

Boudin found him working in the laundry.

Onesiphorous did not mind the duty. It was hotter than midsummer, and the wet was enough to make you feel as if you were drowning, but no one ever came down there but servants. He wasn't likely to be bothered by bluecoats or corsairs. Most especially he would not be accosted by the Openers who reportedly swaggered along the bridges and walkways of Port Defiance, terrorizing their fellow dwarfs.

The Boxers and their allies on the citizens' council had disappeared into attics and locked rooms, or thrown into what few cells the Harbormaster possessed. The servants in the Flag Towers whispered that there had been talk of a prison hulk, somewhere to set the filthy traitors to rotting.

Everyone among the palace staff seemed to know that Onesiphorous was working in the lower halls at menial tasks. He was kept safe by the fact that they held little enough love for the Harbormaster and nothing but venom for the corsairs. Still, he knew he had to move on soon. Eventually someone would sell him upstairs for greed, or out of sheer panic. But he had no place else to go. And here he learned so much.

Gossip had always been a dwarf's stock in trade, but usually from the front office or behind an account book. Working with servants belowstairs was a novel experience for Onesiphorous. When one was little more than mobile furniture, prop for an oil rag, people would say anything without consideration.

The walls might have ears, but as far as those in charge were concerned, the servants did not. And so he heard everything that happened in the Flag Towers, and by extension Port Defiance.

If only he could do something with the information.

"She send me back, ah," Boudin said apologetically. He wore grubby whites and carried a kettle—nothing more than a drudge out in the halls on some errand.

"It's your head, boy." Onesiphorous stirred a huge pot of linens with a long wooden paddle. He hadn't bothered with the wig down here, but still wore his smock.

He made a very ugly woman indeed.

"She say plantation men not happy. Rock men not happy either."

"Rock men." He hadn't heard that term before. "I presume you mean Jade miners?"

"Yes, ah."

"Nor are there a lot of happy people here in Port Defiance." Onesiphorous had taken refuge in fatalism of late. It seemed safer than optimism. The corsairs talked of raiding the City Imperishable, but that was like wolverines attacking a beached whale. Nonetheless, they could certainly fire the docks and create havoc. The tightening blockade was much more damaging at both ends, in less obvious ways.

Few in Port Defiance bought and sold goods for local use, or with local money. Now that the City Imperishable was cut off, trade was much more difficult here as well.

Somebody was definitely going to betray him to those upstairs, soon.

And then there was Ashkoliiz.

Boudin went on. "She say you come back to green shadows. She make you welcome, take you round find friends in the white houses and the rock tunnels."

"I need to leave soon," Onesiphorous said. Though in truth, right now he mostly wanted to meditate on the patterns of the linen in his vat. "They will catch me before much longer."

"She say that too, ah. You be found, you be floating on the tide. Crab food."

"Ah." He looked closely at Boudin. The boy seemed a bit older. Maybe it was the stained uniform he was wearing.

Anyone could wander in to the Flag Towers if they dressed invisibly.

"Have you seen Big Sister?" he asked.

Boudin shrugged. "Maybe she fly away home. Me, I got a boat, got a place to take you where the corsair-men don't sharpen they swords on dwarf spines. You coming?"

Onesiphorous shouldered his paddle and picked up his wig. "Perhaps my time here is done. Lead on."

He'd survived two weeks in this damnable place, living in fear but without incident. On the way to Boudin's boat they ran into two corsairs.

Onesiphorous and the boy turned a corner as they headed for one of the understairs which would lead them down to a walkway. A pair of blade-thin men walked the other direction. They were tanned dark by the ocean sun, their muscles like ropes, dressed identically in black silk trousers and leather vests. They were deep in conversation, barely glancing at dwarf and boy.

"You," said one behind Onesiphorous. From his accent, he'd been born in the Saltus basin—it wasn't a Sunward Sea voice. "You're either the shortest woman I've ever seen, or by Dorgau you're a dwarf."

Onesiphorous stopped. He didn't turn around. *Wait*, he thought, but he didn't know for what.

"She is being the ugliest woman as well, yes," laughed the other.

"Let's see you."

Onesiphorous spun as hard as he could, swinging the laundry paddle wide. One of the corsairs caught it open-handed with a rough laugh as Boudin threw his kettle.

The lid flew off and a rank green fluid spilled across the second corsair's face. He shrieked like a girl and clawed at his eyes.

The first man released the paddle and drew his blade. "You are to be going nowhere!" he shouted as he stabbed at Onesiphorous.

The dwarf tried to block with the paddle, but the first impact shattered it in his hands. Boudin put his shoulder down and crashed into the corsair's groin, catching the cutlass in his shoulder.

"Go," the boy groaned, sliding to the ground with his arms tangled around the corsair's legs. "She waiting."

Torn, Onesiphorous went. He ducked into the next corner, threw open the door, and clattered down to the underslung walkway. He could see Boudin's boat tied up at the next rock pillar.

Behind him, the screaming continued. Someone else keened in agony as a counterpoint. *Symphony of pain for two voices*, Onesiphorous thought. Scored by him.

He tried to row toward the western bank where Boudin had previously taken him. He didn't have the trick of the oars, though, and the tide was running out. Onesiphorous couldn't beat the current, so he headed for another stand of rocks with the hope of hiding among the boats tied there. He wasn't even sure where he was going, just away from the Flag Towers.

If it had been night he might have found some hope of getting away. As it was, all they had to do was look out a window to find him.

Trying to make a dock against the pull of the tide, he bashed the hull of a small, ragged fishing boat.

A dark-haired woman sat up. She blinked sleep out of her eyes to look over the side. Her shoulders were bare. "Hai!" she shouted, then launched into a stream of sibilant curses from far down the Sunward Sea.

"Help," he said quietly, fighting with the oars to keep the tide from pulling him away.

She glared, then slipped over her rail with a line coiled in one hand. She was naked except for a pair of tan trousers torn off above the knee. Waist-length brown hair trailed behind her. Dark aureoles were two blind eyes upon her chest.

"Hold water," she hissed, working to tie her line off to the cleat on his bow. Onesiphorous paddled as best he could. The southern woman somehow got the line secured. Almost immediately it went taut, forcing a groan from both hulls.

She kicked back to her boat, climbed in, and hauled him close. Onesiphorous tried to help, but she cursed again, so he lifted the oars free from the water as he'd seen Boudin do.

Their boats bumped once more a moment later. The woman threw a sausage-shaped wad of netting over the side to keep the hulls from banging together further, then lashed his line down.

"Come," she said.

Onesiphorous let himself be dragged over the side. There he dropped into the bottom of her boat. A tiny cabin with a chimney perched amidships, topped by a single mast. Coils of netting surrounded it, along with several large wooden boxes. The deck looked like a fishing vessel, but it didn't *smell* like a fishing vessel.

His rescuer shrugged into a dark grey silk vest, dyed with pale streaks. He didn't recognize the fashion of the cloth. "You dwarf," she said. "Sit now." She sat with him and tugged a sheet of canvas over them both.

They were enveloped in a beige light. He couldn't shake the image of her breasts bobbing as she'd slid into the water—this woman was slim, and either young or extraordinarily fit.

"Dwarf row boat from palace, not know oars from ears. You running away."

Onesiphorous didn't see any point in denying the obvious. "Yes."

"City man?"

"Yes."

"Hmm." She studied him. "You make ugly woman. Call me Silver. I call you Oarsman, yes? No names."

She was no more a fisherman than her vessel was a fishing boat. "From the Sunward Sea." He made it a flat statement.

"Home port Bas Gronegrim." She patted the deck. "Sail close to shore, go far, not get lost. You home port City Imperishable, you already lost so close to home."

"I need to get back," he said.

"Everybody here want somewhere else. I not care your politics. *Ssardali.*" That was obviously another curse, just from the tone. "Brothers fight, neighbors stay away, yes? I care *dessai*. Eh… no… corsairs, you say. Big problem home now. Make bigger problem home when settle in here."

"I don't care about the damned corsairs," Bijaz said. "I just want Port Defiance back under the City's flag, and my people headed home."

"Same same. I want take black flag down, you want put your flag up."

"Yes. Can you help me travel upriver?"

"No one go up less they have inspection, papers. *Attalassi.* Everything control now, yes. Little boats go little places, still good. You got little place?"

"The swamps. Would we be able to reach the west side of the delta?"

"By night, sure certain. But you." She grinned. "What you do for me, Oarsman? Yet can I sell you to bluecoats, yes."

"I have no funds." Which was not strictly true. He still had the money he'd tucked away when he'd left his office for the swamps, the day of the coup. And the silver bells were likely worth something. But that wasn't what she meant, not even if he'd had an entire strongbox with him.

Except, in a sense, he did. "I can speak for the Lord Mayor of the City Imperishable."

"Imago." She said the word oddly, slowly, like it was something she'd read but never before used in conversation. "His words have power now?"

"Right here, right now, no." Onesiphorous thought quickly. "But I can pledge substantial funds to hiring a fleet if Bas Gronegrim can supply the ships."

"My city not fight *dessai*. Not open battle. Princes sail the decks." She touched his nose. "Do better, Oarsman. I already spend risk to save you from tide."

He could draw on power of the City Imperishable, except it was all money and trust. Manufacturing, too, but electricks and gun barrels were scarcely at issue right now. Not directly.

"Monopolies," Onesiphorous offered. "Trade concessions. Not for gunships in open battle, but enough pressure to force the corsairs out. If princes sail the decks, then people move back and forth between that black fleet and the palaces of your city. Am I right?"

"Dwarf knows politics." She looked thoughtful. "I got no power make treaty. I just sail, look, make letter home. *Ssardali*, little man, I send letter home say I find trade or patents, maybe they pay good attention, yes."

"One hopes."

"You got City Imperishable *attalassi*? Official papers and seal?"

His thin hopes collapsed. "In my office. Which I was chased out of two weeks past."

"Where your office?"

"Under the bridge between Axos and Lentas."

"Fine. Little Oarsman, we go look. Find you stuff, you tell me no lies, you write letters. Everything good."

Everything was far from good, but for the first time, he saw a path forward. "One thing," he said. "I write you letters, I also write letters home to the Lord Mayor. Maybe they go upriver, maybe not, but I have to try."

She tucked her hair behind her ear, then reached back to coil it up. "Everybody try."

The last thing Onesiphorous wanted was to return where he could be found. Heading for his office seemed the height of folly. Still, he'd stayed away since the corsairs took over. And it didn't seem likely the two in the lower halls would have any idea who he really was.

Silver rowed Boudin's boat, leaving hers tied up with a cluster of small fishing craft. The looks she got as they cast off told Bijaz that none of the locals were fooled by her pretense of fishing, any more than he had been. *These were poor people*, he thought. The poor never went to authority if they could help it. Far too easy to get in trouble themselves.

It took her about fifteen minutes to reach the base of Axos. That rock finger was forty feet in diameter, and had stone steps carved up to the Tidewatch.

He wore a cutting of one of Silver's unused fishing nets like a shawl, and still had his wig on. She took his elbow as they mounted the stairs. "Step wise, Mother," she said, but he could hear the giggle in her voice.

Onesiphorous figured he might as well play into the role, so he shuffled slowly. A young woman and her mother weren't likely to raise suspicion.

It took a while at his pace to make the walkway outside his office. Someone had nailed boards across the doorway and affixed a poster over them. That in turn had been scrawled over with enough graffiti to render the message unreadable.

"In there," he said.

Silver stepped casually onto the little rope bridge which connected his office to the walkway, and tugged at the boards. More sibilant cursing.

"I back soon." She trotted off.

Onesiphorous looked around. The walkway was on the east side of his office, so his view was mostly of the nearby islets, with the Jade Coast beyond. A storm worked itself up to the south, and little shipping was in port. There was almost no incidental traffic.

Port Defiance normally bustled day and night. The factors and syndics were no doubt feeling the financial pain daily. Somehow he didn't think the corsairs would care overmuch. Silver had implied that they needed a home port, but within the Flag Towers, they'd seemed violent and disorganized—hardly interested in settling into a long-term occupation.

Finally, Silver returned with a metal bar. Blood glistened on one end, and a few shreds of hair. He didn't ask.

Wordless, she popped the boards free and threw them into the water. When she had removed them all, the metal bar followed the wood. Onesiphorous had been in Port Defiance long enough to wince at the waste of good materials, but he couldn't disagree with her sentiment. Not to mention getting rid of the evidence.

"Now," she whispered.

Within, his office had been vandalized. It certainly hadn't been stripped—frustration or anger, rather than a thorough search. The tall windows still stood open as he had left them.

His seal had been in the strongbox at the bottom of the desk. Imago's letters, blank sheets entrusted to him with the Lord Mayor's signature at the bottom, were in a small cardstock portfolio. "We look for a folder," he told Silver. Onesiphorous opened his hands about a foot apart. "This size. It is a buff color."

She gave him a blank look.

"Tan, like your trousers."

"Yes." She began digging through the scattered papers.

He checked his desk. The drawers had all been yanked out, but the strongbox was still there. Definitely vandalism. A political raid would have carried the secured container away on principle. Onesiphorous adjusted the dials on the little lock, which popped open.

Sixty gold obols, the seal, his commission as the Lord Mayor's personal representative.

"You need money?" he asked. "Gold?"

Silver laughed as she tossed her way through the piles of paper. "Gold? They call me thief if I have gold. Poor fisher girl."

"Right." Onesiphorous looked down at the coins. They weighed too much to easily carry with any discretion. He scooped the bright gold into one of the upper drawers then carried the impromptu box to the windows. Reaching out, he dumped the money into the ocean.

"Sea King blesses you." Silver held up the portfolio. "You did good to give that to the ocean. We go now, before they come."

He wondered again who she'd killed to get that metal bar, but decided he didn't care. When had he become so brutally indifferent? "Let's go."

Imago

All the Lord Mayor could do now to salvage the situation was ensure that Ashkoliiz did not come before the Assemblage of Burgesses. Otherwise, the cause was lost. Imago turned to Enero and pointed at the steamer as it was tying up.

Enero whistled. The horsemen rode out onto the quay. At Imago's nod, they used the flats of their swords to clear a path to the base of the lowering gangplank. "Aboard," Imago shouted. The freeriders reined their horses up the plank one by one. The crowd cheered behind them.

The horses jostled nervously together on the foredeck of the steamer, facing a crowd of full-men. Imago was pleased to see they were an assortment: young and old, thin and fat. Not likely a corsair raiding party. Traders and clerks from Port Defiance, rather. About a dozen carried instruments—her band, ready to march.

Ashkoliiz appeared in an expanding circle of silence, followed by her bear and two of her Northmen. "I do not believe we have had the pleasure." She approached his horse from the left and lifted her hand.

Imago leaned down, took her fingers in his grip and brushed his lips across the back of her hand. "Lord Mayor Imago, of the City Imperishable."

The mountebank glanced at Bijaz, whose expression was dark enough to concern Imago. "I have met your creature before. You are entirely different." Her blue-white eyes sparkled with the swell of the moment. The crowd ashore continued to cheer. "I'm afraid that I must show myself to my public now," she added, winking.

Imago tried to bow without falling off the saddle. "Would my lady do me the honor of presenting herself at the Rugmaker's Cupola when it is convenient?"

"Why, you seem worried." A big smile. "Surely you don't think the old fossils at the Assemblage would be any use to me? A few hours, perhaps."

The band struck up a jaunty march. Ashkoliiz walked down the gangplank. Her ice bear followed, the creature bending low to clear the overhead. The Northmen gave Imago long looks as they followed the bear. Most of the rest of her men trailed the blare of the music.

Imago was left looking at a handful of sailors. "Are you all of Port Defiance?" he asked.

One answered, his face drawn. "Some are City men, taking the chance to come home. The dwarfs paid for this circus, but Harbormaster's men wouldn't let none of them board the steamer. Neither wives nor children."

Imago lowered his voice. "How stands the port?"

The man shook his head. "Poorly. But I cannot say more."

"Why not?"

"My wife—" He broke off and glanced around nervously. "Leave off. Please do not speak to me."

Moments later the horses picked their way back down the gangplank. Ashkoliiz and her procession were already moving up Palatine Street, away from the waterfront. Her band tootled merrily in the spring sunlight.

Imago couldn't actually *see* Imperatrix Park from his office, but he could spot the tops of the poplars that grew there. He could certainly hear it, even from halfway across the City. Ashkoliiz, her voice projector, and her marching band were making quite a stir.

At least Enero had agreed to hold his forces here in the City Imperishable until the woman had departed once more.

"Sir." It was Stockwell, the clerk. Acting acting chamberlain, as it were. Though he might well have one more "acting" on his nonexistent title than that. Imago had lost track.

"Yes?"

"There's a... person. Here to see you."

"One of the Northmen? Tell me it's not that dancing bear."

"No, I'm afraid this is one of ours. Says you know him well." Robert's pursed lips gave his opinion of that statement. "A fellow by the name of Saltfingers."

"Ah." Imago felt a mixed flood of relief and guilt. Saltfingers, dwarf and chief dunny diver to the City Imperishable. He worked for the Water Captain, but through that office the dwarf was responsible to the Lord Mayor.

More to the point, without Saltfingers' help Imago would have been dead half a dozen ways, and never met the Old Gods in their tombs beneath the City.

Yet he hadn't seen the old dwarf since the battle at Terminus Plaza.

"Send him in, please."

Stockwell looked as if he wanted to question the order, but withdrew. Saltfingers entered a moment later. The dunnyman was a strange one—the only albino dwarf Imago knew of. His skin was pebbled and shiny from some disease.

He was also one of the bravest, most resolute human beings the Lord Mayor had ever known.

"Hello," Imago said, rising to greet his visitor.

Saltfingers hung back, hands clasped behind. "Your worship."

Imago veered away from a more personal greeting. "May I offer you a drink?"

"Begging your pardon, no. I'm a-working soon, and with that ruckus down at Imperatrix Park the Old Twins will be running thick this evening. The boys'll need me."

"It's always a pleasure to see you." Imago paused, then forged on. "My debt to you is bottomless. Whatever your need, just ask. If that is within my power to grant it, it is yours."

"Ain't got no needs, your worship." Saltfingers grinned, teeth broken and rotted as Imago remembered. He held out a hand. "Got this instead."

Imago took the withered green mess from the dunny diver's hand. "A water lily?"

"'S right."

He went to his chair again. "It's, well, green."

"'S right."

Why had the old dwarf felt the need to bring this to him? "And you found it in the sewers somewhere."

"Quality will out, I'm always saying. Usually when cleaning the grates up on Heliograph Hill, mind you, where most of the quality's let out, if you take my meaning." He cackled. "Glad to see your worship's still sharp as a crocodile gaff."

Imago was starting to remember what a conversation with Saltfingers could be like. All he could do was press ahead. "Not a lot of light in the sewers as I recall."

"That's what I was thinking. I says to myself, Saltfingers, here's a thing to see. A whole lake of water lilies in the number four stormwater catchment, here sixty feet and more beneath the cobbles. Dark as a whore's cootch down there, and don't smell much better. No light but me little lantern, but there they is, pretty as a spring sunrise."

"Yes," said Imago. "I can see why that would be puzzling."

"Especially since there was hundreds of the bastards, some the size of barrow wheels, yet a week gone by I'd swear on your sister's thighs there weren't nothing there but black water and mossy stones."

The Green Man of spring walked somewhere beneath the City Imperishable. That thought gave him great comfort. "I believe I know who did this," he said. "You won't be needing your steam gun just now."

"Well, and that's what I figgered. Ask his worship, get an answer. If you'd looked at me and the lily and said it was crazy, I'd call out the boys and be hunting something with a green thumb and a black heart."

"Green thumb, yes. Black heart, no. And Saltfingers…"

"Yes, your worship?"

"If you see him, or a dwarf woman with him, give them every courtesy. They deserve it."

"Yes'r." The dunny diver turned to go, then stopped. "One more thing, your worship."

"Mmm?" Imago looked up from the withered water lily.

"It's no mind to me whether the crazy woman down in the park is crooked as last year's blackberries or right as rainwater, but you might give thought to the fact that himself, the last Imperator—" Saltfingers paused for a moment. "Excuse me," he said, interrupting himself. "I tells a lie. The last true Imperator I meant to say. Himself, when he went off, was headed north beyond the Silver Ridges. Through Endres Pass. He wasn't in no mood for trees though, whatever that might mean to you."

"And you are certain of this?" Imago asked, though he knew better than to question Saltfingers.

The old dwarf laid a finger beside his nose. "We got our own histories down beneath the stones. You of all people knows that. The dunnyman remembers everything, because he never knows what will save him."

"I understand. Is there anything you need, old friend?"

"Only to get to me work. And not to have another run of freshwater squid 'd be favorite, too." The dunny diver bowed and saw himself out.

"Jason," Imago said, looking at the lily. "Maybe you're doing her some good down there. I hope you come back soon. Both of you."

Imago spent most of the afternoon staring out the window toward Imperatrix Park. Music erupted from time to time. Flights of birds were released twice.

Ashkoliiz was making a show of things.

She was certainly closer to the Limerock Palace than to the Rugmaker's Cupola, but he couldn't force her next direction. Not when she moved with a brass band, a dancing bear, and the company of hundreds.

He could only hope the Burgesses were disinclined to invite her into an Assemblage session. Zaharias of Fallen Arch was no fool, but he was surrounded by them.

The telelocutor failed to jangle as well, further sign that this latest riot was beneath the notice of the Burgesses.

Just after the evening bell erupted above his office—nearly deafening Imago for a few moments as always—the affair at the park ended in a burst of fireworks. What *had* she brought on that damnable steamer?

Insurance, he realized. She would not be run out again, not after such a huge display. The band commenced a marching tune. They were coming up Orogene Avenue toward Lame Burgess Bridge.

Coming to him as she'd said. Imago found himself quite surprised.

He resolved not to meet the mountebank in the street. He had no desire to compete with her musicians and a rowdy crowd of cheering drunks. Instead he rang for Stockwell.

"Please bring a selection of the better wines. Borrow from the rugmakers next door if need be. Also, ask their kitchen for a tray of food. *Not* the special dishes, rather the usual fare." The Tokhari idea of delicacies did not always sit well with a city-bred palate. Though Imago had the feeling Ashkoliiz would cheerfully eat raw scorpions to face down a confrontation, he didn't mean to spar with her over food.

"As you request, sir." Stockwell scuttled off.

It was time to wait. Imago swept his paperwork into the wicker baskets next to his desk. The bare surface made him look unengaged, so he fished the papers out again. Then he made himself cease fidgeting.

Eventually Stockwell returned with the tray and a statement that the procession had arrived at the Rugmaker's Cupola. That was clear enough from the racket coming through the window.

"The wine, then, and show her in," Imago told him. "While you're at it, tell Enero to make sure she comes without her hangers-on."

"Sir." He bowed his way out.

Imago listened, refusing to be seen leaning out the window like some overeager child. The voices died to a mutter.

There were arguing tones.

A flat blast from some horn in the band, quickly hushed.

More argument.

Crowd noise.

The self-satisfied hum of agreement.

It was a discussion of terms, obviously. He wondered how much he'd given up.

Stockwell threw open the door again and drew a deep breath. "The Right Honorable Imago of Lockwood, Lord Mayor of the City Imperishable, bids welcome to one Ashkoliiz, gentlewoman-adventurer from Northern lands, and invites her to speak of affairs of moment to City and citizen alike. She attends with her closest advisors."

Ashkoliiz entered. She was wrapped in her fur-trimmed cloak once more, presumably to ward against the chill of the evening. As she shook it off into Stockwell's waiting hands, Imago saw the mountebank wore a blue silk dress the same shade as her eyes. A frosted gem hung at her neck, pale and cloudy like winter ice stored too long.

Her closest advisors turned out to be one of the dark-complected Northmen along with that ice bear. The creature had to bend low to fit into Imago's office, and seemed to occupy half the space. In such an enclosed area, its musk was powerful enough to make him want to sneeze.

The bear slumped to the floor. It crushed a bookcase to kindling, spreading its contents like so much stable bedding. The Northman stood by the door with arms crossed tight. Ashkoliiz took a chair before Imago's desk.

She did not offer her hand this time.

"Welcome to my humble office," he said.

"Indeed." She made a show of looking around. "So this is where the City Imperishable takes its direction."

"Or at least leaves notice of where it seems to have lately gone."

Stockwell turned on the electricks, then withdrew.

Imago launched himself into the silence that followed. "I see that you have raised interest and funds for your expedition to the North."

"Yes. We have been most privileged. The consideration extended to me in Port Defiance was far more favorable than my previous reception here in the City Imperishable."

"Strange, that," murmured Imago. "An unfortunate oversight on our part."

"I am certain." Her smile dropped away. "I think we understand each other, my Lord Mayor. Despite your efforts to the contrary, my expedition is already well subscribed. It is secret to no one with ears."

"I can see that. Though I continue to believe that Bijaz was correct. You might have been better off peddling your maps down the coast, where no one would be in a position to verify them." Saltfingers' words about the Imperator Terminus, spoken just a few hours ago in this same office, haunted him now.

"Perhaps. Nonetheless, we will take *Slackwater Princess* upriver to the cliff cities. From there we plan to cross Endres Pass into the high countries, and follow the routes which I have discovered."

Imago was grateful for a decade's experience running grifts before suspicious judges, else he would have started at the mention of the name of the pass. A part of him was eager to ask her about trees and why the Imperator Terminus would have been moved to avoid them. He settled for something far more noncommittal: "It sounds a wondrous plan."

"Wondrous indeed. I am here to raise additional funds and hire swords. Would you object to me recruiting the last of the tribesmen lingering beyond your River Gate?"

That took him by surprise. Imago had rather expected her to try to draw off some of the City Men. "Not that they are mine, but may you have the joy of them." That solved some of his other difficulties in the face of Enero's imminent departure.

"Excellent." She rubbed her hands together, then glanced back at the ice bear for a moment. "I shall not trouble you for gold from your City coffers, but there is one favor I would ask."

And here is the rub, Imago thought. She didn't need him except for this segment of the con. "What favor would that be?"

"There will quite possibly be old magick or restless spirits from another age of this city when we find the Imperator." Ashkoliiz looked uncomfortable. Imago found it interesting that her poise slipped, especially now. She continued: "I would take it as a great display of confidence if you could send someone well-versed in the City's lore. Ideally they should have some role or station of birth which places them in the City's heart."

"Lest you meet an angry ghost?" He didn't bother to hide his smile.

She became deadly serious. "The North is stranger than you think, Lord Mayor. Do not smirk. You of all people should understand how curious the world can be."

Dorgau only knew what gods Terminus had hauled off to dump into the frozen crevasse. The City Imperishable had made a point of forgetting as thoroughly as possible, even to razing the old Temple District and burying it under the New Hill all those centuries ago. He should not mock her fears.

"That you even express such concern does much to convince me of your genuineness," Imago said slowly, lying with his old courtroom grace. "And while I am not especially inclined to extend support to your venture, I have an idea. When do you depart?"

"We would like to cast off at dawn," she said with another glance at the bear.

"Of course you would." Then they'd be a nine days' wonder, talk of the City. The easy money had already flowed in. Leaving so soon would make the reluctant regretful, and the contributors smug. Staying risked some flaw in the plan becoming all too evident. "My deputy will meet you in the last hour of the night."

"Thank you." Ashkoliiz departed. Her bear and her Northman followed. The tray of chickpeas and flatbread and olives remained untouched.

Bijaz, thought Imago. You will travel further from the writ of the Burgesses than you ever imagined. Work your miracles in the empty North. Who better to contest with the lost gods of yore than the City's own burgeoning godling?

It was a terrible idea. But the very thought made him smile.

Imago went to look at the wine selection.

BIJAZ

He was angry.

Livid.

Wrathful.

Sparks spewed from his fingertips, setting Imago's office carpets to smoldering.

"I am *not* going with that woman!"

Wine bottles danced in place. An inkwell cracked. The bells on the roof of the tower hummed.

Imago stared at Bijaz, face set. "Are you done?"

"*No!*"

Window glass shattered as the wine exploded. Half a dozen bottles sprayed their varicolored contents around the room. Bijaz snapped his fingers. With a hollow sucking noise the dribbling wine condensed into bunches of grapes scattered across the floor.

He felt large now, larger than he'd been since he was first touched by the Numbers Men. In his anger he contained multitudes—every fist raised for a desperate cast of the die, every soul wagered on one last attempt. Bijaz towered over Imago, rage and frustration boiling within.

"You cannot turn me aside with those powers, friend," the Lord Mayor said. "I've been touched by the gods, just like you."

Wheat, Bijaz thought, remembering the field. The scythe fell where it would. Some grains tumbled to the miller's sack, others spent another hour or season in the sun. He saw that horizon, the path which rose where the reaper man had just passed, and knew his own way lay North.

With that thought, a ball which he had not heard circling fell into a slot. The wheel clicked to silence. He did not need to look to know it was the White Table, setting another pass of his life.

"I am sorry, sir," Bijaz said quietly. The air in the room was acrid, tangy, metallic—reeking of the noumenal. His anger was gone, his heat drained. "Every day I live is time loaned me by the Numbers Men. Sometimes I forget why they remade me."

"They did not remake you," Imago said gently. "You remade yourself. They merely set you a new direction."

"Path," said Bijaz. "Kalliope says I must be on a path. My path lies North."

"See? It works."

"I go." To his own surprise, Bijaz smiled. "Besides, that will allow me to jump those writs you keep receiving from the Burgesses."

"Every well has its coin. Go do what you need to prepare. I recommend sleep.

I'll have Enero escort you to *Slackwater Princess* an hour before dawn."

"Is he not already away?"

"Not yet. Our friend has stayed on a bit longer to see this latest affair out. Ashkoliiz alleges she is taking the last of the Yellow Mountain tribesmen with her, as hired swords."

"There's a neat trick," Bijaz said with grudging admiration. "Picking our pockets with an ancient lie, then using our obols to buy off our latest enemies."

"Pity the Burgesses couldn't do half so well." Imago shooed Bijaz away. "Go now. Unless it is your fondest wish to spend your evening bantering with me, tend to your own affairs. It may be a very long time before you can pursue them again."

"Thank you," said Bijaz. "I think. I only have one question before I leave."

"Yes?"

"What has become of Jason?"

Imago looked away, unwilling to meet his eye. "I believe he is well. I do not know everything I should."

"So you did not have him killed again?"

That made the Lord Mayor look up. To Bijaz's surprise, tears stood in Imago's eyes. "No. I set him to saving a life, in fact. That journey took him farther than I expected."

Bijaz felt a sort of obscure betrayal. "I would have liked to bid him farewell."

"I am sorry." Imago came round the desk and they hugged. "Now go," the Lord Mayor whispered. "I have an office to clean up and a city to run."

"And a war to win, I think."

"You go North. I'll turn my eyes south."

Bijaz nodded. "Good luck locating Onesiphorous."

With that, they parted.

On the long, slow walk down the spiral steps of the tower, Bijaz pondered what might be done on his last night in the City. All he really wanted to do was talk to Kalliope.

They stood in moonlight on opposite sides of the table. It was a tableau in pewter, color leached by night. Two giants facing one another across the plains of the world. Not agreeing, not arguing.

"I am unsurprised," she said. "Imago can see your road more clearly than you do."

He'd expected her to protest. Or possibly rejoice. Things had not been right between them since they'd brought Jason back only to lose him once more. This genteel acceptance confused him.

"I don't want to leave the City Imperishable. You helped me settle in to what I am. No more parlor tricks. I've more control now. I am *of* the City."

"And that is why you must go." Kalliope smiled as she traced her fingers across the northern edge of the map table. He stood at the southern edge. The world of the old empire stretched between them. "Who else would he send? Archer vanished during the late unpleasantness. Onesiphorous is lost to us in the south. Jason is missing once more. Imago would hardly send Ducôte or one of the Tribade, and I am not to be trusted. There is none but you. That you are bound so close to the City only increases your value in this game."

"I *know* the logic. I was teaching cats to hunt mice before any of you were born." Bijaz was aware that he sounded desperate. "It all makes sense. Just not to my heart."

She gave him a long, slow look. "You are afraid."

Bijaz bit off an angry response. Was he? "Yes," he said slowly. "I am a creature of the Numbers Men, the only Old Gods left. If Ashkoliiz is right, I may bear our banner to the resting place of their enemies. Whatever terrible creatures Terminus carried off. Consider this: When I leave, what if my powers remain behind?"

"Then you will be a cranky old dwarf, just as you have been for years. It is a role well-practiced."

She had the right of that. He was almost sixty, too old to be adventuring farther than the nearest tavern.

"You're afraid of something else, too," Kalliope added. "When you say that woman's name, there is a catch in your voice."

Those ice-blue eyes. "She has made some glamer on me."

Kalliope laughed. "A very common glamer, I'm afraid, casting a tight net over your little head."

"I've never—" he began hotly, but she cut him off.

"It does not matter to me if you ever do. I merely say there are some people who fit others like a lock and key. When lock and key match, you may have a love for the ages. When one fits and the other is indifferent, you may have a tragedy for one. It's in her walk, the line of her jaw, her smell. She has snared you, old friend. And she will never have a care for you, until she needs you for some trifle. Such as your life."

"No." Bijaz felt a swell of wounded pride. "I have bedded women, men, boys. You and I have coupled. I know love. This is some other form of fascination."

Kalliope passed around the western edge of the empire to meet him. "Listen." She held out her hands. "We should not fight. I don't suppose we'll see one another again in this life. The ways forward are tangled beyond remedy."

"Is that sandwalker wisdom?" he asked bitterly, not responding to her gesture.

"No, just common sense." She took his hands anyway. "Go, defend the City, follow your path, discover what she means to you. I will find Jason. I no longer expect to see my desert again, but then I was born in this city. Perhaps I am fated to die here."

He stepped into her arms, face pressed against the front of her vest. "I'm sorry," Bijaz said in a muffled voice.

"So am I, my friend." Kalliope ran her hands through his hair awhile, then pulled him to the cot.

This time as they made love, she called him Jason. As for Bijaz, he tried to imagine Kalliope with ice-blue eyes, but when he did that all he saw was her brother resurrected. So he made love to the storm he could see in her face by moonlight, and let the seed of the City flow freely deep within her.

Bijaz idled in the central hall of the Rugmaker's Cupola. It was well before his appointed hour. Kalliope had kissed him good-bye then slipped into troubled sleep. Imago was absent, hopefully also sleeping. There was a murmur of challenge at the door, then a freerider strode in—Malvo.

"You are to be going now. A dwarf is having great luck, I think."

"We all go somewhere," Bijaz replied. "As I recall, you are bound for the road home."

"Perhaps." Malvo sounded doubtful. "The captain is to be keeping us here by days. I am thinking he is being unwilling to leave you uncertain."

"If it is certainty that you await, you will die of old age here in the City Imperishable, my friend."

The Winter Boy laughed. "Maybe yes. As for now, I am having four men to be playing knives-and-smiles with the bailiffs outside. We are to be departing before they are tiring of the game, yes?"

"Yes," Bijaz said. "Let us away."

Malvo looked serious a moment, then handed a small dagger to Bijaz. "Captain, he is sending this for you. We are all knowing you to be a god, but even gods are needing a knife sometimes."

"Thank you." It was the only going-away gift Bijaz had ever received in his life. He'd never gone anywhere before.

They stepped into the predawn fog. Malvo's men were closed around a pair of bailiffs. One made a show of wiping his sword with a rag. Malvo hoisted Bijaz on a horse and whistled.

The freeriders were off. Looking back, Bijaz could see the bailiffs trailing on foot, but the redcoats seemed in no mood to tangle with five mercenaries.

Down at the Old Lighter Quay, the boilers on *Slackwater Princess* rumbled. She was recently built and so sported the most modern electricks. Pale lights outlined the wide, flat main deck and the three decks above in gleaming array. The wheelhouse gleamed from within. She was more a floating structure than a ship—a riverboat lacked the knife hull and raked masts of a Sunward trader.

Sparks floated into the dark sky from tall stacks amidships.

No one was at the gangplank. Malvo helped Bijaz slip from the saddle. "To be having a care, yes?"

"To be having a care," Bijaz replied. "And thank you."

Malvo saluted.

Bijaz trudged up the board, finding his way onto a lower deck crowded with supplies and sleeping men. Someone cursed quietly as he stepped too close. He located a narrow spot between two bales and sank down into it.

He barely heard the whistle shriek as the steamship cast off. The thump of the paddles became the heartbeat of a continent in a dream of frozen mountains and a fire in the moon.

ONESIPHOROUS

They huddled in Silver's little deckhouse as the boat rocked in a nighttime storm, arguing out the details of the letters of patent and the trade monopolies. Even their shouting could barely be heard above the wind. Her cabin was too low to stand up in, lined with silk and several long, narrow chests of the sort one might use to store rifled muskets. The cabin smelled of spices as well, mixing with the tang of her in a scent which gave him the shivers.

Onesiphorous concentrated on the business at hand.

"I cannot grant you the shipping of lumber, grain, or meat," he yelled into her ear. "Those move in quantities too large. I think I can reserve certain manufactured goods."

It was all lies. They both knew that. Onesiphorous figured if he made a deal which pried Port Defiance free, he could sell the price to Imago and create *post facto* truth from this paper. If nothing changed, the lies were meaningless anyway.

"Small things, yes. Electricks and metalwork."

"Those can be smuggled."

"You commission us to be inspectors, we inspect smugglers." Her easy smile slipped back onto her face. "Everybody make more money except poor smuggler. That is very special *attalassi*." She looked thoughtful a moment. "*Detta*... no. Eh... Letter of marque and reprisal!"

He was incredulous. "You learned that term in Civitas just in case of need?"

"Fisher girl got to know her business."

Onesiphorous chuckled. "You're probably a princess in Bas Gronegrim or something."

"*Ssardali!* No joke that, Oarsman."

Oops. There was something not to step in. He wondered how close to the truth he'd landed, then put the thought out of his head. Even if it *was* true, he didn't want to know.

"No joke," he agreed. Then, changing the subject: "So we have a letter of marque and reprisal granting what? A ship flagged from Bas Gronegrim the right to enforce trade agreements on behalf of the City Imperishable?"

"To full extent required."

"Guns *and* money," he said. The storm outside had found a moment of calm, except for the tiny, rippling drums of the rain.

"Oarsman got to know his business, too."

He went on. "Then we have a letter of patent granting Bas Gronegrim duty-free trade and sovereign soil within the City Imperishable, at a location of the Lord Mayor's choosing. We also have trade monopolies on small goods and metalwork shipped to the cities of the Sunward Sea."

The boat shivered in a particularly violent gust. When the noise dropped off again, she added: "And finished cloth shipped to City Imperishable."

"All right." Here was the difficult part. "In return, Bas Gronegrim will work to remove the corsairs from Port Defiance, and restore the rule of the City Imperishable. These letters will be worthless until that happens."

"Feh. I not got fighting ships in my pocket."

"You don't even have pockets," Onesiphorous pointed out. "Nonetheless, that is what must be. Otherwise make your own deals over in the Flag Towers."

"We want them gone," she admitted. "You letters make deal sweet, buy certain people who otherwise love the princes of the deck."

Now that made sense. He just hoped that Silver, or at least the letters, made their way to Bas Gronegrim and into the hands of whoever sat in judgment on their fleets.

"My regards to your admiralty," he said. "I will write out two copies of everything over the Lord Mayor's signature. We'll both witness the seal. I keep one copy, you keep one copy. Then you'll take me into the swamps."

"Yes. You crazy go there, dark water swallow a man like shark swallow chum."

"We're all crazy these days."

"True, Oarsman."

They had to wait for the storm to slack off, dozing quietly in the cabin. Much later he was able to work at the documents. In two hours with quill and inkwell Onesiphorous scratched out four letters—the patent, the letter of marque and reprisal, and two separate trade monopolies—in a pair of copies each. Onesiphorous had been on the wrong end of enough writs to have a sense of the rhythm of the language, but he was hardly a lawyer. And he had no familiarity whatsoever with the nautical realm.

Nonetheless, he did his best. They could all happily sue each other someday if the language he coined this night was at issue. That would mean the City Imperishable had prevailed, after all.

He wasn't upset about selling rights which weren't his to give away. What sickened him was leaving the City dwarfs behind. It didn't matter that the Openers had rebelled—they'd been sealed out again right quick, while the Boxers cowered in hidden rooms praying for relief.

There would be denunciations soon. With the money not flowing the port already carried an air of desperation. Going to the swamps might aid Imago but it did nothing for his people here.

He wrote out another letter to the Lord Mayor, explaining everything. That the report was over Imago's own signature seemed strangely fitting. He didn't bother to copy that one—Onesiphorous certainly didn't need to carry about his own testimony. He countersigned the letter with a flourish, then set the pen down to rub his cramped hand.

"All done, yes?" she asked.

"Yes. Now I need wax."

They sealed each letter, and wrote their mark beneath each seal—some southern glyph for her, and an O for him. Onesiphorous drew a tiny oar beneath each O.

Quill. It was so old-fashioned. He would have been happier for a ball-calligraph, but somehow it seemed fitting to use an old implement for such plotting. The luxury of the modern was already lost to him.

"Tide turn before dawn," she said. "I show you one thing by daylight, then we go swamp."

"Shouldn't we leave now?"

"No, sleep now." She blew out the lantern and settled to the floor.

Onesiphorous tried to match her even breathing. Her scent mixed with the smell of spices to excite his imagination until his cock swelled. He dared not touch himself, not in her presence. Instead, he lay in a quiet fever until the water changed directions beneath the hull and she awoke.

They set out in Boudin's boat while dawn was still a ragged pink gleam in the deepest east. Silver paddled quietly to work her way back and forth across the tide's incoming current. They passed between eyots he didn't recognize. Perhaps it was the curls of mist, or the dim light, but Onesiphorous felt as if Silver conducted him through an entirely different city. The water ran heavy with storm wrack, shapes half-familiar and fully strange.

"Where are we going?" he asked in a low voice.

"No talk," she whispered. "Only look."

Eventually he realized they were heading out to sea, at the west end of Port Defiance. They passed the warehouses and traders' offices of the Loska District. Silver rowed better than Boudin, with swift, quiet dips of the oars.

"See toward the middle," she said as she turned the boat to scull east. "Front of Barlowe's Finger."

He looked. There was sufficient light to make out the rock half a mile away.

Something dangled from the seaward face. Two somethings, in fact. He started to ask, then closed his mouth.

She rowed on, letting the tide carry them back in toward the city at an angle with respect to the Finger. There were at least half a dozen other boats out here. Most drifted as they did, but two backed water to keep a consistent station near the rock.

People, he thought. They've chained two people beneath the high tide line.

"Not go close," she muttered.

They were youths, or women. Not large enough for grown full-men. He was glad that neither was a dwarf.

The sun cleared the horizon. A rich golden glare showed the pale faces of Big Sister and Boudin, already chest deep in the incoming tide. Swells slapped against the rock, covering them a moment before withdrawing.

A youth *and* a woman.

"By my dead gods," Onesiphorous whispered. This was no simple hanging, but a slow death by cold, malicious torture.

She dug in with the oars. "We go now."

The other boats were also moving away with the daylight, all but the two keeping close to the rock. Not meant to chase away watchers, Onesiphorous realized, but to discourage a rescue.

All he could do was watch the water take them again and again. He tried to imagine the cold hand slapping his chin, sending stinging spray up his nose and down his throat over and over. Would he swallow enough to drown quickly, or would he slowly choke on the encroaching saltwater?

Onesiphorous vomited over the side, his stomach heaving as tears streamed down his face and terror weakened his arms and legs.

Silver said nothing. Instead she rowed silently into the shadows of the city's islands.

Out on the estuary in the full light of morning, well away from Port Defiance, Onesiphorous finally found his voice. "Is that a corsair execution?"

"No," she said shortly. "Your people make that. You never see it before?"

"I never *knew* it before." Both had died for him, in truth. The execution was a message to him. The Tribade would avenge Big Sister, he knew, but no one would raise a hand for Boudin. The swamp people hadn't lived this long by striking out against injustice.

They died for him, and for the City Imperishable. He felt ill, far more than he ever had during last autumn's fighting back home.

"When we retake Port Defiance," he said, "that will end forever."

"Good plan, Oarsman." She made another long pull. "Now you got to win war."

They finally glided into the treed shadows. Silver looked at him. "Now we do what?"

"No oars here," he said. "Use the paddle. Too many vines, and the water's slow and close."

"You got land? Or you climb tree like monkey?"

"Go in as far as you can and still find your way out."

"Hmm." She took up the paddle and worked the boat like a canoe. When the long, sinuous fin appeared, Silver gave him a hard look. "I hope you know what you doing, Oarsman. Don't want lose my letters."

"Don't let them chain you up," he told her.

They eventually bumped into a hummock large enough to have actual dirt. Silver looked distressed. "No more. This bad place. You sure you not sail with me? We both go Bas Gronegrim, I buy you short woman lick you all night long."

"As attractive as that sounds, no. I need to find the swamp people, and through them the plantations. Those are City men and dwarfs out there, for all that they've gone to seed. Miners, too. If I can raise an army in small boats, perhaps I can rescue my dwarfs."

"Your dwarfs dig own grave."

"Not all of them, Silver, not all of them."

He steadied the boat and grabbed a vine dangling from one of the knob-kneed trees. Once Onesiphorous was ashore, Silver turned her hull stem to stern, then blew him a kiss. "You find way back, we have drink fine wine together, laugh some, yes?"

"A much better invitation," he said. "Smooth sailing to you."

"Walk safe."

He watched her slip into the green shadows, headed back toward sunlight. The long fin circled three times then vanished without pursuing her.

It had been following him.

Onesiphorous explored his little piece of land. It was scarcely larger than his office in Port Defiance. Curiously, several pieces of dressed stone protruded above the mounded soil. He wondered what he would have uncovered if he'd had the energy to dig.

Instead he settled down and waited to be found. He had a death to tell them of, though he imagined the old woman already knew Boudin's fate. Then he needed to persuade them to action. These people would never fight, but they could help in other ways.

He glanced over his shoulder one more time. Silver was long gone, but looking after her was still better than staring ever deeper into the swamps, waiting from something woman-shaped to spring from beneath the surface.

IMAGO

He approached his office door a dozen times, wanting to head below and bid Bijaz farewell. Instead he kept delaying until hooves echoed loud on the cobbles below his window. Then he stared down at the river until a whistle shrieked and the steamer sloshed its way out into the current.

Imago continued to stare until the morning bell rang, startling and deafening him at the same time.

"By Dorgau's cherry tit," the Lord Mayor shouted. It was time to eat something, and bid Enero farewell.

Everyone was leaving him.

Kalliope met him downstairs. "Come. I want to sit in a café and hear the birds."

They walked into the morning air. The bailiffs who had been dogging the Rugmaker's Cupola for weeks were gone. That meant the Limerock Palace knew Bijaz had taken ship.

Enero's men were gone. No one insisted he ride in the enclosed fiacre. It was good to walk, as if he were just another city dweller.

They wandered down Filigree Avenue toward the river. Several cafés near the Spice Market catered to traders and immigrants. People from far beyond the old Empire's writ lived here at the end of a long caravan trail bringing sweet peppers and a dozen exotic seasonings from their countrymen. Jewelry, small metalwork, and hot spices from the Sunward Sea were sent home in return.

He followed Kalliope as she ducked into a little place smelling of steam and kava. They used cinnamon from the south and Rose Downs cream to flavor it here, he knew. Other varieties were available, made with far western spices, that only foreigners drank.

Kalliope negotiated for two mugs and a narrow twist of bread with strands of herbs baked in. They sat in silence awhile.

The drink was rich and dark and pleasantly bitter. Imago studied the habitués of the café—mostly westerners. They were short, broad and stocky, with muted gold skin and eyes darkly red as pomegranates. Their tongue, spoken with quiet ease, sounded to him like the gabble of geese.

"Did you ever wonder how many different peoples there are in the world?" he asked Kalliope.

"As many as there are grains of sand in the desert." She took a sip. "That's what the Tokhari say, and they've made war with a hundred tribes and nations. Might as well ask how wide the world is."

"North to south, or east to west?" He smiled over the rim of his mug, trying to appreciate this drink.

"Heh. You play the fool poorly. One only need watch the sun and moon to know that question is falsely stated."

There was an infinite east, and an infinite west, though north and south were bounded by ice and stars. Everyone knew this. A few had even gone and looked. No one had ever proven the world to be otherwise.

He thought of the Alates with their wings. "We are not all children of the same gods."

"How could we be? No god is wide enough for the endless whole of the world."

Imago knew enough gods personally to be glad of that. They were bad enough lurking in the sewers beneath his city. Bijaz was all right, but he could see in his friend the seeds of a god much like the Wolf or the Little Man—the dwarf could easily grow to an ancient, terrible presence without ever understanding why he was hated.

"Now what?" he asked. A far larger question than the conversation which had gone before, they both knew.

"You're the Lord Mayor. That's for you to decide."

"I have a blockade to the south. I pray that the Northern Expedition never returns, though I still must count the cost of whatever their enthusiasm raised yesterday. Everyone I care for is departed or dead." He looked uncomfortable. "But for you, of course."

She laughed. "I am scarcely of your inner circle. A season ago we were set on killing one another." Kalliope set down her mug to lean forward over the untouched bread. "But hear this now, Lord Mayor Imago of Lockwood. Find me my brother again, bring him back from whatever hole you sent him down, and I will stand beside you until these affairs are settled, both north and south. Continue to keep him from me and I will dog your dreams like a wolf on winter sheep."

"Ah, Jason." He sipped again. "I have a friend who knows where your brother has been recently. He's safe beneath the streets."

She pointedly looked downward. Imago took her meaning. He'd lost almost two feet of height and much of his mortal soul beneath these same streets.

"No," he said, "the Old Gods will not trouble him. He follows a different path. I sent him to someone in great distress. Someone I have need of again. I asked Jason to heal her."

"That dwarfess who worked in your offices? Marelle?"

"Yes, her. She is old."

Kalliope's brow wrinkled. "Old? Everyone grows old. Lost youth is lamentable, but scarcely something to be healed."

"No. *Old*. She has lived centuries."

"Oh. That sort of old. Is she an immortal?"

Imago shrugged. "After four or five centuries, who knows? She gave us those archives. The City needs her memory."

"Be careful. She may be a failed goddess. Like Bijaz, but in long decline."

"Bijaz was in decline *before* he became a god."

"As may be. So now, where is my brother?"

He pushed his kava aside. "I shall take you to the Water Captain. He has a dwarf named Saltfingers you need to meet. Stranger than a hen with three beaks, but he found Jason's trail."

"And you?" she asked softly.

"I will go plan a war I cannot fight, as I have no troops or ships."

"Money. Coin wins many battles."

Imago sighed. "Only if I have someone to pay for serving under my banner."

"It could be worse." She rose, smiling. "You could have gone north. Or south. Now show me this Saltfingers."

"You may be sorry," Imago warned her.

"Me? Sorry on account of some happening in the City Imperishable? This place has been cream and roses to me since my birth."

He laughed, then was grateful that she had been able to make him do so.

Outside the sun was warm and the Spice Market in full cry. Down here, he could almost pretend things were normal.

He already knew that it was going to be a long, hard summer. Here spring was barely settling in.

II

GERMINATION

BIJAZ

When he awoke from his doze, *Slackwater Princess* was passing among low, wooded banks. He could see occasional great stumps or the long hump of a massive, rotted log. There had once been lumbering here. Towns, too, for they passed stands of wooden pilings dotting the current like old soldiers drowned at their posts.

North of the City the land was mostly empty. The northbound road ran close to the river, sometimes bending further east to pass a bluff or cross a swampy tributary.

The steamship made very good time, which became apparent as he watched a group of riders work their horses to match *Princess'* speed. Occasionally the mounted men cut overland to beat the river's slow curves.

Hirelings, he supposed. He didn't see the point of raiding the boat, not with a hundred armed men aboard her.

Bijaz stayed on the main deck that first day, sitting among his bales and watching the river go by. Electricks were strung along the ceiling, but in the bright sunlight the crew had not bothered to turn them on. He shared the space with several dozen men lounging about, talking, smoking, and maintaining weapons; as well as bales, baskets, chests, and every kind of supply.

Back at the City Imperishable, this had all been numbers in a ledger, goods to be accounted for and taxes to be levied. Out here, it was life.

As for Ashkoliiz, Bijaz figured the mountebank knew exactly where he was. She would send for him in time. Based on the scale of the great table map back at the Rugmaker's Cupola, he reckoned a thousand river miles from the City Imperishable to the remains of the cliff cities where the Saltus made its closest approach to the Silver Ridges. Perhaps seven hundred as the pigeon flew. Their pace was abut fifteen miles in an hour even against the current, which meant that running dawn to dusk, they'd make close to two hundred river miles on their best days.

Around the noon hour, the signal gun fired. The loungers made no show of jumping up, so he assumed the shot was a greeting.

Nothing was ashore except limestone bluffs topped by grasses. Bijaz's curiosity got the best of him. He turned to a man polishing the barrel of a rifled musket.

"What was the gun, sir?" he asked politely.

"Signed on in the City, eh?" The musket polisher grinned to reveal a mouth sadly bereft of teeth. "When she makes better'n twenty river miles in an hour, they fires off the gun. Herself has promised the boat a bonus for every fast hour."

"Ah." Ashkoliiz was in a hurry. Had she fled Port Defiance ahead of some retribution?

"Didn't know they was taking on dwarfs," the gun polisher added. "You's not much to look at."

"Little but useless, that's me." Bijaz settled back into his bales and pretended to sleep.

He woke as the movement of the ship changed. They turned across the current. Had something happened?

The deck loungers again did not seem concerned. Bijaz looked to see what the ship was headed for.

A crude wooden pier stuck out from a shingle beach. At the head of the pier was a very large stack of cut wood. Fuel for the boilers. The City Imperishable burned a great deal of coal, but out here on the river that commodity would be almost impossible to procure. Though there seemed to be no one on the beach, or indeed, anywhere near the wood.

The ship made for the pier, angling upstream so the current nudged her into place. Sailors leapt from the bow with hawsers, while chain rattled as a drag anchor was dropped.

At that the waiting men stirred themselves.

"Load 'em up," bellowed a red-faced officer.

A line formed quickly enough, though some hung back. Bijaz fell in just as a blue-capped sailor caught up to him. This fellow was little more than a boy, with skin so dark it was almost black.

"You're wanted abovedecks," he said in a voice that echoed far more of the Sudgate than it did of the Sunward Sea.

"Thank you." Bijaz found his way aft, looking for stairs. Behind him the human chain groaned and chanted its way through taking on the great load of firewood.

Ashkoliiz had not been shy about having *Slackwater Princess* well-provisioned down in Port Defiance. She sat in a lounge on the third deck, beneath the pilothouse and the hurricane deck—the one nautical term he'd picked up so far. Beautiful Tokhari rugs covered the floor. The interior walls were paneled in wood the color of old whiskey. Tall, narrow glass windows made up the forward wall, through which the mountebank could watch her men swarm over the wood.

She wore white linen trousers and jacket, her clouded gem at her throat. A tray with several decanters of wine was laid next to her, along with bowls of bright southern fruit. A curl of smoke betrayed a cigar—a vice he had never pursued.

The bear was not present.

"I have noted something interesting." She leaned forward to pour a fresh glass of fluid the color of cranberries. Her blue-eyed gaze pierced him like a bat on a hook. "This landing is normally the end of a day's run out of the City Imperishable."

Bijaz could play the game of old friends. "I understand that the captain has been given significant motivation." He accepted the glass. Their fingers brushed with a spark. *It is the carpets in this room,* he told himself. He did not believe that.

"Amazing what people will do." She nodded out the window. Men worked like ants on a corpse in the gutter. "The captain is happy because he earns his exorbitant fee, as well as bonuses. The sailors are doubly happy, for they share in the captain's bonus, and the passengers perform their work for them. The idlers are happy, for they are on an adventure which will take each of them into the pages of history. I am happy, because the Northern Expedition is finally under way." Ashkoliiz took a long sip of her wine, a golden vintage. "And you, sir godling? Are you happy?"

Bijaz sniffed his drink. A Rose Downs wine, not some southern import. One of the good, earthy reds from the higher vineyards. He was never such an expert as to tell the label from the taste. "I don't suppose my happiness is at issue," he said slowly. "If you are making history, I am along to witness it."

Ashkoliiz laughed. "Your Lord Mayor wanted eyes he could trust. Not that he expects any of us to return. That does not speak so highly of his regard for you."

"Lady, I know what Imago thinks of you and your purposes. But I also know you travel with an impossible monster, and three quiet men who could be assassins or wizards or tax collectors for all I can tell. You are far more than a simple grifter come to cheat a few gulls in a meeting hall.

"As for me, Imago knows what I am. I think he sees my fate better than I ever shall."

"Come now, friend Bijaz." She set her glass down. "Do not be so dour! The Northern Expedition *is* a grand adventure, whether or not you choose to celebrate it. Your city has not mounted such in centuries. They loved us in Imperatrix Park yesterday, after all."

"And yet you slipped the moorings before dawn."

She waved off the objection. "Excited men buy in with funds or their own sword, then slink home again heavy with second thoughts. We kept the greatest number that way."

It was all just a little too pat, somehow. Was her supreme confidence a bluff? Bijaz didn't plan to call her on it, but he had to ask about the men. "Did you *want* the greatest number?"

"Do you think we can make the Rimerocks without loss?" She gave him a long, slow look. "Would you rather lay down your own life, or have some willing boy bound for glory lay his down for you?"

"That is a cold calculation, lady."

"How many did you lay down, when first I visited the City Imperishable?"

Bijaz felt himself blush with shame. So she'd heard. One of her men *had* come back to the City long before *Slackwater Princess*. Something about this woman deviled him. "I do not criticize," he said. "Only observe. My own slate will never be clean."

Ashkoliiz's mood fled as quickly as it had come. "So long as we understand each other. Oh, look!" Her voice feigned surprise. "We have taken on wood in under twenty minutes, when the captain assured me it would require an hour at least."

"I believe I shall go down to my place on the main deck." He set his half-empty glass on her table.

"I assure you that travel is far more comfortable up here."

"Either way, I am certain I will be broadened." Bijaz retired with what little remained of his dignity.

That evening the captain did not bring the boat to shore, but anchored instead out in the current. The main deck idlers were offered a meal of fresh fish and stale cornbread, washed down with some liquor that tasted like a gluepot compared to the wine served above.

Afterwards the cards and dice emerged. He resolved to stay well away from any games of chance. Bad enough he was a dwarf. These were City men for the most part, and even Port Defiance had seen dwarfs aplenty these past few years. If he were to run uncommon lucky, he might find himself waking up in the river.

Bijaz had no doubt whatsoever that his luck would be amazing, were he to sit in a hand or two.

And so it went, for six days. *Slackwater Princess* called twice at riverside towns but passed by many more. Sometimes the locals stood on the docks trying to flag her down. Bijaz presumed the captain would make amends on his return journey, once freed of the invisible lash of Ashkoliiz's gold.

The towns themselves were curious. Most settlements had been built in the lap of cities long gone to ruin. He didn't know the names, though he should have after spending so much time at the map table.

History was a pond into which great treasures had been cast. Smooth and unremarkable at first glance, but on closer examination, one gem after another was revealed deep as one cared to reach.

Instead of watching history, Bijaz was called upon to arbitrate disputes among the men. Though he had kept his hands away from the cards, the deck idlers knew that as a dwarf he was educated in numbers, and could likely be trusted to be fair-minded. So he had become their judge when such was needed.

That kept him busy. It also gave him a footing with men who might be protecting his life in the future. Ashkoliiz's words stuck with him, about who would survive as the journey grew difficult.

In quiet moments, Bijaz saw trees reflected in the eyes of the men around him. He kept to himself the dread that inspired.

As they journeyed, mountains which had been distant shadows slowly found silhouette, then shape. Bijaz calculated that *Slackwater Princess* would reach the bend at the cliff cities in another two days at most.

The Northern Expedition would put ashore there. Then it would be a different journey indeed. One foot at a time, and no lounging on the bales.

ONESIPHOROUS

He spent the day wondering when someone would come for him. He was hungry, and felt very lost. The swamp was darker and deeper than memory had painted it.

Eventually he scrambled to the top of his little island and sat until he fell asleep. He dreamed of towers drowned between a slumping shore and a rising sea. The waves wore a crown of coins—his coins. Each building boomed as it sank, crying woe in a secret language of stones.

When the stones began to pinch him, he awoke. A monkey loomed close. Even in the dark he could see it well enough. It had a face like an old woman's, though small as the palm of his hand. The wizened visage was surrounded by a dark tufted mane.

"Have you been sent for me?" Onesiphorous felt like an idiot talking to an animal.

The monkey picked a nit from its fur, cracked the insect and ate it. The deep eyes glowed silver and black with the shadowed night as it stared at him, jaw working rhythmically. Then it turned and ran away, tail twitching.

Onesiphorous followed. He tried not to slip. He didn't fancy a nighttime dip in the toothy waters.

At the bottom he found a canoe scarcely longer than he was tall. The monkey sat on the bow and scratched at its ear, now blankly devoid of its earlier purpose.

The dwarf tried to climb into the canoe. He nearly flipped the little craft. The monkey screeched once, then settled down again. Onesiphorous sat quietly for a few moments, breathing.

How would Boudin have handled this boat?

That thought brought a stab of fresh, guilty pain.

Onesiphorous grabbed the paddle and pushed himself off. He dipped to one side then the other, as Boudin had. Where the boy's strokes had slipped into the water like a knife into warm butter, his own splashed high and wide.

As a drowning boy might, fighting the inexorable tide.

He dismissed that thought as a luxury for another time. Much like the hunger pangs in his gut.

Onesiphorous had long since lost all sense of the compass points. He paddled only because it was what he was meant to do. Out on the black water, the monkey seemed willing to offer advice. When he dug out too much water, the miserable little beast gave a toothy snigger. When the canoe drifted thanks to his inept paddling, the monkey pointed out where his next stroke should fall.

He began to watch more carefully. The monkey was not only offering advice, it was giving directions. The dwarf steered as the monkey pointed. As before, the islands grew more numerous, the water began to find channels.

The drumming grew stronger as well.

Was this the drowned city the queen of Angoulême had claimed for the site of Port Defiance?

Rivers could move, everyone knew that. Floods carved new channels, banks collapsed, dams grew from debris. Maybe the city at the mouth of the River Saltus had once been here.

If this was that lost city, it was now drowned in the swamp's verdant riot—blood-warm by night, green-shadowed by day.

The monkey screamed and leapt up to disappear among low hanging branches. Onesiphorous nearly fell into the water before righting his craft again.

A fire blazed ahead, the drumming loud now.

He found a firmer stroke and moved almost silently toward the light.

The gold-skinned dancers around the fire did not break step to acknowledge Onesiphorous as he beached his canoe. He managed to fall into the water while getting out. Something sniggered in the darkness above him.

The monkey, of course. He wished it ill, then tried to slap himself dry as he climbed a set of broken stone steps to where they danced.

A huge log stood upright in the fire at their center. It was big around as the greatest of the knob-kneed swamp trees. Drummers, each armed with a single long pole padded at both ends, swung at the log in a looping motion. The strikes came in different rhythms that combined to call the measure of the dance, though no one of the drummers carried the entire beat. Each stroke sent sparks spiraling out of the top of the log.

The flames lit the swamp jungle canopy above in a bright, stark relief of muddy red and green-black shadow. Eyes gleamed there, large and small.

He hoped they were animals.

The drummers and dancers were all dressed in pale swathes of cloth belted at the waist, which dropped free to a skirt. Some wore only one cloth to expose their flanks. Others were swaddled. It was not a difference between men and women, for he saw swaying breasts as well as flatter chests. Taste, preference, role. He didn't know.

There were no children here, but some dancers seemed in their teens. The oldest were balding, though as spry as their youthful partners.

The entire company moved with the beats of the fire-drum. Each followed the compound rhythm in their own way, swaying and twisting like flags in the wind. Just as with the music, the separate movements of the dancers combined to form a coordinated whole which could not be adduced from any one of them.

After a time, he realized that an old woman sat in a chair on the far side of the drum circle. Knitting needles flashed in the firelight.

The swamp-mother. The thing from beneath the quagged soil.

Onesiphorous trotted around the perimeter, keeping a close eye on the swirling limbs lest he be struck down or drawn in. They'd marked their ring with a cord, which he stayed away from.

"Greetings," he yelled over the thunder and crackle of the fire-drum and the slap of the dancing feet.

"Little City man." She nodded. "You learn much benny-benny, ah?"

Onesiphorous knelt. "It is my sorrow that Boudin is lost."

The swamp-mother cackled. "'At boy? He no lost. He with the Sea King. Somebody pay his fare, I hear told by the squid. He comin' back on the dark moon."

"I saw him drown, mother."

Her needles stopped. "I tell you true thing, little City man. Him that drown live another life beneath the waters. You try sometime, surprise what you learn, ah. 'Sides, you know 'nough to pay his fare."

The gold tossed into the tide. "As may be," Onesiphorous said. "It was my honor to serve him. But now I am cast out. I must return to the City Imperishable, or find a way to retake the port."

The needles resumed clicking. "Black ship men walk the river. They cut you throat faster than a City man shave him coins. She say you throw them from port city, you take them from river. She say you die on river, nothing go happen."

Onesiphorous recalled Boudin's hints that the swamp-mother *was* the "she." As if she spoke of herself from another place, sometimes.

"I'm a dwarf," he said. "No one raises a sword at my word. I've made what bargains I can in Port Defiance. Now I need to move ahead."

"Sun princess, ah." The swamp-mother nodded. "She silver, move quiet as morning fog, where gold's bright fire be taken and locked away. Smart woman." She grinned.

Onesiphorous saw that her teeth were needle narrow and far too numerous. "Her, yes. I've made promises far beyond my faith and credit. Still, I did what needed doing."

"So now you little City man swim upstream like bright shad come home to spawn. You lay your eggs at the dock and die, ah?"

She made going home sound so unappealing. "You've told me your people will not fight," Onesiphorous began, then trailed off as he realized the drumming had stopped.

He turned to look. Ranged around the burning log, four drummers and ten dancers stood smiling at him. Their teeth were filed to points in imitation of the swamp-mother's.

As one they opened their hands to show the gold each carried. Each slipped the coin between their filed teeth. Together they picked up the cord which marked their circle. In a single rippling motion transmitted from hand to hand each looped the cord around their neck. In the shadows above, the monkey screamed. All fourteen dropped to their knees to lean backward, away from the log and each other. The cord stretched tight and crushed all of their throats with a tearing noise that turned Onesiphorous' guts to water.

"Ah," said the swamp-mother behind him. "We fight. You not worry, little City man. We just not fight your way."

He turned back as she slithered beneath the earth, folding into a fist once more. The hollow log burst to send shards of flaming wood into the air. He crouched down, covered his neck with his hands, and waited for the fall of burning debris to stop.

Onesiphorous finally stood and brushed himself off. He tried to quell the roil in his gut. When he looked, the bodies were gone. Only the cord remained, a loop of loops around the smoldering mound of the fire.

"Hey, City man," said a voice in the darkness. "You Boudin's friend, ah?"

"Um…"

The speaker stepped close. Visible now in the flickering ember, he was clad in trousers ripped at the knee and a linen shirt. He was gold-skinned and dark-eyed just as Boudin had been, just as the dancers had been. "Next time, don't make so much a fire."

"It w-w-w-asn't my fire," the dwarf stammered.

"Oh, just you pray it was, City man. No one see one of her fires and live to tell the tale, ah. Me, I never seen one, and if I did, I never say it." A large hand thumped him on the back. "You been lost long time. Want some dinner? Come,

132 — JAY LAKE

I take you to shelter."

Onesiphorous followed, stumbling and shivering even in the oppressive warmth of the night.

IMAGO

He and Kalliope found the Water Captain knee-deep in mud at the grate of a pumping station along the Little Bull, just above the Bridge of Chances. Their quarry was a large man named Fencarro, who currently struggled with a long-handled wrench and the help of two wretchedly muddy dwarfs. Imago's guards hung back, fingering their pistols and watching the rooftops for stray spies or assassins out of the North.

It was hot and foggy here, though the day was still crisp elsewhere on the streets.

"The steam is troubling you?" Imago called down.

"Leak burned two men bad this morning, Lord Mayor," Fencarro replied. "I was saving the report 'til we were done, in case we killed anybody." He set down his wrench and smeared mud across his face with the back of his hand. "Kind of you to inspect our work, sir."

"Aye, his worship's always had a keen interest in the power of steam," cackled one of the mud-drenched dwarfs.

It was Saltfingers, Imago realized. "Hello, friend," he said. "I have someone you must meet with, but I'll leave you to your work until then. Do you require more men?"

"Not unless they fancy being cooked like lobsters." Fencarro grinned. "I believe this has been shut off."

"Overpressure from Lightfoot Lane number two boiler," Saltfingers added. "Check valve rolled over on them like a three-chalkie whore on festival night."

"Very well." He and Kalliope stepped away to look for a seat on the bridge rail.

"Most of your City desk warmers won't get into the muck," she said. "But that's your Water Captain and your chief dunny diver down there. They risk their lives instead of sending lesser men."

"And strangely enough, their bureau functions better than any other in my government." Imago settled against the stone of the bridge in a leaning seat. He wished that the gods who'd shortened him to a dwarf had left his joints with less of a hard, brutal ache.

"Thank you for helping me with this."

Imago smiled. "What else am I to do with you? General of a vanished army, sister of a hero of the late unpleasantness, mighty sand mage. If I don't help you, I'm liable to be made over into a camel blanket. And I've had sufficient transformation to last me the rest of my days."

"Surely you'd be a fine, hand-knotted rug," she said with a laugh.

"A right honorable one at that, no doubt."

Saltfingers found them soon enough. He was soaking wet, but most of the mud was gone. The dwarf was as strange and ugly as ever. "Hello, your worship," he said, touching a finger to his forehead. "Twice I sees you in two days. My stock must be rising up on the hill."

"It has always been high." Imago nodded politely. "How were the Old Twins last night?"

"Clogged," the dunny diver announced cheerfully. "Piotr Sharpshoes and Big Denis had to go for a swim to manage the clearing out, poor them. Did the job, but they tell me the smell was a thing of itself. A few days of steaming herbs and decent rest and they'll be right back at it."

Imago felt vaguely queasy at the description. He'd spent enough time down in the sewers to have a personal appreciation for what went on there. "Give them my thanks, and the gratitude of anyone who lives near Imperatrix Park. Meanwhile, I have a great favor to ask."

Saltfingers gave Kalliope a long, slow look. "You'll be wanting something for the foreign sand lady, then?"

"Yes. She seeks her brother, him that you've seen trace of beneath the stones."

"So you think you are one of us," Saltfingers said speculatively. "You're a creature of light and air, sand lady. Down there's no place for a woman. Even less a place for a desert rat."

Kalliope met the dunny diver's look with a cool appraisal of her own. "I'm also responsible for Jason. Thrice over. Once as his sister, twice as his killer, and the third time because it was I who helped Bijaz to raise him again."

"You quality gets up to strange doings, but I reckon that's none of my concern."

"Probably not," she said. "Still, I have nothing to hide."

"The tunnels hide everything as it is. They don't need no help."

Imago cleared his throat. "Since you both are getting along so famously, perhaps I can leave you to it? I've a need to assess the damages from that little rally last night. I want to know if we lost anyone or anything important."

"We'll make our way when we're ready," Kalliope told him.

"Blessings on you, your worship," Saltfingers added.

Imago resisted the urge to bow, and instead simply walked away.

He was surprised to find Enero waiting in his office. "You've been leaving for days, now," Imago said as he took to his chair. "Not that I wish you ill, but are you planning to have done with it anytime soon? I can't miss you until you go away, you know."

"To be sure," Enero said. "A man's mind is to always be changing."

"Like the weather, I suppose."

Enero slapped a leather book onto Imago's desk. "Notes. Maps. Codes. Who can be trusted. I am thinking this is to be a bad time for you."

"Worse than what?" Imago asked. "We've had armies at the gates, monsters in the streets, gods in the sewers, and a revenant madman in the Limerock Palace. Is someone planning to set fire to the entire city?"

"It is being a stranger thing, subtler than that. The Northern Expedition is to likely be stirring up more than they are having bargained for."

"That wouldn't surprise me," said Imago. "A not unreasonable speculation. What is your source?"

"Ulliaa."

He tried to parse that, decided it was a name. "Who?"

"The Northman who was to be staying behind when the mountebank was to be fleeing south. Last night he was coming to Orlando, of my freeriders, with a message for me."

"He ratted himself out?"

"No. They are being in disagreement. Ashkoliiz is to have one purpose, that bear to have another. The Northmen are fearing what might be to come with this fracture."

"What precisely did this message say?"

Enero tugged a folded piece of parchment from the book. A note was written on it in a strange hand.

> She bethrais ore purpos for glori. We feir Iistaa tchanjing also. She will waik
> what we did not seik. Gaard your threis.

After puzzling for a while, Imago looked up at Enero. "You obviously read more into this than I can. I don't understand this last bit. 'Guard your threes.'"

"Here is what I am to be fearing," Enero said. "You are having succeeded in laying old power to rest. You are having balanced the Burgesses. If Ashkoliiz is to be waking some terror in the North, the City Imperishable will to be rising to defend itself. Our work of last winter is being undone then."

"Of course we'll defend ourselves." Imago almost sputtered. "We are already in a war to the south, if you haven't forgotten. I'll even be sure to guard the threes, if I can figure what in Dorgau's hells those are. And I'd love your help. But you've refused to let me pay you to stay on. Repeatedly."

"I am being for hire now." Enero leaned down to face Imago, hands planted wide. "Extending the contract of last autumn to a year. Same terms as before for my men, but being different for me. I am needing one copper orichalk in payment. I am also needing a reliable messenger to Bas Luccia."

"You can be buried in orichalks for all I care," Imago told him. "I'll even give you the keys to the mint if need be. But I can't get anyone through to Bas Luccia. I can't even get a cutter down the River Saltus."

"Tokhari caravans are already to be coming and going."

"They pass hundreds of miles to the east of Bas Luccia. They don't go near the coast. They can't compete with the shipping trade. I would have to pay a fortune—" He stopped. "There is no shipping trade now. It's under blockade. For all we know, it will stay that way for months, since we've no way to break it."

"You are to be thinking again, Lord Mayor," Enero said. "As am I. The Northmen are being made of frozen iron. Anything to frighten them is being like terror to me. Anything to break down your walls is being like worry to me."

"I'm glad you have your priorities straight," said Imago.

"I am to be writing messages. You are to be finding me a caravan."

"And an orichalk," the Lord Mayor reminded him.

"I am not objecting to it being delivered in a gold casket."

He smiled. "I'll see what I can arrange."

Enero nodded and left.

Imago breathed a heavy sigh of relief. He would have been down to almost no support at all, nothing to balance the bailiffs or supply his own force to keep the peace.

Or break it, if needed.

The afternoon brought him a succession of Tokhari caravan masters, two complaints from ships' captains trapped by the downstream closure of the river, news of a house fire near the Potter's Field, and a summons to appear before the fraud court of the Assemblage in answer for the misdeeds of his ward, one Bijaz the dwarf.

"It never ends," Imago growled, after being refused for the fourth time in his request for a caravan to Bas Luccia. "How am I to get this through?"

"It is not a matter of willingness," said the caravan master. This one's name was Quaals. "There are no trails, no serais." He lacked any Tokhari accent. But for his copper skin and swarthy cast and the almost exaggerated traditional Tokhari vest and flared trousers, he could have been a born City man.

Of course, with all the Tokhari living in this place, he *could* be a born City man.

"There must be roads. People live everywhere."

"Certainly." The Tokhari spread his hands, gesturing to emphasize his words as if signing to a fool. "Every farmer walks his pig to market. Every town has a track to the next town. A man on foot or ahorse might go anywhere he pleases, if he is patient. Four dozen camels and horses with a mounted escort? No.

"And there is more, your right honorableness. Some lands *are* empty. The east bank of the Saltus south of here is, so I am told. Beyond it lies trackless swamp and open prairie to the Yellow Mountains. Likewise long leagues of the route you propose. I am to follow my usual trails, and double back after Cairn Pass or the Glass Monastery? Thus the distance is even greater, and no profit there to be had."

"Do you have any suggestions?" Imago asked, frustrated.

"I am crippled with regret in having failed you, Lord Mayor." The caravan master managed to look desolated. "Send trusted riders with me. I will show them the trails leading back west and south where we pass them. They can make their own choices. Bas Luccia is not some dog-infested pit, it is a great city by a great sea. But it faces the water, much as the City Imperishable faces the River Saltus, and takes as little care for its roads inland as you do."

"I will send a boy to you later," said Imago. "Please hold places for me until tomorrow."

"We leave at moonset two mornings hence," the master said. "For the Lord Mayor I will charge a most special, favorable rate in escorting and advising his riders."

"I've got a better idea," said Imago. "Charge me nothing, and I'll make sure you're at the top of the muster lists in the future."

More desolation. "A promise is a glorious investment, but a payment can be spent on feed and weapons today."

"And what would that payment be?"

"Forty gold obols for up to four riders. Payable on depositary draft to Azure Expedition and Trade at Dawes, Toombs, Mousely, Grubbs. I do not carry my funds where bandits can steal them." Quaals smiled ruefully. "At least not bandits of the mountain kind."

"This must be done," Imago said ungraciously. "Never mind waiting for my runner. I'll send Stockwell to the bank with your fee before the windows close. My riders will find you tomorrow."

"You will not regret this."

"Don't tell me what I will and won't regret," Imago muttered, but he rose to shake hands. "The City Imperishable is in your debt, sir."

"Not once the draft has cleared."

BIJAZ

Slackwater Princess came upon the cliff cities near sunset with her whistle screaming and bells clanging. The river was narrower and faster here, so the paddles thrashed hard. Swallows circled in flocks so thick as to cloud the light. The air smelled of the sweet sap of scraggly evergreens for which Bijaz had no name, of the tingling scent of the river where it broke over rocks along the south bank and mixed tumbling with the air until the two became one.

Excited men lined the rail speculating on the adventure to come. They had to shout over the river's roar, the thrash of the paddles, the chatter of swirling swallows. Bijaz could see little but broad backs and supplies already shifted to be offloaded. His opinion varied from the prevailing sentiment on deck. It was perfectly clear to him that the safest, simplest part of the journey was just behind them. Everything from now on would be uphill, increasingly cold, and if successful, likely to culminate in the unpleasantly noumenal.

He figured he'd see the cliff cities soon enough. Right now Bijaz aimed to enjoy his last moments of relative luxury. He'd successfully avoided Ashkoliiz and her invitation to return to the upper decks, and so had partaken of neither cigars nor wine. The sour mash and roasted fish of the lower decks had been filling enough. Meanwhile, he'd noticed the men going up in fives or tens.

She was making the acquaintance of every one of her troops. He had no doubt Ashkoliiz would know each man's name and have an assessment of their character. He knew little of soldiers and generals, but the great syndics of Heliograph Hill did not invite their clerks and stevedores up for drinks. Could one woman lead so many men on charm and wit alone?

With a great clangor and a groan of distressed timber *Slackwater Princess* came to a shuddering halt. Sailors communicated in whistles over the noise of landing, lashing the boat tight. Even from his limited view, Bijaz could see that they had laid out more lines than normal, making the boat fast against whatever forces of the river might pluck her from the bank.

The vessel settled in place. Men poured down the gangplank. Some leapt overboard in their haste. The birds swooped low, darting under the ceiling of the main deck, alighting on the rail, circling Bijaz with whirring wings.

He realized then they were not swallows, but bats little larger than a man's hand. They shrieked and piped as they flew. Tiny monkey faces glared at him with glittering eyes the color of clouded citrons.

Bijaz stifled a shout and began to swat them away.

Some burst into flowers. The rest quickly veered off, leaving Bijaz in a shower of rose petals that no one but him seemed to notice.

He finally made his way to the rail. The docks here were substantial—stone jetties of riprap much like those at the City Imperishable. A few rotting piers protruded from the fast water, showing that there had been wharves in the River Saltus in older, better days.

The cloud of bats still circled *Slackwater Princess*, but they spiraled ever wider into the sky. Late afternoon's slanting light flowed golden bright across the faces of the roofless white buildings behind the docks. This port had been burned out. Facades were damaged. Curving columns broke off halfway up.

A hill rose steeply behind the buildings, stairs climbing to meet the cliff which carved the northern sky here. Bijaz followed their line upward. That slope was nothing more than a skirt for the vertical face, he realized. The buildings of this port were a veneer for what had been built above.

The cliff cities—he had never heard another name for them—were great, bulbous structures which clung to the wall of rock. Bubbles of brick and mud and stone strained a half-mile and more toward the heavens. The globes varied in size, but even the smallest could have contained *Slackwater Princess*.

Bijaz realized the larger ones were demiglobes, domes set vertically instead of horizontally. He wondered if those opened within the cliff face to complete the spheres beloved of the architects of this place.

Each globe had an entrance in the form of a flanged tube, rather like the flare at the top of a vase. Various of the tubes faced upward, outward, or down, though all were roughly at the waist of their respective globes. The monkey-faced bats issued from the globes in spiraling clouds.

This had been a city of some flying race. Perhaps the bats were degenerate descendants of the builders. Bijaz recognized the power and skill it had taken to raise this place.

It was one thing to call a flower into being within cupped hands, or even to raise the dead. It was quite another to build an entire city such as this.

The Northern Expedition assembled itself on the docks in the failing light of day. The stone waterfront ran a mile along the bend of the River Saltus. Flowing by the City Imperishable it was slow, sullen, louche. Here at the cliff cities, the young Saltus was narrow and fast, filled with bright promise and a manic momentum.

A cheap metaphor for life itself, Bijaz thought sourly.

He seemed to have been spared any particular assignments thus far. The only dwarf in the expedition, and presumably the only god as well, he could see why the others would work around him. It didn't seem to be in Ashkoliiz's character to leave a piece on her board unused, but lurking belowdecks he hadn't been in a position to know whom she might have been checking by his very presence.

He found his way to a half-ruined balcony overlooking the bustle and watched.

About a hundred men had shipped upriver with Ashkoliiz. Most had signed on in Port Defiance, seeking a way out of the troubled city. The rest had been swept in from the rally at Imperatrix Park. Bijaz knew forty or so riders were coming upriver, though he hadn't spotted them since *Slackwater Princess* had last called ashore. The cliffs there would have forced the horsemen to swing wide to the north. They had not caught up with the boat since.

That made for a hundred forty men, plus Ashkoliiz and her personal party, including Bijaz himself. He doubted any crew from *Slackwater Princess* would be joining them. Adventuresome as they might be, sailors would have no great love of walking empty miles.

A gross of mouths to feed, plus several dozen horses, required a considerable wealth of supplies. Bales, barrels, boxes, satchels, sacks, saddles, weapons, washtubs, wheels of cheese. Ashkoliiz's five-score hirelings swarmed around the docks, directed from the upper deck by her with her electrick voice projector. Bijaz watched her three dark Northmen move among the work parties, touching an arm, pointing out the needed direction of supplies. A few of the sailors helped as well.

Then the ice bear lumbered down the gangplank. Men scattered in a controlled panic, reluctantly reforming out of the path of the bear.

That was why she'd called the men up to the upper decks in small groups, he realized. To introduce them to the ice bear, and show that it was tame—or civilized?—enough for them to work with.

The bear was unmistakably working. It moved from stack to stack, inspecting supplies and the effort being done to bring them ashore. Every few minutes it would stop, stand to its full height, and stare up at Ashkoliiz. In those moments, her attention would come to a precise focus as her voice boomed from the voice projector.

"Hargraves, Donati, restack those fur bundles!"

"You two, in the green—Arcus and Orcus—count those axes again. See that we're not missing any."

The ice bear would move on, poking and prodding. Everyone gave it a wide berth. Not panic, but more like frightened respect.

And so it went until full dark, *Slackwater Princess* emptying out her belly for the first time on this journey.

Ashkoliiz stood at the gangplank and paid the riverboat's captain by the glare of the electricks. She walked ashore, the last member of the Northern Expedition to debark. The crew began the process of casting off.

Slackwater Princess had not once sailed in the darkness the entire eight days of the journey upriver.

The boat didn't sound her whistle, either, just slipped into the current and thrashed her way upstream. The moon was not risen yet, but Bijaz had no difficulty following the vessel's progress by the glare of her electricks.

Ashkoliiz stepped onto his balcony. "So," she said, her voice clotted cream. "What do you think so far, little god?"

"I think that's a tall cliff ahead of us," Bijaz said, ignoring the insult. "I think we've mislaid some horsemen. Most of all, I think half of what I see here is more show than substance."

She laughed, her voice thrilling with chills upon his spine. "You misunderstand.

Everything you see here is for show."

Definitely not cut from the same mold as a canny old syndic, he thought, for all her strong words.

The riverboat's whistle began to screech. Something was wrong. The sound was throatier and pitched higher than normal. He could see the dots of light moving oddly. Was she spinning? In the current this far up the Saltus, that could be deadly.

Slackwater Princess broke apart with a rumbling flash of orange and white. In a moment, the riverboat was gone. A cloud of fog and steam rising into the starry night.

"Boiler explosions are a terrible tragedy." Ashkoliiz's voice was as cold as the ice in her eyes.

Bijaz could say nothing to that. He watched the current, wondering if anyone would survive, and what story they would carry home.

Of course not, he realized. The woman was far too thorough. He turned to her, fearing the expression he would see upon her face, but she'd slipped away once more.

He spent another bad night amid the bales, worrying about a slim knife in the dark. Bijaz's own small blade would be useless against treachery. He knew she was fatally ruthless. She knew he knew. Destroying the boat had been a stupid mistake, to boot.

What mattered to her?

Bijaz could scarcely guess.

Nor could he come to a good reason for her to destroy the riverboat. She might be able to escape blame, it was true, but why even do the deed? Was there some secret of hers that the captain or crew might have betrayed?

It could be as simple as her paying the ship off in bags filled with stones, then ensuring that the captain never returned to the City Imperishable to blacken her name.

These thoughts kept him twisting until dawn arrived with its own flying horrors returning home on the wing.

The next morning Ashkoliiz led a memorial for the captain and good sailors of the late, lamented *Slackwater Princess.* She stood on the balcony he'd used the night before. The men assembled along the docks with their backs to the water.

"Northern Expedition!" Her voice carried in the dawn air.

"And bears," shouted a wit amid the ragged, groaning rows.

"And bears." Her tone could have frosted iron. Then: "We gather now to pray mercy for the souls of our departed helpers and servants. They were not the first to lay down their lives that the Northern Expedition might prevail."

Oh really? Bijaz thought.

"They will not be the last," she went on.

At this the men murmured.

Prophecy, or threat. He interpreted her statement in either light.

"Without their brave sacrifice, there would be no Northern Expedition. There would be no history to be made and remade. There would be no fortunes to be brought home upon our straining backs."

That got a cheer from all except the most thoughtful.

She lowered her voice so the men had to strain to hear. "Today we thank them, and speed their souls onward in care of whatever caravan may convey them across the black deserts of the next world. Today we climb the stairs they have built for us, sailing the course they laid down their bodies to chart. Today we let them make us great." Then: "Hip-hip…"

"Hooray!" screamed the men.

She led them through the traditional three cheers. Bijaz had never seen anyone so happy about the death of a boatload of people.

Later a grubby little man who'd lost quite a bit of money gambling on the river sidled up to Bijaz as he sat sorting tent stakes. "Herself wants to be seeing you, sport." J. Quesenberry, Bijaz recalled.

"You running messages now?" he asked with a smile.

His jocularity was rewarded with a whine. "Everybody's got to pitch in." Quesenberry cast an injured glare and wandered away.

Bijaz picked his way amid men laying out loads along the dock. They were preparing for a line of march. He could not see how the supplies were to be carried.

There was very little food, he noted. He presumed that Ashkoliiz planned to live off the land. This wasn't such a large group to make that impossible, but nothing he'd read back in the City Imperishable about the high desert country behind the Silver Ridges suggested a useful degree of fertility.

Ashkoliiz had set up a temporary headquarters just inside the gaping doorway of some old temple or commodities exchange. Snakes and cattle intertwined the surviving pillars of the facade, each bearing blossoms in their mouths.

The interior was roofless. They were under the same sky as the men outside. As with the docks, virtually all the rubble had long ago been removed. Vines grew from cracks in the floor, spreading like a green carpet with flowers the color of muskmelons. The blooms were tended by small, dark insects.

Ashkoliiz had papers laid out across a stone table just inside the entrance. The ice bear and one of her Northmen were there, along with three of the expeditionary hirelings.

Bijaz knew two of them from the card games on the main deck—toothless

Carmen Priola, and Wee Pollister, a dark-skinned giant with a dreamy expression and shaggy straw-colored hair. Wee Pollister was easily the biggest man in the expedition and the only one Bijaz would have backed in a bare-knuckled bout against the ice bear. The third was a dapper, twitchy fellow in a deep blue velvet cutaway and mismatched gray twill trousers with braiding along the seam. He was of ordinary build, badly shaved bald, his scalp covered with scratches. He turned to examine Bijaz, with one dark blue eye and one pale gray eye. They were slightly crossed, which might explain the poorly shaven head.

"Ah, friend Bijaz." Ashkoliiz smiled. Somehow he didn't find her winter-eyed gaze so compelling this morning. "Welcome to our councils."

"Am I to be your court dwarf?" He hadn't meant to be so sharp, but the bald man's gaze was disconcerting.

"Not at all." She remained silk-smooth as ever. "Perhaps our consulting deity." Ashkoliiz looked to her deputies. "Gentlemen, allow me to introduce Bijaz the dwarf, a longtime leader of the minuscularian community in the City Imperishable and of late blessed by divine powers. He is here as the representative of Lord Mayor Imago of Lockwood. I have invited him to sit on our innermost councils. He has graciously accepted my poor request."

It was a declamation worthy of a hearing before the Assemblage of Burgesses. Bijaz was fairly certain the mountebank's words had skimmed past all the listening ears but his.

Of course, it was to him she was primarily speaking.

"My good Ashkoliiz," he replied with a slight bow—moderated by degree, to indicate courtesy only and not the respect due to higher rank—"I take great pleasure in overseeing your affairs on the part of the City Imperishable. As it is in our name you act, we have been most gratified to be invited into the governance of your Northern Expedition."

She nodded, her sunny expression slipping momentarily. "Fair enough." Ashkoliiz indicated her hirelings. "Do you gentlemen have any questions for Bijaz?"

"'S an odd one," Priola said with his soft-edged grin. "But he been fair belowdecks in sitting judge on our games, and never got all dwarfy on us."

"Ya," rumbled Wee Pollister.

The rest waited to see if he had anything else to say, but Wee Pollister subsided to inertness.

"I'm thinking something." The bald man tossed a narrow, hiltless, leaf-shaped blade in one hand. It had not been there a moment before. Bijaz wondered how difficult handling such a knife would be, even without sending it spinning by one's fingertips.

Ashkoliiz nodded slightly. Bijaz was not sure for whom the signal was intended. "I believe you have the advantage of me," he said brightly.

"And I aim to keep it that way. Whump's the name." A couple more slips of the knife. Then: "What's a squat-bodied defect like you doing walking into the high, hard country anyway? I don't aim to see us slowed to carry your larded arse on the backs of good men."

This was familiar territory. Years of struggling with First Counselor Prothro and the rest of the Inner Chamber had inured Bijaz to insults, albeit usually somewhat more nuanced. He had plentiful practice in cutting to the heart of fighting words.

Bijaz kept his voice level. "If you are suggesting that you might be obliged to help me up the mountains, I assure you that I shall pull my own weight and more."

"I'm suggesting you don't know how to *survive*." The bald man's leaf-bladed knife snapped through the air with a faint whistle.

The path through the wheat field loomed large in Bijaz's mind. This was only a scythe, a blade to cut the grain, and he was not yet ripe. He reached out and blocked the edge as it swung close. The scythe took another stalk instead, which broke with a scream like a rabbit trapped in a burrow beneath burning stubble.

The bald man staggered backward, his eyes crossing. The blade was stuck in his sternum, blood soaking his ruffled silk shirt. He dropped to his knee and opened his mouth to gasp for air. Tendrils of green emerged from his throat and slid out of the rent in his shirt to wrap his knife.

Bijaz felt no twinge of regret at all. He watched the bald man collapse. The tendrils writhed to wrap him tightly.

"Does anyone else wish to question my survival skills?"

Ashkoliiz continued to smile at Bijaz fondly. Priola and Wee Pollister both had found architectural detail to study. The bear favored him with a level gaze, while the Northman waited at the door.

The mountebank nodded. "Fetch the next one, please."

The Northman nodded and departed.

"I expect my councilors to exercise a modicum of judgment," Ashkoliiz told the room at large. "Anyone who sees fit to draw weapons against a divine figure has failed a most basic test of intelligence."

Wee Pollister's gaze drifted back down from the stonework. "All's know him what was touched by the Numbers Men," he said. His voice was like millstones grinding dry. "Some's don't believe what they been told is all."

Bijaz looked at the man-shaped cluster of vines. Tiny red blossoms the color of shed blood covered him. The black insects were already exploring. "I should hope belief will not be in such short supply now."

He wondered if he ought to be regretful, or afraid, but if he felt anything at all, it was an angry sense of justice having been done.

Onesiphorous

"I am Clement." His guide paddled them in a dory much like Boudin's boat. "You are that little man with the strange name."

"Onesiphorous," the dwarf said glumly.

"City name. You got a water name?"

He thought of Silver, with her strange intensities and curious priorities. "I've been called Oarsman."

"Oarsman you are now." Clement laughed. "You want to paddle?"

"No, no thank you."

"Oarsman who sails no boat. A person could make a song of that, ah?"

"Be my guest."

Clement hummed and paddled, guiding them through apparently blind channels without pause for thought.

"You knew Boudin?" the dwarf finally asked, picking at the misery of his guilt like a child worrying at a scab.

The humming stopped. The paddling stopped, too, missing a few beats before it resumed. "Boudin is my sister's son."

"Was." Onesiphorous was thoroughly miserable now. "He drowned for me."

"No man drowns who does not live again, ah." Another stroke of the paddle. "Corsairs stick him in the belly, that be great mourning. Drown in the honest sea, ah."

Despite his words, Clement gave out a heavy sigh.

"I'm sorry." Onesiphorous huddled around his knees. "He was taken trying to help me."

"You force him help?" Clement asked sharply.

"No."

"You catch him in irons?"

"No."

"You tie him before the tide?"

"No."

"Then you got no right to be sorry. You got right to be angry, if you want. These not your regrets, City man."

They slid among a grove of narrow trees unlike any Onesiphorous had yet seen in the swamp. He looked up to a close blackness. He realized that these were not trees, but houses on poles. This was Clement's village.

Clement took Onesiphorous to a long, low room with half-walls that let the night air move. Several trestle tables were set up, along with an oven of stone and clay. It was a refectory—he didn't think the swamp had much room for restaurants. A huge pot steamed over a banked fire, from which Clement ladled stew into a wide wooden bowl. It was dark, tasting slightly burnt but in a tangy, satisfying way. There were several vegetables he couldn't identify, and clumps of rice. Peppers too, spicier than what he was used to, and bits of fish and crustacean floating about.

At least he hoped they were crustacean.

His host offered Onesiphorous a piece of bread. This was torn ragged from a flat round which had been baked clinging to clay walls within the oven. It tasted of some dark-green herb, and was the best part of the meal.

The fact that he hadn't eaten since the day before might actually have been the best part of the meal. Onesiphorous would have gladly gulped down catmeat soup from the worst Sudgate potshop.

He sopped the last of his stew with the bread fragment, then looked up at Clement. The swamper's face was set.

"So I am here," Onesiphorous said. "And I must ask you a thing."

"Ah." Clement nodded very slightly. "And this thing?"

"You told me no one sees a fire in the night. Not one of her fires. Whoever *she* is." Onesiphorous waited for a reaction, but Clement said nothing, just continued to stare at him. "But I did see it. I'm not one of her people. Maybe I'm permitted to see more than you are. She promises a fight, but not armies at the City's command. All of these things I think I understand. I do not understand how Boudin knew to bring me to her, the first time. What was the boy to her?"

Clement cleared his throat. "See, you dangerous, little City man. You ask questions we know not to. You see things we allow to cloak our eyes. Whatever she let you see, let you do, that be her judgment, ah. But these strange times now. Hard times, live on sword edge instead of by casting of nets. Boudin. My nephew." He stopped, breaking eye contact with Onesiphorous, then paced the room.

The dwarf waited him out in turn.

Finally the swamp man tore off another piece of bread and worried it in his hands. "We got no standing temples here. Everything is sacred. Every shadow is altar, ah. You understand?"

"Yes," Onesiphorous said, though he didn't yet understand at all.

"We got no priests, neither. No fat men in cloth-of-gold. No crazy women cutting chicken necks. Just us and the swamp. So when she come among us, she got to find horse to ride. Boudin, he be one of them horses."

"Is there more than one horse?"

Clement's eyes shifted as he continued to pace, not looking at Onesiphorous at all. "Everything with eyes can be a horse, ah. Carpenter got many tools, she got many horses."

He had to know. He needed to understand. So he pushed a little harder. "Is there more than one of her?"

"Is there more than one swamp? Moonrise in spring not the same as storm off the ocean in autumn. Mists of winter different from daylight in summer. How many faces the world got, ah?"

"How many faces does any man have?" Onesiphorous muttered.

"Maybe you understand." Clement stopped pacing. "Maybe you need to know. Whatever you see around fire, that between you and her. I already say too much. I don't want hear nothing. When she angry, she ride horses into deep water, leave them there."

He tried for reassurance. "She'll forgive you. If she needs you to tell me, she'll forgive."

Clement laughed, a hollow sound. "You crazy little man. Tide raise him boats, drown him boy, forgive nothing. Why she be any different from wind and water?"

"Why indeed?" He set his spoon inside his dry bowl with a click. "It seems best to leave you swamp people to fight your own war. I will stop asking foolish questions."

"Where you go, then?" Clement glanced out at the night-black swamp.

"The plantations, the mines. See who I can raise among the City folk here to fight."

"Them? Failed parasites, ah. Live off your City power without no respect for him."

"As may be," Onesiphorous said. "But I have experience in organizing people to do things they might not see as desirable. I believe I can find a way. Will you take me to one of the settlements?"

"We sleep. Then I take you to Lost Receiver Mine, ah. Got one thing to ask you first, me."

"Yes?"

"Don't say no more we are swamp people. Our people, we the Angoumois."

"Angoumois. My apologies." Onesiphorous rubbed his aching temples. "You mentioned sleep?"

He awoke to the squawking of birds. Onesiphorous blinked his eyes open. A strong green light showed outside the refectory. Two women in dresses much like the swamp-mother's worked at the cookpot. They chattered without ever turning to glance at him.

Four red birds clung to the top rail of one of the half-walls. Did she ride behind those bright black eyes?

Onesiphorous sat up, wondering where to pee. He slipped out the trap door in the floor and climbed down the ladder to a little landing where several boats were tied up. The tide was high again, judging from how close the water came to the boards beneath his feet. No one seemed to be around, so he unbuttoned his pants and urinated directly into the swamp in a steaming arc.

"That a bad idea," said Clement behind him.

Surprised, the dwarf splashed on his pants. "My thanks, sir," he replied bitterly.

"Candirú fish, he swim up your little yellow river. You one unhappy man after he climb inside."

"How lovely."

"Angoulême have many gifts, City man. We all she children."

Onesiphorous tried to figure if Clement was twitting him, but his host seemed positively lugubrious this morning. "Is there anything else I should do before we go?"

Clement nodded solemnly. "Get in the boat."

Insects whirred like a steam engine with bad bearings. Clement paddled again, though today the little boat also had a pair of oars shipped. They slid between narrow passes walled by root balls and lumps of clay. Onesiphorous watched for more stony evidence of the drowned city, but he saw nothing certain.

They finally came to a halt in the mossy shadows of a stand of trees. A large channel opened before them. A visible current disturbed the water's dark surface.

"Listen, ah," said Clement. "The mine, she just up this stream. I take you there but fast. I must go back to her. I already say too much to you, she will take price from me."

"How are you going to find her?"

"She everywhere, City man. I open my arms and close my eyes, she find me."

Onesiphorous felt a sense of dread. "You take care. She has too much to say, she can ask me. You are helping me and repaying the death of your nephew."

Clement smiled sadly. "The tide, she got no forgiveness." Then he unshipped his oars and put his back into moving the boat out onto the open water.

Free of the trees, Onesiphorous could see the outcropping of the Lost Receiver Mine. It rose from the swamp like a black stone thumb, taller than even the Rugmaker's Cupola and at least as wide.

He wondered about the resemblance to a tower as Clement made for a dock sticking out from the flowering bushes at the base.

Good as his word, Clement crabbed the boat close enough to the dock to let Onesiphorous climb out. The Angoumois then slipped away on the current. The dwarf watched his guide find his way back into darkness. As Clement rowed into the shadows of bushes, something followed that left a long, narrow vee of ripples on the surface.

If Onesiphorous had possessed another coin, he would have paid it to the water right then in case Clement was in need of a fare all too soon. She could not be trusted in a way that made sense to men. He wasn't sure she could be trusted at all, even though he had been allowed to walk free of the swamps.

Not the swamps. He'd walked free of Angoulême, drowned lands that yet lived in green shadows under her protection.

Once Boudin's uncle was gone, quite possibly forever, Onesiphorous made his way to the curtain of vines where the dock met the rock. He was surprised at how rickety the structure was, until he reflected that this was a jade mine. They did not bring heavy ores out to barges here. What came from within the rock could be carried by a man with a padded valise.

The vines masked a recessed entrance where a door made of stout planks stood propped open. A sun-browned dwarfess sat on a cane-bottomed chair in the middle of the doorway. She smoked a long, thin clay pipe as she tipped her seat back on two legs.

"You're that Slashed fellow." She spoke around the stem of her pipe, narrow trails of smoke coming from her lips as she talked. "Long way from home, aren't you?"

Onesiphorous made a tiny bow. "I don't believe we've had the pleasure."

"You've got a strange definition of pleasure." She tilted the chair onto all four legs and set the pipe on the stone flooring. "I'm Beaulise. I believe you know my father."

"Beaulise?" He drew a blank on who her family might be.

"Bijaz, late your enemy. Now a crazed, god-touched old man."

"Ah." He wasn't sure what this presaged—irritated rebuff or welcome. "Bijaz, yes."

"Yes?" She snorted. "That's all you can say about the strangest transformation in the City Imperishable?"

Onesiphorous decided to try for a change of subject. "Was I expected?"

She pursed her lips. "Not exactly. Come in, we can talk in the coolth."

"Of course," he said, and followed her inside.

IMAGO

He ignored the writ from the Assemblage. The Burgesses had managed to dither themselves into irrelevance after the disgrace of the old Inner Chamber and the overthrow of the Imperator Restored. The rest of his immediate troubles were dispatched by relatively simple decision-making.

By Dorgau's brass hells, he missed Onesiphorous. There had been nothing from the south but silent blockade.

Imago decided to step out for dinner. He wanted to stretch his legs again. He took a cloak and made his way down the spiraled stair. His usual guards were not at the door—confusion with the changeover regarding Enero's men. Now that the Winter Boys were staying on another season, Imago would need to make the City Men a greater priority. He didn't intend to be caught short yet again.

Cork Street was deserted. He wondered if a riot had erupted somewhere.

Imago found his way into a steaming, high-windowed café with the menu painted on the glass in gold lettering. It was reversed from within, intending to appeal to passersby, but he could still read it. Besides, he'd eaten here often enough.

"Pease soup," he told the server, a narrow-faced woman with a strange cast to her skin. Yellow Mountains? If so, she was a long way from home. "Tell the cook to throw some bacon butts in it if he hasn't already. Also half a long loaf, honey butter, and a kava, please."

She grunted and moved on.

Imago stared out the window. The street was still all but deserted, and he was the only customer in the cafe. This was like the bad old days when the threat of noumenal attack hung over the City in a miasma of fear.

The clink of cooking in the kitchen ceased. Imago stepped to the door to peer outside. The downhill stretch of Cork Street amid the gaming parlors was empty, the narrow park in the middle of the boulevard quiet as well.

A mob was gathered at the bottom of the hill on the Bridge of Chances. *Again.*

Something towered above them—a plant. Well, a tree, at that height.

A horse galloped down from the crest of the hill. "To be coming!" shouted the freerider in the saddle.

Imago darted out the door and allowed himself to be hoisted ungraciously onto horseback. At least this wasn't a war saddle—otherwise he would have been sharing space with a number of uncomfortable implements.

They raced down along the center of the streetcar tracks until they reached the edge of the crowd. The freerider wheeled his horse so that Imago could get a good view.

A tree grew out of the Little Bull and through the east side of the Bridge of Chances. It had destroyed a good portion of the center span in the process.

Imago knew who was behind something like that. "Jason!"

"Excuse me, sir." Someone tapped him on the elbow.

Imago turned to see four large bailiffs right behind him. One of them swung a brass-shod staff to knock the Lord Mayor's freerider escort off his horse like a dropped sack of grain. The other three dragged Imago down after him.

"I do believe you're under arrest, sir."

Imago recognized the grinning bailiff who led the squad. Serjeant Robichande, one of the deepest Assemblage loyalists in the City Imperishable.

He started to yell, but they stuffed him into a huge wad of burlap meant for baling indigo and hauled him away from the shouting crowd.

The Lord Mayor of the City Imperishable was unwrapped and dumped without ceremony onto a marble floor. Groaning, he looked up to see a ceiling painted with a mural of Balnea Meeting the False Riders. The artist had expended considerable effort on the goddess's rosy nipples.

A red-coated bailiff stood over him, staff now pressed against Imago's chest. A judicial bench loomed behind the bailiff. Imago looked the other way. A familiar gallery rose.

He was back in the fraud courts before the bench *dolus malus*. He'd nearly died in this room the night the crowd had stormed the Limerock Palace. Jason the Factor had rescued him, unknown and unknowing who he was.

The night Imago had declared himself for Lord Mayor.

He was certain that the symbolism was utterly intentional.

"Welcome," said a very familiar bald judge. Judge-Financial and Burgess Alois Wedgeburr, syndic of a metals-trading cartel, oldest son and heir to the Horse Street Wedgeburrs of Heliograph Hill. The man who'd ordered his death once before.

Also known as "Crusty Alice" in certain clubs in the Sudgate districts where decent men went to spend an hour or an evening—or sometimes a weekend—as indecent women.

Imago kept that little fact close to hand.

"So?" Once again, Imago was playing for this life before this man. Once again, he hated it. This time, however, Imago held many more cards. "I trust I am about to be accorded the honor of my office, released from this ridiculous position, and receive an abject apology."

"Fine words for a man on the floor," said Wedgeburr. "I understand you are styled Lord Mayor of the City Imperishable, but my clerks have been unable to find any evidence of your election. So before you plead immunity of office, as you have previously done before this court, I would suggest that you take that fact into account."

"What elections?" Imago asked, surprised into speaking unwisely.

"And you used to follow the minutes of our sessions so closely." The judge sounded almost loving. "The edict of 42 Imperator Arnulf regarding elective office in the City Imperishable was voided this past week by an act of the Assemblage. Noon today was established declarations of intent by candidates desiring to seek elective offices covered by the act."

"We don't have any elective offices."

"Somehow the title Lord Mayor springs to mind." Wedgeburr stroked his silver-wrapped thighbone gavel. "A fine young man named Roncelvas Fidelo has declared himself. He is a candidate, with official immunity from prosecution. You, Imago of Lockwood, are a private citizen who has been pretending to public office and expending valuable resources required for the defense and enlargement of the interests of the City Imperishable."

Fidelo was the little buggerer who'd been dogging Bijaz, Imago realized. He had to think quickly. It was likely none of his people knew he was here. The freerider had been clubbed from the back, and would remember nothing. *Play for time, play for time.*

"You know that won't hold up under any review whatsoever," he said in his smoothest voice. "The law has always recognized that a thing established without objection creates a precedent for its own continuation. When the First Counselor of the Inner Chamber negotiated a settlement with me in my capacity as Lord Mayor after the battle of Terminus Plaza, the Assemblage of Burgesses waived any objections to my office."

Wedgeburr grinned. "The actions of this court will eventually be subject to the review of history. My rulings may well be found wanting, in which case I shall be saddened by the cloud upon my name." He pointed his gavel at Imago, his voice thickening. "You made a mockery of the proceedings in this courtroom. You incited an invasion of the Limerock Palace. You were instrumental in the murder of a bailiff, on that very floor where you now loll so disrespectfully. Your actions that day and subsequently led directly to the murder of all but one member of the sitting Inner Chamber. This court cannot let such insults to its dignity stand. This court will not be made a laughingstock." He hammered the gavel down repeatedly, his face blooming red.

This was no legal hearing at all, Imago belatedly realized. Only Wedgeburr and the bailiffs were present. "You declaim from a bench like a judge," he said quietly, speaking to the redcoats more than Wedgeburr himself. "But I see no office, nor dignity of the court. There is no transcript being taken for review. There are no clerks sitting in the gallery. You and these fine gentlemen are consp—" Imago cut off as the staff jabbed hard into his sternum. His breath left him and would not return.

"Beg for your life," Wedgeburr growled. "Beg for your life, and I might let you stand on your own feet again before the good serjeant and his men have their way with you. Beg for your life, and I might tell them to kill you before they set fire to your hands and feet, crush your knees and elbows, pluck out your eyes and your tongue and your cock. Beg for your life well enough to please me, or they will do all these things *before* you die."

Robichande stirred uneasily, a look of slow alarm dawning on his face.

Imago, still fighting for breath, gasped, "The…" There were no reasonable defenses. He tried for an unreasonable one—secret passion and shame. "The dead man. Was he a favorite of Crusty Alice?"

Wedgeburr screamed and vaulted over the front of the bench, landing heavily on the marble floor before Imago. He raised the thighbone gavel over his head in a two-handed stroke, but Robichande caught it and held it high.

"Him that killed Marko, he gets his punishment," the oxlike bailiff said. "But we ain't breaking kneecaps here. That's not how it's done."

The judge quivered with rage .

"Who cares," snapped one of the other redcoats. "We're in for it now. Keep his honor happy. Let the little pecker have it."

"I will forget every name and face here," Imago said quickly, "except his honor's. Only let this end, on your oaths to the law."

"He. Is. *Mine!*" Wedgeburr shouted, struggling with Robichande.

The big serjeant snatched the gavel loose from the judge's grip and hurled it across the gallery, where it shattered against the back wall. He sacked Wedgeburr hard with his shoulder and stuffed the judge in the witness cage, which he then locked. Robichande walked back over to Imago and dropped the key on his chest. "Sword's behind the bench. You decide. Giving that choice to a complicated man like you is revenge enough for me." The bailiff walked slowly up the stairs. "Come on boys. We'll let them two sort it out."

Imago regained the last of his breath as the courtroom door snicked shut. He stared up at the painting on the ceiling. Balnea was particularly well-endowed, and could probably suckle an entire village. He found his feet, as always off balance due to the loss of so much of his length of leg, then staggered to the cage.

Wedgeburr leaned against the back of the bars. It was deliberately too narrow to allow him to sit. Imago was intimately familiar with how that position felt. He'd nearly lost his life in that exact spot.

"I could leave," he said quietly. "Place the keys on the floor right here in front of you. Arrange with Zaharias of Fallen Arch to have the room sealed. You'd starve to death right there, piss running down your leg, shit stinking between your ankles, licking the bars for cool moisture. All a few feet from the keys of freedom. I could keep you locked here until there was nothing between you and the deepest brass hell save another breath. Then I could walk in, drink a tall glass of water, and watch you die. No broken elbows, no fire. Just a slow starving. What do you think of that?"

Wedgeburr's face was tight now. "Everything I said was true."

"A man was slain here the night of the riot," Imago told him. "I did not kill him. I wanted to kill the other fellow, but I was restrained from my anger. The man who did kill your lover died during the Tokhari assault." Which was technically true, though Jason had certainly pursued a lively career since. "As for mockery, it has never been a capital crime to mock. The rest of your charges were not my doing in the least."

He approached the cage, leaning close. "Now the clever Serjeant Robichande has set me a pretty problem. I daresay any doctor in this city would give you strong philters and send you to your bed for a year or two in hopes that you might recover from your madness. I even know the one to do it.

"But alive you would continue to boil against me. I suspect you have already lost your bench. Robichande is no fool. He will be sure that Zaharias hears this tale. Even impeached, with you alive and in the funds your family holds, I would not be safe from bullet or poison.

"Or, I could kill you now. It would hardly be self-defense with you locked in a cage. I could wrap myself in the dignity of my office and the crises of these terrible times and postpone investigation until no one cares.

"So tell me, Syndic Wedgeburr. Am I a good man, or an evil one? Am I a killer, or a merciful gentleman? I will act upon your judgment in this matter."

He stepped away from the cage and found the sword behind the bench. It hung in a wooden scabbard built into the platform. *Curious*, Imago thought. What purpose did this serve in the ritual of the law? The implements of the question were openly racked near the cage.

Approaching the cage again, Imago dangled the sword in his hand. "Well?"

"You are a smug, trite little parvenu," said Wedgeburr. "Those Burgesses not too far gone in vice or dementia have long hated you. You have made us over from proud rulers of the City Imperishable to a debating club confined within these crumbling walls."

"Then you are idiots!" Imago shouted. "I am Lord Mayor of this city. I do not control the waterways, I do not administer the Rose Downs, I am not responsible for the loss of Port Defiance. You Burgesses are. *Everything* beyond these walls is yours. The City Imperishable sits like an aging spider in an empty web, at the center of the vacant lands of our old empire. Your debating club could do anything, could rule a thousand leagues at a word. Instead you fools plot to bar the Portmaster's office from me, and niggle at the hours of the closing of the gates. Everything for pride, including your attempt to have me murdered." He poked through the bars with the sword, jabbing Wedgeburr in the stomach. The judge's eyes were wide as two moons.

"Everything for pride and nothing for sense." Imago drew a deep breath. "Tell me one thing. Is it true, about the elections act?"

"Yes." Wedgeburr snickered, vainly attempting to show a game face. "We made you over into history."

"As a private man, I have no role here." He tossed the sword to the ground next to the keys. "I suppose the charwoman will let you out."

As Imago climbed the steps to the door, passing the shattered bone and links of silver chain, Wedgeburr called out. "What about the bullets? The poison?"

Imago turned and stared back down at him. "If you think you can do better than I at running this madhouse of a city, then strike me down and take my chair. Otherwise leave me to the business of keeping us all alive."

He left. The doors were not even locked.

Robichande stood between two of the broken idols which lined the hallway, his arms folded. He was not carrying a pistol.

"Serjeant," Imago said with a nod.

"Lord Mayor."

Imago spread his hands. "See? No blood."

After a moment, Robichande answered him. "I am surprised."

"I have to ask. Did you know what Wedgeburr was about?"

"It was a writ, duly served." Robichande quirked a small smile. "We had to work a bit to get at you, sir."

"So you were not a party to murder?"

"I am a party to justice. A loyal bailiff, sworn to the law."

"We are not friends, Serjeant, and I don't suppose we ever will be. But I respect your oath. I am also tired, and have larger battles to fight than warring over the wounded pride of Burgesses."

"Fair enough." Robichande stared at him a moment longer. "Then I have a suggestion, sir."

"Yes?"

"Petition to address the Assemblage. Bring it out into the open. Tell them what you told Wedgeburr about empire and empty lands. Remind them who we are."

"You don't like being a shadow of a shadow of power, do you, Serjeant?"

"I am a loyal bailiff, sworn to the law. But the law could be more than it has become these days."

BIJAZ

He knew the dead man's replacement from the river cruise—Sammael Pierce. The new man was quite deferential to Bijaz.

Ashkoliiz led a brief discussion of supplies and food consumption and the logistics of keeping twelve dozen men alive in an unpeopled wilderness. As Bijaz had figured, it was her intention for the Northern Expedition to forage for everything but a few key necessities.

He was far more interested in her statements about their line of march.

"I shall split our force into two columns," she said. "The riders should be here within another day. They will be bringing pack strings with them if all has gone well. We'll load the majority of the gear onto the animals and send them north and west along with a screening force of forty men under Priola. There's a trail which will get them up and over the Silver Ridges at Jarais Pass.

"Our own group will ascend the cliff cities here. A much more direct route above will take us up to the old Imperator Paucius nickel mines, and through the mountains there. We will save two weeks' time and build an advance base on the north side of the Silver Ridges to be prepared for the arrival of the mounted column. Wee Pollister will command the heavy troops, who will do the primary load bearing. Pierce will command the light troops, who will range ahead to mark the ascent and set ropes as necessary."

"We're not heading to Endres Pass?" Bijaz asked, surprised.

She gave him a long, slow look, those ice-blue eyes narrowing. "Why would I do that? Endres Pass is a hundred and fifty miles east of here."

"Of course," he said blandly. She'd said Endres Pass, back at the City Imperishable, which corresponded with what Marelle had told him. Where *was* she going? Certainly not following the most likely path of Imperator Terminus.

Of course, there was always the question of trees.

Whatever the hells that meant. Though it was true he kept seeing trees where they did not belong.

The tribesmen on their horses rode in at dusk, just as the horrible little bats were rising from the globe houses above their heads. The riders led several dozen animals of a kind Bijaz had never seen before. They resembled camels, with their spade feet and their broad, long faces, but they had a pair of floppy humps rather than a single high back.

Bad tempered, too, Bijaz observed as he watched Priola and his men try to wrangle the strange camels into a temporary corral. Several of the men got bit, and there was one fairly serious trampling. The horsemen just sat in their saddles and laughed.

Bijaz managed to avoid the bats that night by sleeping in the shelter of a shallow portico with a roof too flat to attract them. He supposed that as one of Ashkoliiz's councilors he would be entitled to more sumptuous quarters, complete with wine and cigars, but he wasn't interested.

The next morning brought chaos, pure and simple. None of Ashkoliiz's commanders had apparently ever led anything more disciplined than a bar fight. Their men saw no reason to take orders from someone they'd just recently shorn at dice, or tussled with over a ration of sour mash. A number of thrashings were underway, to varying result.

Only the horsemen were ready. They contented themselves with a knife-throwing contest at the far end of the docks, away from the muddle.

The men were avoiding Bijaz like a dockside whore with cuntburn. Word of yesterday's argument with Whump had gotten around. He gathered what little kit he had accumulated thus far and climbed to the balcony he had used the night of the landing.

There he was surprised to find Ashkoliiz. Unusually, she was alone. No Northmen, no bear. She wore traveling leathers trimmed with small scraps of her signature blue silk. It was the first time he'd seen her dressed in a practical manner.

The outfit did nothing to diminish the lurch of his heart.

"What do you think of my men?" she asked.

Bijaz glanced upriver. The foredeck of *Slackwater Princess* protruded at an angle above the surface, the current of the River Saltus breaking in white spray around it. When he turned to meet her gaze, Ashkoliiz was smiling. Those ice-blue eyes seemed the size of frozen lakes.

"I think they are all fools," he said slowly. "And I do not see why you have brought such an ill-matched set of misfits."

"Well." Her lips quirked tighter. "I *am* a woman after all. Perhaps I am no judge of men, easily swayed by a pretty face or a tight arse."

He thought of the bald man, angry and stupid. "No, no. You have done this on purpose." Bijaz certainly hoped so.

"Indeed. They are fools, friend dwarf. Hired as such and meant to be such. But consider this: from any crop of fools will rise a few sensible men. And this crop shall be winnowed in the weeks and months to come."

"Months, eh?"

The smile faded slightly. "Were we hiking to Endres Pass, yes. Months indeed. You and your strange little Lord Mayor have done some pretty guesswork."

"What else would you expect of us?" He snorted. "You come to town and set a stout problem to hand, one which is equally dangerous whether true or false. Of course we look into understanding what you meant. And while the City Imperishable has not set its eyes northward in centuries, we are not entirely bereft of maps or histories."

"I but seek to restore what was lost." She spread her hands. "Should I not profit thereby?"

"You seek to upset the order of half a thousand years, lady." In that moment Bijaz felt his age. This woman could have been his granddaughter. She was caught up in the romance of her cause, the wealth and fame at stake. All her thinking was in the present. It took a tired old man like him to look and see what her deeds would mean to history, to the future of the people she purported to help. "Besides that, there is more at play than your desires. You do not travel alone, and you do not take your counsel only from your conscience."

To his surprise, she struck at that bait. "The bear is something you would not understand. A tutelary spirit. He holds my wisdom."

"I know what a totem is." Bijaz knew what an overseer was as well, and he was certain the ice bear somehow filled that role. He had not yet tasted the tang of the noumenal in the bear's presence, but they had never had a direct confrontation. Of course, at thirteen feet and better than half a ton, he would pray to any god who had ever darkened his door that such a confrontation never take place.

"If you understand," she said, quite serious now, "then do not challenge how I tread the measures of my dance. It is a matter of the North, where life is different."

"Naturally," he said. "Life is different everywhere, lady."

She pointed down to the docks. "Watch life be different here, now, as I make a point to my men."

Bijaz turned his attention back to the shoving, milling mass below. The ice bear and the three Northmen were fanning out from yesterday's meeting hall. They waded in to separate knots of arguing or idling men. All the bear need do was loom overhead and everyone hopped to attention. The Northmen were forced to work a little harder to capture the fractious attention of their targets, but they were all three masters of a fighting style Bijaz had never before seen. With open hands and rapid spins they were able to lay out three, four, even five men each in quick succession.

After the first few rounds of this, the columns began to fall into shape. Even the odd double-humped camels were frightened into submission by the ice bear.

In less than ten minutes Ashkoliiz's lieutenants had accomplished what two hours of pushing and shoving and yelling had failed to do.

"What they have all just learned," she said quietly, "leaders and men alike, is that they need *me*. Only I speak with my Northmen, only I command the loyalty of the bear. Only I can make their fellows obey."

It seemed to Bijaz they needed the Northmen far more than they needed Ashkoliiz, but he held his counsel in that regard. "Leading from fear is not the position of greatest power."

"Hmm." She gave him a brisk nod and turned to find the stairs. "The command section will be forming up in about ten minutes. You might wish to center on my banner. That will be a position of strength in times to come."

The pack column set out in the bright fullness of morning. The camels were restive and braying. The mounted warriors rode three times around the moving column before pulling ahead, leaving the west end of the dock and kicking dust as they followed a long, shallow slant up the hill beneath the cliff face.

The camels followed, Priola's forty men spread among them. Bijaz figured this was seen as scut duty, but then they weren't climbing through an abandoned city, and might have a better chance of living to see the back of the Silver Ridges.

Ashkoliiz's banner was a long whiptail of blue silk. It streamed from a tall pole capped by a round brace with four dangling white horsetails. She held it herself, surrounded by four large men picked from Wee Pollister's heavy troops. They wore blue silk hats atop their otherwise irregular expeditionary kit. They all looked distinctly uncomfortable. None would meet Bijaz's eye.

All the musical instruments seemed to be among Pierce's light troops. The tune soon trailed off as the scouts scaled the steps north of the port, climbing toward the base of the cliff cities complex. The plan was obvious. They would go higher and set the lines to draw the rest of the men up from below.

He wondered how many among them were mountaineers, or had ever climbed anything higher than the steps to a flatback room.

They reached the top of the first stone globe in an hour. At this rate they'd be a week climbing the cliff. Nonetheless, the men cheered. Lines were dropped down and stouter lines drawn up. Despite appearances, *someone* knew what they were doing.

The scouts had set the climb so that the ascending heavy troops would have access to the globe's spout-entrance. Once they were up, the lines could follow.

"We go after everyone else," Ashkoliiz said as the first of Wee Pollister's men began beetling their way along the ropes.

He didn't answer. It didn't seem necessary.

ONESIPHOROUS

Behind the door was an irregular cavern which seemed a natural formation. It had been walled off from the outside by a course of dressed stone. Half a dozen full-men and another dwarf sat around a table playing cards in a pool of light, though he could not immediately spy out the glow of a window or airshaft. Wooden partitions along the stone walls allowed for curtains to define private spaces. Larger tables stood near the back of the cavern, where several ladders and tunnels led off. Dividers ran across them, with bins beneath.

Sorting tables for the jade. Though no one seemed to be working at the moment. It was a very lazy mine.

The men glanced up at his entrance, but Onesiphorous marked that they looked to Beaulise. She nodded and they went back to their cards.

"Your day of rest?" Onesiphorous asked. He had no idea what day it in fact was. He was three weeks or more thrown out of his office, but the time had since become a blur.

"Every day is a rest day now," said Beaulise. "Boat's two weeks late. We're already out of wine and milk and butter. No point in bringing down even more rock if it's just going to sit here waiting to be stolen. It's safer in the ground."

"So you know what's happening in Port Defiance?"

Beaulise shrugged. "I know what I heard. Don't know what happened. Corsair banners flying on the Flag Towers, dwarfs in hiding around the port. Some other strangeness back in the City, but it's another one of their twists far as I can tell." She snorted. "You know, like the Drover's Heresy or that business with the soul bottles when I was new in my box. There's a reason so many of us came down here over the years."

He pursued her earlier remark. "But I was expected?"

"Last assay boat here, crew said a City dwarf was making trouble for the Harbormaster. You're not the most ordinary fellow, you know, and half of anyone up the Saltus knows of you. Besides, that new Lord Mayor hasn't got a lot of people to trust."

"No." Onesiphorous wondered what new strangeness she was referring to in the City. "When last I saw your father he was well enough, considering the facts of his condition."

Her smile crooked. "If it's not strange when your Da gets elevated to godhood, I don't know what is."

"Perhaps. Nonetheless, I am here. I must ask, do you have any way of communicating with the City?"

"No. Everything always went by boat to Port Defiance and up the river from there. With the port in unfriendly hands and the river closed to traffic, we're lost as dwarfs in a desert."

Onesiphorous still couldn't figure where her sympathies lay. "I am hoping for shelter," he said slowly, watching to see how she reacted. "And help, perhaps. Either in moving on…"

After a moment, she said, "Every 'either' has an 'or,' Sir Slashed."

"Yes, well." He took the plunge. "Either help moving on, or help mounting a restoration movement to strike the corsair colors."

"Hmm," she said. "Well, shelter, and maybe a bowl of whatever watery gruel we still have. I believe the boys are playing Beggar's Chance over there if you'd care to lose a fortune or two."

"I am not your father," he said, thinking of Bijaz's uncanny skill at gamesmanship since the old dwarf's transformation.

"Something we should all be thankful for," she muttered darkly, her first real reaction to anything thus far.

Beaulise had not been joking about watery gruel. It was a thin soup of oats, onions, and dried apples, with too much salt. The Angoumois made feasts of what grew all around this mine, but these were still City folk, for all that they were hundreds of miles from home sweating for treasure in a hole in the ground.

Onesiphorous sipped and looked at the other miners. Eight full-men in total, plus the two dwarfs. They were a motley lot, to be sure. Two were pale-haired Sunward men who could have come from whatever clan or family had birthed Enero, though they dressed the same as any ordinary laborers from the City Imperishable, in canvas trousers and cotton shirts. Another was a dark-skinned fellow with the look of someone from much further down the Sunward Sea, wearing wrapped muslin grubby with sweat and rock dust. The other five seemed men of the City to him, the typical disaffected younger sons and bankrupt clerks who'd moved south in waves since the eruption of the Jade Rush.

It was the dwarf he could not figure out. He was young, glitter-eyed and red-faced, with pale blond hair over a pale complexion. While the others chattered softly of their card games over gruel and hard biscuits, the dwarf miner remained silent. He cast occasional resentful glances at Onesiphorous.

Time to sip politely and say little. These were bored, angry men who were running out of food while being cut off from their livelihood and dreams of avarice. Not to mention whatever pleasures didn't fit in the palms of their hands.

"All right, boys," said Beaulise as they finished eating the terrible little meal. "We got us a real celebrity here. Ikaré here already knows Onesiphorous, I believe. As for the rest of you, he's been a mighty big dwarf back in the City Imperishable. Used to be a genuine revolutionary before the new government made him a minister."

"I'm hardly—" Onesiphorous began, but she cut him off.

"This is a shareholders' meeting of the Lost Receiver Mine. You're a guest, here on sufferance. When it's time for your testimony, you'll be told."

He wasn't sure what that implied. Even working as the Lord Mayor's chamberlain he'd had little to do with the jade mines, which fell under the jurisdiction of the Assemblage of Burgesses.

But shareholders? He'd never worked as an accountant, at least not until becoming Imago's man, but still, Onesiphorous was fairly certain that shareholders were wealthy men smoking in their clubs on Heliograph Hill, not grubby pick-and-shovel types.

"I'll go last," muttered Ikaré, still glaring at Onesiphorous.

Beaulise nodded. "Ikaré has invoked privilege. I shall grant it unless someone objects."

As far as Onesiphorous could tell, none of the rest cared.

"Do I hear any other testimony?" she asked.

One of the pale Sunwarders leaned forward. "I am to be wondering if this mighty dwarf is to be restoring our contracts."

"I don't know." Beaulise glanced at Onesiphorous. "The witness may address the question."

"Um…" Onesiphorous had no prepared answer. His wits caught up with his lips. "If I am successful, with or without your help, your contracts will be back in force. If I am successful with your help, there will also be recognition and remuneration from the Lord Mayor's office."

It was hardly the most stirring speech he could have delivered.

A City man wiped a bit of soup from his mouth. "You got anything to offer besides your hard-working self, dwarf?"

Ikaré stirred at that, but said nothing. Onesiphorous thought he was seeing the lay of things. "No. Just my word. But it's my word as chamberlain to Lord Mayor Imago of Lockwood. Not just my word as a hard-working dwarf."

"Hot air's no contract," said the City man, but he settled back in his chair.

"Anyone else?" Beaulise asked after a moment. The dark-skinned Sunwarder grinned, but that was the only reaction the dwarfess received.

These aren't desperate men, Onesiphorous thought. *These are defeated men.*

"Ikaré, you may have your privilege now."

"I say toss him in the river and let him walk home," the other dwarf snapped. "His little ruckus back in the City Imperishable this past winter killed my parents and one of my sisters. This one and his precious Lord Mayor both are no better than the damned Burgesses, and probably a sight worse."

"So you wish to eject him from the Lost Receiver Mine?" Beaulise asked softly. "Is that a formal proposal?"

"No, of course not." Ikaré kept his temper barely reined in. "I'm no fool. Anything's better than sitting here waiting to starve. Since Malcolm took the boat, we couldn't leave on our own if we tried. Nothing but leeches and snap-jawed eels out there in that black water. So this little prince of the City arrives with promises and a beggar's hand of cards, he's still more than we had before. At least he's got a boat."

"Ah..." Onesiphorous began, then shut his mouth.

Beaulise shot him a look that suggested he keep that mouth firmly shut. She slapped the table. "You have used your privilege, Ikaré. I will not entertain your proposal unless another shareholder advances it." She looked around the table. They were all sober-faced now, but no one responded.

"May I speak now?" Onesiphorous asked, keeping his voice calm and quiet. "I wish to address this good dwarf."

"The witness is granted privilege." She obviously thought him a total idiot.

"Ikaré." He wasn't sure what to say, but he could not let that kind of anger smolder here at the heart of whatever effort might be built to unseat the corsairs in Port Defiance. "I worked very hard over the years before the Trial of Flowers to spare as many dwarf lives as possible. There are hundreds of dwarfs and dwarf families in Port Defiance because of my urging, my cajoling, my lobbying of the Inner Chamber, and my endless arguments with almost everyone in the City Imperishable.

"I regret beyond measure what happened to your family. But please, believe me. People were already dying in the most horrible ways from noumenal attacks. The Inner Chamber was stirring terror against the City dwarfs to distract from their own plottings and failings. If we had not risen, if we had not fought in Terminus Plaza, many more would have died."

He thought of Boudin with a curdled feeling in the bottom of his gut. "I know they are dead all the same, and the reasons do nothing to ease your anger. But the City Imperishable is not your enemy. I am not your enemy. We hung the old Inner Chamber from the walls at the Riverward Gate of the Limerock Palace that day. Your enemies died that day. I can give you no more solace than that."

Ikaré turned his seat aside, so he didn't have to look at Onesiphorous. "I got nothing to say to you. I'll say to the chair that we'll do what we must, and I'll not fight it nor make trouble for the Lost Receiver Mine, but that's the whole of it. Unless you can bring back my dead, you are nothing to me."

"I've seen what happens to the dead when they're brought back," Onesiphorous said, his voice low. "You don't want that."

"No, we don't." Beaulise's voice was bright, almost forced. "What we want is to return to our work, and get back to what's ours. I propose that the mine's company place its resources at the disposal of Onesiphorous and through him the Lord Mayor of the City Imperishable." She turned to him. "In return for lending our attention and our good name, we will expect full reimbursement for expenses, as well as additional consideration."

"Propose the same," said the City man who'd spoken before.

They all muttered "aye" except Ikaré.

"Are there any nays?" she asked.

He shook his head. "Nothing. I got nothing."

"That's nine for, none against, one abstained, and four not present. A majority of the shares of the Lost Receiver Mine have voted to carry the proposal." She slapped the table again. "This meeting is adjourned."

Onesiphorous looked around the table. He saw Ikaré's back and shoulders, and a tired but triumphant expression on Beaulise's face. It was the hopeful look in the eyes of the rest of them that worried him most.

"First of all," he said, "thank you. Second of all, there's a problem with the idea of a boat."

"What idea?" snapped Ikaré. "It's wood, it sits in the water, it floats. Not much thinking there, is it?"

Onesiphorous felt himself flush. "I'll need to call it back."

"How'd you get here, then?" asked one of the City men.

"An Angoumois rowed me here."

"An angry moth?"

"One of the swamp men. It's what they call themselves."

Everyone in the mine stared at him. "You passed through the water rats?" Beaulise finally asked. "And survived?"

This was as bad as the way some people treated the City dwarfs. He let his exasperation into his voice. "They're just people."

"They're snake-eating, food-stealing, boat-sinking, half-lizard bastards," the City man said with venomous conviction. "You go into the shadows, you don't come out."

Onesiphorous stood firm. "I did." Though he had to admit that he'd seen enough in those shadows to understand how a rational man might take fright.

"And what does that make you?" whispered Ikaré.

They drifted away, muttering, but no one, not even the obstreperous dwarf, seemed interested in reopening the business meeting. They were growing desperate, and he was the only hope that had presented itself.

Beaulise took him on a tour. "This is nothing like the mines of the Silver Ridges," she called down to Onesiphorous as they climbed one of the ladders at the back of the main gallery. "Up there, the name of the game is volume. They move a ton of ore to realize less than ten pounds of silver. That's in a *good* seam. Similar ratio for gold. Copper's easier, so's nickel, but it's still bleeding great masses of stone."

They stepped off the ladder into a tunnel so small anyone much larger than a dwarf would have been required to stoop. Beaulise raised her gas lantern to show him how the cut curled upward.

"Jade's a precious stone." She corrected herself: "Semiprecious. But valuable enough, especially for the Sunward trade. They carry it from there on out into the endless oceans of the world, where a good piece can be worth more than its weight in gold." She laughed. "Not *here* at the mine, of course, but we do well enough when the shipping is running right.

"In any case, these mines are small because the seams are small. Every few years a mine brings out a good boulder, but almost everything that is traded away could be carried by a small man."

They advanced slowly up the narrow passage. Even Onesiphorous felt pressured, closed in by the narrow rock.

"These rock outcroppings are called 'thumbs.'" Her voice echoed in the enclosed space. "Cores of old hills maybe. The thumbs rise up out of the swamps. They're veined with jadeite. We dig out the veins. Simple, eh?"

Onesiphorous ran his fingers across the chopped-out wall of the tunnel. It had been done by hand—who would blast in here? One stroke at a time. "Simple enough, I suppose. If you've got time and tools and the skill to delve. How many people get rich enough off this to bother?"

"You'd be surprised," she said. "Are you a jade collector?"

He snorted. "Until six months ago, I was lucky to eat decently every day. Since then I've been far too busy for hobbies. I've never had the luxury of, well, luxury. It's shiny and green, that's what I know. People carve beads and little gods out of it."

"They call it kingstone down along the Sunward Sea." Her voice drifted a little, almost meditative. "The princes there are buried in suits of it. Armor, though you wouldn't care to stop a blow with the stuff. There's a lot of green jade. A fair amount of white jade. Those are your nickel and your copper, really. Enough to make a living, but it won't buy you a villa."

People had always been his business. Still, Onesiphorous had to admit this was interesting. "So what's the jade equivalent of gold? Or diamonds?"

"Red. Orange. Jadeite comes in many colors, but white and green make up most of it. The rest is far more valuable. Now—" She stopped.

Beaulise was obvious weighing the significance of sharing some secret. One-siphorous waited her out.

"Blue," she finally said. "Blue jade is the diamond strike."

"Where is it found?"

She sighed. "In shards, among the tailings of jade works from long ago. The water rats, or someone else, worked the thumbs in the distant past. They didn't have steel tools or much engineering, so they didn't get far. We think they broke out accessible portions of the seams with fire, then hauled the rubble away from the thumbs to be sorted. Their scrap piles are on little islands up and down this coast rather than at the mine sites. People have found chips and slivers of blue jade. They mined it *somewhere*. That means some of it's still here."

Beaulise gave him a long look. "His Serenity, the Anchor Prince of Bas Engarin, has offered his own weight in gold for a piece of blue jade the size of a grown man's thumb." She laughed. "And His Serenity is said to be an individual of extremely generous proportions."

"Dreams," he said. "It's all dreams."

She seemed intrigued. "All commerce is dreams. Dreams of profit, dreams of success. No one sets out in their youth intending to end their life as a third clerk in a shipping office. Down here, our hands are closer to the dream. That's the difference. Labor and value, in one transaction."

He was surprised at that final comment. "You're an economist?"

Her tone was scornful. "I am my father's daughter. He was one of the better business managers in the City Imperishable for many years before he took up politics."

"And so here you are in the swamps, chipping away rocks looking for the blue vein."

"Here I am. I was chipping away happily enough until my father's politics interrupted us." She pushed forward, worming her way up a sharply angled rise in the tunnel. "Follow me," she said, her voice muffled.

He followed.

IMAGO

He found his way out of the South Doors of the Limerock Palace to discover a rally in progress. Someone he didn't recognize addressed a crowd of clerks, bailiffs, and servants. Zaharias of Fallen Arch stood in the shadows of a pillar just by the door.

"First Counselor," said Imago politely.

Zaharias jumped as if he'd seen a fetch. "What are you doing here?"

"An appointment with one of the judges-financial," Imago replied blandly. He had not checked his clothing carefully and itched to pat himself down.

"When I am Lord Mayor," the speaker began.

"Ah," Imago said. "Fidelo."

"…ensure public order takes a firm priority."

The crowd gave a dull cheer.

Imago stepped out of the shadows behind Fidelo and grabbed his sleeve. The young attorney looked around. Imago slugged him in the chin, then tripped the full-man, kicked him again in the side of the head. He stepped onto Fidelo's back to address the crowd.

"I still retain the office of Lord Mayor," Imago shouted. "If the Assemblage desires elections, we shall have elections. But not now, and not with this moronic popinjay conspiring in secret."

The muttering turned to scattered laughter.

"Would you want to be led by a man who could be so easily dropped by a dwarf?" Imago stepped off, leaned close to Fidelo's ear, and whispered, "Cease sending those ridiculous writs, or I'll have you flogged for a pederast and hanged from Lame Burgess Bridge."

The people made way for Imago. He stepped between two bailiffs at the Costard Gate to find Enero and Kalliope on horses, backed by several dozen Winter Boys.

"Reports of my arrest are sadly exaggerated," he told them. Then, more softly: "Take me home."

"We found Jason," Kalliope said as Enero hoisted Imago up onto his horse.

"I never would have guessed. Somewhere near the Bridge of Chances?"

"So you were being with Zefat," said Enero. "We were to wonder very badly."

"So was I. How is your man?"

Enero's face closed briefly. "Alive, but being unable to awaken."

"I am sorry. These bastards did for him when they snatched me." Imago waved at the bailiffs and the crowd behind them as the freeriders wheeled and headed across Terminus Plaza, away from the Limerock Palace. "Just once," he said, "I'd like to both enter and leave that place in good order."

Well after the evening bell, Enero, Kalliope, and Imago returned to the little café for Imago's much-delayed dinner. A crowd of Winter Boys blocked the door as they ate. He had noted crossing the Bridge of Chances that the tree was already being cut for lumber.

"Repairing that stonework is going to be expensive," Imago said as they waited for their food.

"Don't change the subject," Kalliope snapped. "What were you doing in the Limerock Palace?"

"We were to be considering you in grave danger."

"Oh, I was," Imago told them. "I talked my way out of it. Suffice to say that if you ever see Syndic Wedgeburr anywhere near me, he should be detained and stuffed down the nearest well."

"Permanently?" Enero asked.

Imago considered that a moment. "Yes. He's had his chance."

They badgered him until his pease soup came, but he would not say more. Steaming hot, it smelled both salty and green—exactly what he wanted. Digging into the meal, he gave them both a long look. "Enough. What happened to Jason? Why that ridiculous tree?"

"Saltfingers took me below." Kalliope shuddered. "I still don't believe what you did down there last winter."

Imago waved a chunk of bread at her. "Continue."

"We went to the number four stormwater pond. I had no idea there was such a city beneath the City. The lilies were dying for lack of light, but they were still there. Then he took me to a vault down somewhere near Terminus Plaza. Said his boys had been hearing voices in the area. We found books and maps spread out on boards along a walkway. Food, too, and a still-warm candle.

"Saltfingers went stalking then, with me behind him."

"I've had that particular thrill," Imago said dryly. "I trust you stayed out of the flow."

"Yes." She snorted. "We caught up to them as they tried to come up by the Bridge of Chances, where Saltfingers had taken us into the tunnels in the first place. Jason didn't realize it was me at first. He made a green…" Kalliope paused a moment. Then: "It was a tiny forest in his hand. Only he held it for a weapon. Then Marelle told him to stop, that it was me. He looked set to toss it anyway, 'til Saltfingers told him not to be every kind of idiot at once. So he threw the thing down the tunnel the other way. It burst into that giant fir tree that shot upward through the stones like a festival rocket, sucking up water and dust and anything around it.

"We climbed out through the hole."

Imago took a long sip of his kava, savoring the additions of goat's milk, Sunward cinnamon, and red pepper. Much better than being locked in a courtroom with a psychotic judge and several angry bailiffs. Much, much better. "Where are they now?"

"Marelle is being at the Rugmaker's Cupola, looking into the offices," Enero said. Imago's heart started at that news, though he didn't want to think too hard on why. The freerider continued, "Jason is being at the Potter's Field. I am being told he is to be talking to the plants there."

"He's not been the least bit right since Bijaz raised him," said Imago. "Again."

Kalliope looked down at the table. "He wasn't right before, either. All this is to my account."

"Some of it," the Lord Mayor told her.

"I'm thinking of sending him after Onesiphorous." Imago stirred more sugar into his kava. "Someone needs to go find if my chamberlain yet lives."

"He can't go alone!" Kalliope almost shrieked.

"She is having the right of it," Enero added. "Jason is being as bad as Bijaz. Uncontrolled power and poor trustfulness."

It occurred to Imago he could solve two problems at once here. "Will you go with him?" he asked Kalliope.

She stopped cold, then looked thoughtful. "I have been abiding here, awaiting some purpose." Her expression seemed relieved. "May I sleep on it?"

"Don't sleep long," Imago said. "Once I talk to Jason again, that decision may be made."

"I will find you at the morning bell."

"Very well."

On his way back up the hill to see Marelle, surrounded by a mob of Enero's nervous horsemen, Imago found himself delayed yet again. Biggest Sister slipped through his security like they weren't there and fell into step with him.

"Lord Mayor." Her voice was clipped. She was dressed in her usual gray leather, like a high-class footpad except for the close-spiked hair. Her intense gaze would have frightened off victims and rescuers alike.

"Ma'am." He'd learned to be cautious with her.

"Have you heard word from Port Defiance?"

"No." At the pained look on her face, he added, "I'm sorry. I can't help but think Onesiphorous is dead or imprisoned. I would not know of the sister you sent with him."

"I hear nothing either."

"It is about time for me to send someone else there to act as my eyes," he said. "And possibly my hand. Prepared for the worst, which Onesiphorous was not." Imago sighed. "I sent him down the river to deal with the absent dwarfs, persuade them home. Not to halt revolution and invasion."

They fetched up in front of the Rugmaker's Cupola, Enero eavesdropping shamelessly.

Biggest Sister ignored the freeriders to focus on Imago. He knew that look, had seen it during their long night together when she had told him again and again what to do to her, with her, inside of her.

She broke his thread of memory: "How will you get your agent there?"

"Agents." Imago realized that he had made up his mind about sending Kalliope, assuming she had made up hers. "I have not thought on that yet. Perhaps overland, though the road south dies long before Port Defiance."

"I may be able to offer assistance." Her face was hard now. "The Tribade aims to rescue our Big Sister there. If she is beyond help, we will claim her price tenfold and tenfold again. I can take one or two down the river with mine, if they are patient and tolerate discomfort."

That certainly described Kalliope. As for Jason, who could say of him these days? "I believe this will suffice." He bowed. "I thank you for your generosity. What support do you need from the City Imperishable?"

"Only to give us undisturbed run of the docks two nights hence. I would prefer to have as few eyes as possible looking on."

"Where?"

"South Quay. Closest to the winch tower."

"I cannot answer for those within the Limerock Palace, but my people will keep their attention elsewhere that night. The burglars will be pleased."

"The Tribade will take care of them." She was deadly serious. "Have your agents to me at the morning bell that day."

"So it will be done."

She nodded and stepped between two horses, vanishing from one stride to the next.

"How does she *do* that?" Imago asked Enero. He didn't really expect an answer.

"I am thinking it is a trick of light and shadow and the twisting of the eyes," the freerider answered quite seriously. "This is not to be done in a bright, empty room."

"Very few things are, my friend." He stopped. "Too much, today. I already intended to tell you that I have secured your message to Bas Luccia. I will need three or four riders to see it through. Do you want to send your men, or hirelings?"

"To be sending one of mine, with hired horsemen filling out the number."

"See to it to your satisfaction."

Enero nodded and wheeled his mount away. Imago headed within for the long, winding climb to his office. He hated those stairs, but it was probably good for his wind.

He couldn't decide if he hoped Marelle was up there now or not. He might rather see her in the morning when he was rested, but his curiosity burned.

The question answered itself when Imago arrived at his empty office. He looked into Onesiphorous' old space, but she was not there either. Even Stockwell was gone. Only the night duty clerk at the head of the stairs was present to nod him good evening. He crawled onto the divan in his office and was asleep in moments.

BIJAZ

When it came his turn at the ropes, much of his sanguine demeanor evaporated. It was one thing to be blasé about the competence of the Northern Expedition's mountaineers when he was safely at the docks. It was another to be lashed to a slack line, handed a pair of gloves, and told to get on with it.

Bijaz spun as he ascended, climbing and kicking off the rock, until he passed into shadow. The ascent merely took an eternity. As he approached the belled entrance, a shorter rope was thrown out, with loops tied near the end.

"Grab on," someone shouted. "We'll pull you in. Climbing the lip is a mother bitch."

Bijaz didn't fancy stepping from line to line, but he didn't have much choice. He disengaged one hand to lean across empty air. The actual transfer was simple enough, then he was being hauled over the lip.

"There you—" a sweating man began, then stopped when he saw who it was.

Bijaz became very aware that he scrabbled for purchase on a rounded surface which wanted him to slide backward into empty air. His helper stood just on the inner slope, eyeing him speculatively.

"Please," Bijaz said. On impulse, he added: "I'm afraid."

The moment of decision passed as the sweating man reached to pull him all the way in. "Whump was a right bastard," he muttered, "cross-eyed freak and all. But what you did…"

"What I did was not allow him to kill me."

"Aye. He ever was one for making points the hard way." The sweating man clapped Bijaz on the shoulder. "I'm Mattieu Gambardella. I know full well who you are."

Still conscious of the immensity of open air not far behind him, Bijaz gasped for the breath he didn't realize he was holding. "Trust me to do right by those who do right by me."

Gambardella laughed as he untied the rope around Bijaz's waist. "There's little enough being done right before we get home, I'll wager. Maybe you need to watch your back, sir dwarf, but in time there'll be those to watch it for you."

Bijaz returned Gambardella's clap on the shoulder.

Light streamed through the opening, setting the rest of the globe's interior in dark shadow by contrast. Bijaz shaded his eyes until he could get a decent view.

It stank. He could see a teeming mass of those horrid bats in the upper arc of shadows, furry maggots clinging to the ceiling. The entire top of the globe was alive. Worse, the bottom arc was deep in their scat. It formed a putrid, pale mass with an awful life of its own. The smell was rank to the point of sickening.

Protruding wooden posts and brick stubs gave evidence that there had once been interior structure. The supports extended at odd angles and random intervals.

Bijaz sat on a stub along the downsloping curve, well above the faintly luminous mass of guano. He was comfortably far below the bats squirming on the ceiling.

"Come on, dwarf," shouted someone. It was Orcus, standing in the glare of the entrance gripping three lines. "Your turn, your shortness."

Bijaz waved. He clambered back up to the opening where he was lashed in and dropped outward to make the next stage of the climb. The moment when he slid past the last of the crumbling stonework and into the open air nearly forced his guts between his teeth. He settled in and resumed his climb, this time always tugged slightly upward by the rope.

The man who hauled him in at the next globe—Arcus, Orcus' twin—had a sour expression. "We've lost two up here," he warned. "Mind your step real good."

Bijaz knew it wasn't personal. On board the riverboat the twins had been kind enough, for all that they weren't City men.

"I'll be careful," he said. "And my thanks for the warning."

This globe was different. Irregular holes punctuated the shell where chinks had fallen away. The monkey bats didn't seem to favor this place. The ceiling was clear, and there was no steaming pool of pale sludge at the base.

Most of the interior stubs and beams were gone as well. He realized their decay must have caused damage to the shell.

The expedition warped its way up to two more globes before nightfall. These were at roughly the same level, perhaps a third of the way up the cliff face. The men spread out between the pair.

The globe in which Bijaz found himself stank. That meant bats would soon be dropping from the ceiling, but it also probably meant a safe footing on the shell. This time he climbed up the curve until the wall arched over his head. He secured a length of rope to a substantial stub of old stone, then wound his chest and waist tight.

That left him closer to the little horrors, but it took him above the restive, irritable troops. Judging from the calls at the entrance, Ashkoliiz and the ice bear were in the other globe, though one of the Northmen arrived here, alongside Pierce. There was a great stack of supplies, too—tenting and bales and food sacks, which Pierce directed be spread out.

The sunlight began to fade. Waiting for the monkey bats to leave their nest was like waiting for the rain. The first drop would come unnoticed. You might think the second a fluke. But when they tumbled like autumn leaves from the ceiling, bringing a shower of dust and guano with them, Bijaz felt as if the storm was breaking.

The air moved in strange, fitful gusts. It set his hair standing on end and made his mouth dry. When their squeaking began to echo, he nearly panicked. That was thunder to the furry rain, a thousand lancets of noise instead of an honest rumbling. He felt as if his ears were bleeding.

Bijaz huddled close to the curve of the stone, watching men scramble below. Two full rope lines of men slid down the curve into the roil of guano. Others screamed.

The skin on his neck prickled with the rush of wings, the flash of tiny eyes.

He had to stop this. He couldn't stand it any more.

Bijaz reached one hand out into the open air and thought of wheat fields and the reaper on the crown of the hill and blood draining down the furrows to ensure the summer harvest and where the bones came from that were ground to feed the soil, until he found the green, and behind the green all colors.

He pulled those colors into the world with him.

The bats fell silent between one heartbeat and the next. Where there had been swirling, chittering monkey-faced horrors, a blizzard of rose petals now swirled in shades of gold and tan and brown and yellow.

The flowers settled quickly, already graying in the last of the light, to cover the white lake of shit at the bottom of the globe. They encased the dozen men struggling upward with flecks of fading color to drown their curses.

Bijaz, still clinging to the wall like a muscular spider, looked down to see every pair of eyes inside the globe staring up at him in utter silence.

The magick had more than one price, of course. He did not sleep at all that night, not with a watch armed with torches and spears keeping its attention on him instead of the door.

The next day, Bijaz continued to find himself the object of a very focused, respectful attention. The Northern Expedition hadn't reacted to his killing of Whump. The late thug had been unpopular, a knife-edged bastard. Transforming a few hundred thousand bats into rose petals had been somehow worse.

Today they'd treated him like a bundle of explosives—touched at their peril, but dropped at their greater peril. If the men of the Northern Expedition had been certain he couldn't fly, someone would have cut his rope.

Late that afternoon Bijaz struggled over a hummock of rock when he realized he was at the top. A wide ledge sloped upward. A wooden frame stood before him, tree trunks the thickness of his thighs lashed together supporting the climbing rope above the rocky edge. Several of Wee Pollister's heavies belayed the line. One of the Northmen was prodding exhausted troops into stacking their supplies. Others worked different sets of ropes.

More cliffs rose to the north, nothing like the sliced-away face they had just ascended. These were knees, with valleys and folds between, that promised access onward and upward. Somewhere in those further heights was the nickel mine Ashkoliiz spoke of. He saw trees, too, so different from the bare face of the cliff and dry prairies along the river.

Bijaz turned from his view of the next ascent. Here at the top, he could see the whole operation in a way that had never been obvious while beetling up a stone face.

They had six of the frames going. Some hauled men, some hauled supplies. It hadn't been the random climb-and-pray he'd thought from below. Even so, given that they'd covered a thousand feet of altitude, he would have thought to send scouts to set the frames, then haul everyone up directly and at less risk.

Ashkoliiz had her reasons. The men had bonded on the ascent, already much closer than the rowdy, mismatched toughs who'd debarked from *Slackwater Princess*. Whatever strategic mistake it might have been, tactically speaking, blowing the riverboat was brilliant. In one move, she had made it clear there was no way home except to follow her. Otherwise many of the men would have sat on the docks and waited for the vessel's return, rather than climb the cliffs or ride off with those dreadful camels.

Even in her eccentricities, she would have made a frightening general. She would have been even more frightening had she been born to rule.

Ashkoliiz came over the edge soon after, up a different rope line. She was followed by Wee Pollister and her picked bodyguards. He saw no sign of the bear.

Bijaz approached her. "I was wrong, lady," he said. Flattery was an old skill, and he judged that her pride would never refuse a polishing. "You are a smith, forging a weapon. Spinning your blade from dross in which I might never have found faith." He bowed. "I learn ever more from you."

"And I from you," she replied. "For one, you have a novel approach to pest control." She returned his bow, her smile pure mockery.

He felt a flash of hot, hard anger. Bijaz took a deep breath. She was working him, too, annealing his nature in the forge of his own anger. He might not know what her goal was yet, but he knew her methods.

Knowing them did little to bank the fire within.

He turned away and studied the sky, looking out over the miles on miles on miles of land stretching to the south. One advantage of his age, Bijaz reminded himself, was that he need not be enslaved to his passions.

Still, her eyes bored into him even when he could not see them. They left smoldering holes in his soul.

ONESIPHOROUS

The tunnel wound upward. It crossed two shafts where chains had been hammered into the wall for grab-ons, and several side-tunnels. Beaulise moved with a purpose, delivering no more narration. Just climbing.

Onesiphorous was beginning to wonder exactly how tall the thumb was when Beaulise stopped. "Cover your eyes," she told him. "I'm going to open a hatch. The sunlight will hurt if it strikes you in the face before you are prepared."

He turned his head and raised his hand to shield himself.

She had not exaggerated. When the trap slammed open, light flooded like an explosion. Onesiphorous closed his eyes and watched the blood-warm glow of his lids for a moment.

Beaulise grunted, then called, "Come on up."

He opened his eyes, lids narrowed to a tight squint, and climbed a short wooden ladder.

They were atop the thumb. This was akin to being atop Barlowe's Finger, except that the thumb stood larger, and the sea surrounding it was a deep texture of treetops that swayed with the wind instead of the tide.

He looked at Angoulême from above. The knob-kneed trees with their deep shadows and unquiet waters seemed a different world up here. Bright birds screamed and fluttered like flowers on the wing. Clouds of butterflies moved through the dark green valleys where the canopies dipped and met. Even the open channel next to the mine was nothing more than a vein of silver-black in this high green sea.

Rocky thumbs stood as far as his eye could follow east to west. They resembled the remains of an ancient fortified wall defending this whole coast.

If the Angoumois lived up here, he thought, *they would honor very different gods.*

"Look north," said Beaulise. "You can see hills rising up thirty miles further inland. That's where the water runs out and it all becomes dry soil and stone. If you look south, you see the Sunward Sea—those silver depths beneath the distant clouds. We're here between the land and water, plucking riches from the bones of the world. A jade miner sees the margins, friend Onesiphorous, whether he acknowledges it or not."

"They call it Angoulême," he said. "Those who live beneath the trees are a more ancient and proud people than any of us. They live in the margins. You merely dig for bright sparks within their shadows."

Her tone grew hard. "You presume we come to dig out our riches and leave."

"You would prefer it here all your life?"

"Have you *been* to the City Imperishable? It's a giant sewer, filled with plotters and counterplotters and superstitious fools all too willing to fight one another for coin or glory. Too many people in too small a space, playing a game for stakes which dried to dust centuries ago."

"I would not think of it that way." His feet missed the cobbles, his taste buds missed the cook shops. "The plots are politics. No different from what Ikaré was playing at belowstairs. Just writ larger."

"Ikaré." She gave him a shrewd glance. "He and I were lovers awhile. I think he fears hours spent with me almost as much as he fears hours spent away from me. You, being a dwarf, have inflamed his jealousy beyond reason."

"And you stay in a hole in the ground with this madman? Picks and axes close to hand, no less."

"He is not mad, just jealous. There is a difference."

"Perhaps," said Onesiphorous. "My point still holds. Right here you have plots and counterplots and at least one fool willing to fight. It only takes one."

She sighed. "In any case, I hoped you would see what I see when I come up here."

"Beauty?" he asked. "Certainly. The shape of the world? Yes. Something worth fighting for? That is up to you. As for me, I fight for the City Imperishable, which will complete its centuries-long withering if Port Defiance remains in unfriendly hands."

"Then we understand each other without agreement."

Onesiphorous had to admire the irony of that. "Much the same relationship I had with your father for a number of years, actually."

"Blood will tell." She clasped his arm a moment. "Unless you have a deep interest in mining technique, let us go back down and plan your little war."

He was sorry to step away from the god's eye view of the jungles of Angoulême, but duty called.

Ikaré packed away his resentments for the discussion. Onesiphorous did not care for the unpleasant little buggerer, but the dwarf was sharp enough.

"The big claims," Ikaré said, "have twenty-five or thirty working them at the most. The smaller claims like ours number ten or twelve. Much less than that and you can't keep a decent watch."

"Jade pirates," said one of the pale Sunwarders.

"People steal your haul?" To Onesiphorous that implied armed men in boats, both of which were in short supply.

The Sunwarder shook his head. "They are being raiders. Maybe miners who are to be losing everything."

"Not a big problem," Beaulise added. "But one reason we don't just load up a dory and row for Port Defiance. Also why we don't let the jade pile up here if the shipments aren't going out."

Ikaré continued. "Over one hundred active claims in a fifty-mile stretch of coast. Average fifteen men per claim. That's a good sized recruiting pool."

"If we had boats, and weapons, and a workable plan." Onesiphorous wasn't trying to argue against his own goals, but he saw no point in pretense.

"Oh, there's plenty of boats along the Jade Coast," said the other dwarf. "They just mostly don't belong to us. The plantations have barges and lighters in great strings."

Onesiphorous knew perfectly well how the plantation men felt about the miners. The South Coast plantations had been the refuge for generations of disgraced families from the City Imperishable. Even many of those at the height of their power maintained winter residences here, as income producing properties and private resorts. "They've got the old money, the servants and field hands, and the better real estate in Port Defiance. But they've never had any interest in working with your lot."

The miners all chuckled. "I am to say not," said the dark Sunwarder. "I am to say they think us thieves and foulers of water."

"Doesn't stop them buying nice pieces off the dock at cutthroat prices," Beaulise added.

Onesiphorous shrugged. "Doesn't matter how much moss they've got in their hair. The plantation families are still City men. Most with their money managed by City dwarfs."

"Lord Mayor's mother and brother live up along the Eeljaw," said Ikaré.

Interesting, thought Onesiphorous. Imago had never mentioned that. He wondered if the Harbormaster or the corsairs knew. "May they stay there," he said. "Tell me, do the plantationers have a legitimate problem with the mines, or just sheer snobbery?"

Ikaré drew lines on the table with his finger, as if marking a map. "They live deeper in, where the swamp's more of a marsh. Grow indigo, water cotton, tobacco, turkweed, hemp, and rice, mostly. Depends on the drainage, I believe. The thumbs don't stand that far back. We're in a belt near the open ocean."

Onesiphorous nodded. He'd seen that in the view from above.

"But…" Ikaré made a shorter line cutting across his long lines. "Everything they load and ship out comes past the mines. Most of the thumbs stand in or very near open channels. And the other way around as well."

The problem remained opaque to Onesiphorous. "So? You're inside, chipping away, waiting for the assay boat from Port Defiance. Their straw bosses pole by outside with a load of indigo. Who even notices?"

"Plantation men claim we stir up the water rats. Swampers didn't used to attack the barges. Not back in the old days. Since the Jade Rush, they do."

"Too many people wandering around Angoulême?"

"Especially the latecomers," said Beaulise. "They go dragging through the swamps looking for smaller hills or islands to dig into. In case there's jadeite down there."

"Is there?" Onesiphorous asked, thinking of the hints of buildings he'd seen deep inside the shelter of the trees.

"Who knows? I don't fancy catching a few swamper darts in my neck and dreaming poison frog dreams for the last few hours of my life. Plenty here for us."

"But not for the people who keep coming."

"The thumbs go on for a dozens of leagues," said Ikaré. "Most of the way to the Yellow Mountains, actually. We could open a hundred more mines without digging up the swamps. Newcomers with foresight and sense make their way further down the coast."

"Further from Port Defiance, and with fewer neighbors." Onesiphorous nodded. "I can see why some might get lazy about that."

Beaulise gestured across Ikaré's imaginary map. "It all fits together."

Onesiphorous reminded himself that most of the people who'd moved down for the Jade Rush were educated, accomplished citizens looking for better luck. The migration hadn't been a surge of disaffected laborers and peasant farmers at all. Quite the opposite.

Listening to these people explain their situation to themselves and to him was something of an education in its own right.

The next morning he stood on the little dock with Beaulise and Ikaré and looked out across the water. Great dark trees loomed perhaps thirty yards to the east.

"The tide is up?" Onesiphorous asked.

"Yes," said Ikaré, "though the swamp mostly absorbs it."

"What's this channel called?"

"The Honeywood River."

He had to laugh. "There's water everywhere. How does anyone know this is a river?"

"No trees in the middle," said Beaulise. "And it's got a current."

"Fair enough."

"What it hasn't got," said Ikaré pointedly, "is a boat."

"Yes." Onesiphorous stared into the shadows. He was certain she would have eyes on him. He couldn't just wave his arms and shout. Beaulise and Ikaré would think him a fool.

So how to signal for help?

"I must build a fire here," he said solemnly. It was bunkum, of course, she had asked him for no such thing. But a fire would give them something to do.

Ikaré snorted. "It's a wooden dock."

"You've got a mountain of rock back there. Surely we can lay out a hearth. Are you doing anything else today?"

Imago

Kalliope burst into his office before the morning bell, awakening the Lord Mayor from a dream of being chased by women with knives where their breasts should be.

"He is a mad fool!" she shouted, then let off a long string of profanity in Tokhari.

"He is not the only one," Imago muttered, still webbed in sleep. "Of whom are we speaking?"

"My brother."

"Jason. Of course."

She sat on the edge of the divan and patted his arm. "I am sorry. This place makes me crazed. Too much stone, too much rain, too much coolth. I long for my desert."

He blinked away sleep. "And so you want to go to the swamps of the Jade Coast? That is hardly an improvement."

"I *want* to walk once more among the empty streets of the Red Cities. I am *called* to follow my crazed brother, who would probably go to every brass hell if you asked him to."

"I need kava if I am going to have this conversation so early."

"Oh, I sent the night clerk out," she snapped. Then, more softly: "There's a bakery on Filigree that never closes. Doesn't even have a door anymore. I think they made it into a table. He should be back shortly."

"For a wild woman of the distant deserts, you are most assuredly a City dweller."

"Mmm." The intense energy of her entrance seemed to have spent itself.

"Have you slept at all?" he asked.

"No. I've been following Jason around the Potter's Field all night."

"What is he doing?"

Her voice hitched. "A-asking the dead if they've seen our father."

"Ah, me. I'm sorry."

"That's the foolish part," she said. "The mad part is he gets answers. Not the ones he wants, but they talk back."

"Is he another Bijaz?" Imago asked.

"No. He's not a miracle worker. More like the consequences of a miracle."

"Most people would consider forcing a two-hundred-foot fir up through pavement to be a miracle."

She shrugged. "He is the Green Man of spring. A creature of your time and place. Beyond the Redrock River, we have the jinn. Spirits of the dust and sand, with a hot malevolence. They are the land out of balance. My brother is your land out of balance."

"But why?"

"I do not mean the balance of men and their worship, as we fought over last winter. This is the balance of seasons and time, water rising to the sky to fall as rain, the dead being plowed under to fertilize the living. Something is out of place here, badly so."

"Is that mystical sandwalker wisdom?"

She found a smile for him. "Actually, yes. Though any noumenal operator could tell you something similar. Including your krewe kings."

Imago knew something of the balance of force. "Is Jason the cause of imbalance, or an effect of it?"

"That would be a very, very good question to know the answer to," she said.

"Perhaps I should not send him away."

"No." Kalliope pursed her lips, thoughtfully. "Best he go, and I with him. The genius of this place will draw him back if it needs him."

The door creaked open. The night clerk, a thin man with a balding scalp and a limp, slipped in with two tall, lidded mugs and a steaming basket covered with black cloth.

"Thank you," said Imago.

"Lord Mayor." The night clerk bobbed through a half-bow intermittently aimed at both of them. "Ma'am."

He withdrew. Imago followed the odor of cinnamon. "If you are going downriver," he said, "you'd best be on the South Quay at the morning bell tomorrow. The Tribade has some secret ship, but they are willing to take you two."

"Do they know it's *him?*"

"I do not think that will matter. I have never seen Biggest Sister so upset. I rather imagine she will look at his strangenesses as one more plague to visit upon Port Defiance."

"And several problems solved for you," Kalliope said. "If I were a man, there would have been much more said about me staying on after my army departed. Having a losing general around can't be the simplest thing."

"Losing general, Tokhari sorceress, and killer of a war hero." Imago watched her eyes.

She didn't flinch, but neither did she welcome the words. "You may be seeing the last of us."

"For my own part, I would greet that prospect with sorrow. Still, it will be nice to have my City Imperishable back to the usual drunkards, muggers, and Burgesses. Without magickal trees erupting, or Bijaz making men into thorn bushes." He paused, studying Kalliope. "Please do find out what happened to Onesiphorous. I'd like him back. Even if only for a funeral."

"I will do as I can." She finished her roll. "Right now I should go find my brother and try to keep him out of trouble for the day. Do you need to see him again?"

Imago considered that carefully. "Sad to say, probably not. He seems to bear trouble with him everywhere, as do I. The two of us together always bodes poorly."

Kalliope opened her arms. He leaned forward to hug her. She grabbed him fiercely around the shoulders, her breath smelling of kava and cinnamon. "Find another line of work, friend. This one will kill you."

"You too," he whispered, and kissed her ear.

She pulled away, smiling. "A different time, with luck. I have something of a taste for small men."

With that, she was gone.

He picked at the rest of the rolls, trying to decide if he would miss her and wondering where Marelle had gotten to.

The pale dwarfess came into his office a few minutes later, just as the morning bell on the rooftop erupted into its usual racket. She seemed to be vibrating, as if it was she being rung.

"Cullingford said you were here," Marelle announced in the thick silence which followed. She spoke very quickly. "Have you seen today's broadsheets? They're terrible. You look like the hells, too. Go wash up." Despite her words, she shoved a stack of papers in his face.

Imago took the stack and studied her carefully. Marelle's eyes shone. She was smiling. "I see you've returned."

She seemed seized by an attack of bashfulness. "Yes."

"Welcome back." Imago turned the papers over.

Broadsheets. *The Revelator* was on top, with a headline that screamed, *Baillifs Murthered in L. Palace!!!* The next had a similar lead.

"Who?" He squinted at the sloppy printing of the top story.

"The big serjeant that hated you, and one of his men."

A cold chill stole down Imago's back. "Robichande?" He began looking for Wedgeburr's name.

"Yes." She stared at him, her happy enthusiasm drained. "You know something."

Imago felt sick. "Judge-Financial Wedgeburr tried to have Robichande kill me last night. The serjeant refused. I was left with the balance of power. I turned my back on the man and walked away." He clarified: "When I could have killed Wedgeburr myself, I mean."

"The Lord Mayor does not kill people."

"No," said Imago. "He has others do his killing for him. I could not see slaying a Burgess as being a useful thing for me to have done."

"So Wedgeburr killed Robichande?"

"The man was small," Imago said, lost in regret as to what he should have done. "I'm not sure how it might have been accomplished, but yes. It must have been him." He focused on her. "Are you back? Here, working with me?"

"Yes," she said simply.

"Then send a note to Provost Selsmark and First Counselor Fallen Arch. Tell them that I am certain the killer is Wedgeburr, and will swear that out before a bench." He tapped his fingers together. "Make sure also that Enero knows this. I'm far more afraid of Wedgeburr than I have been of anything or anyone else in recent times. The man's cracked, and he's quite wealthy. It's a terrible combination."

"He's a judge. Is this something from your old days as a barrator?"

"Wedgeburr tried to have me killed when I was first making trouble last fall. Jason saved me the night the riot burned part of the Limerock Palace. The man's come quite unhinged since then." He snorted. "Assuming he was fully hinged before."

"Right." She made a note on a foolscap pad.

"And for you, is there anything I should know?" The question assumed a disproportionate import as soon as it left his mouth.

She eyed him with speculation. "Perhaps. Enough that I am back, for now. Also, I accept your job offer. I will be your chamberlain. I should not have fled."

"Thank you."

"As your chamberlain, I insist you look through those broadsheets. There's another set below the ones about the murders. Probably more important."

Nothing was more important than murder, at least to the victim. He flipped down until he came to *Truth's Silver Horn*. Not one of Ducôte's, he noted. The headline read: *Elections to Unseat LM Imago.*

Imago groaned. "Another note, if you please, to Fallen Arch only. Please tell him that I beg the courtesy of an address to the Assemblage of Burgesses in full session. Indicate that soon would be excellent, but do not make it appear that I am in a rush."

"Are you?"

"Of course. You did read these, didn't you?"

She snorted. "The broadsheets have also reported on giant beavers in the sewers. I do not believe everything I read."

"I might believe giant beavers," Imago said. "In this city, especially. But no, part of Wedgeburr's little maneuver yesterday presumed my being thrown of out office by an act of the Burgesses. That little shit Fidelo has declared for Lord Mayor through some secret process known only to the Burgesses and their toad-eaters. I believe I damaged his candidacy yesterday, but anything's possible."

"That would be the next paper down."

He looked, dreading what he would find. *Sudgate Seeker. Lord Mayor Brazenly Batters Hapless Youth.*

"Thank you. I needed that. Now you know why I generally don't follow the broadsheets." Imago set down the papers and extended the basket. "Roll?"

"No, I have memoranda to compose."

He stood and attempted to hug Marelle just as she turned for the door. The moment was awkward, stretching out in a painful silence. "I'm glad you're back," Imago said, abandoning the effort.

"Me too." She did smile then, for a moment, before departing.

Imago found that he had a headache. "I believe I shall leave my post," he told the empty office. "And let someone else take up the scattered threads of this city."

His office made no answer. Instead of quitting, Imago worked his way back through the broadsheets, to see what else the City Imperishable was telling itself about him.

BIJAZ

They camped far enough from the cliff edge to avoid an unexpected fall by a late-walking piss taker. Bijaz was exhausted from his watchfulness the previous night. He didn't bother with a tent—the stars were clear and cold, without even a mist to trouble him.

Wolves howled all night. The sound was lonely and frightening, but Bijaz still found it oddly comforting. Other creatures snuffled in the high country darkness as well.

The faint whistles were most disturbing. They floated on the night air from indeterminate distance. He counted shooting stars until sleep took him into deep dreams of blood-filled furrows, tall trees reflected in the pooling carmine by the dark of the moon.

Ashkoliiz seemed confident of her course the next morning. The column formed up at dawn without any casting about. The ice bear had reappeared overnight, come by a secret path.

The creature led that morning. Wee Pollister and a wedge of his heavy troops made up the van. Here in walking country, the light troops shared the supply loads.

The column moved up a valley which narrowed and deepened as the day went by. They followed a dry watercourse. The banks exuded a loamy scent, underlain with rotting algae from the stones beneath his feet.

Bijaz found himself walking alone near the column's tail. That was fine with him. The rearguard pretended indifference, never coming closer than a dozen paces behind.

He watched the trees. Something waited here in the North. It likely wasn't on this side of the Silver Ridges, but he detested the thought of being surprised.

They marched for hours, deep into shadow. The sun was lost behind bends in the towering rock walls. If there really had been a nickel mine up here, Bijaz couldn't see how they'd gotten the extracted metal anywhere useful.

Orders passed down from ahead called the column to a halt. Bijaz turned to look for the rearguard. They were nowhere to be seen.

Damnation.

He hurried forward, shouting for Pierce, Wee Pollister, or the Northmen.

The sky above had darkened to a narrow river of stars. Evening brought mist and the scent of wet stone, but also panic. A search party had been sent for the rearguard. Everyone kept staring at Bijaz.

He assumed the searchers were looking for unaccountable sprays of rose petals further down their line of march. Bijaz was forced to take company with Ashkoliiz and the one Northman she hadn't sent out.

"You continue to escape my hospitality." She studied a small leather-bound book.

"It is not for a lack of gratitude, lady." He looked at what she was reading. The leather binding was slick and oddly grained, the folios yellowed and brittle, covered with a mixture of black letter presswork and copperplate script.

She turned a page, still not looking at him. "If you desire reading matter, I have a small traveling library. Largely historical topics, I am afraid."

"Thank you."

Finally she glanced up at him. "I trust you did not improperly dispose of my rearguard?"

Anger made Bijaz's temples pulse, but he held his tongue.

Another of the Northmen slipped into Ashkoliiz's pavilion, speaking in a low-voiced language of clicks and sliding vowels. The Northman's fingers moved with his words.

Ashkoliiz answered the Northman briefly in the same language. He then departed with a thoughtful expression that left Bijaz wondering who had been reporting to whom.

She spoke up. "Iistaa says they were taken about three miles down the trail."

"He's Iistaa?" Bijaz tilted his head to indicate the departed Northman.

"No." Ashkoliiz sounded distracted. "The ice bear. Six men, taken within seconds of one another. Little blood, no dropped weapons, and no broken trail up the banks on either side. The search party ranged a mile further back but found no evidence that the men had been dragged that way."

Alates, he thought. "Snatched from the air?"

"Perhaps." Her gaze was long, level, and cool. "You will be pleased to know they found no rose petals."

"At least they checked." He didn't bother to mask his sarcasm.

"You are a most troublesome little god."

"I am hardly a god."

She reached into a nearby traveling chest and held up a glass jar stuffed with gold and brown petals. "No man made flowers of bats on the wing."

He let that pass. "What will you do now?"

A chuckle. "Put out word that the rearguard was taken by the mountain teratornis. That story is as true as any other and it will keep the next rearguard doubly alert."

"How do small miracles and the secrets of roses fit into this? I am concerned for my own safety, as you might imagine."

She steepled her hands. "You are free to make your doss with the command tent. I will allow rumor to resolve your worries, so as not to create false concern with an official announcement."

"Your generosity is exceeded only by your thoughtfulness, lady."

He sat awhile, watching her read and pondering what it meant that the ice bear had a name. By the time Ashkoliiz went to address the men, he was dozing off.

So it went for two more days. They marched up an increasingly rough trail, thick with trees. When the Northern Expedition crossed burn-scarred clearings, they only saw other higher ridges. He twice glimpsed a distant flatness behind them brown as summer grass—the plains of the Saltus basin.

No more mysterious casualties occurred. A number of non-mysterious casualties did happen, including a shooting.

Bijaz heard the gun go off. He followed close when Ashkoliiz and Iistaa moved back down the line to investigate.

Several of Wee Pollister's heavies held Arcus, the twin from Port Defiance. Gambardella, one of the few Bijaz could still hope to count as a friend, lay on the rocks. His forehead was shattered. Brown foam oozed from his mouth. Ashkoliiz exchanged a long quiet look with the bear.

"Have him made comfortable and bound to a sledge of poles." Ashkoliiz nodded at Arcus. "He and his brother will carry the wounded man. If Gambardella dies, the twins will draw straws to see which one's life is forfeit. The loser will execute the winner." She looked around slowly. "There will be no more such stupidity."

"Lady," Arcus gasped, "it was—"

The ice bear growled, silencing the man.

Ashkoliiz's voice was as frozen as her eyes. "Does any man here doubt my command of the Northern Expedition?"

No one in the ring of watchers would meet her gaze.

"Good," she said. "Here in the wilderness, I am guide and judge and sage. No other. Heed me well, and we shall all live to be rich and famed. Heed me poorly, and you will die unremembered on the hard rocks of the North."

She turned and walked away.

For his emerging doubts, this was the first outright misstep Bijaz had seen her make.

That night they camped in a long, sloping meadow. Arcus and Orcus refused to draw straws over Gambardella's fresh-dug grave.

"As lief, kill both of us as one," Arcus shouted. His eyes were wide, the sweat of fear coating his face like lacquer in the firelight.

Orcus stood silent and close to his brother.

Bijaz saw no way for Ashkoliiz to salvage this. It was a bloody business at best.

She stalked around the twins. The mountebank wore her finest silks tonight, with gems at her ears and neck and wrists. Judge, sage, or priestess bent on sacrifice.

She stopped behind Arcus and leaned in close. Her voice was pitched low, but with that trick of speaking that had every man around the fire straining at her words. "Tell me why one should live, when another has died at his hand?"

"Accident, lady." Arcus' voice shook with fear. "A mercy, p-p-please…"

"Mercy!" She pointed at the mountains bulking higher above them. "Do the stones have mercy? Does the mountain teratornis know pity? What of the wolf and the bear, each hunting for her clan's blood totem?"

"Mercy, lady," said Bijaz, stepping close so that he faced her across Arcus' shoulder. He could not let this go on. She would tear the men apart, and doom him with herself. "Mercy because you are not a mountain, nor a great bird, nor a dark forest full of fangs and leaves."

She started slightly at those last words, which gave him brief pause. She had felt something of the same fear of trees which had deviled him.

Bijaz continued: "Mercy, because mercy makes us human. And good sense, because the mountains and their beasts will tear at our numbers like dogs on a dying horse." He pointed at Arcus. "This man, or his twin, might be the one who can see us all home. If you must have justice, whip him to his knees or proclaim a were geld from his share. But do not be cruel. Not when it is in you to show your love for your men, and your sense that any of us may hold the key to life for all."

Ashkoliiz stared him down. Then she winked. Turning with arms spread wide, she made her pronouncement: "The godling dwarf speaks well. I forgive Arcus of Port Defiance his life, and the life of his brother. I fine him one gold obol, to be paid from his share to come. I fine Orcus one silver obol, and charge him with his brother's parole. Their money I grant to the dwarf as gift for his defense of their misdeeds."

The men roared. The fatal fascination of an execution had given way to relieving drama. Bijaz knew theater when he saw it. He'd been played again. First she built him up, then she tore him down.

Had the whole thing been a trap for him? He doubted that. Ashkoliiz was capable of making an example of both brothers. But she never pursued merely a single purpose.

The mountebank was not the sole dramatist around this fire. Nor was she so clever as he'd believed, to let affairs come to this pass. Bijaz played his part, bowing with arms spread to match Ashkoliiz's. He turned to Arcus, wiped the sweat from the man's astonished face, then flicked the drops away as a spray of fireflies that rose in a pale green swarm.

"Your life is your own," he said quietly.

The men made way for him with a muttering, fearful respect that was far preferable to knife-pointed hatred.

Dawn's bright fire threw the cliffs ahead in sharp relief. Bijaz stood outside Ashkoliiz's pavilion staring north, wondering where the path went next. They confronted another face as sheer as what had met the Saltus at its northmost bend. No globe cities were here, nothing but vertical scoring in the rock as if the mountains had been poured into place. The nearest cliff rose from the sloping meadow topping the network of canyons they'd been climbing for days.

Would they climb this, too?

Bijaz looked south. Somewhere beyond the mountain and prairies lay the City Imperishable, Port Defiance, and the Sunward Sea.

He wondered how things stood with Onesiphorous. Hopefully his old rival was even now arguing his way through gatherings of the plantation landholders.

The Northern Expedition formed their usual line, except the vanguard and rearguards were more spread. Bijaz walked with Ashkoliiz, Iistaa the ice bear, Pierce, and one of the Northmen. The men had grown less fearful, but he felt safer among the dangers he knew.

They cut across the slope toward a darker patch of rock where the pillars in the cliff face bent aside. As they approached, what had initially seemed little more than a shadow resolved to a black plug, then back to shadow.

A cave.

Bijaz looked up. He was no judge of mountains, but thousands of feet loomed above. This cavern could not possibly pass completely beneath the peaks.

Ashkoliiz had mentioned the Imperator Paucius nickel mines.

Bijaz wished he'd come to trust her more.

ONESIPHOROUS

They set a fire using scrap wood, piling vines and leaves to make it smoke. Onesiphorous let the flames burn freely for about an hour before smoldering down to a bed of coals. "I don't know when the Angoumois will come," he told them. "But they will be here." He tried to sound confident.

He spent the rest of the day sitting watch in the shadows of the entrance where he'd first encountered Beaulise. The Honeywood River brought nothing but the occasional branch. There was no sign of the Angoumois.

Near dusk the miners came outside to share a few pots of ale. They set their lines as the evening's insects summoned fish to the surface. Ikaré stirred the ashes. Pale plumes rose on the night breeze.

"Call up any swampers?" he asked with false pleasantry. "Or did all your boats burn upon their beaches?"

Onesiphorous let that pass. He worried that she wouldn't bother to send someone for him. He worried that he wouldn't find his way upriver to the plantations. He worried that his efforts at fomenting uprising had already reached their peak.

Most of all he worried that this angry crumb of a dwarf would poison his work. Back home, Bijaz had been the one who tried to find the good in everyone. As far as Onesiphorous was concerned, destructive little buggers like Ikaré could drown in their own piss.

Except for the lack of any sign from darkest Angoulême, it would have been a pleasant evening. Beaulise sat on the end of the dock with her knees drawn up, smoking her long clay pipe. The miners rebuilt Onesiphorous' signal fire to cook the sinuous fish they'd pulled from the river. Onesiphorous wouldn't have eaten them, just from their pallid look, but they smelled good.

The last of sunset stained the west a pale azure. He watched the stars. Even with the fire's glow, little light competed with the diamond brightness above.

"Quiet," Beaulise said.

The miners ceased their chatter, except for Ikaré, who drew a breath to protest.

"Say it and I'll cut your lips off," Onesiphorous hissed.

Ikaré shot him a dirty look, but held his tongue.

The sound of rowing echoed off the river. With the noise, they were enveloped in mist.

Onesiphorous could see little except an orange glow from their fire. Beaulise wasn't even a shape to him. Only Ikaré was close enough to make anything of.

Another dip of oars. Someone was rowing out in the current. A slow series of scrapes echoed as the miners reached for their weapons.

"Wait." Onesiphorous barely whispered. "She sends aid to us."

"Could be corsairs," growled Ikaré.

The spark of Beaulise's pipe flared. "Icky, I'll hold you while he cuts if you don't shut the hells up."

Another dip of the oars, closer now.

"Hello the dock," said a voice. It spoke with the accent of the City Imperishable, rather than the Angoumois that Onesiphorous had been expecting.

The mist shifted again to open a line of sight onto water shimmering with reflected stars. One of the narrow Angoumois boats glided close. Someone stood in the bow wrapped in a cloak. The pale oval of a face showed in the darkness. "Onesiphorous, old friend."

The boat slid next to the dock and Jason the Factor stepped up in one smooth motion.

You're dead, Onesiphorous thought. The man had been a miserable, dried-up walking corpse when last seen.

This Jason almost glowed. A green fire danced in his eyes. He stood tall.

He wasn't dead.

"Jason—" Onesiphorous tried for more, but words seemed to be failing him.

"Who's your friend?" Ikaré asked nastily.

A spare woman in leathers climbed out of the boat, graceful enough but not so deft as Jason had been. "He's my brother," she told the dwarf. "*Sula ma-jieni na-dja*. If you don't know what that means, I suggest you find out before you pick a fight." She glanced around the dock. "Hello, Onesiphorous. You're looking well."

"Hello, Kalliope." He glanced down at the boat, worried that he would see drowned Boudin with a paddle in his hand.

Clement stared back with ethereal calm. The swamp-mother was riding behind the Angoumois' eyes.

"Ma'am," Onesiphorous added. "My thanks."

The Angoumois nodded, unsmiling, then backed water and paddled into the mists.

"More mouths," Ikaré said, "but no more boats, I see."

Jason walked over to the obstreperous dwarf and took his chin in both hands. "Silence is like a garden," he said pleasantly. "Let it grow and you will harvest endless bounty."

In a moment Ikaré's mouth was filled with a tangle of leaves. Panic flooded his eyes.

Someone snorted with half-suppressed laughter.

"It's been a difficult trip," Kalliope said. "I smell fish. May we beg something to eat?"

With that, the night became normal again. Ikaré noisily spat out the leaves then stamped off into the darkness. The miners made way around the fire, Sidero the dark-skinned Sunwarder reaching up with a wooden plank on which pieces of fish steamed.

"Here is being some," he said pleasantly. "But you are please to be paying with a story?"

Licking the last of the fish from her fingers, Kalliope told of the coming and going of the Northern Expedition, and how the Lord Mayor had sent her and Jason south to seek out Onesiphorous and lend aid to the effort of unseating the corsairs in Port Defiance.

That the Northern Expedition had apparently departed the City Imperishable in both high style and good order was news to Onesiphorous. He couldn't imagine what Imago was about, letting such dangerous foolery pass.

"In Imperatrix Park?" he asked. "Truly?"

"With fireworks," said Kalliope.

"And what happened when the mountebank left?"

Kalliope shrugged. "She loaded a riverboat full of men and supplies and headed north. Nothing more has been heard. Enero and Imago were quite relieved that the woman took the last of the Tokhari and Yellow Mountain tribesmen with her."

"Good riddance."

"Not exactly." She looked uncomfortable. "Imago sent Bijaz on the boat."

That gave Onesiphorous long pause. What could Bijaz do in the North? He was surprised to find an intense sadness welling up within. "I don't suppose we'll see him again. The North has swallowed armies. A boatload of men following a confidence trickster are scarcely going to prosper."

Beaulise snapped her clay pipe in half and tossed it in the river. "My father is an old, tired dwarf with delusions of divinity. It was cruelty to send him on such a farce."

"He is more than you know," said Jason kindly.

Onesiphorous looked closely at the dead man. "I wager you have come to understand much. What has happened to you?"

"Bijaz happened to me." Jason extended a hand toward Beaulise. "Believe me when I tell you that your father is growing."

"He was still better off as an old, tired dwarf," she grumbled.

"No." Onesiphorous felt the need to defend his former enemy. "I found him rotting in an alley near the Green Market. He was not better off then. Whatever else the Numbers Men did to Bijaz, they gave him back his spirit." He glanced around at the eager audience of miners. "And I believe we have spoken enough of that worthy dwarf. How did you get down the river and across the swamps of Angoulême to us?"

"The Tribade sent their turtle," said Jason. "Biggest Sister meant to have her women come to Port Defiance in darkness, sailing beneath the waves. Imago believed that if you yet lived you must not be in port anymore, so we saw no purpose in following their plan. They discharged us at Sandy Banks. We'd planned to walk west over the hills above the swamp country and come down to the plantations from the north."

"What's a turtle?" asked Sidero. Onesiphorous had been wondering the same thing. Big Sister would have known, before the tide had stolen away her life in corsair chains.

"A ship which travels on the bottom of the river."

"They also call it an intramarine," Kalliope added.

That was an unfortunate thought, given Big Sister's fate. Onesiphorous tried to work out how such a ship could be. "Doesn't it flood?"

"And so you see why they call it a turtle," said Jason. "It has a shell above and below, with steam screws where the flippers might be."

"Another wonder of the modern age." Onesiphorous wished he'd had one that morning in Port Defiance. A secret way into the city had a distinct appeal. Especially if he succeeded in raising a broader resistance.

"Indeed," said Kalliope. "It was a bloody-eyed bunch of women that went down to the port, at any rate. They're looking for one of their own gone missing."

"Big Sister is not missing, she's dead." Onesiphorous' old misery surged. "I saw her chained to a rock and taken by the tide for the crime of helping me."

"Ah, my friend," said Jason. "I am sorry."

"A boy died with her. Nephew of your boatman. For the same crime, though he didn't understand the chances he took."

"I also am sorry, my friend," Kalliope told him. "The Tribade will doubtless make every effort to foster their regrets. Perhaps that is a measure of consolation."

"I too plan to foster as many regrets as I can." Onesiphorous' heart was leaden.

"The boatman was strange." Jason looked thoughtful. "Almost noumenal."

Onesiphorous nodded. "He was a horse. For *her*, the mother-queen of Angoulême."

"In the deserts we call that eyes-of-the-sand," Kalliope said quietly. "So the genius of the world can see within each soul."

Onesiphorous wondered if Clement was just a horse, or if some deeper geas had been laid upon the man in punishment. The Angoumois had certainly expected to meet his doom at her hands.

"You didn't walk west," he said, prompting a return to their tale.

"No. A mute boy met us as we climbed the banks." Kalliope stared at her hands in the light of the rising moon. "He was soaking wet, though he came down from above. A sword cut gaped on his shoulder, untreated. He gave me a gold obol, freshly struck from the mint at the City Imperishable. It was wrapped in seaweed."

"I am something of an expert on being dead." Jason didn't even look at his sister-murderess. "This boy was not with the living. His wound was neither healed nor corrupted."

"Boudin," Onesiphorous told him. "The drowned boy. I paid his fare to the Sea King to buy him back from drowning."

"On purpose?" Kalliope asked.

"No. Not at all." He added miserably: "I know better, believe me."

"He did not seem in torment." She reached toward Onesiphorous, then dropped her arm as he made no response. "The boy led us by quiet paths to a little bay. A narrow boat was there. He took us into the swamps, where he slid over the side."

She paused. "He did not come up again."

"No," said Onesiphorous. "I don't expect he would."

"We paddled on, though neither of us had the trick of it. After a while we met that big man who brought us here. It was a night and a day through the swamp, but he never stopped. We saw many fires, but did not approach them. Our boatman said not a word to us the entire journey."

"No wonder you were starved," Beaulise said. "Two days with the rats and their magicks, and no food."

"Angoumois," said Onesiphorous. "They are Angoumois and their swamps are called Angoulême." She was owed respect.

Jason nodded. "The bones of a proud and ancient kingdom lie beneath those spreading shadows. They were rulers of wave and water long ago, when the City Imperishable was nothing but a shepherd's hut near the river."

"Rats, Angoumois. It makes me no matter at all." The dwarfess waved off their objections. "They can sit amid their proud history and dream of better times for all I care. But they've burned our boats and attacked mines. They're trouble."

"Listen." Onesiphorous' anger rose. "You can wish us all to Dorgau's brass hells. And when everything is settled, I'll pay the bar tab and stand to take your blows. But now…" His voice dropped to a growl. "Now we need to take on the corsairs, throw down the Harbormaster, restore trade between the City Imperishable and Port Defiance, restart the assay boat runs, and put the world back in order. If we fail at that, everyone loses. The mines, the plantations, the swamps, the City Imperishable. Dwarfs everywhere lose.

"Ikaré can keep his anger, I want his clever tongue. You can hide forever from your father, but I want your sensible thinking.

"Every last one of you needs to pull together, or we'll all wither and die. Some chained to rocks, some broke and starving, some old and regretful in distant ports. But we're *done* if we don't find common cause."

He stopped, out of breath and out of purpose. Anger drained as suddenly as it had risen.

Ikaré walked out of the deeper shadows, clapping slowly. "You should have been a politician. No, wait, you *were*. Or at least a rabble rouser." The dwarf turned to his fellow miners. "Consider this rabble of one to have been roused. When it's all over, I'll be pleased to take my swing at mister City dwarf here. But we haven't seen an assay boat in weeks. Even if they start anew, I can't think that them now running Port Defiance will show any more kindness toward us than they have to anyone else that's crossed their path."

He turned again, stepping past the coals to jab Onesiphorous in the chest. "So I won't like you, dwarf. But I'll heed you when it's sensible, and challenge you when I think you're wrong. Follow you, no. But I'll go where you're going, 'til the cause is lost or I can finally take that swing at you."

Onesiphorous grabbed Ikaré's finger. "You can take me on, then, *dwarf*, but only if you hold to your word."

"Fair enough."

They glared at each other, two wrestlers just stepped back from a bout of shoving.

"Then get my friends here fed and bedded down," Onesiphorous said. "Tomorrow we'll plan our moves. Clement will be back. The Angoumois can take us over the water wherever we decide to go."

The miners headed within. Sidero dipped a bucket and poured more water on the hearth.

Onesiphorous looked up to see a spray of shooting stars. Ice, it was said, fell from the heavens. He wished Bijaz a sound journey in the North, though he had little reason to hope for such a thing.

He was the last man in. One of the miners waited with an iron rod to bar the door. "Good night, bull baiter."

"They call me the Oarsman," Onesiphorous replied with a smile.

IMAGO

Marelle returned with a new set of despatches. "Would it be wrong of me to have someone killed so that I could keep my office?" he asked her.

"That Fidelo fellow? Enero says he's hiding in the Limerock Palace. They're putting it about that you've sworn to finish the job you started yesterday."

Ah, thought Imago. "So you've checked."

"Of course."

"You have a lot of experience," he said cautiously. "What's your interpretation?"

"The Assemblage can amend its own prior acts. By extension in its role as the collective proxy for Imperator Terminus, it can also amend prior acts of Imperators past. I don't think you have a basis of formal challenge, though it is probably worth your effort to pursue that route as a form of negotiation."

"Were you ever an attorney?"

"An archivist," she said. "And stop treating me like I'm old."

"But you…" Imago's voice trailed off.

"No." Marelle's tone was dangerous. "I've lived a long time. I'm not old. Do I *look* old?"

"Not at all," Imago said quickly. "Frankly, I'd expected you to come back changed." *If you came back at all.*

"Jason was persuasive."

"I certainly hope so. I've sent him south with his sister to look into Onesiphorous' fate."

"Not so wise." She bit her lip. "He is of this place, you know."

"*I* am of this place," snapped Imago. He paced. "Irrevocably. And if this place wants him, it will bloody well call him back. The City Imperishable has a way of doing that."

"My life, in a word," Marelle said. "And I believe the City Imperishable wants you in charge. If the Assemblage of Burgesses were capable of running things, they'd still be doing so. If the City wants you as Lord Mayor, you'll stay Lord Mayor."

"You speak as if the City were a very large dog. It doesn't have thoughts or dreams."

Marelle smiled again, wicked this time. "What are the gods sleeping beneath the streets, but the dreams of the City? What are you and Bijaz, but thoughts molded to their purpose and set back into the world?"

"Jason, too," Imago muttered.

"Jason, too." She patted his arm. "You will still be here when the Limerock Palace has been razed to a grassy field."

"What of you? The City Imperishable has kept you around for a very long time."

"If you are one of its ideas," she said, "I am part of its memory. Both more and less than the sum of myself."

He wanted to comfort her, but that road was already closed. Imago fell back on business. "So you think I should ignore the Burgesses?"

"No. You must argue them out of this foolishness. How long will we have before things go badly wrong?"

"Around the end of the spring the economy will give out," Imago admitted. "Trading houses and banks already keep short hours, or shutter on certain days. Without the ships from the Sunward Sea, the river trade is drying off. The lumber trade won't make the trip if there's no market to sell at. Soon we will be reduced to eating our own crops and buying our own goods. That is not enough. The only bright spot of the moment is our shortage of skilled clerks has eased, due to a decline in work for them."

She shook her head. "So you have solved the unemployment problem for any dwarfs from Port Defiance. Everything else is in abeyance."

Imago spread his hands in helplessness. "I asked Bijaz to head north and Onesiphorous to investigate the south. The letters I send to Port Defiance go unanswered, my couriers do not return. I cannot tell if the corsairs mean to starve us out or mount an attack in our weakness. Without forces of my own, or the means to hire them, I am stuck waiting for an offer."

"And what have the Burgesses done?" she asked.

"Passed an election reform act aimed at unseating me."

"Then don your chain of office and go rally them. Offer to resign if they fail to respond."

"I *can't* resign," he said. "We'll call the Old Gods back again if we let the Lime-rock Palace take command. That was the lesson of Prothro. At the same time I have to find an answer which does not raise me too high."

"Maybe you're asking the wrong questions." Marelle's voice was patient. "Have you gone to see the Card King? Remember what *we* are? He does."

Dwarfs. Priests, once, to the gods that Imperator Terminus had carried away. Those days had been lost even to memory, that the suffering of the dwarfing box was a sacrifice to the City Imperishable and its blood-drenched stones. Imago had rediscovered this beneath the flint knife of the Little Man when he tried to battle the Imperator Restored.

"Go," she said gently. "You are nothing sitting in your office. You are everything walking the streets."

Everything, he thought, *including a target for that buggerer Wedgeburr.*

Still, he stood and took up his chain of office, donned the cleaner of his jackets, and thanked her. "I shall go walk a bit," he said, "as I once did. The City will speak to me."

"And its paperwork will speak to me." She kissed him on the nose. "Now go."

He forced his guards to follow on foot at a discreet distance. Imago wanted to make his own way through the streets just as he had when he was nothing more than a citizen, hard on his luck and working for his next obol.

The Rugmaker's Cupola was something of a prison, he realized. Comfortable, distracting, but always with walls around him.

First he walked north, to Filigree Street, then along to the Root Market. Imago avoided the streetcars. They seemed to be running behind anyway. No surprise that, as an unusual number of large carts were in the road.

No edge of panic hung in the air. This end of the City Imperishable was never as crowded as the Sudgate districts or the area around Terminus Plaza, so Imago did not have to push his way along. Instead he walked slowly and just watched. Jason had once talked of listening to the City—Imago tried to see with his ears as well as with his eyes.

Three boys playing cock-a-hoop, chasing an iron wheelband off a small cart. Each had a stick. "Bijaz, Bijaz, dead as a nail," they chanted. "Raised up my sister by his long shirt tail."

A Northern woman, carrying a tray of cardamom buns from some southern bakery, hawking them for three chalkies each.

A double handful of drovers with their morning beer, dicing against the lip of a stone horse trough. "Double the dwarf," one shouted as Imago passed, but they were not looking at him. "Three says he'll never climb," another answered. They laughed as the dice clicked again.

Passing a little fruit stand redolent with the odor of early berries and a few melons, a tired woman's voice saying, "…fool ran away on that steamboat. Her bear will eat them all, mark my…"

The City was being itself. The financial difficulties of the syndics and the factors and the waterfront did not mean so much in this part of the City Imperishable. These people would begin to suffer when the manufactories shut down for lack of contracts for finished goods. Then there would be less money for rolls and fruit and sidewalk games.

He passed into the Root Market. Great piles of potatoes were in from winter storage. Imago wondered if that was panic selling or good business.

There were rutabagas as well, reeking of soil and stacked twice as high as he was—had been. Kitchen carts from all over the City Imperishable threaded through the pyramids of tan and brown and gold. This was his city. He'd loved it as a man, and he loved it as Lord Mayor.

Imago sat on an overturned half-butt. He'd seen no one reading broadsheets here—a pursuit of dockside idlers and the self-important.

"You buying or trying?" asked a gruff voice.

Imago looked around to find a squat man in a dirt-stained apron. The moon face was a City-born classic. This man's family had probably been selling potatoes here when the legendary Imperator Osric had first declared himself.

"Resting weary feet," Imago said. "My pardons." He gave a slight nod to the two Winter Boys trying to appear casual near a stack of something long and purplish-white.

"Mine, too." The potato seller puffed out a great breath. "I figured you dwarfs was always busy."

"Sometimes a man needs a minute." Imago smiled. "I'd buy, but I'm not sure what I'd do with a potato or two."

The man laughed. "As I sells by the twentyweight, you'd have to do it with a lot more than two." He reached under his apron. "You smokes?"

"No. Never found that habit."

"Filthy, it is," the man agreed. He struck a lucifer match against his shoe and lit a fat, hand-rolled cigarette. The odor was sweet and light, not the tobacco Imago was used to in bars. "'M Gordon Huxford," the potato seller said around his cigarette.

"Imago."

"Same as him that's Lord Mayor?"

"Yes. Or was." Imago couldn't help but try his luck. "I heard the Burgesses cast him out."

"Eh, they's all the same. Takes your money and sends around a boy to shill for sewer cleaning and it's always too long to fix the cobbles."

"You won't miss him?" Imago was vaguely disappointed.

"He does well enough, I reckon, but so will the next fellow."

Imago rose, half-bowed. "Thank you for your time."

Gordon tossed something at him. Imago barely caught it. His reflexes had never recovered from what the Old Gods had done to him.

It was a potato.

"You don't look like a man in need of twentyweight," Gordon told him, "but anyone can throw one of them in a fire and get some decent eating."

"Thank you, sir."

Walking away, he wished he had mayoral kitchens so he could send the man business. A citizen untroubled enough to think anyone in charge might do a decent job was what the City Imperishable needed more of.

BIJAZ

They stopped before a cavern shaped like an inverted vee. The base was thirty yards wide. The stone showed the marks of tools and blasting.

"Behold the lower entrance to the mines," Ashkoliiz said quietly.

Bijaz thought that over. "So we climb up through a passage within the guts of the mountain, lady? Forage will be scarce." He didn't fancy miles in the dark, either.

"There is a lift, godling. Though you perhaps could fly up the shaft like a thistledown."

The others laughed. Bijaz resolved once more to keep his own counsel.

Darkness was not so bad, marching with a hundred jostling men. Ashkoliiz had forbidden torches, for the sake of the bad air, but they carried lanterns.

Soon their tunnel broke out into a great bubble beneath the mountains. The lower ends of the mining operation were here.

Wooden beams broader than Wee Pollister's shoulders gleamed black. Thick metal braces showed the patina of age. The lift was a platform about six yards square, large enough to accommodate three dozen men with supplies. It was secured by great chains to a set of metal cables threading up into the darkness.

He could not identify the power source. This place was centuries old. No steam engine would have survived down here unmaintained.

"I require a volunteer from the men," Ashkoliiz said quietly. "To climb to the base of the shaft and throw open a great valve there. It is controlled by a bronze handle wrapped in rotten leather."

"And this will make the lift go?" asked Pierce.

"Yes. The engineers of the old empire diverted an underground river to power the platform. The control links are long gone, except below at the source."

"How will he get up?" Bijaz asked. "Can the valve be set in place?"

"That is why I require a volunteer." Her voice was patience itself. "One who is none too thoughtful, or perhaps pines for a life of solitude in the high country.

We will not likely be returning to the City Imperishable by this path."

Bijaz had a brief, crazed notion to set himself to the task.

He went up with the first party to secure the top of the shaft. Wee Pollister commanded the platform, along with two dozen of his heavies, a scattering of the light troops and one of the Northmen.

Ashkoliiz stayed below. This was a machine which had spent the last four centuries rotting in the dark, after all.

Arcus and Orcus had volunteered to go down the shaft and hold open the hydraulic valve. Ashkoliiz had been almost resentful, as if she was somehow being cheated by them, but acquiesced when faced with a lack of competing volunteers. Bijaz hoped that the twins could make their way back down the mountain again to the River Saltus and home.

The platform swayed and shuddered as it rose. The men stood with weapons ready. Bijaz was far more practical, sitting down at the center.

He wondered how far they would ascend. Possibly a mile, from what had been discussed. Even though they had lanterns with them the shaft walls were nothing but glittering darkness.

Oddly, while the lift rose within a squared frame, the shaft itself was roughly hexagonal in cross-section. That seemed less than logical as an engineering decision. He was unsure what natural process would create something so regular and deep.

The platform groaned, a deep noise accompanied by a popping twang from the cables. Bijaz became aware of a pattering sound.

He stuck out his hand.

Something small and pale wafted into his palm.

Snow? he thought. *In here?* He looked at the little flake closely.

It was raining tiny bits of paper.

Bijaz stared up the shaft. The lanterns vaguely lit a descending flurry of shreds. Some seemed brown or black or gray.

Paper, in a hexagonal shaft. He had a sudden, horrible vision of being trapped inside a hive with bees the size of ships.

"We have to get back down, right now," he told Wee Pollister in a low whisper.

The big man stared at Bijaz as his jaw worked in gelatinous thought. That millstone voice rumbled into motion. "No way back."

A paper chunk the size of Bijaz's chest landed next to him. It was brown and shiny.

"Then draw your swords, by Dorgau's cherry nipple!" the dwarf shrieked. "Flame and blade up high. We're about to meet something very, very bad."

The lantern light began to reveal a shiny mass blocking the shaft above them.

The platform continued to shake, moving upward far too fast.

They were going to be crushed.

"To arms," Wee Pollister shouted. "And fire a volley so's them below knows there's trouble!"

The platform crashed into the paper wall with the inevitability of a toppling building. Bijaz pressed himself flat, face buried in the crook of his arm to trap some air. The paper pushed down tightly against him as the curses around him were muffled. The platform bucked hard.

Everything stank of rot and acid and a smell like old crab legs, a nose-wrecking reek, bad as a urine vat behind a papermaker's shop

Bijaz kept his face hidden and sobbed his fear. He should have stayed below and worked the valve. He could have walked home, or at least died in the open air. He could have done anything besides be crushed by this—

They broke through with a great tearing noise. All lights had been snuffed. Though the lift continued to rise, the advance party was in absolute darkness now.

There were no gleaming eyes. There was no heavy strain of wet breath. But he could hear faint clicking. A woman's heels on distant cobbles. Or a carnie counting the rubes. Anything, that clicking could be anything at all.

"Little god," said Wee Pollister in a slow and heavy voice. His millstones seemed nearly ground to dust. "Do you live?"

"Yes?" Bijaz whispered.

"Do something, little god."

The Northman hissed in his sliding, strange language—a prayer or a spell.

"Wh-what would you have of me?" Bijaz asked.

The clicking grew louder.

"Light, for the love of all the hells," wailed a different voice, before breaking into a shriek that quickly ended in a muffled thump.

The clicking stopped at that outburst. The only sound was the chains clanking. A breeze stuttered, that might have been made by the fanning of great wings.

"Are you sure you want light?" Bijaz asked.

His only answer was a whimper.

The clicking resumed. Bijaz withdrew to the wheat field. The golden light there had dimmed to gray. The reaper stood close by, scythe on one shoulder, dark cloak billowing.

Bijaz found himself using fingertalk. IS THE APPLE TREE READY TO FALL? Meaning: *Is it my turn to be harvested?*

The reaper reached into the clouds and broke off a fragment of the sun. He handed Bijaz a brilliant jewel that smoked and burned. The dwarf turned it in his closed hand.

His fist glowed a faint red, like a candle held behind an arras. When he started to open it, white light streamed between his fingers. The shapes around him caught his breath flat, so Bijaz tightened his grip once more.

Bijaz wondered once again what price he paid for the visits to the wheat field. Kalliope might have been able to tell him, but he hadn't thought to ask.

The air was even closer and more stale. The acrid paper smell sharpened. Bijaz cupped his hands and gazed up. Armor clinked as every man on the platform looked with him.

Another wall, combed and dripping. Great pale shapes the size of cattle were tucked close within gigantic hexagons. Their guide cables ran into scabbed orifices at the comb boundaries.

The lift was about to drive them into a wall of grubs.

"To arms once more," shouted Wee Pollister. "Make a flame, little god!"

Bijaz opened his hand wide and tried to recall exactly how the reaper had broken off a piece of the sun.

Light erupted from his hand. The men cried out. Around them a thunder made of wings began to echo.

Mercifully the glare kept him from seeing.

The comb burst into flame where his hot beam struck. A grub began to blacken as the wax holding it dripped in a burning rain.

"Push them over the edge as they fall!" Bijaz shrieked.

And fall they did, like flaming, boneless, albino cattle. When the first of the grubs slammed into the lift, its progress stalled a moment. A blessing, really, as they were a dozen yards from the comb, but then there was a thousand pounds of sagging insect to shove over the side.

The second grub crushed two men. Wee Pollister and the Northman levered it over, then tossed the bodies after. Let Ashkoliiz make what she would of the falling corpses.

The grubs' caretakers spread their wings. Bijaz could hear the buzz as they dropped away, but none had yet climbed onto their platform.

Two more grubs dropped, killing another man and setting the wood smoldering. He realized something was wrong at his feet.

A quick glance down showed the wood evaporating where he stood. His footing was fast becoming a dusty lattice. Was this reaper-magick taking its fuel from the deck?

"Wait," he shouted as four of the heavies groaned to shove the next grub over. Bijaz leapt for the huge, smoldering corpse and plunged his free hand into its side. He tried to envision the circuit, like an electrick light—the generator inside the grub, the bulb his open right hand.

The grub sizzled as it contracted.

Bijaz looked up again.

They were too close. He'd burned partway into the comb. Half a dozen grubs still clustered above them.

"To me," Bijaz called, stepping away from the grub's collapsing shell. Wee Pollister and his men formed around Bijaz, swords and spears braced upward. The Northman stepped close, too, hands open as if ready to catch a great burden. Some prayed. The troops were a metal thistle with a shaft of light in their midst.

Bijaz was losing the wood beneath his feet, but that wouldn't matter in a moment or two. They'd bump up against the plug. At that point he could use the plug itself to feed the fire. If it wasn't two dozen yards thick, or capped by stone.

Too late to worry.

Swords and spears around him sliced into the burning paper and hot wax. Men cursed as their cloaks caught fire. Bijaz could feel his hair smoldering. Goo and grub bits encased them. The platform slowed to nearly a halt, shaking as it strained upward.

"Get down," he said, and stretched to touch the paper.

A thought came unbidden to his head. *Enough fire.* Transformation was easier than heat and light. His fingers brushed tons of paper. From this madness of insects he would make instead a madness of flowers.

With that, it was done. The paper exploded in roses the color of light and flame, twisting in a whirlwind as the reaper touched Bijaz's shoulder to claim back his fragment of the sun.

ONESIPHOROUS

Morning brought a lean breakfast of thin soup and a tasteless flatcake made from chopped grasses and old crusts. They had only water to drink, with a few drops of wine to cleanse each cup.

"We need to move as far and fast as we can," Onesiphorous said. "I will go among the plantation men and appeal to their old ties to the City. You miners split up two or three together and make for the other thumbs. Tell them what we are doing and raise their support."

"What *are* we doing?" asked Ikaré. "I can talk of turtles and drowned boys, but that won't mean much in honest daylight. Not to sweating men with jade where their brains should be." He glanced around at his fellow miners.

"A question well asked," replied Onesiphorous. "We are gathering weapons and people to wield them. We will need to meet somewhere not far from Port Defiance. The boats and barges of the plantationers will be our navy."

Ikaré persisted. "Where do we meet?"

"You tell me." Onesiphorous stared him down. "Your first assignment is to figure our assembly point."

Someone snickered, but Ikaré subsided with a thoughtful glower.

Onesiphorous looked to Beaulise. "The rest of you should prepare to travel. Gather your weapons and food. I am taking Jason and Kalliope to the top of the thumb, to show them what you showed me."

"Mind your step," the dwarfess told them with a sly glance at Onesiphorous.

Everyone grew busy then. He grabbed a lantern and led the newcomers to the upward ladder he'd used before.

Both Kalliope and Jason were sufficiently compact to make their crouching way through the tight, winding tunnels without resorting to hands and knees. Somewhat to his own surprise, Onesiphorous found the way without having to double back.

Condensation covered the walls. Tiny runnels slid down the floors, pooling to glistening puddles that seemed to have no depth at all. Or possibly too much.

Onesiphorous didn't bother with half-remembered commentary on jade mining. He wanted them to see the world from atop the thumb.

When they reached the trap door, Jason had to help him push it open. Out onto the thumb the air was gusty and wet. He stood and looked around—a dark gray storm line was moving in off the Jade Bight.

The thumb was still bathed in sunlight. The green billowing roofs of Angoulême spread around them like an arrested sea. Birds spiraled in shrieking flights, seeking shelter. Distant rock towers were outlined in an eerie chiaroscuro. The light had a curious, vitrified quality.

"Strange taste in parlors you've developed." Kalliope hugged herself against the wind.

Jason turned, smiled. "It's beautiful. I can see the mother of swamps at her sleep, her dreaming thoughts leaping from tree to tree."

"I wanted you to spy out the lay of the land." Onesiphorous shouted over the rising wind. "The Jade Coast is a very long, very narrow place. These people think long, narrow thoughts. Angoulême dreams and resents us all. The miners have their own concerns. I can't say what the plantation men believe."

Lightning struck not far to their south. The thunder which followed was close enough that Onesiphorous could feel the pressure of the air upon his skin.

"Let us go below," he shouted. "Before we are stricken."

"No," said Jason. He raised his arms and faced the oncoming rain. Kalliope watched her brother intently, ignoring Onesiphorous.

Rain slapped the top of the thumb. Jason shifted his weight so as not to tumble backward. Water sluiced through the open trap as Onesiphorous dropped into the tunnels. "Come on, you fools!" he screamed.

Lightning struck so close that all the hair on Onesiphorous' body was raised. The rock around him was strangely slick, and his teeth buzzed. It took a few moments for him to refocus his eyes. When he did Kalliope was standing over him, oddly pale in the lantern light. Her leathers smoldered as her lips moved silently.

Somewhere in the middle of her tirade his hearing returned. "…which case I *will* kill you, you little Slashed bastard."

"I'm a Boxer now."

That stopped her. "What?" She sat, heedless of the water coursing down the tunnel. "You never did make any sense. Daft buggerer. Right now my stupid twice-born brother is outside calling down lightning and laughing."

"What did Bijaz do to him?"

"It's my fault." Kalliope tucked her head down. "When they found him, he was almost finished dying again. Bijaz was in a sweat to bring him back, make something more of Jason than he had the first time. The old bastard used my brother, you know, when he was a boy. Used him like a greased rag to spill his own lusts. Jason cried himself to sleep licking dwarf come off his fingers."

That explained much about both of them.

"If you don't believe me," she went, "ask that angry little dwarfess down there. She grew up listening to my brother whimper. I believe he took her virginity, and her sister's as well." Kalliope shuddered.

"They didn't seem to recognize each other last night."

"It's been close to fifteen years. This morning, she might have been pretending not to care. As for Jason, well… I've been traveling with him these past ten days. His memory has holes. They're getting bigger."

"Is he still your brother?"

"Not for much longer. Bijaz reached into him as he was dying the second time and made him into something green."

"Green?"

"He was the *sula ma-jieni na-dja*. The dead man of winter. Now he is the Green Man of spring."

"*Bijaz* did that?" Onesiphorous didn't know whether to be astonished or horrified.

"I showed him how." She cupped her hands and spilled golden sand. The water flowing around her steamed. The sand glowed a moment with the light of the distant desert before it became a thread of pale sludge in the runoff. "You forget, my friend, that I am a sandwalker. I have been taken down into the dark and made my way back into the light again. Thinking to help, I showed him a path to make his power more than parlor tricks and the death of longshoremen. He needed to control what he was given, not be subject to the whims of amusement and panic."

"You showed him a path to raising Jason?" Onesiphorous' head was spinning.

"No, I showed him a path to his power. He raised Jason all on his own. But in doing so, my brother was changed."

"Changed again," Onesiphorous said gently. "You had already changed him once, sandwalker."

"I should have left him alone." Her voice rang with a familiar misery.

"As may be," he said roughly, trying to draw her out. "But here we are now. What will he become? Is he our friend or our enemy?"

"I have no idea."

They stared at one another as lightning continued to flash outside the open trap. The thunder was growing more distant, though the water had not slackened.

"So we watch him as if he were a drawn weapon," Onesiphorous said quietly. "I have no noumenal powers. I am just a dwarf with a purpose. Can you match him?"

"On hot sand under a snake-eye sun, certainly. Here in the swamps of Angoulême where the power of green trumps bright, hard sand and stone, I doubt it."

Onesiphorous tried a different approach. "Was Bijaz seeking more than emotional reparation? Did he have some purpose to which he raised your brother?"

"I don't know that, either. He said he wanted things to be right. Then that woman came to town, and the old buggerer was gone." She stood, brushing wet sand from her leathers. "Enough. I will say no more. Just watch Jason awhile. You'll understand. As for me, I think the hairs in my ears are singed. I'm wetter than a fish. My brother can take care of himself up there. Are you coming down to dry off?"

"Yes." The wet chilled him. "Let us go down."

The tunnels wound strangely, the water changing the lay of the shadows from his lantern. He turned and turned again, trying to find the way down, but was quickly lost.

They came to a shaft which dropped in front of them. A dead end, unless he wanted to fall free. Another tunnel stubbed off the shaft on the far side, though he couldn't see any way to cross.

Not that it mattered. They'd never crossed a shaft coming up.

He peered over the edge. Light flickered forty or fifty feet below, and voices echoed indistinctly. Water dripped rapidly from above.

"What's over there?" Kalliope asked next to his shoulder.

Despite himself, Onesiphorous startled at her presence. "More tunnel," he said, "but we didn't come this way."

"Something glistened."

"Half this mine is wet."

She took his lantern and tried to angle the light. "I tell you, something is over there."

He tried to keep exasperation out of his voice. "This *is* a jade mine. Beaulise told me they'd stopped extraction until the assay boats were running again."

Kalliope groped to the right and then to the left of the mouth of their tunnel. "Ha," she whispered, and pulled a well-slimed rope into view.

She handed him the lantern. With effort she knotted a large loop in the rope near their floor level. "Sucker's heavy," she grunted. "Long."

She knotted another loop about her shoulder height. "Pull me in if I mess up too badly."

"Right." Onesiphorous figured on finding her body in the main gallery later. "Try not to kill anyone when you fall."

"Your faith is inspirational." Kalliope stepped into the stirrup formed by the lower loop, grabbed the upper loop with her right hand, and kicked off. She spun into the middle of the shaft with a slithering noise, then swung back to their opening.

"Done yet?" he asked. "It's not hung right from above. You can't swing across like an acrobat. And that rope is rotten."

Kalliope tugged slack in from further down and made a second loop around her foot. Then she crouched on the edge of the shaft.

"Why are you doing this?" Onesiphorous asked.

"Because I'm angry." She kicked into open air.

The woman had muscles, he would give her that. It was a strong jump, but the weight of the rope pulled at her. Kalliope milled her free arm, grabbing for the edge of the opposite tunnel. She was tugged upward by the rope, robbing her of forward momentum and lifting her over the lip of the shaft.

Onesiphorous watched Kalliope reach one hand into the darkness, then slip back. He grabbed at her shoulder as she slammed into his tunnel. A loud snap echoed. The rope began to tumble.

"Kick it free," he screamed, fearing the dead weight.

The coils slithered into the shaft. Onesiphorous crabbed backward, trying to drag her with him. He nearly lost Kalliope when a loop of the rope tugged her toward the edge.

She slashed at the coils with a thin knife. He braced heels but simply slid after her.

"Stop, by Dorgau's rotten nipple!" he shrieked.

They were both leaning over the edge before she finished sawing the rope away. Onesiphorous could feel his balance shifting into the shaft.

Kalliope threw her arms out. They wriggled away from the drop. Once out of danger, they lay gasping in the stink of fear-sweat.

Somehow the lantern had survived.

"You are as crazed as Jason," Onesiphorous finally said.

"Look." She opened her fist.

He plucked a three-inch lump of dark rock and held it up into the light.

It was dusty and fractured, but it was unmistakably blue, with gold flecks.

Onesiphorous chewed his lip. "Beaulise told me that stuff was mythical."

"Mythical to you and me, perhaps." She smiled. "Trust my intuitions, friend. I paid a very high price for them."

When they finally picked their way back down to the main gallery, Jason was already there examining the weapons and equipment. Onesiphorous saw no sign of the rotting rope they'd dropped.

Ikaré swaggered up to them. "Found something to keep yourselves busy, I see," he said with a leer. "Though there must be better places than a mine gallery."

Onesiphorous opened his mouth, but Kalliope beat him to it. "Do not mock what you only can dream of."

The dwarf gave her a sour look. "Indeed."

"Where did the rope land?" asked Onesiphorous, trying to change the subject.

"What rope?"

"Don't play the innocent. We dislodged a long section of rotten rope."

"Nothing here," Ikaré said. "Maybe you threw it down some other mine."

"Possibly." Onesiphorous felt a sudden need to drop the discussion. He exchanged a long look with Kalliope. There had been lights at the bottom of that shaft. And voices.

Another mystery in a life full of mysteries, he thought.

IMAGO

He wound up at the Potter's Field, along the northeast corner of the City. The air was colder here. The roads curved on themselves and ended in odd places, graves placed in haphazard arrays. The district was dotted with little groves, accidental orchards, colonies of flowers and shrubs. Pale poppies unlike any he'd seen before grew in abundance—petals almost waxy white, with a blood-red dot at the center of the flower.

The wealthy interred their dead in the catacombs of the Temple District, or private ossuaries on Heliograph Hill. The poorest simply laid theirs into the River Saltus, to the occasional dismay of boatmen. Here lay the ordinary citizens, paupers buried by the City Imperishable, foreigners, and executed criminals—hence Jason's search for his father.

Imago wandered among the markers. Many were wood, rotting away in a decade or two. Bones were piled where old graves had been dug up to be reused. Some were overgrown with berry vines already showing pink and purple fruits.

These were the City's people. The gods had their magnificent tombs deep beneath the New Hill. The rich slept armored in splendid gold until their grandchildren crept down to steal their rings for pawn. These bones here kept watch beneath the old walls forever.

He sat amid a bed of ferns and looked toward the Rugmaker's Cupola. It rose atop Nannyback Hill, sheltering the Root Market and all the northern districts from the endless machinations of Limerock Palace syndics in their silk-walled offices.

"I cannot quit you," Imago said to his city. He patted the ferns and by extension the bones which slept beneath them.

Though he waited awhile, no answer came.

Eventually he tired of watching flowers grow. The Lord Mayor stood, waved to his guards. It was time to resume his duties.

Imago and his escorts arrived at the Costard Gate along Maldoror Street, at the south wall of the Limerock Palace. Enero had mustered an entire squad of Winter Boys for the Lord Mayor's escort. Marelle was present, with two clerks carrying armloads of cloth.

Formal robes, Imago realized, and a fresh cloak for him. His chamberlain was not going to allow him to enter the house of his enemies in ordinary street wear. He mouthed his thanks.

A crowd had gathered. Two-Thumbs, from Jason's warehouse. Men and women and dwarfs he recognized from the neighborhood around the Rugmaker's Cupola. Ducôte even, the old dwarf dressed in formal muslin wrappings and leaning on a cane as he whispered to a young dwarfess close by his side.

Imago slid off the pony to find that Marelle had pushed close.

"You won't have time to change," she said. "Put your arms up."

A robe was tugged over him and pulled down as if he were a child. Imago was about to object when he realized they'd done the deed surrounded by freeriders. No one could see much of him.

Marelle set his chain of office into place, and slipped the flat fur cap of the Lord Mayor's ancient regalia onto his head.

"Go, now, and force them to hear you." She pushed him gently away. The Winter Boys opened up, and Imago stepped before the Riverward Gate.

The way was blocked by six bailiffs with staffs and pistols. Imre stood at their head. A decent man, the Lord Mayor recalled, if a bit of a fool. He had been close to Serjeant Robichande.

"Well met," Imago said. "I offer my sorrow at the death of your serjeant."

Imre seemed surprised. "Hello, your right honor."

"I am here to speak before the Assemblage of Burgesses."

"Are you on the docket, sir?"

"No."

"Do you have a writ of summons?"

"Imre," Imago began, his voice lowering with frustration. He caught himself, tried to recapture the sense of peace he'd found at the Potter's Field. "You know who I am, what office I hold. The welfare of this city is my business, much as the Burgesses think otherwise. Do not conspire with them at pretending me away. I am here, with my people behind me." *The live and the dead*, he thought.

"I have been ordered not to admit private citizens."

"I am no private citizen. I am Lord Mayor Imago of Lockwood. You yourself called me right honorable just now."

Imre looked nervous. "In accordance with the Electoral Reformation and Civic Governance Act of seven Mars, *anno* 618 Imperator Terminus, your claim on that office has been voided. You are enjoined to hand over your keys and regalia."

"Let me in," Imago said, feeling less reasonable by the moment. "I will speak to the Assemblage. If they do not express a revision to their will afterward, I will surrender my keys and regalia to you." To his surprise, he realized that he meant that. "If they do heed me, all will be well." He jerked his head slightly, indicating the freeriders and the gathering crowd behind him. "These are not angry people, they are curious people. Perhaps you recall what happens when people grow angry in my name."

"Do you threaten riot?" Imre asked.

"I threaten nothing. I merely point out recent history." Imago stepped close, until his face nearly bumped Imre's chest. "Let me pass, or haul me away in chains. I shan't be going anywhere else this afternoon."

Imre retreated into his own line of men. Enero and the Winter Boys surged forward, followed by the chattering crowd. In a moment they were all inside the cobbled expanse of the South Garden.

This face of the Limerock Palace still showed scars from the fires of last winter. Even the stones remembered.

"Onward to the Assemblage!" he shouted.

A ragged cheer arose.

Attended by several hundred of his citizens, the Lord Mayor of the City Imperishable entered the South Doors of the Limerock Palace, intent on taking a stand before the rulers of his city's vanished empire.

Imago followed a mass of retreating retainers down a wide hall floored in black marble. Electrick chandeliers hung from the high ceiling—the rooms in this portion of the palace were two and three stories tall. Large, irregular sheets of leather stretched on frames were hung on the walls every few feet. Glancing at them as he walked, he realized they were from the hides of executed criminals. Each was inked with a recounting of the decedent's crimes.

He came to a wide gallery where the functionaries had made a stand before a high pair of wooden doors which were scarred with axes and fire from some battle of old. The gallery spread out to his left and right, stairs leading to upper doors. Weapons and flags were racked upon the walls.

"I seek admission to the Assemblage of Burgesses," Imago announced.

"You-you are denied," squeaked one of the pages.

He wasn't going to have the same argument twice. Imago beckoned the freeriders to spread out. At a sharp word from Enero, they drew their pistols.

The defenders scampered away. Imago tugged the ancient doors open.

The Great Hall had been the seat of the Imperators. The Bladed Throne was poised high on a dais a hundred paces before him. It had rusted in its centuries of vacancy, now far more relict than instrument of state.

The Assemblage of Burgesses was in session. Each sat behind his desk with a high-backed chair surrounded by little stools for his clerks. The desks were arranged according to the political parties of the Assemblage.

Imago smiled as broadly as he could, and walked down the center aisle. First Counselor Fallen Arch stood at the base of the throne, with Provost Selsmark and another man—small and bald, though certainly no dwarf.

Wedgeburr, Imago thought with a hard and sinking heart. The judge-financial had not been ruined. Rather, he stood here at the front of the chamber in robes of silk and velvet.

The Lord Mayor's only comfort was the shuffle and clatter of feet behind him.

The upper balconies were screened with wicker. Their balustrades were carved with scenes of forests—marble trees greened with emeralds and jade, gem-bright birds in their leaves. The ceiling above vaulted to meet pillars, then vaulted again. The highest reaches were a deep purpling blue, stars inset as discs of crystal. Constellations had been picked out among them with silver lines, though not the traditional images of the night sky. Instead of the Archer, the Horsetail, and the Crown, he saw a rose, a wasp, a bat.

Someone else's view of the world.

Imago stopped three paces before Wedgeburr, Fallen Arch, and that fool Selsmark. He felt like a man arriving for his own hanging.

"My good Imago of Lockwood," exclaimed Wedgeburr with delight. He actually pressed his hands together. "It is always a pleasure when the citizens of the City Imperishable come to view their government at its work. I believe, however, that you have been misdirected. The galleries above are reserved for persons in their private capacity."

"First Counselor," said Imago gravely, with a slight bow to Fallen Arch. That man he could work with—they had conspired at the overthrow of the previous regime.

Zaharias returned the bow. "No longer, I am afraid. Burgess Wedgeburr has just been elevated to my former dignity by virtue of his Imperatorial party colleagues."

A gleam of desperation shone in Fallen Arch's eye. Imago was suddenly struck by the fact that he had no idea what game was afoot. Two dozen armed men at his back seemed remarkably insufficient.

"I see," he said, racing to find a line of argument which would run in his favor. "So the rivers of change have flowed within these halls."

"Certainly they have." Wedgeburr rubbed his hands, knuckles whitening. "I see a man in borrowed robes with a misplaced jewel of state around his neck, who has brought armed rowdies into the presence of the Bladed Throne. That is an offense punishable by quartering and being cast into the River Saltus."

The buzz of angry voices behind him was both encouraging and worrisome. Imago set his own loud and hard. "Which offense would that be?"

If the game were to be played rough, rough he would play. He could always have a man killed. Marelle had said so herself.

"Which offense?" shouted Wedgeburr. "You are a fool as well as a madman, Lord Mayor, to bear arms in the Great Hall."

Imago raised his arms and turned away from Wedgeburr. "See, even the First Counselor acknowledges my office," he called loudly. "Burgesses and citizens alike take note!"

There was snickering from the Boyarist side of the aisle. Enero grinned but kept a grip on his pistol. Clerks, mostly from the Imperatorial party, pressed in against the citizens who'd followed Imago. They avoided the armed freeriders.

He turned back to Wedgeburr. "Note, sir, that I bear no arms. And you yourself have just given voice to my claim of office. I see no trouble here. Only the two legs of government met in solemn council."

The First Counselor looked triumphant. "I will not brook your sophistry." Wedgeburr tilted his head back. "Now!"

A tearing noise echoed from above. Imago turned to see the wicker screens tumble away from the witness galleries. Several dozen bailiffs stood on each side, rifled muskets raised to train on Imago and his followers.

"I—" Imago said as the first volley echoed.

Enero fell without ever firing his pistol. His Winter Boys tried to return the attack, but they were cut down. Something stung Imago's arm with a hot, hard slap.

Another volley. Clerks died, as did Imago's people. The survivors stampeded toward the doors, only to be met by another line of bailiffs with pistols in hand.

He could not allow this to go on. Imago turned and dropped on one knee to Wedgeburr. He dipped his head and drew off the chain of office, knocking loose his broad-brimmed fur hat.

"The day is yours, First Counselor." He tried to humble his voice through his tears for Enero, and the senseless waste.

Selsmark kicked Imago hard in the ribs, knocking him to the ground. He landed on the aching arm, which blossomed into great pain. He was shot.

Fallen Arch was aghast.

As Imago was dragged away by bailiffs, he glimpsed Enero face down in a pool of blood. He searched for Marelle, but she was not to be seen.

He wished that Wedgeburr had been willing to settle for the assassin's bullet after all. Enero dead and Marelle lost once more was too high a price to pay for anything.

BIJAZ

He found himself alone in a stone room without knowing quite why he'd been asleep. No memory of dreaming told him what his soul had recently been about.

He was lying in a nest of blankets.

"Bijaz." One of the Northmen squatted over him, pronouncing his name with flattened vowels and a stretch of the final sibilant.

Bijaz? "That's me." The dwarf looked curiously at his right hand, which was wrapped in a great length of silk. "Isn't it?"

A long, sliding string of sentences this time. They meant nothing. The Northman stood, clasped his free hand a moment, and matched gazes.

Memory came to Bijaz then in a burning flash of terror. "We lived!" he shrieked.

The Northman nodded, giving Bijaz the first smile he'd seen from any of them. The man then turned to call for Ashkoliiz.

She swept in moments later with an expression he didn't recognize. Moments later it dawned on Bijaz: respect.

"You are present in your own head once more, little god." She sat on the floor next to him.

"I was absent?" It was a foolish question, he realized. He already knew the answer.

"You spent time crying about the wheat. Whatever that meant." She looked him over. "I'd also guess you've lost twenty pounds. Your skin will hang slack when you decide to stand." Her hand reached out tentatively. Those ice-blue eyes caught him once more. "You saved many lives. Offerings have been left at your door."

"We are all at the top of the shaft?"

"Wee Pollister rode the platform back down to us once he'd signaled for the descent. I do believe it was the bravest thing he'd ever done in his life. But you opened the way, and the fliers were gone."

"Did you mean to send us into them?"

Her eyes slipped away. "No. I had not taken this way before, but had been reliably informed it was open."

Another mistake, with all their lives in the balance. "Not so reliably as all that." He tried to hold in the laughter bubbling inside, a gibbering primal terror seeking escape. It came out a snort.

"No. But here we are, holding fast in the upper galleries in hopes that you would wake. Can you travel?"

He tried to sit up, but a spinning sickness took him. After heaving his empty guts a few minutes, Bijaz lay back down. "Not now, I think."

"I will have Ulliaa bring you something for that." She rose, dusting her hands. "We must go soon. You will be better on your feet than on a litter, but either way we must go."

"Ulliaa?" he asked.

"One of my Northmen. You have earned sufficient respect to merit knowledge of their names."

"He said my name. The one who was in here."

Her smile seemed real. "You have also earned sufficient respect to merit the remembering of *your* name. It means they believe you will survive long enough to matter to them."

"I am overjoyed." Bijaz immediately regretted his tone as her smile closed.

"Rest a bit longer, and eat whatever he brings you."

Ulliaa came back with a dark wad the size of a stuffed grape leaf, tightly rolled and very sticky.

Bijaz took it and sniffed. Honey, though not so sweet as he was used to. He had a sickening feeling he knew where this had come from. The wrapping was not a leaf, but rough, charred paper.

The Northman remained impassive. He merely watched Bijaz.

The dwarf wondered if this was medicine or a test. Probably both at once. Bijaz could not imagine Ulliaa and his fellows being any less clever than the woman they served. Her actions always fulfilled multiple purposes.

He ate the wad in three bites. The charred paper was filled with something that stuck hard at his teeth the way bones in a baked fish might.

I will not look, I will not think, I will not ask, he told himself, chewing and swallowing. It tasted of ash and that unsweet honey, having a mealy texture punctuated by the sharp crunch of chitin.

Bones, he told himself. *Think of them as fish bones.*

The bolus hit his stomach like last week's pork, but he clenched his jaw. This was no different than swallowing his hysteria, really.

The Northman nodded.

"Thank you, Ulliaa," Bijaz said.

Another nod, then he was gone.

Twenty minutes later, deep-stabbing abdominal cramps drove the ailing dwarf in search of a latrine.

"I see you are on your feet now," was all Ashkoliiz had to say as he staggered past her.

She had been right. Still with an itching in his guts, Bijaz inspected the little shrine outside his chamber. Insect parts and nest paper shards were scattered around. Some had been folded or twisted into little homunculoid shapes that were probably meant to be him. Two silver obols and a scattering of copper lay shining among the tiny figures. There was also food and drink: a leather-bound flask of something doubtless too strong for him right now, along with bread, dried meat, and a twist of honey candy someone must have carried in their pack ever since leaving the City Imperishable.

"How is it, being a god?"

Bijaz straightened as he met Pierce's gaze. The light troop leader squatted to meet the dwarf face to face.

"I would say that I tire of it, but I truly don't know. Within, I am still a dwarf of the City Imperishable."

Pierce looked thoughtful. "Maybe all gods say this. 'Once I was a shepherd.' 'I am a carpenter who set down his plane too long.' 'Give me back my ship and I will quit this temple.'"

Let me tend my wheat field, Bijaz thought. That would make no sense to anyone but him. "We have a dwarf god," he said quietly. "Sleeping these long centuries. I don't think my purpose will extend thusly through the deeps of time."

"Maybe." Pierce nodded slowly. "I could not say. But the men who were on the platform with you?"

"Yes?"

"They call you their patron now. You seem to bring them more comfort than burning joss sticks to some dead cavalryman at an altar behind a stable."

The very idea horrified Bijaz. "I'm a stupid little god. I mostly cheat at dice and cards, and make flowers."

"You kill, and you make life. That's all one can ask of any god."

Bijaz had never *made* life. He had only called it back once. "I am no one's god. People near me get hurt."

Pierce smiled. "People everywhere get hurt, but people near you live, too. You can be a blessing and not realize it."

"Then blessings upon us all," he said, trying to disguise the bitterness in his voice.

With Bijaz up and walking, the Northern Expedition decamped from the great gallery where it had sheltered. He tallied eighty-nine men, plus Ashkoliiz and her councilors. That meant eleven deaths so far, unless he'd mistallied.

Even with the losses, everyone was in high spirits. Surviving the shaft had been a signal honor for those who had gone up first. Everyone had seen the smoking grubs, the shattered bodies of the dead, the blizzard of roses from on high.

They were still talking about it.

The gallery itself was a wonder. Several districts of the City Imperishable could have fit within. A dim light showed from a distant bend high up on one wall. The ceiling seemed to belong to a natural, if enormous, cave. The original mine must have been worked from the floor down.

They followed a roadway that passed between great pillars carved with faces of men and animals. Their track ramped up along one wall to rise toward the lighted bend.

It took over an hour's walk to leave the gallery. The roadway wound up and out to a paved opening similar to the one through which they'd entered far below, but much larger. This vast cavern mouth contained an abandoned town. The buildings were roofless and slumped but partly protected by the shelter of the stone soaring above them.

Bijaz missed a step as he took in the view ahead.

They faced north, that he knew from simple logic. An arid plain below him stretched for miles on miles. A gleaming ridge of mountains rose on the horizon, white with faint lines which might be cliffs of stone showing through their mantle of snow. Those distant peaks had to be the Rimerocks.

Nothing could be seen upon that plain—no fields, no roads, no towns. Just a nearly endless stretch of broken gold and brown. What had been a few feet of olive-and-tan paint on a tabletop back in the City Imperishable was here a wide wilderness of near-desert.

"He's out there somewhere," Bijaz muttered.

"He's out there," Ashkoliiz agreed, walking next to him.

They strode onto the apron of the cave. The sun was above and behind them, a bit south of the Silver Ridges.

Bijaz was looking for the trees when the buzzing erupted from behind him. That was when the screaming began.

The enemy was as big as he'd feared. Great, glittering eyes bulged from rounded heads slick with chitin armor. Vast wings wide as a building shone translucent in the late afternoon light. The buzz was the same manic thunder he'd heard in the shaft, magnified by the cave, layering echoes on echoes until the noise was a creature of its own. The attackers swooped low, legs longer than lamp posts reaching down to snag men between cruel black pincers.

These were not bees, but wasps.

Bijaz hadn't the least idea what to do. He couldn't strike down dozens of the giant creatures. Transforming the paper plug within the shaft had left him unconscious for two days. That didn't seem a trick to be played again.

He compromised by hurling himself to the ground.

The rest of the Northern Expedition fought. Iistaa reared to his full height and actually pulled down a wasp. The insect slammed into the ground with a crunch of shattering chitin. Pale goo shot out from it. Bijaz noticed other wasps dodging the spray.

He crawled toward the nearest yellow-white puddle. It had a familiar reek. Bijaz rolled through the puddle. The stuff was warm and sticky, and acrid enough to burn his skin.

Manic inspiration overrode his sense of self-preservation. He stood and waved, screaming, "Come get me, you big buggers."

A giant wasp dove toward him. Bijaz windmilled his arms wide as he could, wondering how stupid he really was. Maybe he should have reached for his powers after all.

The wasp pulled away at the last moment with an uncoordinated buzz of those great, pale wings. It made a running skip over him, then took off again.

"Kill more," Bijaz shouted. "Cover yourselves in their guts!"

Wee Pollister rolled into another steaming puddle of goo. "Get it on yer!" he roared. *His* voice carried.

The ice bear brought down another wasp. Men dashed toward the broken abdomen, sliding into the oozing puddles.

Then they were gone. Three insects were dead, while the Northern Expedition had lost at least a dozen men, including Pierce the light troop commander. Bijaz watched the wasps fly away over the open country to the north until they vanished in the endless distance.

One of the Northmen loomed next to him, still coated in wasp guts. Ulliaa, Bijaz thought. The Northman nodded once, a note of respect more profound than any celebration, before turning away to help sort out the chaos.

He could see why Ashkoliiz had not worried so much about supplies. Her men would attrit fast enough on their own.

If only a few survived to return with a cartload of gold and history, they might be very rich indeed. Who would there be to gainsay them?

By the time the Northern Expedition double-timed away from the burning corpses of their friends and enemies, everyone seemed to know that bathing in the wasp guts was Bijaz's idea. Though the ice bear had been the true hero of the battle, the men preferred to confer their gratitude upon a fellow human being.

And once again the losses seemed only to bolster their spirits. Thirteen dead or taken, and here the troops were belting an off-key song about a general's sister and a one-legged Tokhari.

Bijaz never would understand soldiers, let alone these ragged brigands.

Wee Pollister stuck to him like a shadow, to the point of gathering irritated glances from Ashkoliiz. Bijaz was certain she had not factored either encounter with the wasps into her calculations. Perhaps the men were dying too fast. Perhaps he was growing too popular.

He wondered what the Northmen thought. He increasingly suspected them of independence from Ashkoliiz, and possibly even holding some hidden authority over her.

A road led down this side of the mountains, with its head at the cavern. Though centuries old, many of its embankments had not crumbled. A number of bridges were intact as well. Bijaz noted a few trees. They made good time, reaching the escarpment's base around full dark.

As the men set down their gear, Ashkoliiz met them with a torch held high so that her face was lit from above. The leaping shadows made a mask of her. She became something bloody and old rising up out of the sere soil of this high, dangerous place.

"We have come to our meeting place," the mountebank announced in her quiet, calm tone. "Here we will build our advance base. The mounted column and the camels will arrive soon."

Bijaz had his doubts about that.

"Our journey is half done," she continued, looking first one way then the other. "*He* is here. Out there in the darkness somewhere, he is here." Her voice pitched higher and louder. "Where is he?"

"He is here," replied the Northern Expedition. Even Bijaz found his lips moving.

"Where is he?" She was shouting now.

"He is here!" The troops shouted back.

"*Where* is he?"

"*He is here!*"

Her voice dropped to the quiet of a spring rain, barely audible over the crackling of her torch. "Yes. He is here. And we shall bring him home."

They cheered madly, the sound echoing to the cold stars overhead. All Bijaz could think of was how far noise might carry in this high, deserted country where even ship-sized wasps could vanish like dust. Anything might be listening. Anything at all.

A thought came unbidden, much as the swing of scythe upon the grain: *Even the trees.*

ONESIPHOROUS

Five flatboats approached at dusk, each poled by an Angoumois. They all wore undyed linen cassocks, with long white scarves around their necks.

These were the fire dancers from his passage through Angoulême, Onesiphorous realized. Men who'd cut their own throats on a single cord.

He shivered. She was strong tonight.

"I'm impressed," said Ikaré in a tone which clearly indicated he did not mean any such thing.

"Whatever it is you need, I'd go find it now." Soon Onesiphorous would be rid of the intransigent dwarf.

Sidero pelted out with the other two Sunwarders, carrying one of the mine's precious few rifled muskets and an array of tools. They also toted the bulk of the food supplies, as their group faced the most distance to travel.

"West," said Onesiphorous, "as far as you can go. Find the most distant thumb being actively mined. Work your way back from there."

Sidero nodded, then looked at the boatman. "Is this to be safe?"

Onesiphorous turned to address all of the laden miners returning to the dock. "These folk will aid us, but they serve another master. They move in silence. Respect that and do not fear them."

He was answered by muttering.

"You have come too far to stop now," Onesiphorous added. "There is nothing more to keep us here. We must go."

"He is to be having the right of it," Sidero said loudly. "I am to be going." The Sunwarder stepped down into the first flatboat. Sidero helped his fellows down, then looked up as the flatboat poled away, the Angoumois boatman still staring at the water.

Onesiphorous had already divided the rest of the miners in three groups based on their destination: south to the coast, further upriver to the other thumbs in the immediate region, and west to the nearer mines. Ikaré went south with two of the City men, for once holding his tongue.

Beaulise was among the last to depart. She looked up at Onesiphorous from her chosen boat. "When it's over," she began, then shook her head.

"When it's over," he told her, "we'll find a way to make things right."

"Fifteen years too late for that, dwarf." Her flatboat glided off into the mists.

Onesiphorous, Jason, and Kalliope stepped one by one down into the final boat. They would head upriver to the docks at the Fallow Acres plantation. They'd brought no weapons and no food, for they had the shortest journey.

He looked at the boatman. This one raised his head and met Onesiphorous' eye. "You going far, little City man, ah?"

The face was a fire dancer's, but the voice was the swamp-mother's.

"You said they would not fight," Onesiphorous told her.

"They no fight. These horses my eyes."

"Then you know where we go."

"I know," said the swamp-mother. "Now show me. I would see it."

It what? Onesiphorous wondered.

Kalliope reached forward and opened her hand. The blue jade shard sat glittering within.

The horse stared awhile, though he kept his hands on the pole. Finally he spoke. "That has not been seen in a thousand years, ah."

The horse's lips didn't quite match the sound of her voice.

"And it won't be seen again if we fail in our purposes," Onesiphorous said, with a glance at Kalliope.

The sandwalker's expression was set. Of course, one of her training would know the grip of the noumenal. Jason just smiled, his eyes nearly vacant except for a faint green glow.

Their boatman poled away through the mists, keeping to the edge of the night-dark water to avoid the fastest reach of the current.

The journey upriver lasted well into the next morning. Stretches of open space populated with sedge and cattails spread before them with the dawn. White wading birds stalked in the first light, catching the fish which followed the morning's rise of insects. The dank, muddy dark reek of the swamps shifted to a grassier scent, mixed with the dirt-and-water of fresh-fallen rain.

The boatman poled mechanically as any engine. Onesiphorous, Kalliope, and Jason shared a water skin and dozed. There seemed little point in conversation.

Eventually he saw a wooden dock extending from a high-banked meadow. They'd reached the edge of some plantation's outlying fields.

Fallow Acres, he hoped.

The river had grown much narrower, too. Tributaries flowed from recognizable banks, not just seepage from tree-bounded marges. Even the trees themselves looked more homelike, except for the beards of moss clinging to their branches.

The air was also much hotter.

"I can hear the beating hearts of the trees," said Jason.

"Of course you can," muttered Onesiphorous.

They passed a bend in the river to see a cluster of buildings close by the water. Several docks had barges tied close. A town lay behind a series of whitewashed wooden warehouses. Farther up the hill, the uniform green of young crops was a tinge on the plowed fields.

An Angoumois waited at the first of the docks. He wore canvas trousers and a denim shirt. When he got a closer look at the flatboat, he hurried back toward a two-story building tucked in among the warehouses.

The flatboat glided up to the dock. Jason and Kalliope climbed the ladder. Onesiphorous paused to glance at the boatman, whose chin was tucked on his chest as his face tilted down.

"Are you there, ma'am?" he asked politely.

The boatman looked up. Nothing was in his eyes but the deep shadows of Angoulême.

Onesiphorous scrambled up the ladder, allowing Kalliope to help him over the edge. When he regained his feet he saw that a dozen Angoumois were arrayed at the far end of the dock with field implements braced as weapons.

"We are expected?" Kalliope asked.

"I believe they caught a look at our boatman and panicked." Onesiphorous considered who he was traveling with. "Let me do the talking. Don't, ah, do anything surprising?"

"Of course not." Kalliope glared at her brother.

IMAGO

His cell was four paces wide and three deep, and shorter than the height of a full-man. There was no light at all. Imago's fingers told him that the ceiling curved upward. The wall within the implied arch was brick, the floor a very thick wood, the other walls dressed stone.

There was no door.

The bailiffs had banged his head on steps as they dragged him down into the palace basements, until he'd thrown up. As a result, Imago wasn't sure if the brick had been laid after he'd been placed here, or if they'd breached the floor.

There was no bed, only a pallet of increasingly foul straw. A bucket came up through a small hatch in the boards once a day. It usually contained a cold roasted potato and a leather bottle of water tinged with wine. He'd tried grabbing the edge when the hatch opened, but someone below had slammed it shut on Imago's fingers. That happened twice. Going without food for a while, not to mention the pain, convinced him to desist that effort.

He had nowhere to shit or piss but in the food bucket. He left it and the empty bottle beside the hatch. They disappeared when new food came. Whoever was below worked in their own darkness—Imago never did see light. One time he left the bucket directly on the hatch so it spilled downward. He'd gone without food, water, or a pot to piss in for quite some time after that.

Imago didn't know if a day had passed each time he slept. He wasn't even sure he did sleep, really. His dreams and his waking hours had a terrifying sameness.

Black, dark, black.

He counted the brick courses. Nineteen of them, cut off at the highest point. He counted the bricks, seeking a loose one. Sometimes there were two hundred and thirty-eight. Sometimes there were two hundred and thirty-seven. Every so often there were two hundred and thirty-nine.

When he became bored of freelance masonry, he counted the dead in the Great Hall. How many of his own had fallen? All of the Winter Boys? What of the others, servants and sailors and people of the street? Had any of the Burgesses died?

Where was Marelle?

Had they sent Enero's body home?

Imago surrendered himself a sliver at a time to the shadow, until despair found him. He'd raged and screamed under the altar knife amid the tombs of the Old Gods, but there had been purpose then. Even the pain served a need. This was just torture for its own sake. His captors would have been kinder to kill him.

Once he woke to find his legs spasming to curl under him. The scars where skin and bone had been fused ached almost as badly as when he was first cut by the Little Man. He cried. That didn't help, so he tried brave memory instead. All he could think of was Enero riding, Jason so crumpled and slow after his murder, Bijaz with that strange pale glow about him.

Not things he wished to have in his head.

"Not so easy, is it?"

A very gaunt, naked dwarf with tangled hair and a nest of a beard squatted at the far side of his cell. The visitor carried a little candle. That light hurt Imago's eyes.

"No." He waited to see how quickly this dream evaporated.

"Dark gets to you." The dwarf was familiar beneath the sores and the sadness and the encompassing grime.

"Wh—" Imago's voice failed. He hadn't spoken in a long time. He tried again. "Why..." One word, a ragged whisper. "Why d-does..." Another deep breath. "A gh-ghost..." *One more time,* he told himself, *hold fast to this thought.* "Ghost need a c-candle."

"Candle? Don't need one at all, me. It's you who needs the candle, Lord Mayor."

"Why?"

"'Cause you're still alive, I expect." The dwarf made the two steps to Imago's side and set the little brass chamberstick down next to him. The flame flared as he did so, recasting the visitor's features.

Imago *knew* this dwarf. Saltfingers? No.

"I'm being called," the dwarf whispered. With a miserable expression, he disappeared into the shadows.

Imago hobbled to his feet and searched the cell before the candle burned out. Nothing but stone and brick, brick and stone. He'd heard no creak of a trap door, nor the sound of stone sliding.

A hallucination, then.

He sat down next to the candle, which was close to guttering. Thoughtfully, Imago touched the flame.

His hand jumped back. For something imaginary, it hurt like the hells. The little rush of air from his reflex pulled the flame after, and it flared out to leave a tiny red coal. Sharp-scented smoke hung in the air.

He covered his fingertips in the hot wax just to feel the tightness as it cooled and set. Then he hid the candle holder in his rotting straw.

Every time he awoke thereafter he reached for the last stub of the candle and the little brass dish. The wax casts of his fingertips he placed in the mortar below the top brick course, to help him climb out someday.

One day shortly after a gobbet of meat had appeared in his bucket, he heard a scraping of stone. Imago froze. He then reached for his treasures. If they came for him now, he was ready to die with dignity. He just wished he could shave.

Stone scraped again. Someone cursed quietly.

A man whispered, *sotto voce*. "Are you sure?"

Another voice: "It's what *they* told me. I doesn't asks a lot of questions when dangled by the scruff of me neck like a pup over the drowning barrel."

A third voice, female. "I'll show you a drowning barrel if this goes any more wrong."

They didn't sound like jailors. Or bailiffs. Or Burgesses.

"You in here, your worship?" asked the second voice.

"He's not going to answer," snapped the woman.

Another scrape. A thin knife of light stabbed Imago in the eyes. He cried out, then covered his mouth with both hands. The brass chamberstick dropped, ringing to the floor.

"That's torn it," said the first voice.

"Open it, now," the woman told him.

After a series of grunts and a crunching scrape, a very pale, ugly dwarf crawled into the cell, holding a lantern in one hand. The light burned Imago's eyes.

"Your worship is alive."

Imago dredged up a name. "Saltfingers." He was right, this time.

"Come on, then," the woman said. "And quiet while you're about it."

Saltfingers tugged at him. Imago found that he couldn't move correctly. The dull ache in his arm flared at their touch.

"Come," they whispered. "Wasting time, wasting time."

"My c-candle."

The woman scuttled in and grabbed it. "We'll never get the stone put back."

"There's always time to set a job to rights." Saltfingers tied a rope to a bar set in the back of the stone, and began tugging the block into the little space where they were crouched.

Imago realized he was looking at Marelle. The other person was Biggest Sister.

"I can remember." He stopped. "You're dead."

"No, fled." Marelle touched his lips. "Silence now."

Saltfingers set chocks behind his stone. "Back out the way we come in, right to the Maldoror Crossover. Once we's in the tunnels, we's in dunnyman's country and ally ally oxen free."

"H-how long?" Imago managed to ask.

Marelle touched his lips again. "Shh."

"Thirty-six days," answered Biggest Sister. "Your funeral was magnificent. First Counselor Wedgeburr himself delivered your elegy."

"That…" Imago was appalled.

"Come," said Saltfingers. "Now."

"First we go to my doctor," Biggest Sister added.

Imago woke up, unsure where he'd been. Or where he was now. Narrow windows above him admitted a vague light. Rain drummed not far away. The room was high and long, though not wide. Suits of plate mail stood racked—empty, weaponless armor guarding an empty room.

And one very exhausted Lord Mayor.

He took inventory. Left arm in a cast and sling. Both hands bandaged. He was going to have all the hells of a time doing anything personal. He seemed to be naked under several layers of blankets. And he felt very, very thin. Ribs strained against his skin.

"You yet live," said Biggest Sister.

Imago would have sworn on raw gold she hadn't been there a moment before. "How do you *do* that?"

"A simple 'thank you' should suffice."

"Thank you. And yes, I seem to live. Which is more than some."

"Seventeen dead in the Great Hall. Ten of your freeriders, including Enero, the Burgess Subat Mykos, two clerks, and three of your followers. Wedgeburr hanged the surviving freeriders from the Costard Gate, though I don't suppose they would have lived long in any case. Put bullets in the heads of the rest of the seriously wounded. Another nine, all of them yours. Burned the bodies in the South Garden." She wrinkled her nose. "It made a horrible stench."

"I led them there," Imago said quietly.

"Yes, you did. But the First Counselor would have come for you wherever you were. Wedgeburr's dismissed everyone who worked for you in any capacity, declared a dusk-'til-dawn curfew on dwarfs and foreigners, and has men drilling down by the docks for an assault on Port Defiance."

"I should have killed him when I had the chance."

"Mmm." Biggest Sister crouched and took his chin in one hand. She tilted his head, looking into his eyes. "Your pupils match. Doctor said to watch that carefully. Not for me to say what you should have done, but I would have slit Wedgeburr's throat on principle."

"I tried to be a better man."

She clucked sympathetically. "Character flaw, that."

"How stands the City Imperishable otherwise?"

Biggest Sister shrugged. "Northern Expedition's in the North. *Slackwater Princess* is far late coming home. Port Defiance continues to blockade the river. There's trouble among the dwarfs there. Your man might have made it into the swamps, but if so, no word's come back. Here in the City Imperishable potatoes are still for sale in the Root Market. Most people live their lives every day."

Which was true enough. Away from the docks with their fresh-off-the-boat rumors and constant broadsheets, the average citizen had little to do with politics. Only people of a certain set of interests concerned themselves with events in the Limerock Palace. As Gordon the root seller had said to Imago, the next fellow would do just as well.

"Did your vessel make it south?"

She nodded. "Your two debarked at Sandy Banks and struck out into the swamps. I'm not certain what that was about, as my women had other concerns to communicate. The Tribade is now active in Port Defiance."

"Good." Talking was tiring him out. Imago lay flat, thinking. It was time to return to his brother on the Eeljaw. Humphrey would lord it over him, while Belisare the family dwarf would scorn him, but that was a quiet existence. He could weigh seed and count harvests and never put anyone's life in the balance again.

"You're heading out in two days, three at the most," Biggest Sister told him. "The Festival of Cerea is three days hence."

"Five Mai," he croaked.

She seemed surprised. "Yes. Good, your brains aren't all scrambled. The Card King will take you on. You will pretend to be pretending to be yourself. Marelle thinks it best to show you to the people thus. If things go badly we can retreat and claim you are an actor."

He remembered all too vividly the last time he'd had the krewes at his back. "Is that wise?"

"Marelle says you're going back to the beginning again. Will of the City." Her smile was crooked. "Me, I just want to see the look on Crusty Alice's face. You know it's forty lashes and a swim in the river now to say that name in public?"

"The River Saltus? With a bleeding back? The sharks would feast."

Her smile had vanished. "Exactly. We've been counting. Two hundred and seven killed or executed since you were murdered."

A thought passed by, fluttering strings of memory.

"Somebody mentioned my funeral. Do I have a tomb?"

"You were buried in the Potter's Field beneath some pale poppies."

"Oh, good," he said. "I like those flowers."

"And unlike certain people, you didn't have to die first in order to come back to life." She stood. "To answer your very first question, it's all in the shadows, and knowing how people pay attention."

BIJAZ

The new light troop leader was a man named DeNardo. He was a beanpole with curly blond hair who always wore a red vest. He also looked vaguely familiar to Bijaz.

Under DeNardo's leadership, the men logged a clay-walled canyon, felling trees whose tops rose no higher than the surrounding land. Posts were stripped and shaped and built into a stockade about the muddy pool which was the closest they could find to a spring.

The weather ran colder here than Bijaz had expected. His cloak didn't cover enough of him. One of the heavies lent him a felt hat which flopped around his ears, but kept him more decently warm.

One morning a few days after they established a permanent camp, he headed out into the open country to see what might be seen. Just past the partly built wall he chanced to pass close to DeNardo drilling his men with stick-swords.

"You are to being slow upon the left!" DeNardo shouted. "I am thinking you are women with poor complexions and no men at all!"

The accent, the strange command of verbs. DeNardo was one of Enero's men.

That was why the man looked familiar. Bijaz must have seen him around the Rugmaker's Cupola.

He walked on. It would do DeNardo no good for Bijaz to call him out. The man knew it, or he would not have been so carefully keeping his distance.

The desert to the north wasn't a landscape of sand, like the fabled dry seas of the Tokhari. Here the ground was graveled in place of good, honest soil, as if the whole world had been paved. The scattered plants were set apart from one another. Each was jealous of its own water, he supposed. They were thick and spiky and difficult-looking, with narrow leaves and sharp thorns.

Bijaz missed the straggling grasses and struggling lindens of the City Imperishable. Though more gray stone than any kind of growing green, the City never expressed such a harsh character as this place. He wondered if Kalliope's Red Cities had once been something like the City Imperishable, before the green faces of their lands had turned away.

Bijaz could not imagine a forest having ever grown here. The endless land was sparse, while the rain fell scarce as fog inside a tavern. Still life found a way to prosper. This place was alive, just not as he understood the word.

He could feel the green lurking beneath the soil. What would Jason have made of this?

When Bijaz turned back, he found he'd walked much farther than he realized.

He had a decent view of the Silver Ridges from here. The fortress-camp of the Northern Expedition seemed little more than a hut. He also had an excellent view of the line of horseman approaching from the west.

The mounted column had finally caught up. A rising dust cloud trailed them by miles.

They were fewer than the forty who had set out from the riverfront. Followed by the camels. At least there were enough of the filthy beasts to make a dust cloud. That meant they hadn't all been eaten by wasps or fallen off the trails.

He ran back to the camp.

That evening launched a long night of tales fueled by ale from barrels which had come up on camelback. Ashkoliiz had marked them as lye, and so they'd remained unbreached on the journey.

Priola told their story in the form of a running argument with Azar, the Tokhari who'd led the cavalry column. The third Northman whispered with his fellows at the farthest edge of the firelight during the recounting. Bijaz would much rather have heard *that* story, but he did not speak their language.

"So then's we come to the second waterfall," Priola was saying.

"Water no!" Azar roared. "You Stonesource men piss your pants so much it flow down mountain!"

That drew a round of laughter.

Priola grinned. "Piss, water, you camel herders drinks anything."

A greater round of laughter.

And so it went through the evening, a mix of hard-edged banter and a certain respect. The camels and the horsemen had ridden a hard track into Jarais Pass. There they were hunted by snow leopards, and fought a pitched battle with a tribe of men the color of chalk who had two knees in their legs. There had been landslides, drownings, three fatal fights between horsemen and camel drivers—the last one, surprisingly, won by the camel driver.

Some of the animals had foundered in the high pass. Of the two-score foot soldiers and the same number of riders, Priola had lost eleven, while Azar had lost six.

Eventually Ashkoliiz declared herself pleased with their efforts. Standing silvered in the light of a three-quarter moon, she blessed them all.

"I declare a day of rest in honor of our efforts. Then our true work begins. We will bring your history home."

Once more they cheered her. Bijaz wondering what might be listening out in the darkness.

Ashkoliiz redivided their forces. Priola and Wee Pollister remained in the encampment. The big man had been reluctant to let Bijaz go, but the mountebank insisted that the heavies defend the stockade.

Bijaz wondered if they would ever return to the camp. Wee Pollister must have thought the same, though the big man didn't voice any objection.

All the horsemen came, and thirty of DeNardo's light troops. They crossed northward into the wilderness. The horsemen rode as scouts, pickets, and re-arguard, allowing the marchers to maintain a strong pace. The ice bear ranged wide as well.

Still, they encountered checks—canyons too deep to simply scramble through, and miles-wide stretches of tangled thorn. On the fourth day north they entered a field of smoking mounds which gave off a reeking yellow fog, and were forced to find another route.

All of which made Bijaz doubt whatever map Ashkoliiz was using to guide them. During the climb she had been in firm command, testing her men and their mettle. Here she appeared less certain.

The closer they drew to whatever remained of the Imperator Terminus, the less resolute Ashkoliiz seemed in their course. Bijaz pondered what that might mean, while keeping a sharp eye out for trees which he never saw.

The land rose steadily over a fortnight's travel. There came a day when the scouts turned their mounts and dropped their reins to await the column. The land simply ended, sheared off as if by a knife. Far below was a broad plain gleaming bright in the sunlight.

Ice.

A vast expanse of ice stretched to the north, pushing a cold wind up the cliff. The rough surface was the blue-white of Ashkoliiz's eyes. Broken chunks rose upward, seams opened, darker patches and great ripples and strange ridges. It was a frozen ocean. If he'd thought the North chill before, this was winter incarnate.

Had this desert once been a high sea, trapped between the two mountain ranges until all the water had been drawn down into this cold prison? Perhaps skeletons of leviathans were scattered across the wastes behind him, if only he knew where to look.

"A great forest grew here," Ashkoliiz said softly next to Bijaz. "Right where we are standing. He marched out of the trees and saw the waters, and he knew that it was good."

Her words had the ring of scripture more than of history. Bijaz stared sideways. The mountebank had lifted her face to take in the cold wind, but her eyes were closed. She looked into the past.

Bijaz realized he was feeling the touch of the noumenal. The cold wind had a faint, flat taste. His hair prickled. The reaper man's scythe was close, the grains of all their lives tossing on that cold breeze.

In that moment, for all its bright and sunny openness, this place frightened him more than the wasps in the mine.

"Where is the Imperator?" Bijaz asked. "We cannot march across this. It buckles like a thing alive. Or more like a thing dying. I do not even see the far shore."

"We are here," she said. "Your precious Imperator reached the Rimerocks, then turned back in the face of what he found there. He had thought to bind himself and the powers around him to the roof of the sky, amid the highest mountains in our part of the world, but he had to settle for this instead."

"The ice?" Bijaz tried to imagine the magick that could bind the strength of an empire, freezing it into place beneath all these tons of water.

Ashkoliiz nodded. "Down there." She turned to her ice bear and her Northmen, releasing a torrent of tangled speech in their sliding tongue. Her hands flickered in their fingertalk.

When Ashkoliiz finished her impassioned speech, Ulliaa glanced at him briefly, then answered.

This was a far more complex discussion than he'd previously seen among them. An argument, he was sure. Iistaa began to growl, then the Northmen shifted into colloquy among the three of them, punctuated by further growls from the ice bear.

He looked around to see DeNardo and Azar using the interruption to rest their men. The Winter Boy and the Tokhari walked amid their troops, inspecting gear and talking to first one then another. The two groups glared at one another and at the little knot around Ashkoliiz at the cliff's edge. There was no camaraderie today. Everyone felt the wrongness of the ice.

The argument subsided. Ashkoliiz looked annoyed—she'd lost ground. He realized in that moment that she answered to the ice bear, and not just as a tutelary spirit.

Something had changed here, something important to Ashkoliiz.

Venal as Ashkoliiz was, Bijaz understood her purposes. Still, he wondered what she truly sought on this greatest of fools' errands. He wouldn't frame the question in front of the others.

"We will strike east to find a gentler descent which can accommodate the horses," she announced. "Once we have reached the ice, we will open the riches of history."

Bijaz wondered what had possessed the Imperator Terminus to find his resting place between nowhere and nowhere else.

ONESIPHOROUS

The Angoumois braced their weapons in an eerie silence.

"Children of Angoulême," Onesiphorous said. "She has brought me here to you. I need to speak with the plantation master."

"You cross water with a fetch, ah." A pruning hook waved nervously.

"One of her servants. I had no other way to reach you."

"Who you be?"

"I am Oarsman, a dwarf of the City Imperishable, though lately much here along the Jade Coast. I have passed through your dark kingdom on my journey."

"Who them, ah?"

"Ambassadors of Lord Mayor Imago of Lockwood, come to meet with the lord of the plantation."

One of the defenders lowered his scythe. Another sheathed an old sword. In moments the barricade was gone.

"Come then," said an unsmiling man with the same golden complexion as Boudin's.

As Onesiphorous walked forward, men behind the front rank cast weighted nets over him, Kalliope, and Jason. The weapons were up again in a moment, poking close enough to draw blood.

"May I do something surprising now?" Kalliope asked through clenched teeth.

"If it's not too late," whispered Onesiphorous.

Their captors parted once more. A thin, pale man with a lugubrious face regarded them from atop a very high horse.

"Welcome," he said in a drawl that smacked of the most affected families of Heliograph Hill. "I apologize for the hospitality. These are dangerous times."

Onesiphorous summoned his tact. "We must treat as equals."

"But why? We are most demonstrably not equals." He looked to his mob of servants. "Kill the big one."

A long pruning hook stabbed close in to the netting, catching Jason deep in the chest. He grabbed the haft with a broad smile. Leaves burst from the wood, crackling like bacon frying. The wielder dropped his weapon with a shriek.

The blooming pole rattled to the ground. Its blade was a smoking fog of rust. The mob of servants fled, leaving their weapons behind.

"Perhaps I shall let you free after all," said the horseman, now alone with his visitors.

Kalliope cut them out without a word. The look she gave Onesiphorous should have flayed the skin from his face.

The rider led them through the now-deserted town. He didn't look back. Onesiphorous was willing to follow—they had not come to fight.

A large mansion loomed at the crest of the hill. It was built high off the ground, with a wide, low roof and huge coastal windows. Most of the latter were thrown open.

Their host rode his horse onto the porch, where he dismounted and showed them to a set of wicker chairs. "Stewart Greathouse, of Honeywood," he said, sitting down. He pulled a large pistol from beneath his own chair. "And you must be traveling magicians."

"We are of the City Imperishable," said Onesiphorous. "Come to restore the Jade Coast to its rightful state."

"You plan to close the mines and ship all those dreadful miscreants home?" Greathouse asked.

Kalliope snorted.

What little patience Onesiphorous still possessed was rapidly eroding. "You are aware of events in Port Defiance?"

"Politics." Greathouse waved a hand airily. He hefted his pistol, sighting down the barrel at Onesiphorous. "If I cared about politics, I'd have moved to the City Imperishable."

"They've stopped all trade along the coast."

"Trade will be back. I've got first quality hemp and indigo here. It can wait in the warehouses awhile longer. The markets will only pay greater prices then." He pointed the pistol at Kalliope. "I can afford to—"

She moved so fast Onesiphorous saw only a blur of leather. The pistol wheeled to one side, discharging through the porch roof in a shower of shattered wood. Kalliope followed up with a hard slap to Greathouse's face. She was back in her chair before anyone else could react.

"Never point a weapon at me unless you are planning to kill me."

Jason just kept smiling.

Onesiphorous decided he was doomed.

"What about you, dwarf?" Greathouse rubbed his cheek. Kalliope's fingertips had drawn blood. "Is this some children's tale where the three of you each demonstrate a mystical power?"

"No," said Onesiphorous. "I've got no power but conviction."

Greathouse raised his hand and snapped his fingers. Gunmen stepped out of a dozen of the coastal windows onto the porch, Angoumois and City men alike. They surrounded the little cluster of chairs in a moment, keeping their distance from Kalliope and Jason. All but one of the weapons was trained on those two.

The last was shoved in Onesiphorous' ear. He could too readily imagine what a pull of that trigger would do to his head, his brains, his thoughts.

"In that case," Greathouse said, "convince me."

Words raced through Onesiphorous' head, pursued by the imminent possibility of a bullet. His legs trembled, his colon clenched, and all he could smell was the sour acid of his own gut.

Greathouse of Honeywood did not care about the City Imperishable. He did not care about Port Defiance. Onesiphorous wasn't even sure the man cared about himself. His captor was embedded in the warm ennui of the south, living out the quiet, dead-end dream of a plantation lord.

He followed that logic. "Nothing will convince you, I'm afraid." Onesiphorous tried to keep the quaver from his voice. "You are beyond passion."

Greathouse yawned. "What? No appeals to my patriotism?"

"You said it yourself. If you cared about politics, you would have moved to the City Imperishable. What you care about is a private place here at the head of the swamps where you can pursue your own indolence without interference."

"Oh, very brave. A nod from me and you'll be wearing your face in your lap, so what do you do? You go on the attack. I *am* impressed."

Onesiphorous cast his eyes at Jason, then Kalliope. She sat almost perfectly still. He figured her for a killing rage, but not even her unnatural speed could outrun bullets.

Jason continued to smile, vacant as ever.

"Attack?" Onesiphorous paid no mind to the cold gun barrel in his ear, or the little clicks which echoed nearby. None whatsoever. "Hardly. I go on the descriptive. You want nothing from the world except a ready market for your crops and an unreasonable distance otherwise. I'm here to help ensure that fulfillment of your desire continues unabated."

"I can see why I haven't had you killed yet." Greathouse steepled his hands and closed his eyes, as if resting. "You are interesting. Do go on."

"If we do not prevail," Onesiphorous said fiercely, "your markets will fail. Someone may yet send a boat up the river, but that will be the last journey, not the first. Your money will run out. There will be no trade in whiskey, silk, or other luxuries. By Dorgau's brass hells, there won't even be *bread*. You'll be eating hemp and indigo, or dining at the Angoumois table."

"Hardly." Greathouse shuddered. "I've no fondness for stewed snake heads."

The gun barrel on Onesiphorous' ear shifted slightly.

"Then help us," he said. "Our little war relies on the hulls the plantation lords can put in the water. We'll fight and win, or we'll fight and die. We win, you get your river trade back and people leave you alone. We die, you get to eat snake head stew and people leave you alone."

Greathouse stared at him awhile. "You *are* a political little animal," he finally said. "Filthy, filthy, filthy. I like that in a man." A smile quirked. "Or even in a half-man. Keep your servants leashed. We shall dine and speak more of this."

Onesiphorous gave Kalliope and Jason a long, searching look. Her lips were pressed white, but she nodded. Jason continued his amiable vacancy.

"Very well," said the dwarf. "Let us reason like men."

"Oh, no, that's what we've been doing." Greathouse waved his hand. The guns were withdrawn. "Men reason with their fists and the size of their throbbing cocks. Now we will reason like women, who talk their way free of their troubles."

"What do you know of women?" Kalliope demanded.

"When you've chained as many to your icehouse walls as I have," Greathouse replied with a slow, malicious smile, "you learn a lot about women. At least while they still can talk." He looked thoughtful for a moment. "Though there's more to be learned after that, too. Just of a different nature."

Kalliope kept her silence this time. The armed servants stepped back through the windows.

Greathouse gave her the vaguest ghost of a bow. "I believe we're having roasted heron stuffed with water chestnuts and fingerling eels. Will you join me?"

They followed him toward chiffon curtains billowing from a wide-thrown double door. As Onesiphorous passed Jason, the dead man threw out an arm.

Onesiphorous met the green glow in his eyes. Jason was back from wherever he'd gone. He pushed a fist toward Onesiphorous. The dwarf opened his hand. A dozen heavy little balls dropped onto his palm, some rolling to the floor of the porch with loud clacks.

Bullets, he realized. From the guns. "You conjured these out of the barrels?"

"I live this borrowed life like a plant in spring," Jason said. "Blooming now in the madness of flowers, soon to go to seed and die once more." He grabbed Onesiphorous' arm so tightly that it hurt. "This is not yet my time."

"Tell me when your time comes," Onesiphorous told him. "I don't want to be standing nearby."

"Believe me, you will know."

They followed Greathouse into the wicker and velvet darkness of the house.

Greathouse finally broke the silence of their meal while rolling up something blue-green from his vegetable plate. "I always like to see a healthy appetite. Who knows when we may meet with an accident? Best to die on a full stomach, I say. With a glass of wine and a woman in hand, if possible."

Onesiphorous suppressed his irritation. "The meal stands quite well with me. My thanks to you and your cook."

"Indeed." Greathouse bit off his *crudité* and chewed slowly. "So tell me. Should I choose to lend you my barges, with whom would you crew them?"

"We are raising the jade miners."

"You do not propose to strip me of my men?"

"Your men are welcome," Kalliope said. "As are your weapons, frankly. But we have been told the Angoumois will not fight shoulder to shoulder. We did not presume to raise troops from the plantations."

"Mmm. And what is in this for me?"

"Restoration of the status quo," Onesiphorous said roughly. He wanted to cut off that line of reasoning before it began. He could not afford to make promises at every plantation.

Assuming they managed to escape Fallow Acres alive.

"Yes." Greathouse's voice was filled with exaggerated patience. "You've claimed that already. I am concerned now with rental fees, degradation of my assets, potential losses due to enemy action, or incompetence on your part."

"I have no monies with which to lease your hulls," Onesiphorous said flatly. "Your boats can rot in their slips, or they can take to the water in hopes of reopening your needed trade." He placed his hands on the table, leaning forward. "You decide, Greathouse of Honeywood. We will be on our way soon enough."

"Not unless I lend my boats," Greathouse said. "You've got nothing but feet. Believe me, they will not get you far without crossing water."

"I can sweeten this pot," said Jason.

Greathouse made a face of mock surprise. "The mute speaks!"

"Hardly. I will raise you a season's crop in one of your fields this coming night. That is the work and wages of your hands for two months or more."

"Then I must incur costs to harvest and store such wondrous bounty," said Greathouse. "So it is not such a great advantage as all that. Still, I would like to see this miracle. Raise me a field of hemp between now and tomorrow's dawn, and all my boats will be yours." He smiled with magnanimity. "I will not even require the loan of your woman."

Kalliope shot Onesiphorous a venomous look. He shook his head slightly. *For the love of the City, woman, do nothing.*

"Meet me at dusk upon your porch with a peck of seeds and a twist of hemp from your most recent harvest," said Jason. "We will walk the fields by moonlight. I will show you true power."

They were escorted to separate rooms by silent servants. The three closeted themselves in the parlor of Onesiphorous' suite. "He is no more to be trusted than a crocodile floating in the river," the dwarf said. "That maniac would gig us like frogs if it suited his desires."

"Little matter," Kalliope told him. "Jason, do you want us to accompany you on this moonlight errand?"

"No." Her brother looked thoughtful. "Let me lead him myself. The lesson will be more salutary when delivered privately."

Onesiphorous marveled. Jason had spent the recent days deep in a spell of his own devising. "Best we spend our evening on the docks. We'll need to cast off at dawn. Kalliope, you and I can ask what water road is best for reaching the next plantation. Names, too, if these people will speak freely."

"Nobody here speaks freely except Greathouse." She stared at her hands. "I for one would like to see the inside of his ice house."

"He was surely making a jest," said Onesiphorous.

"No." She shook her head.

"We need his help, even if he eats babies for breakfast. When this is all over, you can come north with an army and burn him out if it pleases you. For now, hold back."

"And what if it was Beaulise chained inside his ice house?" she asked quietly. "Or me? Would you come back another season?"

"For the City Imperishable," Onesiphorous said gravely, "I would."

"Then you are an idiot." She turned her back on him.

IMAGO

He was tottering around inspecting the armor when Saltfingers arrived. "Your worship's ready to begin the assassinations, I sees," the old dwarf said cheerfully.

"Naturally." Imago shook the dunny diver's hand, then sank to the floor against a plate mail skirt. "And you?"

"Fired from me job by Crusty Alice. Me and the boys went below. We been amusing ourselves closing off the flows from the Limerock Palace and certain quality homes about town."

"Never make an enemy of a dunny diver," Imago said solemnly. "I thank you for my rescue."

"I just crawls the walls. It was them harridan women made me do it."

"Thank you for the candle, too."

"Candle?"

"The little brass holder, with the candle stub. You brought it to me sometime before the rescue."

"Ah. That one. Them what jailed you didn't leave it?"

"No." Imago was too tired for fear, but he felt a cold twinge. "A dwarf came later. Small and pale, much like you. Kept me my sanity, I believe."

Saltfingers glanced about, though they were alone. "Him that's the messenger brung it, I'm thinking."

"The messenger?"

The old dwarf mimed drawing a bow. "We don't say the name, below the stones. It might call him. He's got errands now."

Archer, Imago thought. His companion on that last, mad trip beneath the New Hill. The godmonger had vanished when the Old Gods had appeared with bloody intent, a casualty of the cruel strengths briefly unleashed. "That's terrible."

"That's life as a rent boy for the gods," said Saltfingers matter-of-factly. "Or afterlife, mayhaps."

His world was full of the dead. Far too many of whom were unwilling to remain in that state.

"Will you be at the Festival of Cerea?"

"Would not miss it for all the world, your worship. Now if you'll excuse me, seeing as you're in health, I've got me a chain of office to recover."

The next day the Tribade doctor swathed and veiled Imago in widow's blacks and led him out of the Sudgate. He felt as if each lift of his foot would make him float away. This was as bad as when he'd first been shortened.

Outside, Biggest Sister helped him into a waiting trap.

"Sit quiet, weep some," she told him.

"And don't move that arm about," the doctor added. She pressed something small into Imago's bandaged hand. "A keepsake."

The trap rattled away through the surge of beggars, fishwives, and feral children. He looked at what he had been given. A bullet, deformed and stained. It must be from the wound just above his elbow.

They headed for Water Street and north across town. The quays were chained off, ragged men sitting guard. No more of the blockade-stuck ships had made a departure. Most gangplanks were drawn up. The docks were far more quiet than they should have been, even now.

Heading across the Water Street Bridge, Imago caught a glimpse of the Rug-maker's Cupola looming high above. An enormous banner drooped from the tower—the red crown-and-keys of the Assemblage of Burgesses.

Further north, Imago saw that Ducôte's scriptorium had burned. The great beast of a press slumped among the charred beams. The old dwarf had been alternately a hero and a meddlesome thorn to Imago, but his loyalty to the City Imperishable and its people had been beyond doubt. Imago vowed anew that if given a second chance he would run Wedgeburr through himself.

Waxy white poppies grew in the ashes of the scriptorium. Imago realized he'd been seeing them in the gutters, along little park strips, and even in pots on windowsills. They were everywhere.

They took the Artemis Street turnoff. The driver followed the declining neighborhood to a stand of cypress near the edge of the Potter's Field. He clucked the horse to a halt, then waited.

No questions, Imago thought. He slowly climbed down. Imitating an old woman was not difficult. Out here the widow's blacks made every kind of sense.

He wandered among the wooden markers and the bone piles. It rained; that slow, patient fall with no hint of sunlight. Being outside felt good—he walked in open air, amid the scent of soil and flowers.

Poppies were everywhere. He passed a number of fresh graves, all marked by little stick dolls with curls of blonde-straw hair. Victims of Crusty Alice?

Around another corner he found a patch of turned soil mixed with ash. Before it was a stretch of pavers covered with flowers, food and wine bottles, small coins and toys and papier-mâché roses. Even a plush camelopard with a tiny mummer doll tied to its neck.

His grave.

Many of the offerings had been kicked over and scattered. More had been set in their place. He walked slowly through this evidence of a city's regrets.

"Flowers I brought in the winter," Imago whispered. "In a trial to unseat one madman. Now I will bring a madness of them, to throw this fool out and reopen our ways south."

Imago set his face west toward the River Saltus and the krewe houses, where he might find the Card King and the shelter of the oldest traditions. The Krewe of Faces would embrace him as it had before.

The city is.

Surrounded by half a dozen stubby candles, Imago and the Card King dined that night on pickled mudshark from a great clay jar. It was the first solid food he'd eaten since leaving his cell. At the Sudgate he'd been fed only thin soup. Though the shark tasted vile, Imago enjoyed the sensation of chewing.

Out of his costume, the Card King was just a fat man. Imago, out of his office, was just a bone-thin dwarf with his arm in a sling.

"Your holy dwarf was a terror, there's no doubt," the big man said, chewing valiantly at the rubbery, pale meat.

Imago had been experimenting with sucking on skin, but it mostly tasted of rancid vinegar. The smell had already stunned his nose. His tongue could not be far behind.

"He's off terrorizing the North now," Imago replied. "I miss him, but he needs seasoning."

"Seasoning and a big pot maybe." The Card King laughed. "He took us all for fools and played us as well as the krewes have ever been played. Like I told him, a dwarf is never bound to a krewe king. I can't figure whether you count or not."

"I'm no dwarf," said Imago. "Not in the modern sense, raised in a box and educated a certain way. But I *am* what dwarfs were meant to be."

"The krewes remember." The Card King tore off another strip. "We are making ready a special stage." He grinned, predatory as the freshwater shark they were trying to eat. "Crusty Alice will shit his silk drawers."

"You fancy a lashing and a dump in the river?" Imago asked curiously.

"I fancy getting that fool out of this city's business." The Card King was suddenly serious. "You did a far better job of keeping the sewers clear and the streets paved. And somehow I'm thinking you were making more progress on our difficulties in the water trade."

"We're all going to be killed if we stand openly against him."

"No. Not with you in our midst. Besides, your Marelle has thought up clever surprises for the day of your return."

Imago chewed some more. "Where may I sleep?" he finally asked.

"I threw an armload of straw into Dorgau's Grip." The Card King pointed toward the back of the warehouse where a giant hand hung in the tangled shadows. "It should be comfortable enough."

"My thanks, and good night."

"Don't piss on the floor. Use the jars by the tool-room door."

Imago picked his way among the ropes and cables stretching across the warehouse. He carried one of their candles against the shadows. The dark was difficult for him now.

He was not looking forward to his dreams.

The next day the krewe worked to bring down the costumes and set-pieces. Imago noted no dwarfs among them.

It was a strange sight. Light filtering through high, grimy windows gave everything the faded look of an old painting. The giant heads, the painted backdrops, the huge props violated his sense of scale. They were all dwarfed here. Paint was being lathered about in great quantities, enough to make the wax in Imago's ears run.

He tried several times to offer assistance, but was waved off. "It's a bloody great lot of jobs," the Card King finally told him, "that are mostly held for life. Let them do their work."

So Imago found a seat on an overturned crown and watched a pageant of history being assembled.

Eventually he began to see the pattern in the chaos. The Krewe of Faces was building a new stage out of parts of three or four others which they tore apart with great enthusiasm. It was big, articulated in the center to make the tight corners of the traditional festival processional route. A giant figure stood on each half of the stage.

The front figure was an ugly woman. She was a large puppet, with an operator inside working the ropes and guys to manage the movements. She was designed to lean over and stand back up repeatedly, while bending her head back and forth.

The rear was a dwarf. He was not articulated at the middle, but instead had his arms raised high. A group of women worked on the movement of those arms.

When someone climbed onto the stage to test the fit of a broad-brimmed hat, Imago realized what he was seeing—him as the Lord Mayor striking Crusty Alice in the buttocks. When she bent over, her skirt opened like a pair of curtains.

He went to find the Card King. "We'll all be killed out of hand for that float back there."

"The main stage?" The Card King laughed. "It's naught but a Judy show made large for the kiddies. Ask anyone."

"That excuse will last until Wedgeburr gets a look at it." Imago made a pistol out of his hand. "We know how the First Counselor settles disputes."

"You'd be a man who understands the science of politics. But people are not the same as politics."

"If I knew politics," Imago told him, "I wouldn't be where I am today."

"True." The fat man squinted. "You'd likely be dead in the riots last winter."

Imago wondered where this conversation was headed.

"The krewes have their own lore," the Card King continued slowly. "We never write it down, but true as anything old can be. I'd have the hide off one of mine who told a squid any of this, but seeing as I'm krewe king, I can do as I please when the need is at hand."

Imago waited. Patience wasn't so hard for him these days.

The fat man hummed tunelessly a moment, then:

"When the last one left
"And passed the gates
"Twelve remained
"Beneath their fates
"They crept below
"The cold cold stones
"Leaving only us
"To carry their bones."

He gave Imago a slow, shrewd look. "Your holy dwarf knew the right of it, that winter day we all went down to the plaza. There Jason killed him who was never supposed to have returned, and you came up out of the ground like an early spring bulb. Here was a new day for the City Imperishable."

"Bijaz told me a little." Imago tried to recapture the details of a hasty conversation. "Why you don't have dwarfs in your krewes."

"Right. Because the krewes remember. Old Terminus took most of the gods away. They were a bloody lot in those days, on the back of a big and bloody empire. He saw what was to come, the City Imperishable torn by enemies and time. He aimed to change things while they could still be changed. He did the impossible, and reset the balance."

"You're the old priests," said Imago. "The ones who carry their bones."

"Almost right." The Card King smiled. "I knew you were a smart man. Before Terminus, it was the dwarfs who tended the gods. Cut down in their youth as sacrifices, the pain of the boxes feeding the holy fires. Find an antique growing box and look at the inlays. You'll see the older story there, still remembered for a while after Terminus."

"But no more," Imago protested, "not after the gods left. We—the dwarfs have tended the fortunes of the City Imperishable ever since."

The Card King shrugged. "Waste little, want less. The temples were cast down. The priests of that time were out of work, those who hadn't departed to the sound of trumpets. They knew numbers and letters better than most.

"After, some of us took up the tasks. The twelve Old Gods who had laid themselves down rather than go adventuring need tending as well. That's why there's twelve festivals and twelve krewes. We keep them laid down, and remember what purpose the City dwarfs truly serve."

That sparked another memory for Imago. "Bijaz had told me that the gods of the Temple District were all *arrivistes*."

"Exactly. Come in on boats or the backs of camels or the fevered dreams of street drunks turned prophet. So many that none ever rise to the top. Gods here have the same problem the government has. Bring all the power to one place, and the beast that is our city remembers what it was. The krewes scratch its stone ears and soothe dreams of ancient power. So do the dwarfs, just by being alive."

"And so you aim to scratch Wedgeburr as well."

"Right off his lily arse." The Card King's voice was hard as street cobbles.

BIJAZ

One of the Northmen found him before dawn. How had he ever thought they looked alike as twins? Ashtiili's nose was flatter, where it had probably been broken once.

Bijaz nodded. "You are from the ice, yes?"

Ashtiili met his gaze. Not challenge, just a reminder. *I am human, as are you.* To these Northmen most people were just talking animals. To be human was something deeper.

Bothering to remember his name was a great honor they'd accorded to him.

Finally Ashtiili spoke. "Not this ice." His accent was thick but his Civitas was clear.

"Beyond the Rimerocks?"

Another nod. "Knees-of-the-Sky, we say." Ashtiili set his right hand on Bijaz's left arm. "Stand away from the bindings." He walked back toward the fires.

Bindings, thought Bijaz. *What bindings?*

There were bindings aplenty. The might and majesty of a lost empire, bound to the bones of its last true Imperator. Whatever bound the ice to this great valley in the desert. In all, too many bindings to be wary of.

He held out one hand. Grain flowed from his open palm. A tiny butterfly jittered in climbing spirals until the cold updraft caught it and tore the insect from Bijaz's sight.

The men had abandoned their excited chatter in favor of a slowed step with heads tucked low. Even the horses fought their reins.

Bijaz found himself walking with Ashtiili. Both picked their way through ankle-high layers of rock protruding from the stony soil.

"There is an old word used among hermetic orders," the dwarf said. "*Omphalos.*

It means navel, or center. The ice here is an *omphalos*."

"You southerners hoard ancient words."

Bijaz looked sidelong at Ashtiili. "Hoard them perhaps like family silver, to be drawn out again at sudden need."

"I have another ancient word," Ashtiili told him. "*Telos*. The end."

"How can something be both *omphalos* and *telos?*"

Ashtiili stopped and kicked some gravel aside, then used a rock to draw a spiral in the crumbing gray soil. "Southern world, here." He pointed to the center of the spiral. "*Omphalos*." He pointed to where the line emerged from itself to trail off. "*Telos*."

The Northman scuffed his drawing away, then scribed a series of concentric circles. "*Omphalos*." He pointed at the center. His hand traced the outer circle. "*Telos*. Here, all circles same."

Bijaz stared at the figure as a squad of DeNardo's lights clattered by, gear jingling and leathers creaking. After a moment he came to a conclusion. "And so the worm swallows its tail."

"Southern thought," said Ashtiili. "Not right, not all wrong." He scuffed his drawing again, cast his stone away, and resumed walking.

Bijaz trotted along beside, thinking that over. Was the Imperator Terminus both the source and ending of the empire? That made no sense. No one was immortal, not even the gods themselves. With the passage of enough time one would become so lacquered with the armor of experience as to have no volition left.

But the last Imperator must have bound something to himself far greater than a mere throne. Else he could not have marched into history bearing armies and gods and treasure on his shoulders.

If Ashkoliiz was right, the power of the old empire was trapped here at the center of this desert. Who would want to let it loose?

Northmen, apparently.

He'd been told that if you went far enough into the North you would rise so high that you could see more than one sun. They moved in a line along the axis of the world, spaced a day apart. No matter if that was true, the idea had a certain metaphorical beauty.

The Northmen came from beyond the Rimerocks. Perhaps they stood as children at the gates of their ice palaces and looked southward at the string of suns sliding across the plate of the world.

It would give them a very strange view of life.

Late that afternoon the land opened up into a steep-walled valley that sank into the rise of the hill, leading to a break in the cliff. A cold wind blew out of the gap as they made camp. Frost settled with the darkness to make for the chilliest night yet.

Huddled beneath his cloak, Bijaz awoke with the dawn. His hair prickled again. *This day will bring regret*, he thought.

That was clear enough even without a nudge from the noumenal world. The dangers of the ice were obvious. Ashkoliiz couldn't plan to walk back west across that broken, frozen hell.

Two hours down the valley, as they made their way out onto the ice, that was exactly what Ashkoliiz proposed. "We will break into teams of six," she announced. "Each carrying ropes."

It was cold as Dorgau's hells. The wind blew wet and hard. Bijaz's skin hardened like pebbles.

"Lady," said Azar, reining his horse in tightly. "The mounts will not walk this. Even if we force them, they will break legs or founder with fright."

Ashkoliiz gave him a look which should have singed his moustaches. "I've always heard that Tokhari could ride through the hells and come back with a fire for the night's supper. Perhaps I mistook you for a man."

"I am a man." His voice was tight with shivering anger. "But I am not a fool. Only a fool takes horses over ice. Especially dirty, broken ice like this, shot through with old god magick." He nodded at Bijaz. "Your pardons."

Bijaz smiled politely.

Ashkoliiz was clearly in a killing mood. This close to their goal, her former aplomb had eroded almost entirely. "Then you will dismount and slay the miserable animals here," she declared.

One of the mounts whickered. Thirty-three men, Tokhari and Yellow Mountain tribesmen alike, rested hands on weapons.

It would be rank mutiny, pure and simple.

Bijaz cleared his throat, wondering what in all of Dorgau's brass hells he was going to say.

They all stared at him. "Friends," Bijaz began. *Now there is a classic opener.* "Men of the City Imperishable." *Wrong. None of the horsemen were City men.* "Adventurers." *That ought to cover it.* "We are very close to our goal. In quarreling now, you bicker at the gates of history. Blood shed here will later be remembered in shame. We have traveled and fought and died to come to this dreadful place. Do not discard everything for the sake of pride."

He turned to Ashkoliiz. "Lady, I pray you listen to the horse masters. They know their animals as you know men." Then he bowed to Azar. "Free horsemen. I pray you listen to the lady. She knows history the way you know horse." Bijaz spread his arms wide, addressing all. "I counsel you to detail five men to keep the mounts. The rest may march onward in company. Otherwise, the horsemen will not witness the opening of the gates. Otherwise the Northern Expedition will be too small to break them down."

Bijaz folded his arms and shivered, waiting to see if blood would be shed. He could see the fire in Ashkoliiz's blue-white eyes, the twitch of her face as she struggled to recall her own words.

Azar broke the stalemate first. "I will stay with the horses, along with any others of the riders who wish to." He dipped his head to Ashkoliiz and Bijaz. "You go open the doors of history. I shall be the first to hear your report."

The already reduced Northern Expedition left three more men with Azar. They walked on much of the day, keeping a ragged formation. The pace was poor. Bijaz was distracted by the wind reaching through his clothing straight to his skin, the nagging scent in the air—a mix of the electrick and the noumenal.

Around the middle of the afternoon the bear gave out a bellowing roar, then raced across an ice ridge.

"We are almost here!" Ashkoliiz shouted. "Hasten!"

Bijaz resolutely kept his pace as everyone lengthened their strides. As a result he was the last to see what lay before them: Pillars were carved in the rock face, topped by an entablature. The porch below was lost in the ice. His attention was caught by what was between the pillars, above the ice and below the roof.

Paper.

The wasps had flown here from the mine, then sealed themselves into Terminus' final resting place.

Ashkoliiz was already haranguing the men to attack the paper wall. Ulliaa, Amalii, and Ashtiili were deep in consultation with the ice bear. Bijaz vividly recalled how awful the wasps had been in the mine. Here, now, even though they were on open ground, the fight would be much harder.

He picked his way off the ridge toward the formation. Fire was the answer to the paper. Fire, which cost a godling nothing if an honest man set it with a match.

By the time Bijaz caught up, Ashkoliiz and DeNardo had agreed to storm the tomb before dark. "Tear it open with fire," Bijaz said.

"Yes." DeNardo was focused on the moment. "We are already to be thinking that."

"You knew about the wasps?"

"We knew there might be defense," Ashkoliiz said acerbically.

Of course there is a defense, Bijaz thought. The gates of history did not just sit waiting for any fool with a wheelbarrow to happen past. But giant wasps?

DeNardo set fire to the paper plug on the tomb. With oil splashed freely, it burned merrily awhile until it slumped in a mass of ash like a lava-edged rose. No insects came boiling out. A ragged cheer was swiftly shushed by DeNardo.

Great bronze doors had been concealed beneath the paper plug. They stood open, broken by the long years of ice.

"To be casting in a torch," shouted DeNardo.

A lithe man sprinted toward the open doors, hurled a pitch brand into the shadows beyond. He then turned to run back. The resulting explosion sent a spinning chunk of ice that sheared his head off. Dark red blood sprayed the frozen ground directly before DeNardo's line of soldiers.

The first wasp emerged, flying erratically. The compound eyes were cloudy, wings draggled. Its thorax was visibly swollen. A distended mass the color of rotted flesh swung below the smooth curve of chitin.

Pierce, their lost light troop commander, peered out of the mass. The man's eyes rolled and his lips moved silently. Agony flared in Pierce's eyes as he pled for death.

Half a dozen troops broke and ran screaming. DeNardo shot one in the back with his pistol, shouting, "To be stopping now!" The wounded man flopped on the ice like a landed trout, while the other five dropped to their knees, facing away from the wasp and its hideous cargo.

Bijaz could hear someone crying.

DeNardo turned to the wasp and raised his weapon. The prisoner's face twisted.

Enero's man pulled his trigger a second time. Pierce's forehead shattered. The wasp collapsed in a spray of ice. This time DeNardo let the men cheer.

The giant insect's body shuddered, then began to move in lumpy waves. The swelling peeled off. Chitin flaked away with a startling suddenness.

Small bats flew out of the wasp. They had monkey faces bearing an uncanny resemblance to Pierce. Each screamed, "Ruin, ruin, ruin," in high-pitched echoes of the dead man's voice.

More of the troops broke. DeNardo stood his ground, sword at the ready, as the bats swirled into the sky.

"Eater of Forests," said one of the Northmen in a voice compounded of fear and awe. Three of them set off in a run *toward* the entrance.

Bijaz followed the Northmen. He was forced to duck as the next wasp erupted with another silently screaming face embedded in its thorax.

ONESIPHOROUS

Dawn found Onesiphorous and Kalliope sitting in a dory at Greathouse's dock. They'd chivvied a map from Honeywood's bargemaster, and descriptions of the channels. None of them had experience navigating the swamp country, but overland was no option at all.

They'd also set a date a month hence for the barges to be in the water.

The night had been long and warm. They'd seen nothing of Jason or Greathouse.

"He must be burning himself up," Onesiphorous said as the east stained red.

"My brother?" Kalliope toyed with a paddle. "As he told us, his is the madness of flowers. They give everything to grow in spring, then spend their short lives going to seed. I think Bijaz had a purpose in remaking Jason, even if the old dwarf didn't know it himself."

"He is the luck of the City. Perhaps the City Imperishable had need of whatever Jason is."

"The Green Man of spring," she said. "Who may wither come summer, but blooms now like a colored fire."

When Jason came down the path, he was followed by half a hundred Angoumois field hands bearing long fronds of hemp. Greathouse was nowhere in evidence. The scent of the broken-off plants was overwhelming.

Jason walked out onto the dock and stared down into the boat. "I could stay forever among these fields."

"We have work to do." Onesiphorous kept kindness in his voice.

"Yes." Jason climbed into the boat.

Onesiphorous noticed green stains on the man's hands, and darker ones as well. Soil? Blood? What had he used to fertilize his night's work?

They cast off. The Angoumois lit the green hemp cuttings, though the plants would only smolder. They tossed the smoking bundles into the river to follow the current awhile.

"Are you well, brother?" Kalliope asked, but Jason only leaned to the back of the boat and closed his eyes.

Onesiphorous paddled and wondered what had been set upon the land here. Something that made great ripples followed them closely, but it did not move against them. He figured it for one of her horses and made his peace with the rising dawn.

The weeks which followed were a foetid blur of muddy channels, slow currents, and overgrown riverbanks, punctuated by meals of fish, fish, and more fish, with occasional stops at plantations.

With every visit, the process of negotiation became easier. Arguments were refined, objections answered repeatedly. The most difficult problem solved itself—the price of inertia was growing higher as summer loomed. Still there were no boats from Port Defiance. Any barges sent down did not return. While certain crops could hang in drying barns—turkweed and hemp, for example—others coming in as early harvest from winter plantings wanted shipment to market. Muskmelons rotting by the hundredweight on the docks improved no one's fortunes.

He fell into a rhythm with Kalliope and Jason. The Green Man slept most of the daylight hours, and spent his nights standing knee deep in water staring upward. It did not seem to matter whether the canopy was stars or leaves. He never attracted leeches or insect bites.

Onesiphorous and Kalliope sailed the boat, kept their maps updated, made notes and collated inventories of promised barges and other resources, set up and struck camp, and did what they could to advance their cause.

Jason awoke whenever they approached a plantation or an Angoumois village. Just the sight of his calm, smiling face seemed to be enough to stimulate a flurry of worshipful attention and gifting from the swamp people. Onesiphorous quickly learned to refuse almost all of what was offered.

Among plantationers, the Green Man was a figure of mixed awe and dread.

IMAGO

Imago wasn't certain that a mocking carnival would have the intended effect. Everyone in the City Imperishable preferred that the noumenal remain within its own realm, while their daylight world carried on by sensible and solid paths. The Card King proposed to raise the ghosts of past power against Wedgeburr.

That struck Imago as being the opposite of a solution.

Nonetheless he watched the krewe prepare, sitting idly atop his overturned crown until a harried tailor thrust a pile of black cloaks into his hands. "Here, baste the hems," the man said, then scuttled off with his needle-filled vest flapping behind him.

Imago didn't know what a baste was, but he set to work. The needlework was inexpert, to say the least, but he had something to do.

Someone eventually brought him a small bucket of beef broth and a dark loaf with a wedge of blue-veined cheese. He couldn't yet bring himself to eat from a bucket, but the rest was a treat upon his aching gut. Finally, he had an appetite again.

As the light darkened overhead, a very short woman found him. *No,* he realized, Marelle, wigged and cloaked.

"Hello," Imago said. The stirrings which Kalliope had raised in him a month or two ago seemed to be returning.

"Lord Mayor." She hugged him.

"I'm glad you survived that day," he told her.

"I turned aside for a moment, entering the Great Hall." She looked ashamed. "It saved my life. I was three days leaving the Limerock Palace, but the servants hid me."

"Later, tell me of what happened while I was away."

Marelle sat next to him on the crown. She pulled one of the waxy poppies from beneath her cloak. "Here," she said, handing it to him. "Do you know what they call this now? Lord Mayor's memory."

Imago took the flower and smiled. "Another name Wedgeburr hates, I would imagine."

"Wedgeburr hates much. Even his own party within the Burgesses has sickened of him. Word is that he has not called them into session for several weeks, for fear of being voted out."

He found that news interesting. "Will the Assemblage bring him down?"

"Who knows? We need to retake the city. Soon, I am afraid." She touched his too-thin arm. "Strange flights of creatures are rumored to come out of the North. I fear that Ashkoliiz woman has disturbed something. The tales are fantastic, but their telling continues with every new arrival from upriver."

"I assume the situation in Port Defiance is starving us."

She snorted. "You were imprisoned when the Trade Control Act passed the Burgesses. All foreign assets in our banks and trading accounts have been frozen, pending seizure by the Intendant-General."

"If that process is completed, we are finished," Imago said. "Syndics in this city hold paper on ships and cargos ten thousand miles away. *That* is the true basis of our wealth. A few months' blockade of the manufacturing trades is not enough to unseat a thousand years of trust and well-secured vaults. But such a foolish law would be."

"And so we need Wedgeburr out," Marelle said gently. "And we need you back as Lord Mayor. Believe me, I understand why the power must be spread about. I've seen far, far more of this city than most people ever will."

"But you're not old," Imago teased.

She smiled sweetly. "And you're no liar, either."

He slipped his arm behind her back. She didn't move away.

They talked on awhile, but soon sitting close seemed more important than the words. Later that evening, when the bustle had died down, Imago and Marelle climbed the stairs to the costume racks. They found a little nest of velvets behind an array of woolen plaids. Lying down together, he teased off her wig to run his fingers through her beautiful pale hair.

"You shouldn't do this," Marelle said. He started to pull away, ashamed. "Your health, I mean!"

"I've been too long without." Imago wasn't willing to meet her eye.

"*You* think you have been too long." She reached over and pulled him close. "You cannot imagine how it has been for me."

Lying with his face against her neck, he undid one button of her blouse. She said nothing, so he continued to undress her. Marelle's breasts were as pale and small as she was, nipples barely colored, but they fit well into his mouth. She found his cock soon enough, which fit her hands quite nicely. He ached to take her like a boy, but they had no grease with them, so when they finally coupled, it was as man and woman.

Imago had expected to come on the moment, after so long without—almost a year, he thought—but as he slid his cock into her, staring into her pale eyes in the costumed shadows, he found himself firmer and firmer. He plunged into her until she bucked, clawing at his shoulders and giggling her way into tears. He pulled out and spent himself in the pale fuzz about her cunny.

After, she held him close to her breast.

"I recall," she said, "so much." Tears shook in her voice and her chest shuddered, but she would not let him up to comfort her. "When I brought the archives to the City Imperishable, I was a heroine for a day. Memories of the empire were fresh then, and so reminding them of what was falling quickly soured their affection. The students had no use for me. I embarrassed their tales of their own courage. I made lies of the nobility of their august professors who'd fled like rabbits before the fox.

"No man likes a woman who stood where he would not." She took one hand away to rub her neck. "When they worked up the pot-bravery to beat me to the ground, then showed me the rope, I thought I was ready for it. But the City would not let me die."

"What do you know?" Imago asked quietly.

"What everyone knows," she told him. "The City is. The difference is that I know *what* the City is."

He tucked Marelle close. They lay a long while, breathing in rhythm, until it was time to make love again. This time he used the juices of her cunny to finger her like a boy. He took her the same way without any grease but that, splitting her open like a pomegranate until they both exploded into hot, thrilling agony, her arse pressing against him as she thrashed like a hooked fish, his seed spilling deep within her.

Then they slept, tangled like monkeys, sharing dreams as their breath mingled in the deepening shadows.

The krewe assembled their processional the next day. The light was dim, which spoke of poor weather outside, but the Krewe of Faces seemed unconcerned. The stage with the Lord Mayor and Crusty Alice was being tested.

He watched the puppets go through their motions. They would draw a crowd, even amid the overflowing streets of a processional, but the figures would also draw fire.

They'd tried this before, invoking the old magicks and lore of the City Imperishable. It had worked during the Trial of Flowers and at the battle in Terminus Plaza. He doubted they could pull the same trick a third time.

Wedgeburr might be as cracked as Lord Logdancer's chamber pot, but the First Counselor was not a stupid man.

The Krewe of Faces, like all the krewes, was a marching society. It was decidedly not a military unit. Even Enero's Winter Boys had been slaughtered by Wedgeburr. These people would stand no chance. Not unless Wedgeburr was sleeping and his bailiffs drunk to the last man. Imago pushed out on the floor, looking for the Card King and hoping for Marelle.

He found them inspecting a large crate of black hats. The headwear was made of some cheap fur—rabbit?—in imitation of the Lord Mayor's formal attire.

Imago realized what the Card King had meant by the surprises for the day. "You're going to dress everyone as me."

"Yes." Marelle looked pleased. She was clad from a costume box with bloused pants, a linen shirt, and a leather vest. "That will sow confusion and aid your revelation of yourself. Or your escape. Whichever proves the more needful."

The Card King nodded, a smile on his face as well. He was in his jeweled, glittering red satin, ready for his role.

"I forbid it," Imago said flatly. "They shot two dozen people during a session of the Assemblage for simply following me. The bailiffs will have orders to stop this sort of thing. Quickly and fatally."

"Oh, it gets worse," the Card King said cheerfully. "We've got over thirty Crusty Alices as well."

"You'll *all* be killed!" he shouted. "And your krewe houses burned in the bargain! I will not be a party to this, not in my name."

"You're still dead, dear," Marelle reminded him. "This is in your memory, not your name."

"Are there not enough graves in the Potter's Field for you?"

"I'm afraid we've gotten into the habit of standing up for ourselves." The Card King cracked his knuckles, then made a pair of meaty fists one atop the other. "The City Imperishable belongs to its people, not to its government. Not you, not the Burgesses."

"The City belongs to *itself.*" Marelle's voice was urgent. "Mistake that at your peril."

Imago turned to her. "Is that the secret you have lived so long to protect?"

She glanced at the Card King. "Not now, Lord Mayor."

"Your confidences are your own," the Card King said. "But the krewes remember much that is lost, mistress. We march to keep the memories alive. If we hid when affairs grow difficult, we'd not be worthy of our sacred honor."

"Everyone has secrets," Marelle replied graciously.

Imago was ready to explode. They were not listening to him. "It's no *secret* that Wedgeburr will grow berserk at this."

"Precisely," said the Card King. Marelle nodded vigorously.

"And you have a charm against bullets?"

"Even better." She smiled, her eyes sparkling. "We have bought off the bailiffs."

"*How?*"

"Selsmark is a fool blinded by the power of his office. Most of the Burgesses are not, not when their own skins are at stake. Wedgeburr came to power on the backs of two dead bailiffs. Even the Imperatorials can see how their fortunes will eventually run under Wedgeburr." She leaned close. "He doesn't have the kind of grip on power that Prothro held. This time there's no Imperator Ignatius at the middle of it like some mad spider."

"Wedgeburr stands alone," said the Card King. "But for his lap dog Selsmark."

"The Tribade convinced the bailiff serjeants," Marelle continued. "Robichande was a hard man, and strange in his thoughts, but he was respected. The redcoats know who killed him. Their commanders will ensure the men go out with blank loads today. It won't be a mutiny, it will be an error."

"Better they not shoot at all," said Imago. It sounded insane to him—counting on a handful of notoriously loyal men to betray their oaths to the Assemblage of Burgesses.

"Better," she said. "But we cannot do everything."

The Card King nodded. "The processional is meant to goad Wedgeburr into the sort of angry, lunatic fit you encountered the night you were arrested. If he comes unhinged in front of a street full of people, he is undone. Even his remaining loyalists will not stand with him then."

"They are weak enough already," Marelle added.

"Your plan depends on much you cannot control," Imago warned. "And a great deal of faith."

Marelle reached out and touched his chin. "But no one knows we have *you*." She handed something to Imago—a leather pouch that might hold a timepiece or a compass.

When he tugged it open his chain of office poured out.

"This was dumped into the drains by one of Wedgeburr's men, just after the massacre in the Great Hall," the Card King said. "Your Saltfingers found it somewhere down below. He is a strange little man, but I expect he could find a way into Dorgau's last hell if there was a need."

"If it has a foundation, he probably could," said Imago.

They were all crazed. Absolutely crazed.

BIJAZ

The five of them skidded flat on the ice. A trailing leg brushed Bijaz from above. The wind howled as three more wasps crawled from the smoldering entrance.

In the quiet which followed, the ice bear rose, claws digging into the frozen surface, to sprint for the doors. The other four trailed behind. Bijaz was last.

Where in the brass hells was Ashkoliiz?

Following on the heels of Iistaa, they pelted into the deep shadows within. The ice dropped off in an unexpected slope. Each slipped to plunge into the darkness. Only Bijaz screamed.

He fetched up hard against a solid, furry mass. The ice bear, of course, breathing hard. A stone surface beneath him had taken a goodly toll on his joints. It was slick with thin, frozen runnels. Bijaz assumed from the rustling around him that Ulliaa, Amalii, and Ashtiili were alive. Their small noises echoed in a huge space.

Were an enemy lying in wait, they would already be butchered. His greater fear was that another covey of those wasps hung overhead.

Bijaz reached back into his memory of the fragment of the sun and opened his hand to a bright shining light.

Pillars carved from the living rock rose to a vaulted ceiling. Behind him was the ice slope where the frozen sea outside had pushed in. More pillars receded into distant shadows.

Nothing was here but a dais some distance away in the lung-scraping cold. No wasps, no treasure, no army.

A sharp shriek echoed as DeNardo, Ashkoliiz, and three of her men slid down. One of the men bled from a scalp wound, and Ashkoliiz's coat was torn.

The Northmen caught her, letting the others fend for themselves. She brushed the ice chips from her knees, then looked around. "Are you lighting our way, little god?" Ashkoliiz asked.

He clenched his fist. The brightness faded to a dull red. Glare shot between his fingers. "I am lighting *my* way, lady. If you choose to follow, I shall not bar your steps."

The ice bear groaned. Bijaz looked at DeNardo. Did the man understand that this creature had been the mastermind behind Ashkoliiz's antics? He wasn't quite ready to ask for Iistaa to be shot, and he wasn't certain that he'd be heeded if he did.

DeNardo's gaze slid away without acknowledgment. Bijaz began walking toward the dais.

The platform was topped by a stone coffin. The sepulcher's lid had been drawn out of true. Bijaz mounted the three steps and looked at what he'd come so far to find. The only decoration was a single line of lettering carved across the top that read *Terminus, Ego*.

Bijaz knelt at the corner where the interior was exposed. He raised his glowing hand, flooding the resting place of the last true Imperator with light.

A man lay within, curled on his side. His skin was tight leather over the rack of his bones, stretched open in places. The bottom was filled with fresh leaves, sharp-scented pine needles, and dead wasps of the usual size.

Neither silver nor gold. No battle flags nor temple arks nor jeweled chests. Nothing but a dead man.

Only the bedding made Bijaz wonder. He'd seen no broad-leafed trees this side of the Silver Ridges. Even the last of the struggling desert pines were days of marching behind them.

As for the wasps…

He realized Ashkoliiz, DeNardo, and the Northmen were crowded close, staring within.

"Where is being the history?" DeNardo finally asked.

"Him," Bijaz said.

Behind them the ice bear roared. DeNardo turned, grunted, and fired his pistol twice.

Iistaa was tearing the head off one of DeNardo's horsemen. Bijaz once more called down the fire of the sun. Flames washed over her. The bear dropped the lifeless body of the trooper and stalked toward Bijaz, fur on fire.

"Back!" the dwarf shouted. The reaper man was close, the grain bending flat in the whirlwind of his passing as the moon ate the sun to noontime darkness. "Back! Beyond your mountains!"

Iistaa opened her mouth to roar. Bijaz poured fire into her throat. His legs shivered. The sepulcher groaned as it was eroded to dust by the demands of his powers. Within the ruins of the tomb a great buzzing arose.

The ice bear coughed twice, then stumbled. She fell to her knees before Bijaz in a mass of flame. The sepulcher collapsed in a cloud of wasps and leaves circling one another. Tiny blue and green fires played within them.

His defense against the ice bear had unleashed whatever slept here. Had she attacked him for that very reason? So he could begin the disaster?

"The Eater of Forests!" shouted one of the Northmen.

"No!" screamed Ashkoliiz.

"Run," said Bijaz quietly.

The glissade of the icefall was already turning to slush. Great crackling noises echoed from the doors higher up. Bijaz struggled to climb the frozen slope, desperate to reach the outside before the frozen sea melted and flooded into the tomb. The bright light of his hand stabbed into the ice, highlighting dark shapes trapped within the flow.

Men, he realized. Horses. Banners roiling as if they had been caught mid-flood. Something with eyes that gleamed—a statue, six-armed and glowing.

Here was Terminus' last army with its train of priests and gods and treasure.

He glanced back. Four people clambered after him. Something that sparked fitfully followed at a distance. The damned bear yet lived.

Bijaz climbed faster. The ice beneath his hands was turning to slush. He would soon be caught in a waterfall with a drowned army and its angry gods.

"If I am the City's luck," he gasped, "then this is the cast of my die." He willed the Numbers Men to hear him, though they were notoriously deaf to prayer. "I must carry these tidings home."

A flight of wasps buzzed past. They trailed green leaves glowing with pale fire.

The Eater of Forests.

Bijaz had no doubt that the horrors were bound for the City Imperishable. Trees, it had all been trees from the beginning. Not the march of them, but the death of them.

He stumbled onto the portico, knee-deep in slush. Dead men and open water were spread before him. The wind bore a stale warmth like old, hot iron, reeking of the noumenal. The sound of large things on the move echoed in the distance.

Bijaz struggled away from the porch to gain a solid rock and so pull himself above the melting sea. DeNardo followed close on, dark as a seal with the soaking water. He turned and helped Ulliaa out. The Northman moved as if in great pain. Ashkoliiz was next, cursing monotonously under her breath. Amalii followed, limping badly.

"Where is Ashtiili?" Bijaz asked.

Ulliaa grunted. "We remember him."

Something very large moaned out upon the waters.

"You!" Ashkoliiz's voice was savage as she stabbed at Bijaz with a finger. "You ruined everything."

"I saved *something*. Including your miserable life. Be silent if you wish to retain it any longer."

The ensuing silence could have been measured in blade widths. After a few heartbeats, everyone sagged.

"Now being what?" DeNardo finally muttered.

"Leave," Bijaz said flatly. "Immediately. Get as far as we can, as fast as we can." He stared up the cliff. "Do we have any rope? I don't fancy trying to make it all the way back to that canyon."

Onesiphorous

So it went, throughout the plantation country and well into the month of Avrille. They received occasional word of Beaulise and her fellow shareholders raising the disaffected men of the thumbs. In some cases, miners were coming in to the plantations on their own, poling crude rafts. Onesiphorous advised those planters and overseers who were willing to set aside old grudges to send out boats.

He had little enough notion what he would do with his flotilla of armed men. He wondered what had become of the papers he'd sent on with Silver, whatever kind of princess she actually was, whether a response was on the way. Even if the miners and plantationers struck the corsair colors from Port Defiance, a lasting peace would require the black ships to retreat for good. Onesiphorous had no power to enforce that, not even if the entire City Imperishable were at his back.

He looked to hear from *her* as well—the queen of Angoulême. The waterways were filled with her horses, but none chose to speak.

Their greatest blessing was Jason, settling into a quiet sleep that lasted all the hours of the day and most of the nights. He rarely left the boat, waking only to trail his fingers over the side or mumble to the moon. Onesiphorous was reminded of an insect metamorphosing into something new.

Neither he nor Kalliope were eager to see what Jason would become.

"I have been too long away from the sand," she said as they sat around a fire the night before their last plantation stop. After putting in at the docks of The Fastness, they would turn downstream and east, heading for the rendezvous at the Bay of Snakes.

He poked the flames with a stick. "You told me you'd been called to stay."

"In the City Imperishable." She whetted her knife. "Not here, amid the stench of old mud and the whine of insects. There are no pests in the desert."

"Not even snakes and scorpions?"

"They are not pests. They are children of the sand."

Onesiphorous could see her smiling despite her mood. "The frogs and biting things are children of the swamp."

"Yes. But I am a sandwalker, not a, a, whatever they have here."

"They have *her* here," he said seriously. "Queen of Angoulême. Mother of the swamps."

"Yes, and the only sand here is wet enough to sink a mouse." She leaned against his shoulder. "Jason sleeps amid lengthy green dreams. You chase your city's need through the fogged minds of people addled by heat and distance. Me, I do nothing but wait."

Onesiphorous set his arm around her back. "But what do you wait for?"

Her voice was sad and hollow. "The end of the magick I began when I opened my brother's life to the soil last winter."

"I do not think you will wait much longer." He hugged her closer. "Jason will not sleep forever. Win or lose, the new moon of Mai will draw this to an end. Beyond that, another beginning. Whatever it may be."

She did not kiss him, then or later, but she slipped his hands inside her shirt. They touched awhile, each taking comfort from the other's warmth, though that was the limit of it.

In time, Onesiphorous crouched in the shadows away from the fire and tugged until his seed spilled in dark water. He was shamed at his lust for Kalliope's breasts.

A fish with a wide, pale face surfaced to strike at the floating white dribble which still hung by a narrow string from his cock's tip. The fish burped, then said, "So you found a way to call to me, little City man."

Onesiphorous was so startled he nearly tumbled into the water. Instead he grabbed at a bush, trying to hitch up his pants at the same time. "Hello, lady. You catch me at a poor moment."

The fish laughed.

He plunged onward. "We are almost ready to give challenge."

"As may be. My will and word have passed where they may." The fish's pale eyes gleamed in the light of a moon a day past full.

"Do you have wisdom for me?"

"No," said the fish. "Just amazement at the curiosity of monkeys. As you are free with your seed, you will share it with me back in the heart of Angoulême, ah?"

"When we fight, and have won, I will come back to you."

"You give me a binding, ah. I will not forget." The fish was gone with a flick. Onesiphorous buttoned himself up and stumbled back to the fire.

"You could have done your business here," Kalliope said with a small smile.

"No," he replied curtly. "I could not."

"So you lust to spread your seed within me, but shame to spill it before me? The men of the desert are different." She rolled over and became quiet, but did not move away when he lay down next to her.

He stared at the few stars that glittered through the leaves above their heads and wondered what game he'd just taken on.

Coming back down the rivers, they encountered more traffic. The narrow boats of the Angoumois were out. They saw a few dories as well, and also plantation barges ingeniously armored with bales.

Onesiphorous realized that fire would be their greatest fear.

Barges, boats, rafts—a flotilla spread out on the waters, heading for the Bay of Snakes. Many were loaded with miners, field hands, even Angoumois fresh from the swamp.

"If there are enough men for us to split our force," Onesiphorous said as he paddled, "I would like to assault the corsair ships."

"I have only commanded mounted troops, never on water," she answered, "but I would not generally split a force except at great need and opportunity. I see your need, but what is your opportunity?"

"These barges make me think of fire. If we burn them out, we will have them."

"If we burn them out, they will fight to the last," she pointed out. "That will be bitter and bloody and well beyond what our raw troops will stand for. Look within the other tent, though. If we burn only one or two of their ships, while challenging them hard at sword's point, the corsairs may make a retreat to defend the rest of their hulls. Always leave the enemy a route of escape." She grinned. "Of course, if you have sufficient force, you can cut down every last one of him."

"Then you take command," Onesiphorous said. "You have just shown your fitness over me. Beyond that, I am but a dwarf and mean little to most of our fighters."

"I am but a woman, and mean less."

"I am awake," Jason said. His voice sounded different. It was deeper, and groaned like wood under great pressure.

They both stared. Jason sat up. His skin sloughed away, like a man with a terrible sunburn. The new flesh exposed below was rippled and tan—tree bark.

"We must hurry," he continued. "A death flies out of the North. I can spend little time in this place. I will take on their ships, in keeping with your plan, sister."

Onesiphorous' skin prickled with the noumenal. He felt a powerful desire to slip over the side and take his chances with the mudsharks. All they would do was eat him.

"*Al ka nja*," muttered Kalliope in Tokhari. Her hands began to slide through some complex motion.

"No." Jason reached out. His arm stretched as he did, crackling to extend almost the length of the boat until he closed a fist the size of Onesiphorous' head around his sister's hands. "I am not what you think. This is a magick of the Stonesource, sister. The genius of the desert will not care what walks the soil here for a quarter of the moon."

"You are not meant to be." Her voice was tense. Warm sand began piling around her feet.

One of the paddles sprouted leaves. Jason's fist creaked. She hissed with pain as he tightened it. "You made me."

"Stop," said Onesiphorous. They both looked at him. "Kill each other time and again if you wish, but wait until I've got my thrice-damned City back!" He turned away. Persuasion was the only power he had with these two. "And don't sink this accursed boat, either."

A green monkey sitting precariously on a branch overhanging the water nodded at him. Then it snickered and scampered away.

"We will hold our dispute in abeyance," rumbled Jason. "But make haste. I will soon be too heavy for this little craft."

Two days later, Onesiphorous grounded their keel on a narrow mud beach at the Bay of Snakes. It was afternoon. The tide was slack, beginning to find its way back in. They were still four days before the new moon of Mai, but already over a dozen boats had arrived. Men gathered in temporary camps along the shore.

She would be angry at the mob breaking her trees and fouling her water.

"I am off," he announced. The other two had not spoken in more than a day. "Jason, do you wish men with you, or will you take these ships alone?"

"I will need several volunteers," he rumbled. "Small men who can climb well and do not fear to fight."

"They will be sent to you, with a bigger boat." Onesiphorous stepped over the side and slogged toward the nearest camp.

Kalliope came splashing after. "You're not going to leave him there."

"What else will I do?" Onesiphorous shrugged off the hand she laid on his shoulder. "You fight like children, with the might to level cities."

"I am sorry," she said. "There is too much between us. In any event, I am coming with you. Someone needs to tell you how to hold an army. It is somewhat bigger than a sword."

"I don't know how to hold a sword, either," he admitted. The fight was coming all too soon. He needed to send a message to the Tribade in Port Defiance. He needed to speak with the free Angoumois, or even better, to their queen. He needed to array his men and boats in something resembling battle order. He needed to pray for good weather.

Grasping a sword was the smallest of his worries.

IMAGO

Crazed or not, the processional was ready to march late that afternoon. The Card King rode his huge white gelding in front of the Lord Mayor's stage, surrounded by Crusty Alices. Imago was among a rank of walkers in wide-brimmed fur hats and long cloaks. Children and women, for the most part, pretending to be dwarfs. He wasn't even the shortest of them.

The doors were thrown open to a sodden drizzle. A decent crowd gathered outside even so. Many of them wore black cloaks and hats as well.

A dwarf dashed in from the rain and approached the Card King. After listening a moment, the fat man waved Imago forward. "This one's got a strange tale," he shouted over the noise of the stage creaking into motion.

Marelle stepped out of the Alice line to listen as well.

"There's wasps," the new dwarf shouted. Imago didn't recognize him. "Great swarms of them down near the Limerock Palace. They've settled all over Terminus Plaza."

The Card King looked at Imago. "Is this your doing?"

"Do I look magickal to you?"

Marelle's words were almost lost as the musicians struck up. "We've been hearing about wasps along the docks. Giant ones, though no one knows for sure."

Giant wasps? "Out of the North, I imagine. There's Bijaz put paid to." Imago felt a hot pressure behind his eyes. Worse even than Enero dying. Had he killed all his friends? "We may as well finish it. I still think your plan isn't worth a candied fig, but I don't have a better one."

The Card King gave him a strange look, while Marelle turned away shaking her head. The processional wheezed out into Fish Trap Lane.

Marching amid the Lords Mayor, Imago kept in step with the drums. Someone tossed him one of the strange, waxy poppies. Imago carried the flower high in memory of Bijaz. Soon his impersonators did the same.

The cobbles were slick and the march was long, but he no longer cared.

Imago watched for ambush at Imperatrix Park. All they saw were hordes of shrieking children, laughing as the giant Crusty Alice puppet bent and lifted his skirt to the Lord Mayor's boot. The walkers handed out hats and cloaks which had been tucked into baskets dangling from the side of the stage. There would be dozens more small figures in black by the time they came to Terminus Plaza.

The march slowed near Melisande Avenue. The Lord Mayor's stage inched forward. Volunteers clustered around, chattering. Most clutched poppies now as well. When they broke out into Terminus Plaza, the problem was obvious.

As reported, the Winter Grove was a writhing mass of insects. Wasps hung on the eaves of buildings around the plaza, beneath the arch of the Riverward Gate, everywhere. Their buzzing was a slow, rippling thunder.

The giant Lord Mayor puppet kicked his way into the plaza. A line of bailiffs waited on the wall of the Limerock Palace. Imago felt an intense swell of frustration. He'd trod this measure before.

The Card King led the stage across Terminus Plaza. He avoided the wasp-clouded trees, where some of the palace staff were nervously setting out smoke pots to drive off the insects.

Instead of the mocking laughter they'd meant for this moment, there was nothing but a widening silence. The square emptied as the prudent slipped away.

Only the bailiffs remained. A knot of robed Burgesses stood in their midst. Even in the fading light, Imago could spot Wedgeburr.

The Card King pressed on amid the drizzle which trailed off to an oppressive damp.

The reduced processional creaked to a halt before the Riverward Gate. Without the paraphernalia of jugglers, bead-throwers, walkers, costumes and shrieking crowds, the lone stage was nothing more than a forlorn carnival prop.

Though the sun had dipped below the horizon, a gelid yellow light clung to the sky. The wind had picked up with the sunset to spread the reek of the River Saltus. The cycling hum of wasp wings tore at everyone's hearing.

The bailiffs atop the wall stood at port arms. Wedgeburr, Selsmark, and Fallen Arch stared down, several nervous back-benchers lurking behind them in support.

The Card King raised his fist. "Greetings to the Assemblage of Burgesses from the Krewe of Faces!"

The puppets creaked as the Lord Mayor tried to kick Crusty Alice in the arse. The Alice did not bend and raise her skirt.

"You seem to be lacking a carnival, fat man," shouted Selsmark. Wedgeburr simply shook his head.

A crowd of screaming, laughing citizens might have provoked something, but this was pathetic.

Still grasping his waxy poppy, Imago stepped out of line.

"It does not matter what the people think," the fat man called up, wiping sweat from his face. "The krewes have our purpose, even if we march alone."

"Then rid my square of those horrid wasps," shouted Wedgeburr, to Selsmark's obvious surprise.

Ah, thought Imago, drawing up next to the Card King's stirrup. *They are off their plan now.*

Somehow the Card King managed a laugh. "That is no magick of the krewes. Just the City Imperishable, turning its worst to you. Usurper."

"Treason!" shouted Selsmark.

"Hardly," Imago called out. He dropped his hat and cloak, but continued to cling to the flower. "It was you, Provost, and your pretender there, who committed treason against the City Imperishable by striking down her lawfully appointed executive."

That was hardly a cry to rally battalions, but it made the point.

The wasps continued to hum. Selsmark stood with his mouth open. Fallen Arch smirked. Wedgeburr stared a moment before shouting down, "You are more persistent than a case of fire-piss. I can cure that."

Imago had to believe in the blank cartridges. He raised his flower as if it were a sword. "Strike as you will, cowardly Alice."

"You hide behind flowers," Wedgeburr growled. "Don't you know that the steel scythe always wins?" He raised his hand. The bailiffs shouldered their rifles. Every one of them was trained on Imago.

He wondered how much charge blanks actually held. "I would not do this thing," he said quietly.

"Hold fast," the Card King told him quietly. "Hold fast."

Wedgeburr's hand dropped. The bailiffs fired. Imago thought he felt a plucking at his hair, but no bullets struck. Behind him, someone shrieked.

What?

The First Counselor looked astonished.

The wasp noise crescendoed amid a massive rush of air. They exploded from the trees.

In moments the insects were everywhere. In the press of their bodies, Imago could see no further than the Card King. That was enough. The fat man's horse collapsed as swarming insects burrowed into its flesh. The stricken animal screamed like a woman.

The Card King fell with his mount, also overwhelmed by a wriggling mass of wasps. Sickened, Imago dropped to his knees to spew his lunch.

Though their wing beats were like a lover's breath on his skin, none of the insects touched him.

Imago curled on the stones of the square, still clutching his little poppy. He waited out the horror with tight-shut eyes until only a heavy, terrible silence remained.

It seemed that hours had passed, though the sky was still light. The insects were gone. Next to him, the Card King and his horse were a bloody jumble of bones, hair, clothing, and harness.

Imago retched again. Then he climbed to his feet. Most of the Lords Mayor were groaning and in shock. Likewise the Crusty Alices. Others were bones and cloth.

It was gut-wrenchingly obvious that the puppeteers had died inside their figures.

Everyone who lived clutched one of the waxy poppies.

He turned toward the Riverward Gate.

Red wool and bones were scattered on the battlements or slumped at the base of wall. Rifled muskets lay everywhere. At least one of the Burgesses had been taken as well—Imago hoped he was looking at Wedgeburr's robes.

Across Terminus Plaza the Winter Grove was a stand of ragged spears of heartwood surrounded by mounds of damp dust. The smoke pots were scattered, but the servants who'd been working close by weren't even rag piles.

So close to the swarms, they would have been torn to carmine fog.

Imago stared at the poppy in his hand. The blood-red splotches at the base of each petal had turned black. That damned woman must have done something terrible in the North, to visit this plague upon his city.

He knelt beside the rags of the Card King and touched the broken dome of the fat man's skull. "I should have called you friend," he whispered, "for you have always been true to me."

Looking back up, he wondered where the streams in the evening sky had come from. They were larger and slower than the little flitter mice haunting the abandoned buildings near the eastern wall.

Another plague from the North. He would ask Marelle what she—

The thought broke off with a shattering of his heart.

"Marelle!" Imago searched among the wandering Crusty Alices and Lords Mayor. None of them were her. When he began pawing through the bloody bones, shouting her name over and over, a few other survivors pulled him off.

Being led away, Imago thought he heard tiny voices crying in the sky.

III
BLOSSOMING

BIJAZ

In six panicked days they recrossed what had taken fourteen on the trip north-ward. The nights were filled with the rush of great waters and flashes of light behind them, though the days seemed almost normal.

The two surviving Northmen had turned completely inward. DeNardo was focused on hunting down food and shelter. Ashkoliiz held nothing but venom for everyone and everything.

"Another word from you and I shall make your tongue into a snake," Bijaz finally told her. "I will not kill you, because I want to see you hanged in Delator Square."

"Your precious City is—" she began, but Bijaz raised his finger. That was enough to quiet her.

DeNardo was little better. The freerider ranged ahead for game and water in the high country, generally avoiding their company. He could have survived out here on his own. Likewise the Northmen. Bijaz and Ashkoliiz were at the mercy of their companions. He wondered why the Winter Boy bothered to keep them alive.

That they met no monsters was somehow more frightening than a set battle might have been. Fear built on fear without the release of rage.

Bijaz never would have thought to find himself longing for a fight.

DeNardo brought them first to the splintered ruins of the stockade that had been the Northern Expedition's base camp. "Nothing being there larger than a thighbone," the freerider said, more words than he'd spoken in the past few days put together.

"No salvage," Bijaz added.

The southerner grunted, then headed for a closer look. Ashkoliiz turned on her heel and stalked a few yards along their backtrail. Amalii turned to Bijaz.

"Where do you fare now?"

"Southward," Bijaz said. "Whatever lies beneath all of this is aimed at the City Imperishable. I presume you will turn east or west, so you can eventually make your way North again somewhere past that sea of ice?"

Amalii shook his head. "No. Our triad is broken. Our spirit-guide is lost. The woman has failed. We are no more. Skin-ghost, we say in the North. Hollow of purpose and empty of soul."

Bijaz noted that the Northmen had already set themselves to forgetting Ash-koliiz. "You're welcome to come with me," he said. "DeNardo is surely heading south as well."

"So we stay together," Ulliaa said. "Lead well, little god."

"You are not skin-ghosts to me," he told them.

"Every man judges himself."

With that cheerful thought in mind, Bijaz picked his way down the hill. What had the ice bear intended for this effort? Spirit-guide, killer. None of the five who had originally come out of the North had pursued the same purpose, that was clear.

Cities, forests, life and death. But why? Just because it was time?

No one suggested passing through the Paucius mines. Bijaz couldn't stand the thought of being enclosed within the stone when the wasps caught up with them.

Instead they set out to retrace the route which the supply train had taken over the Silver Ridges. They crossed the mountains via a high, winding pass. The flat-floored cleft was jumbled with rocks and enormous gravel bars.

The fifth day out from the ruins of the base camp, they reached the south end of the pass. The rolling tan prairie of the Saltus drainage stretched below them. At their feet the valley simply ended in a sheer cliff much higher than what they'd climbed so long before. Bijaz approached the rounded edge until he felt the drop pulling at him. For a moment he thought he might be able to fly, but he had no desire to share the air with those wasps.

They did not set a fire that night. Stars glittered cold and hard. Bijaz slept poorly, his throat aching from the chill. The edge continued to beckon him. It was almost a voice, telling him that he'd float forever.

He flexed his right fist to call back his piece of the noumenal sun. When his fingers glowed pink, Bijaz found his way once more to the wheat field.

The reaper man was along the ridge now, cutting rank after rank of the golden grass with wide swings of the scythe.

"Am I doing the right thing?" Bijaz asked, though they stood the length of a furrow apart.

He received no answer but the hiss of the blade.

Of course he had to go home, but to what end?

Bijaz had one more question. "Could I truly fly?"

The reaper turned. The gray hood opened on nothing but shadows. Still, he knew he was being examined.

Bijaz realized he was not quite touching soil. Startled, he looked up to see the nighttime expanse of the south. One foot was raised in the air, ready to step into a long, deep nothingness.

DeNardo squatted nearby. "When someone is to be going for a walk over the edge," he said, "I am always to be curious what they are believing they will find."

"Dreams." Bijaz backed slowly away, then tumbled onto his arse, fingers digging into the thin gravel. He had never been so grateful for solid ground.

"If I am to dream of flying, I am doing it from the safety of my bed." DeNardo stood, heading back for his cloak. "You must be going home, little man. As well me."

"I wish Enero was here," Bijaz said.

"As well me."

Standing near the edge at dawn, he could not imagine how the mounted column had gotten up here. "Are you sure they came this way?"

DeNardo waved him toward the western edge of the pass. "See? There is being a trail."

Bijaz looked. There certainly was being a trail, though he wouldn't have spotted it from any distance. A narrow track slipped past a bulge in the rock and dropped away.

"I am to be going now," DeNardo announced, and headed down.

With a twisting pain in his gut, Bijaz followed.

The cliff face was deeply channeled. He realized this was a very old, very big waterfall. If the entire high desert had once been an inland sea, this would have been the outlet.

Behind him the Northmen toiled at their descent, apparently unconcerned about the half-mile drop beside them. Past them, Ashkoliiz strolled. Only Bijaz seemed to be struggling. One slip and he would either discover flight or be dead. Crawling would only make the descent more difficult.

So he followed DeNardo. Horses had made their way up this path, after all.

Bijaz was surprised when his feet eventually struck level ground three paces in a row. He glanced at the sun. A bit after noon. So it had taken them a good six hours to descend.

The thought drew his gaze to the cliff face. The Northmen were two switchbacks above him. Ashkoliiz trailed behind them.

Something else moved much higher up.

"DeNardo," he said quietly, not wanting to turn lest he lose sight of whatever it was.

The Winter Boy was at his side in a moment.

"Watch up there." Bijaz pointed. "See that column of red rock? Stained with pale streaks? I just saw movement on the trail a bit to the right."

Out of the corner of his eye, he saw the Northmen stop and look up. The four of them watched awhile, but there was nothing else except the occasional flash of Ashkoliiz's elbow.

"It is not being one of our men," DeNardo told him quietly. "And there is being nothing good for us up there otherwise. We are wanting to be on the water very soon."

The River Saltus was shallow here. Long-collapsed pilings showed in the current. Had people once brought metals down out of the mountains by mule? "No boat," Bijaz said.

"We are to be finding trees, making a raft."

"DeNardo, where are the trees?"

The two of them stared awhile, until Bijaz spotted stumps a mile downstream. They appeared shattered, surrounded by shards of wood and sprays of sawdust.

"The Eater of Forests," he whispered.

"It comes this way," said Ulliaa, now right behind him.

They scrambled to the water's edge. No one wished to wait on the trail for Ashkoliiz.

Onesiphorous

News had come in the past days of the Lord Mayor's death. Imago had been killed in the Great Hall of the Assemblage of Burgesses. He'd had a massive funeral in the Potter's Field. Or not. Perhaps the bailiffs had barred the proceedings. Or Imago's corpse had been dumped in the River Saltus.

No one was certain.

Onesiphorous sat on the deck of the assay boat which would be his flagship, *Xanthippe D.* She'd been out on the western loop of the mine run when Port Defiance fell. Her captain had spent two months lurking in lagoons until Beaulise had run across him and brought ship and crew back for the assault.

Onesiphorous propped his feet against the aft rail and stared at the knob-kneed trees. A pair of green-furred monkeys stared back, their eyes filled with mock wisdom.

"It doesn't matter if he's dead," Kalliope said, squatting next to Onesiphorous. "Everything he cared about remains true."

"Who will stand in his place as Lord Mayor?" Onesiphorous wished he had a pipe to draw on, something to do with his hands and his nerves. "The City hasn't been calm long enough to develop an orderly succession of power. Elections are ancient history. We can't keep restaging the Trial of Flowers."

Kalliope placed her hand on his arm. "Without Port Defiance and access to the Sunward Sea, you won't have enough of a city left to govern."

"What in the nine brass hells do you care, anyway? You walked away from the City Imperishable years past."

"I sold myself for some food and a safe place to sleep," she said coldly. "That I did something more than sweating spread-legged beneath a hairy rug merchant is a testament to Tokhari ways. I'm here because the fate of the City Imperishable is important. Your home isn't the ghost of an empire, it's the naked heart. What flows out of there affects everyone who lives within the distance an army can march.

"So get up off your miserable little arse and shout these people in line. You've raised an army. Use it. Or lose everything. Imago wouldn't want otherwise, would he?"

Onesiphorous met her eyes. "I apologize," he said slowly. "I stood for years in adversity with none to aid me. Even my own Slashed spent more time complaining or asking for favors than they did advancing my cause. *Their* cause. I should not punish you for that."

Kalliope snorted.

"I take it you still refuse to take command?" he asked.

"They will not listen to a woman and a foreigner."

"Then you will remain here with me on *Xanthippe*."

"You know how I feel about that," she said.

"And you know how unprepared I am. I can shout 'attack,' but after that I will be helpless against whatever comes next."

"We've been over this," she said. "Port Defiance is a widespread target. There are no walls to scale, no streams to dam. And there's no way to ride them down."

Tactics, tactics, it was always tactics. He fell back on strategy. "Then why are we bothering? We can't hope to prevail in a lengthy struggle."

"We don't require a lengthy struggle. Most of Port Defiance won't defend their city, not if the choice is between the corsairs or us."

"I'll have a banner made today," he said. "Something to fly from this ship. We'll need firepots to go around it. I don't believe she has electricks aboard."

"Imago never adopted a flag for himself," Kalliope reminded him quietly.

Jason left that afternoon, taking a dozen men with him. The volunteers were strong of arm, and apparently limited imagination, for they were forced to heave the Green Man like a log into a little sloop. The vessel sailed with a deck full of fishing nets for pretence.

Dusk fell. The new moon of Mai would be rising soon. Anyone not already assigned a place in the attack was told off to the reserves.

The rest of his jack-hazard fleet circled itself into sailing order. Steam barges, flat boats, sloops, dories, even the narrow little Angoumois boats. The smaller vessels were underpowered. The larger steamers were too heavy to be swift. They'd be making their way slowly across the incoming tide. The corsairs would see the attack coming as soon as they rounded Snag Point.

Onesiphorous fingered the shard of blue jade. The mystery of its finding had never left his mind. The thumbs were strangely interconnected. It was odd how little the miners seemed aware of the curious nature of their adopted homes.

Much like the City Imperishable, the world was filled with strange, half-re-membered secrets.

Xanthippe D.'s boiler hissed up to operating pressure. She would be near the head of the attack line. He clambered up to the roof of the deckhouse, where a red-and-white sheet was stretched across a wooden frame.

"Boudin," Onesiphorous told the noisy night. "I come for you, and Big Sister, and most of all for Imago." A thought occurred to him. "Captain Pottle!"

The man poked his head out of the deckhouse, where he'd been working over the charts one last time. "Sir?"

"Do you have a gold obol? I am in need of a single coin. If we survive the night I'll repay you double."

"I'm more broke than the bride's father on wedding day," the captain said, "but I reckon I can find my reserve. We don't see the dawn, I shan't need it. If we do find daylight again, you're a likely investment."

Onesiphorous watched the phosphorescent ripple in the water where the Bay of Snakes met the Jade Bight. *Xanthippe D.* rocked as she passed the line. Then she was out in open water, flanked by four fast, narrow outrigger boats rowed by Angoumois.

Pottle climbed up on the roof with a wallet. "It's said to be bad luck to have dwarfs or women on the boat. But 'twas a woman dwarf that sent us back, so who knows from luck? Now, what would you be wanting with this gold obol?"

"I wish to pay the Sea King's fare."

The captain's voice dropped. "Where'd you hear that? I'll beat any man of mine bloody who's been talking up such—"

"Stop," said Onesiphorous. "I have friends beneath the shadows of Angoulême who hold faith in such things. I wish to honor their weird, and perhaps buy a bit of the future back for myself."

"Then you'll need two gold obols." The captain's tone was grudging. "One for each eye, to hold them closed so the dead man don't see the green ladder nor the black. Otherwise they won't never come back up." He paused. "You ever seen a man who's returned up with his fare paid?"

"Maybe." Onesiphorous thought of Clement, the boy who'd brought Kalliope and Jason from Sandy Banks.

"Don't know their own mothers, mostly."

That struck at Onesiphorous' conscience. "Still," he said stubbornly, "it's an honor I want to render."

"Here." The captain passed over four gold obols. "This'd pay my crew off for a full voyage. Two for you to throw down in memory of whoever, and two for yourself. Now that I know what it is you want, I won't have you repaying me. Even if we all live to feast like Burgesses, the story will be worth more to me."

"Thank you," said Onesiphorous.

The captain returned below. Onesiphorous watched Angoulême slide past his port rail. He wondered again about the stone traces beneath the swamp. Every city fell in its time. Perhaps if one dug far enough beneath the fields of any land one would find ancient palace floors and the gates of fallen fortresses.

The City Imperishable might have reached the end of its life. Cities were creatures of a sort, with bones of stone and people for muscles. They had many heartbeats—financial, agricultural, military, political—but hearts failed. Everyone lay down to rest eventually, even gods. Even the queen of Angoulême, in her time.

Faint lights danced within the eaves of her swamp. Onesiphorous raised a hand, waving across the darkness. That greeting done, he cast the captain's coins over the starboard rail into deep water.

Doubtless there was an invocation he should utter, but it seemed more honest to hope for a better day and grieve for his friend Imago.

Kalliope came up top. "Jason should have been in position by dusk. He'll wait for our attack before he approaches the black ships."

Onesiphorous stretched. "Are the firepots ready?"

"As best we can do." She sat so that their shoulders and elbows touched. "Now you wait. Others will have to pick up their courage, remember the butt end of their spear, and run screaming."

"I've done some screaming in my life. And a lot of waiting. But never for four hundred men on four dozen boats."

"Any commander sits through this." Onesiphorous swore he could hear her smile. "Usually you've trained them first, and burned a few villages for practice."

"I've never burned anything bigger than a log in a fire. Neither have most of these."

"Oh, there's more retired bandits in this bunch than you know," she told him. "Simple men with simple lives don't wind up working plantations on the Jade Coast. Most people here are fleeing something. Even your precious swampers—Anger Mice."

"Angoumois," he said, obscurely pleased that she'd at least made the effort.

"Even the Angoumois know their way around a knife and a net. Not like the fat, happy factors of Port Defiance."

"I don't really care whose flag flies there," he said. "Not anymore. But the Saltus needs to stay open, regardless of who collects the tariffs. And the dwarfs need to come home to raise their children."

"The City will go on without them."

"Maybe. But dwarfs will not go on without the City Imperishable." He guided her hand to his thigh. "Feel how short and twisted my legs are? Without the laws and customs of the City, in two generations this will be seen as the worst sort of cruelty. As depraved as any father who uses his sons on Saturday night and his daughters on Sunday morning before he goes to a temple to sweat out his virtue. Only the truly disturbed will make their children over, once we are no longer ordinary.

"I want my people to remain ordinary, to remain who they are."

"No one remains," she said. "What do you think has happened on the deserts since so many Tokhari have moved to Bas Gronegrim, Bas Luccia, Sel Biost, the City Imperishable? That migration began generations ago. The City's empire drew off men to fight wars. Instead of coming home, many sent for their wives and children.

"Now more of our people live in foreign cities than in our own honest sand. No one wants what *was*. I'm a sandwalker because not enough desert-born children seek out the apprenticeship anymore. They'd rather go to one of the cities and sit beside a trade factor to learn the counting.

"There's nothing to fight, no port to attack to convince Tokhari to come back to the sand sea. Someday our serais will be empty. The Tokhari will just be dark-haired families with odd names, as much Gronegrii or City men as anyone else. Then someone else will find our lands empty and learn our arts of living, or discover new arts which serve them better. That's the world, Onesiphorous. It may be that your people's twilight has come. They will not vanish. They will simply become something else."

"Perhaps." He suspected the queen of Angoulême would have said much the same thing. "I thank you," he told her, squeezing her hand.

The bow watch scampered back along the deck, having been forbidden to call. "Snag Point ahead," he whispered hoarsely.

Onesiphorous stood. "Prepare to light the firepots. Captain, fight the ship as you see best. Kalliope, are we made ready?"

"See," she said, laughing. "You even sound like a general."

Imago

The wasps were everywhere and nowhere. The City Imperishable had lapsed into panic. Most people retreated to their homes, abandoning carts and baggage in the street.

A squad of the surviving Winter Boys under Astaro found him leaving the square shortly after the attacks. At least he wasn't heading back to the Rugmaker's Cupola alone.

They headed north on Arbogaster Street, angling toward the Root Market along a more circuitous route than he would ordinarily have taken. He wanted to see a bit more of the City, and stay away from the waterfront.

Something buzzed loudly overhead. The freeriders drew their pistols. Imago looked up as a massive shadow crossed the stars. A wasp bigger than a house. It was gone as fast as it had appeared. The horsemen drew closer together.

This was worse than the noumenal attacks of last fall. Those had been random, and fatal only to an ill-chanced few. The wasp swarms had already killed dozens in Terminus Plaza, and could easily have taken the lives of hundreds more. If they were the scouts for an invasion, the City Imperishable was done for.

"You did not call the wasps." Between one moment and the next Biggest Sister was walking next to Astaro's horse, where Imago rode double.

Astaro startled, saw that it was her, and twisted around to grin at Imago. "She is being a cat in the evening."

Biggest Sister smiled sourly. "As I've said before, shadows and focus. What will you do now, Lord Mayor?"

"I do not know. My forces are reduced. I sent my noumenal actors away. There are only the flowers to protect us."

"You take your strength where you find it," she said. "Where will you find more?"

He sighed. In her direct way, Biggest Sister had flushed his deepest thoughts into the open. "If I were desperate enough, I might go down beneath the New Hill and call up the Old Gods once more."

"Are you that desperate?" she asked.

"No." Then he blurted, "But I soon will be."

Biggest Sister touched his hand, oddly tender. "You will hear more from me. Wait, before you do anything drastic."

He nodded, but she was gone.

Astaro turned to him. "We are to be returning to the Rugmaker's Cupola now. Not safe here."

"Not safe anywhere," Imago said.

The Winter Boys grumbled among themselves in their southern tongue.

Passing through the Root Market, he saw potatoes scattered in the street, and many stores shuttered. Somehow that made him as sad as any of the day's other losses. In time he knew he'd grieve the Card King more, and Marelle most of all.

The City Imperishable truly had begun to sicken.

The Rugmaker's Cupola was a disaster. The front doors had been shattered. Debris from a recent struggle was scattered in the great circular hall at the base. Not to mention broken furniture and a blizzard of papers thrown down from above.

This had been a slap at Imago and his legacy.

Astaro sighed. "Nine more of us were dying in the fight. Finally we were to be retreating to the castle beyond." He nodded toward the door which led to the old fortified Tokhari embassy from the days of empire. It had obviously withstood assault quite recently. "They were to be leaving off after a time, but your offices are to having been sacked."

Imago climbed the spiral stairs. Five levels rose from base to top. What wasn't piled in drifts of broken wood and paper littered the balconies as he ascended.

"Bailiffs?" Imago couldn't see Imre and his brothers destroying a seat of government.

Astaro grunted. "Restorationists again. Like the madmen of winter."

"Who else did they kill?"

"Only freeriders. We were to be keeping all the clerks safe."

Imago stopped, saddened by that statement. "Thank you. You have given up your leader and half your numbers for me. The City has shown little for it." More freeriders crowded behind Astaro, staring. "This isn't your fight anymore. It never was but for Ignatius' coin."

"Enero was to being our fight," Astaro said slowly, his voice thickening. "In the case DeNardo is to be returning from the North. He is to be taking Enero's place. Then we will being to decide."

One of the others rattled off something long in their language, but Astaro ignored it.

DeNardo? *Who the hells was DeNardo?* "No one will be returning from the North," Imago told them. "You should make your own decisions."

"Oh, no." Astaro smiled, a hard-edged, predatory grin. "We are to be having word. DeNardo is to be coming."

Imago was astonished. "How would you know?"

Astaro shrugged. "You will to be asking DeNardo himself. All we are knowing is he comes. We are not knowing with who or why."

"Who is DeNardo, anyway?"

"Enero's brother. To be watching quiet what happen here, no attention being on him while Enero is to be leading. Different tales to be told home."

There's always another layer, thought Imago. That was oddly comforting.

His office wasn't the wreck he'd expected. In fact, someone had been cleaning it, or at least arranging the trash. Imago looked into the chamberlain's office.

Stockwell the clerk cowered within, brandishing a letter opener. "I'm warning you—" he began. Then he screamed and fainted.

Of course, Imago thought. Stockwell understood Imago to be dead. The Lord Mayor stepped to Stockwell's side. This office was clean too, and a desk had even been rigged from broken furniture. He knelt beside the clerk and patted his cheeks. "Come on, there."

Stockwell's eyes opened. "You... you were killed."

"A temporary condition." Imago forced a smile. "I've been in prison actually. 'm still slug pale, but very much alive."

"Your funeral..."

"I've been to the grave. Very touching. We have larger problems now, I'm afraid."

"I wouldn't know, sir." Stockwell sat up. "I've been hiding. What else was there to do? And someone might need the files again someday."

"You've done well. It's someday now, as I am back in the Rugmaker's Cupola."

Something big fluttered outside. Imago jumped in panic, fearing another wasp, but it was just a huge sheet of cloth falling past the window.

The Winter Boys had thrown the Burgesses' banner off the roof.

"Good." Half an hour ago he was ready to ask Saltfingers to stand as his psychopomp one last time. He now realized that if this ninny of a clerk could find a way to look to the future, so could Lord Mayor Imago of Lockwood.

Imago found the bear's bell amid the wreckage of his office, and pocketed it for luck. He took his poppy, wilted now but still recognizable, and tucked it into a buttonhole of his shirt. He was still costumed as himself—dark trousers, a white shirt with an untabbed collar and no necktie, with a cloak over it.

He trudged up the wooden ladders to the roof. There had been no morning or evening bell these last few days since he'd escaped. The Temple District as always clattered and clanged away, but Imago was surprised to find that he had missed the bone-shaking racket in his office.

The clouds had cleared, leaving only the stars in their glory with a new moon drifting dark. The City Imperishable doused its lights, huddling in fear, or also a more practical effort not to give the wasps something to home in on. That left the heavens blazing.

Mai, he thought. This is Mai. So much had been stolen from him in that cell. Out here was the opposite of imprisonment—open sky and a far horizon.

He held the tiny bell out, fragmentary imitation of those which had fallen silent. The carillon was still there. Someone had probably stolen the clappers for scrap by now, but the bells remained.

Good.

Imago waved the silver bell at its massive iron cousins. Then he turned to the west, where the sun had fled beyond the far-distant Yellow Mountains, and where the Saltus first flowed from. He rang the bell once, twice, three times.

Then he walked around the tower until he faced south. The Limerock Palace and the Sudgate hulked in the starlight. Onesiphorous had vanished in that direction. Three times again he rang the bell.

West, toward the Rose Downs: sunrise, and the breadbasket that fed much of the City. There he rang the bell three more times.

Finally, north. The Silver Ridges lay there, and somewhere beyond them, Bijaz's grave. He rang the bell another three times.

Nothing happened. No wasps, giant or small. None of the rumored bats. Marelle did not spring whole-bodied from the stones, nor did Enero rise from the dead.

He was a fool. Bijaz might have made something appear. Jason could have turned the bells to melons. The poor godmonger Archer would have found wisdom in the tiny silver echo.

Imago was just a failed Lord Mayor.

He made a conscious effort to cheer himself. The City would live to see another day. Wasps could be killed; people did it all the time. At least Wedgeburr wasn't a threat at the moment.

Voices echoed down in the street, which surprised him. Imago leaned over the decorated battlement. Half a dozen people gathered at the door below, with several lanterns. A few more walked up the street, one carrying a torch.

They slipped into his tower.

More were coming.

More went inside as well, though the crowd outside seemed to grow faster than the trickle heading within. Imago wondered what it meant. Not an attack, not with the quiet talk and occasional laughter drifting upward. Some of his partisans? This was the City Imperishable, and these were its people. They seemed to have visited his grave in numbers, unsafe as that had been with Wedgeburr in control.

Imago thought he glimpsed Imre and a few other bailiffs in their red wool uniforms. They weren't pushing forward with warrants. Rather, they stood amid the others, waiting their turn.

Someone lit the Burgesses' banner on fire. It was almost a party down there. As best as he could tell *everyone* carried a poppy. People glanced often at the sky,

They show courage, he told himself, and headed for the narrow door.

An Alate waited there, wings flexing in the starlight.

Imago jumped, surprised. The day had already been full of frights.

"You called." The Alate's voice was high and narrow.

Called? Thinking quickly, he opened his hand and showed the little silver bell. "Yes, I did. I am Lord Mayor of the City Imperishable. My city is in dire need of aid."

BIJAZ

They walked southward all afternoon, finding no intact wood. In time, DeNardo called a halt. The Northmen were trailing far behind.

Bijaz waited for them as DeNardo made camp and Ashkoliiz sulked. Ulliaa and Amalii finally caught up with him. Ulliaa looked sickly pale. They sat and Amalii laid a six foot snake out. Bijaz couldn't tell if it was dead or just stunned.

"I am to lose my name soon," Ulliaa announced. "The world begins to forget me."

Bijaz mentally translated that. "You are dying."

"Yes." It was Amalii. "Our third had no remembering when he was lost. There is yet time for Ulliaa to remember."

"I am pleased for you," Bijaz offered. To his surprise, he meant it.

"Will you remember as well?" Ulliaa's voice creaked.

The snake was worrisome, but Bijaz nodded.

Amalii stroked the animal. It wriggled back to life within his grip. Bijaz had no idea what sort of snake it was, just that it was longer than he was tall and thicker than his forearm. It flickered its tongue at Amalii.

The Northman began to chant. This wasn't the language they usually spoke. Bijaz listened for something of the meaning behind the words. It was an opening, and invocation. Chilly wind blew as Amalii continued, bearing the hard scent of ice and sharpening some very unpleasant recent memories.

The snake coiled around Amalii's arm. It worked its way up and across his shoulders, then doubled back past his neck and reached for Ulliaa. Ulliaa raised his hand, grasped the snake's neck, pulled it close to his mouth and made a noise such Bijaz had never before heard.

It was as if all the words a man might speak in his life tore from the Northman's mouth at once. A god-shout that could have awakened a Creation from a sleeping, empty sky. Bijaz's ears popped and bled. The air grew so cold that ice flurried around them in tiny crystals. The snake swelled, then spasmed in death.

Ulliaa slumped over.

Amalii laid the snake out on the ground and immediately sliced it open. He cut a great length, examining the organs. Bijaz would ordinarily have been quite curious, but his head was buzzing with thoughts and memories and words which did not belong to his life. A wall of ice like a frozen fall, glittering with colors he could not name. Some great fish, longer than three men, laid out on snow and being butchered. Sex with Amalii and Ashtiili, sharing slick cocks and the taste of one another as they bound their triad with the flesh. A woman crooning as he thrust his hand into a fire, only to draw it out again unburned. The wounded boys ran crying to their mothers, but he was taken down into a hole in the stone to be buried alive and reborn. A seal screaming as he clubbed it to death, then stripped its skin to wear so he could swim beneath the ice for hours.

These were echoes of Ulliaa's death shout, setting themselves into his head.

That was a mighty power indeed.

Bijaz shook the false memories away, retreating to his wheat field. To his surprise he nearly collided with the reaper man, who reached for him with the scythe. Bijaz smiled and stepped aside.

Amalii handed him several purpled gobbets. "Eat now," he said, "and remember." The Northman consumed those he'd kept for himself, then lapsed into quiet.

A liver? Bijaz couldn't tell. He swallowed, letting the thick, sticky meat slide down his throat. He licked the snake blood off his fingers and waited.

After a while Amalii opened his eyes. "His name was Ulliaa."

"His name was Ulliaa," Bijaz repeated.

They both stood. The dwarf followed the Northman, who set off looking for DeNardo. The bodies of man and snake were nothing more than empty flesh now.

The two of them trailed slowly into camp.

"The other is being dead?" DeNardo asked.

Bijaz nodded. "He has been sent to his next trial with honor." A fragmentary memory surfaced of the same ceremony for a different brother, the sacrifice on that occasion an ice bear that had laid itself down for the knife. The snake was all they had here. It must have felt very wrong to the Northmen.

"I'm sorry," Ashkoliiz said in Civitas.

The north bank eventually widened again—a combination of a bay in the line of the mountains and a southward curve of the river itself. The resulting bottomland was filled with shattered stumps and scattered spears of well-gnawed heartwood. Bijaz had been seeing living trees for months, a trick of dream and divination. Now they were all dead. The little stands they'd seen coming on first reaching the river had been stricken, but this was an entire region stripped to nothing.

The Eater of Forests.

He couldn't see how everything fit together. Giant wasps, man-faced bats, tiny wasps, all living out a cycle just as the creatures of garden or field did. But these monsters had a cycle that spanned centuries and encompassed destruction.

The Northern Expedition had raised this killer of trees to head for the City Imperishable. *Why?* To purge the southern ghosts from their ice?

That did not matter now. What mattered was how quickly he could make his way home, warn Imago, and raise a defense. Marelle and her archives might hold answers. Bijaz needed to reach the City ahead of the Eater of Forests.

Slackwater Princess had covered a thousand river miles from the City Imperishable to this region. It would take the four of them all summer and well into the autumn to make their way home on foot.

They walked until sundown, detouring around the marshy outlets of streams, scrambling up and down banks, forcing their way through stands of brush. There were no trees at all, just more groupings of shattered stumps surrounded by a mass of slivers.

DeNardo called a halt atop a little bluff. Bijaz examined a stump at close quarters. Pale globules clung to the debris, ranging from the size of raindrops to muskmelons. When he touched a small drop with the tip of a stick, it quivered before bursting into a flowing mess, like the remains of a garden slug.

There was plenty of firewood from the ruins of a small grove at the base of the bluff. Bijaz set that alight as darkness fell.

Amalii began to chant. This resembled the song he'd sung to the snake. His voice rose and fell in a conversation with the fire. As Ulliaa's memories continued to sink into his own mind, Bijaz found the words tugged at him more and more. Where the other had been an invocation, this was a lamentation.

He was surprised when Ashkoliiz joined in. Her part of the chant was infrequent, an occasional harmony that crossed with Amalii's voice to form something which stirred the hairs on Bijaz's neck.

She seemed genuinely sorrowful, for the first time since he'd known her.

In time Bijaz walked away from the fire, staring north and west. The river was noisy here, talking with its speed. The cliffs held an echoing silence, different from the rustling stillness of open country. Something big moved in the brush along their backtrail.

"DeNardo," Bijaz called softly.

The Winter Boy approached quietly.

Bijaz mimed listening. DeNardo nodded and slipped down the slope. The dwarf wrapped his arms around himself and waited nervously.

"What?" asked Amalii.

Startled, Bijaz hadn't even realized that the chant had finished. "DeNardo is hunting whatever out there hunts us," he whispered.

Amalii nodded, then limped after DeNardo. Bijaz realized he was better off watching Ashkoliiz than facing away from her. He found her subdued.

This seemed as good a time as any to speak to her frankly. He asked the question which had been on his mind since the beginning, in one form or another. "What was it you intended? Truly, beneath all the stagecraft?"

"To prove myself." Those ice-blue eyes gleamed in the firelight. "Iistaa needed me, so she made me need her in turn. The elders of Black Cleft Council sent the triad to watch us both, me for being too flighty and female, the ice bear for being, well, herself."

"And you just wanted to be right? A hundred men have died for that, while an entire city now stands in peril."

"Right. Wealthy. Feted for my perspicacity." She hugged herself. "Who could have known how difficult this would be?"

"What of Iistaa?"

Ashkoliiz shook her head. "I thought I knew. Now…" She took a slow breath. "In the North, entire lifetimes are spent to realize a single moment. I have begun to wonder if she spent us all to arrange what you released."

That neatly paralleled Bijaz's own speculations. "But why?"

"We see time differently, so high above the world. Sometimes that bends a person's reasoning beyond recognition."

"It still cannot be nonsense. A person—" Bijaz was interrupted by a quick, sharp shriek. He grabbed a brand and ran to the edge of the slope. DeNardo ran out of the darkness moments later, Amalii stumbling close behind.

"Who was hurt?" Bijaz asked.

"Not to being hurt," DeNardo said. "Surprised."

That startled Bijaz. "Something surprised *you* enough to make you scream?"

"Iistaa," said Amalii.

"The *bear?*"

"Her spirit is so great it can remember itself, even in death."

"Where is she now?" He hated the panic in his voice.

"We led her into the river."

"She is not to be swimming so well," DeNardo added.

"So now she's in front of us?" Bijaz demanded. "There's no way we can walk home with her ambushing us at any step of the way."

"You'd best conjure a boat, then, little godling." Ashkoliiz's tone was smirking.

Whatever moment of honesty they'd been sharing was lost. "There's an answer here somewhere." Bijaz tried to keep from snarling. "But if you don't know what it is, you might wish to keep your mouth shut."

"Being enough," DeNardo snapped. "Sleeping awhile, then going on while it is still night."

Bijaz lay on his cloak and stared at the stars. Avoiding the endless replay of his aborted conversation with Ashkoliiz, he wondered how to lift them over the miles to home. A memory came unbidden, of the battle of Terminus Plaza. The Alates had sided with Imago.

How in all the brass hells would he call an Alate?

Try, he thought. *Reach out and try.*

He imagined a flying steed. Not like the monkey bats, but something large and graceful, with the dignity of a thinking man. He remembered crows picking through the wheat field when the reaper man had passed. They flew to carrion and war, following the scythe as it hissed through the world.

He'd flown, too, if he'd reached high enough to break off a piece of the sun. How did it feel to fly? How did it feel to have the wind beneath your feet and the world open forever around you as you plummeted toward the ground, beating wings you didn't have and screaming for—

Bijaz awoke with a shriek, startling the others. They were on watch two-and-two now, so only Amalii had been sleeping.

Everyone stared as an Alate landed next to the ashes.

"You said my name," it told Bijaz in a voice like a cliff face, cracked and high and stony.

"Ah, welcome." That was the best he could do in the moment.

ONESIPHOROUS

They attacked Port Defiance with the incoming tide. One of the firepots spilled, setting his banner afire. The men clashed their weapons, shouting fit to raise the dead. The people of the city covered their lights and pulled their shutters to.

That was fine with Onesiphorous.

Further to the east a single white firework lofted to end in a transitory chrysanthemum. Jason was moving against the black ships.

Their attack flotilla split up to weave between the islets. *Xanthippe D.* passed his old haunts, right by Axos and Lentas with their great, absurd wooden bridge.

There was no sign of the corsairs yet.

Most of the boats made for the Flag Towers. The Harbormaster would be holed up with his new friends. If they could get into the waters beneath, they could board the building like a ship.

The first trouble came with a bright flash just north of the Flag Towers. Cannon fire landed among the lead elements of Onesiphorous' little fleet, splintering a fast sloop and sending a steam-powered raft spinning.

He had no plan for that. Everything he and Kalliope had discussed assumed the corsairs lurked in their castle.

"What do I do?" he shouted at her.

"Keep sailing!"

Three more salvos rippled in quick succession—the corsairs had at least four ships out there. *Xanthippe D.* took a hit near the bow that left a sailor screaming like a girl until one of his fellows clubbed him on the head with a belaying pin. Captain Pottle cursed violently and set his men to patching the damage.

They were far too small to carry a chirurgeon. Anyone hurt would depend on luck and a strong constitution for their survival.

Onesiphorous stood in front of his banner, screaming by the light of his firepots. "You want me, then come and get me, you stupid cunt-mouthed, arse-brained, dog-fucking, motherless whoreson suckers of your father's flaccid cocks!"

He seized one of the pots, heedless of how it burned his hand, and hurled it uselessly toward the dark ships. "Cowards! Buttery maids! Rent boys!"

"Get down." Kalliope tackled Onesiphorous as another salvo crossed overhead. The banner and its frame vanished, leaving the roof of the deckhouse in flames.

"I think I sprained my ankle," Onesiphorous hissed.

"It's one thing to lead," she growled. "It's another to make a target of yourself." She kissed him, then let him up.

He tried to stand, and nearly collapsed. Men screamed all around. A steam engine shrieked its way toward catastrophic failure.

Their attack had broken on the rock of impossibility—small boats were no match for cannon.

"Turn the fleet!" he shouted. "Board their ships. We've got no other chance!"

The call was taken up, passed from boat to boat.

"You're an idiot," Kalliope said affectionately. "And you're going to get us all killed."

"We're all going to die anyway. If they've readied their ships, they've also placed snipers on the parapets of the Flag Towers. We might as well die clever as die stupid."

Onesiphorous limped to the bow, slipping on someone's intestines. A sailor brought him a rifled musket. He sighted in on the shadows ahead before he realized he didn't know how to use it. Still, he felt good with the weapon in hand. He pretended to hold his fire while examining the trigger and the tiny levers around it.

"Above and forward, on the left side," Kalliope whispered. "The safety catch. It's intended to keep foolish dwarfs from shooting their own nuts off."

"I'm too short to shoot my own nuts off with a rifle."

"Then someone else's nuts."

"Isn't that the whole point of a rifle?"

As they turned away from the Flag Towers, the fleet was met with a chorus of jeers and a rattle of small arms fire. The ambush would have been complete if the black fleet had let most of the attackers sail into the trap, then cannoned them as they *fled*.

"Hold fire," he shouted. "Wait for close range."

It sounded good. His men weren't going to hit anything in the dark anyway.

Laughter rippled in the distance, followed by another devastating round of cannon shot.

"Are they moving?" he asked Kalliope. "Or have we changed our course?"

She scrambled to check with Captain Pottle, who was directing the effort to fight the fire. A moment later she was back. "He believes they've weighed anchor and are tacking across the current."

"Tacking? That means sails. They've not got steam?"

Kalliope hummed a brief moment while she thought. Then: "I understand that the corsairs run very fast sailing cutters. Given the least bit of wind they can beat anything with an engine. Steam's for heavier, slower boats."

"By all that's holy, why aren't we keel-hauling across the windward or whatever it is steamships do that sailing ships don't?"

"Because that's not what we planned for," Kalliope reminded him. "This was an assault landing, not an open water battle."

"Wait 'til we catch them. We'll see an assault." He thrust the rifled musket at her. "Here. Shoot something. I need Pottle's help."

The captain looked at Onesiphorous as if he were stupid, then the light dawned. "We can reverse back through the islands of the city and head right down the wind at them. It's blowing off the shore at the moment."

"So we'll come right to them if we do that, then be behind them where they can't reach us?"

"It's a suicide run," Pottle told him. "Some captains won't follow you. But some will. And that gets us away from the firing out of the Flag Towers. Even better, if we close in tight on the ships, they can't gun us down so easily with their heavy weapons."

"All they can do is outnumber us." Onesiphorous glanced into the darkness as another cannon volley went wide, crashing into buildings. Now that his fleet had broken formation, they were just so many small boats.

Pottle found a wooden hailer and began shouting over the rail. *Xanthippe D.* came about, chugging toward her next opportunity to be a target. Onesiphorous headed back for the bow.

"Thinking like a general?" Kalliope asked as he crouched down next to her.

"I suppose." He stared into the gleaming darkness between two islands, seeing a pale line of foam as an unknown vessel cut toward the west. No one had their lanterns hung this night. "Do real navies fight in the dark?"

"Of course not. And they don't fight in port, either."

"Speaking of fighting in port, where is your brother? Their ships were out of position, but he had hours to see that."

"Trust him to do what he can," she said.

"I don't trust anyone tonight. It's all up to chance now. Even my last orders probably only got through to a handful."

"Another reason ships don't fight in the dark. Signal flags are difficult to see."

"There's always rockets." He sighted down the rifle again. Someone ran across a bridge, a dark shadow against the gleaming starshine, but Onesiphorous let them go. "Of course, we don't have any rockets."

"Genius," she said. He noticed she'd found another rifle.

"Do you know how to reload this?"

"You are *worthless!*" she shouted, but then she kissed him again.

At least he would die laughing.

All too soon, *Xanthippe D.* slipped into an open channel. Onesiphorous saw the silhouettes of four large sailing ships ahead. They appeared fast and deadly. How many more were in port?

He looked around to see how many boats had followed.

"If you see someone moving on board, take your shot," Kalliope told him.

"I'll be lucky to hit the water. I've never fired a gun in my life."

"You're never going to have a better chance to learn."

The boiler grumbled as they picked up steam. Pottle had decided to lead by example. Onesiphorous twisted to see two motor barges following.

When the cannon fire opened, it took him a moment to realize the shots were going in the wrong direction. The muzzle flashes were *behind* him. The balls struck the ships ahead. Shouts echoed from the corsairs, along with the ringing of a signal bell.

"Full on!" he screamed.

"Shut up," Kalliope suggested. She took a shot, then loaded another cartridge.

Onesiphorous also took a shot, though for all he could tell his round had hit the moon. He turned to see who was firing in support of them. Something caught his eye as he moved, and so he glanced back ahead. A pale figure was climbing one of the enemy hulls ahead. A number of them, in fact.

"Look," he whispered. Another salvo passed overhead.

She was staring the other way. "Who the hells is that? Three big ships, steamers."

"I thought you said steamers didn't fight."

"No, I said corsairs don't use steamers. Other people mount guns on steamers. Slower, bigger ships with heavier cannon."

Ahead, the pale climbers had gained the corsair's rail. Onesiphorous had the sick feeling those were the swamp-mother's fire dancers.

That unlucky ship's mast exploded into bloom. Branches erupted with a noise like ripping cloth. It glowed green as leaves budded amid a thousand tiny crackling pops.

"I know where your brother is," Onesiphorous said.

"Brace for impact!" shouted Captain Pottle.

Impact? He was in the bow watch station and he couldn't see anything close.

Xanthippe D. struck something low in the water that rang like a gong. The boat bucked, drenching Onesiphorous and Kalliope in cold seawater. The boiler shrieked over the sound of a woman cursing.

"I think we hit the turtle," Kalliope yelled above the racket.

The assay boat shuddered as something belowdecks gave way. Two of the corsairs had recovered sufficiently to exchange salvos with the approaching steamers. *Xanthippe D.* listed dead in the water between the two ranks of cannon. Her boiler was howling.

"Abandon ship!" Someone began thrashing the assay boat's bell.

Onesiphorous risked standing. The two barges following were still making way. His boat didn't lack for rescue, but this was no night for a swim.

He realized who the steamships must belong to.

"I think we won," he told Kalliope. "Time to go."

"You're utterly fey, you know," she said. "Battle rage. It kills good men."

Xanthippe D. lurched again. Her list became more pronounced. Onesiphorous set his rifle down and slipped into the water. Kalliope followed him, even while screams began to echo across the water from the corsair which had been boarded.

Panic began to set in as Onesiphorous found a chunk of wood to cling to. What the hells had he been doing?

Kalliope surfaced beside him. "I must be the only Tokhari who can swim," she said, laughing as another fusillade of cannon fire passed overhead.

"I'm a dwarf who can barely swim," he said. Then: "Why aren't we dead yet?"

IMAGO

This close to him, the Alate did not seem so manlike, but more of a very large bat with feathered wings, barrel-chested and narrow-hipped. It wore only a weapons harness over skin that was shadow-dark in the starlight. The face was narrow, almost human except for eyes like yellow fires with no darkness in their center. The great wings moved like a butterfly's, balancing it as it stood. The Alate reeked of wet bird.

"Your city is ready," it said in that strange voice. "Let her rise."

More laughter echoed from the street below.

"We are beset," Imago said. "Blockaded from the south, our politics turned fatal again, and now monsters come out of the North."

The Alate considered that. "They are not as you or I."

A classic political answer. Completely true and utterly useless. Imago knew he must turn around his line of argument or he was lost. "You came to the sound of my bell, yes?"

"I heard the sound of a score of scores of summers lost."

He'd take that as a 'yes.' "What did that tell you?"

No judge sat to accuse him of leading a witness. Of course, Imago didn't know *where* he was leading this witness.

The Alate seemed amused. "That you are ready to reach again for what was taken away so long ago."

"Imperator Terminus took giant wasps?" Surely someone would have made a note of that.

"They are intramothers. Because you do not understand something does not make it wrong."

"Destroying people is *wrong!*"

That drew a long, slow, yellow-eyed stare. "You wash your cattle before you slaughter them."

"I wouldn't know." Imago was feeling less and less in control of this conversation. "I've never killed a cow. But I suppose someone must, since I've rarely found mud or fleas in my meat."

"The fleas might think it wrong. The mud might resent the wash. The cattle most certainly regret the slaughter."

The Alate's logic was leading to an unfortunate place. "The City Imperishable is ours," he said. "We will defend our home."

"You have made one error of thought," the Alate replied. "The City Imperishable belongs to itself. You merely live upon its back."

Imago didn't like that thought either. "The wasps are here to help the City?"

The Alate nodded.

"What of you?"

"We are history," it said, then leapt into the sky.

Both thoughtful and disappointed, Imago tucked the bell into his coat and went downstairs to see what was becoming of his people.

The lower hall of the Rugmaker's Cupola was crowded with men and horses. The men, at least, spilled up the stairs, seated or standing on the double spiral. Imago reckoned there must be sixty or seventy people down there.

The Lord made his way down without announcing himself. Still, they saw him coming. Someone shouted his name, then they took up the old cheer. "Im–a–go… Im–a–go… Im–a–go…"

Inside the tower, the words rang loud.

Imago stopped at the first-floor landing and raised his hands for silence. He looked down at the faces peering upward. Dwarfs and full-men, Winter Boys and bailiffs, longshoremen and clerks, Sunwarders and Tokhari and the pale blond City-born—all waiting.

"Why are you here?" he asked. "This is a night as terrible as any we have known."

"Because it *is* a terrible night, your worship," called someone.

"Yeah, we liked your walls better'n ours," another man added. They all laughed, even Imago.

One of the bailiffs spoke. "You're the only one who's tried to do right by the City Imperishable. For the sake of the City, nothing more. And you are right, Lord Mayor. This *is* a terrible night. So we've come to help."

"I suppose you want to hear my plan," Imago said.

"By my sweet pickle we do," shouted an anonymous wit.

"I don't have one…" He pointed at them. "…yet. There's more here than meets the thought. This is not a noumenal crisis arising from the Limerock Palace, may Dorgau bless the Burgesses with milk from his cherry tit."

They laughed again. *Good*, Imago thought. *Keep it moving.* "I have need of knowing more. Every person with a poppy can venture out on the streets. I need certain things done."

He held a hand up and tucked down his index finger. "First, I need good men to watch over the Potter's Field. We cannot afford to have some fool burn out the poppies, or cut them down. That will only require a handful of you, but you will need to stand watch in shifts."

Middle finger. "Second, I need a good count of how many wasp attacks happened today. Also, whether any were outside Terminus Plaza. Ask people, but look at the trees as well. They destroyed the Winter Grove. Chances are good they'd do the same elsewhere. That will take as many as can be spared to canvass the City."

Ring finger. "Third, I need to know whether there truly are giant wasps somewhere in the City." They murmured at that. "You will need a stout heart and a small imagination for this job, believe me. I thought I saw one, and nearly soiled myself in my fear. They are the size of houses. Did I see but a hallucination? Or is there a nest of them in some empty factory? Perhaps you can make that search as you look for the small wasps."

Pinkie finger. He was running out. "Last, I need two or three men of discretion to search for my chamberlain, the dwarfess Marelle. I do not think she perished in the attack at the plaza." *Hope against hope*, he thought. "She may be on Heliograph Hill, in or around the abandoned Footsoldiers' Guild Hall. She may be elsewhere. She has access to ancient records which can show us how best to carry this struggle forward."

Imago spread his hands wide again. "I name you the Lord Mayor's Own. Every man here tonight will forever be in the first rolls of my company, a name in honor. Now arrange yourselves into squads." He pointed at random. "You, you,

you, and you are the leaders," he said, making sure to pick both a dwarf and a bailiff among them.

The crowd dissolved into excited chatter, comparing weapons and gear and talking of this one's knowledge of certain districts and that one's skill at finding high places to look from.

Astaro slipped close. "That was being well done, Lord Mayor. Enero would to be proud."

"Thank you, my friend," Imago replied. "Perhaps I have learned something from your late captain."

During the small hours of the night men began to trickle back with their reports. A watch was set on the Potter's Field. They used a tumbledown mansion as their post because it had no trees around it. No one was willing to stand outside for any length of time.

Though rumors were rampant, every wasp attack they'd sought out seemed to have been one or two streets away. No other shattered trees had been found thus far. The City Imperishable was a big place, with many alleys and back gardens, so anything was possible.

Likewise the giant wasps. Several claimed to have seen them, but it was impossible to set a number or location on the monsters. Imago reckoned if they were in the City Imperishable they were in the Sudgate—he didn't know where else you'd hide something that big that wouldn't be immediately noticed. He decided to hold off on dispatching his new force there.

One important success came a bit before dawn. A bailiff and two dwarfs, one of whom Imago was certain hadn't been here earlier, arrived with Marelle.

She looked tired, but not angry. That meant they had not snatched her from some private pursuit. She was also clutching a poppy.

"I was afraid to go out," Marelle said to Imago. "After I made my way back to the archives. Your men persuaded me to safety."

"Give your names to Stockwell," he told the three. "I will find you later to commend my special thanks."

They bowed and scuttled away in an excited little knot.

"And you?" Imago had not moved from this step in hours. He wasn't sure his knees would let him up just now.

"We should retire to your office and speak privately," Marelle said. "There is much to discuss."

"Good enough." Imago tried to think through what was needed. "I'll tell Stockwell to send men for the papers there. Can you draw a list of what you need? I won't have you on the streets again and again."

"Yes," she said. "Now come."

He needed help standing, and it was minutes of agony to climb four flights of stairs, but up they went. Short of wasps at his window, Imago figured they were as safe there as anywhere above the stones. He wasn't quite ready to begin governing from the sewers.

After a long and somewhat painful pause in the garderobe, he stumbled into his office. Marelle was on his little daybed. Her shirt was open. She wore nothing else, so that he could see the pale hairs of her cunny.

"Come to bed, you fool," she said.

He felt silly. "I am afraid I shall fail you badly."

"I don't mean *that*. Just for comfort. We can whisper in the dark."

He undressed and settled in beside her. Imago set his face on her breast and breathed across the pert, pale nipple. His will to speak drained away with the closing of his eyes.

They made love with day's first light. Not heaving at one another as they had in the costume racks at the Faces krewe house, but rather a tender touching by the dimness, fingers and tongues and the slow crawl of bodies. Marelle held Imago close and crooned to him, then spread so he could lap at her awhile. He did the same, slipping into her mouth, where he came despite his resolve to save himself for more.

That did not matter. They went on, hoarding morning's first hours for themselves. "Thank you," Imago finally said, his hair plastered to his head. His thighs were slick with both their juices.

"No, thank *you*."

He toyed with her pale hair, touching the crooked scars on her neck. "I thought the wasps had felled you."

"I ran," she said. "They did not follow, I think because I am of the City. That's what the poppies mean. They see them somehow, as how bees know which flowers have given up their pollen and which have not."

"But what are these wasps? Where did they come from?"

"I might have found something," she told him slowly. "I spent my evening in the archives reading on the mysteries of the past."

"And?"

"Records are so strange. When people wish to write about a tax assessment, they say something simple. Perhaps the Imperator Loghead declared a fee of one silver obol on all white dogs. Twelve hundred and three assessments were made, and seven imprisoned for resisting the edict. The monies were used to build a new wing on the Imperator's brothel.

"When people wish to write about something noumenal, outside the realm of edicts and treasures, they seem incapable of using plain language. 'The Imperator Loghead dreamed of a three-headed fish and awoke to find that he had dropsy,' or something of the sort."

"So what you're saying is when they wrote about giant wasps, the archives don't simply say, 'on seven Octobres, six wasps the size of boats were seen above the City Imperishable.'"

"Exactly. Instead there's a bunch of jumble about winged history and stone dogs and intramothers."

Imago felt a chill settle on him. It was as if she were quoting his conversation with the Alate.

"Listen." He drew her close. "There's something you need to know. That cryptic language of the noumenal may not be so cryptic after all."

BIJAZ

He backed away, astonished. The Alate looked as he remembered—thin and strange, like a man with the wings of an angel and an advanced case of the crab disease.

"My pardons," Bijaz told his visitor. "I did not mean to call you down."

"Yet you did," the Alate replied in a creaking voice made of wind. "The intra-mothers arrive. The game is near to ending. You must be on the board."

DeNardo stepped forward, a knife loose in his hand. "This is being a friend of yours, Bijaz?"

"I believe our new arrival has come to give us all a faster way home," Bijaz said.

"They are not of the game." The Alate was almost querulous.

"They are of mine," Bijaz answered. "These three accompany me, or I stay with them."

Yellow eyes stared impassively. "Dawn," the Alate announced, and leapt into the sky with heavy, slow wing beats.

"That gets us away from the bear," Bijaz said in the silence which followed. "Unless you would rather walk."

"Not to be walking," said DeNardo. "Not when there are being other pos-sibilities."

Amalii grunted agreement. Ashkoliiz just glared at Bijaz.

He smiled. "You wanted me to summon something, I summoned some-thing."

DeNardo's teeth gleamed in the darkness. "A boat was being more to the point."

"You do better." Bijaz lay down and tried to work through how Ulliaa's death shout had been done.

Dawn brought four Alates. Four huge birds circled above them, hawks on a scale with the giant wasps.

"We cannot carry you," his visitor from the night before said. "We have brought servants. They may give you fright."

Another Alate dropped a pile of leather. "Put these to your shoulders. They will carry you as they can."

"Like a fish in an osprey's talons?" Bijaz asked. He took up pieces of the leather and set them on his shoulders. They hung over the front and back. He wrapped thongs to secure them, then cut them to length with the little knife he'd been given so long ago. DeNardo helped him tie off the thin strips before picking up pads for himself. Amalii followed suit.

Soon Ashkoliiz stood alone. "I'm not going to do that."

Not petulant this time, Bijaz realized. Panicked. "Then you will walk home by yourself. And you had best hope no sailors find you, or you'll be swimming home tied to an anchor."

She snatched up another set of pads and laid them on her shoulders. Before anyone could help her with ties, the birds descended.

"Mountain teratornis." DeNardo's voice was awed.

The birds' wingspans were at least forty feet. Their pinions were longer than the height of a man. Dark eyes brimmed with cruel intelligence. Somehow the scimitar-sized claws set to his shoulder did not crush him like so much meat.

With two great beats of its wings, the teratornis was aloft again. Bijaz dangled. The river beneath him became a silver thread amid a rumpled blanket of brown and green.

His stomach finally rebelled, spew trailing in a thin, bitter stream.

They flew all day and into the night. Terror became boring, then numbing. Eventually the birds angled away from the river to cut across the sweeping arc of the River Saltus' course. At some point the joints in his shoulder began to exhibit a remarkable pain. At least that kept his mind off the terrible thirst which had turned his mouth to dry cotton. His eyes were old prunes, and his tongue had become a stiff strip of leather.

Midmorning the next day, Bijaz glimpsed the River Saltus again. When he realized that the jumbled terrain at a bend in the river's silver-black thread was the City Imperishable, he burst into dry, heaving sobs.

The teratornis circled downward, escorted by two Alates. He tried to see if the City was intact. People were on the streets. Something had happened to the Winter Grove in Terminus Plaza.

The Eater of Forests.

Fear gripped his heart until Bijaz realized that the streets would not be so busy if a plague of monsters had already stripped the City Imperishable.

He resisted the impulse to wave. The teratornis made for the Rugmaker's Cupola, which was fine with him. After circling the tower, it released him to tumble too far to the rooftop.

The impact knocked all the wind from Bijaz. His vision bloomed red. He tried to move, then lay quivering, wondering if the Alates and their bird-servants had slain him.

The three other teratornis circled close. Each was guided by two Alates. A door slammed open. A dozen men with rifled muskets raced across the roof, shouting. They looked to be a mix of Winter Boys and City Men.

Imago's, surely.

Bijaz tried to stand. He tried to shout "no." They were intent on the sky, raising their weapons for a volley. Bijaz managed to flop like a gaffed mudshark, crawling across the stones, willing the men not to shoot.

Their freerider leader bawled out, "Ready!"

He would not get their attention soon enough.

Bijaz remembered himself and opened his hand to let out a bit of the fire of the sun. Weapon stocks burst into flame. Men cursed as they dropped their muskets. The leader drew a pistol, then stopped with an astonished expression. He opened his mouth to say something when DeNardo fell out of the air between them, the freerider landing flat on his back with a gut-wrenching thump of his head on stone.

ONESIPHOROUS

One of the corsair ships exploded with a blinding white light. Onesiphorous clutched his board as air pressure slapped him hard. A surge of water was close behind, followed by a burning rain of splinters and shards.

Even as he was swamped in the resulting chop, his vision returned sufficiently to see that the blast had left two other black ships afire. Now would be an excellent time for his little fleet to attack the Flag Towers. Unfortunately, in the sinking of the *Xanthippe D.*, he'd lost his control of the battle.

A rowboat pulled up next to him. "Ahoy," said Pottle, reaching down to help Onesiphorous over the side.

The dwarf landed heavily. "Where are those steamships?"

"About a hundred yards behind us," Pottle said grimly. "They're holding fire, giving the black ships a chance to surrender."

"And Kalliope?" He felt a surge of panic. "She was right here with me in the water."

"I don't know." Pottle sounded pained. "All of mine are accounted for, including the three killed in the fight." He gave Onesiphorous a long look. "That'd be Ben Boals, Ghibli the Brown, and Cornelio Rensi. They died for you today, dwarf."

"For me, for Port Defiance, and for the City Imperishable. Now let's find my general."

They circled the black water. "Don't be calling out," Pottle warned in a low voice. "The sound will carry. Someone might decide to investigate with a bullet."

Xanthippe D. hadn't gone down yet, but she was turned turtle. Water around her hissed as the boiler lost its final head.

Pottle's oarsmen stayed wide of the hull, everyone scanning carefully for a bobbing head or a floating body. Light gleamed from Port Defiance as windows opened and walkways became crowded.

"Where is she?" Onesiphorous felt a tightness in his chest. She'd been right beside him.

"I don't know." Pottle had forgotten his own injunction to silence. "And if they start shooting again, we're pulling right smartly for a dock. I won't stay out here under another barrage."

Three long whistle blasts echoed from one of the victorious steamships. The new vessels began closing without more firing. Signal bells rang from the corsairs. They were answered in turn by a more complex sequence of whistles.

"They're using night code," Pottle said.

"Do you understand it?" Onesiphorous asked.

"No." Despite his words, Pottle cocked his head to listen. "Never needed it on *Xanthippe D.* It's a habit of them who sail the Sunward Sea."

Of course the steamers were from one of the Sunward navies, Onesiphorous realized. They had to be, if they were truly Silver's. He focused himself on the trouble at hand. "Could someone else have picked up Kalliope? What about the turtle?"

"Who would have? Either she got swept further away than you, or she's joined my three." Pottle sighed. "Good thing you paid the fare. Davey, Banco, get us to a dock."

Onesiphorous watched the dark water as they rowed away from the ever-settling *Xanthippe D.* Kalliope was in the water there somewhere. He just didn't know what else to do.

The steamships cruised past at dead slow, approaching their prizes. The rowboat was far enough away to avoid being swamped by their wake, but one of the steel prows tore through the assay boat.

"She was a good little vessel," said Pottle quietly.

He had nothing to offer the captain.

The ships continued their negotiations by whistle and bell, until the steamers had closed on their quarry. The vessel with the treed mast had survived, Onesiphorous noted. Let them make sense of that.

"They's someone on the dock, sir," whispered one of the sailors.

Kalliope! he thought.

But it was an old woman in a rocking chair, knitting. A glistening white trunk extended from her back and over the dock's edge into the waters. It was covered with tiny, questing hairs that rippled like grass in the wind.

One of the oarsmen threw up over the side.

"She's a friend of mine," Onesiphorous told them. "Queen of Angoulême."

The old woman laughed, her voice clear even from a distance. "He means I'm the swamp-mother, but he's too smitten to say it of me. Land me my dwarf, boys, then scuttle off if it please you."

They rowed slowly toward the dock again. "You are not from the Sea King?" Pottle's voice quavered.

"That old goatfish? No, he and I was done back when your people still be picking lice from your hairy backs." She put down her needles. "Though you done made him good offerings this night."

The captain sat a little prouder. "Three men, a woman, and my ship."

So he believed Kalliope was lost. Onesiphorous found himself close to tears.

"You got no idea what you fight for, ah?"

"This dwarf of yours," Pottle replied. "The port. And the City Imperishable." The rowboat bumped up against the dock.

She cackled. "You smarter than you look. But I not so sure you take your own meaning."

Pottle boosted Onesiphorous up the ladder. The dwarf was surprised to discover how stiff his joints were. Atop the dock he looked down. "You coming?"

"With *her*? All respects, madam, but I must rejoin the rest of my crew."

"Good cess and fine sail to you, Captain." She winked. "You got my gratitude for to return my dwarf unharmed."

Pottle urged his men away. Onesiphorous watched them go. "So I'm your dwarf, now? I belong to the City Imperishable, you know."

"I know more than you 'bout that," she snapped. "My laying claim to you don't hurt you none in these parts. It don't matter up the river so far from Angoulême."

"Where is Kalliope?"

"I took her scent one time," the queen said absently. "That mean I should always find her again. Her brother, he be on that sloop, fat with sap and growing into the boards of the hull. You with me, wishing you anywhere else. Your woman... I do not know, little City man."

"So she's dead?"

"Oh, usually I got no trouble sniffing out the dead." The needles started up again. "Plenty of 'em in the Flag Towers tonight. Shouldn't ought to have chained my grandson to rock, they shouldn't."

"The fire dancers," Onesiphorous said.

"I have servants aplenty, they both steadfast and true. You don't pass through so many years like me without loyalty growing deeper than blood."

Onesiphorous figured that was all the answer he was going to get. His practical side was reawakening. "I'm here now. What would you of me? Otherwise I shall go and search further for Kalliope."

The swamp-mother gave him another long, slow look. "If I cannot smell her, you cannot find her. Trust in me."

"Then what is on your mind?"

"Your City need you," she said. "Need you now. The intramothers be arriving. People will be fools in they panic. Take that tree man back up the river quick as you can."

"Jason? You said he's in the sloop."

"Yes. Someone must tow him, ah. No sailor would press canvas on that boat now."

"Has he become a monster?"

"Become?" She cackled again. "All men are monsters born and bred. He has become what he could be, that all." She paused thoughtfully. Then: "Go. Now. While there still be time."

With that she folded again. Her face went slack, body, dress, and rocking chair absorbed into a huge fleshy flower which slid backward off the dock.

Someone leaned from a balcony. "Are you that City dwarf?"

He looked up, baffled by far too much, and fell back on an old formulation. "Onesiphorous of the City Imperishable, Chamberlain to the Lord Mayor Imago of Lockwood, come to rally the dwarf refugees."

"You'd best go quick. The short-butts are killing each other in the Flag Towers."

IMAGO

He and Marelle had finished cross-referencing what they knew. Their notes were a mess, and no less cryptic than what they'd thought before.

Stockwell burst in, sweating with excitement. "The roof is under attack!"

Imago stepped into the hall. A cluster of Winter Boys and the Lord Mayor's Own were packed around the narrow stair to the rooftop. They had pistols and rifles. Someone was yelling down from above.

A freerider spotted him across the open well of the tower and shouted, "Bijaz is being here!"

Marelle broke into a run around the circumference of the balcony. Imago stumped along close behind. The defenders opened a path for them. Imago trembled with excitement as he scrambled up the ladder.

He burst onto the roof to see a flight of large birds spiraling away, pursued by sparrows. No, he realized, those sparrows were Alates, and the birds were bigger than anything he'd ever seen fly. Even the giant wasps.

Imago trotted past a pile of smoldering metal toward a knot of men. "I think he's dead, too," someone said.

The Lord Mayor pushed in. They surrounded a small, dark-complected man—one of the Northerners.

"Where's Bijaz?" he demanded.

"Near the edge."

Imago ran to the old dwarf's side and dropped painfully to his knees.

Bijaz was emaciated, his face sun-scarred. His right hand seemed to have been burned. Leather pads were roped to his shoulders over ragged clothing bleached by heat and ill-use.

"Was he left in the desert to die?" Imago asked.

"Don't know," said one of the men. "Some damned big birds dropped them all here." He met the Lord Mayor's eye a moment. "They bounced."

Imago turned to Marelle. "Have Stockwell send for that Tribade doctor." His fingers brushed Bijaz's face. "Who else was returned to us?'

"Just being four," Astaro answered. "DeNardo, Bijaz, one of the Northmen, and that woman Ashkoliiz."

"Are they all like this?"

Astaro shrugged. "They are being too long without food or water, I am thinking. We are working to save DeNardo."

Of course they are. Imago suppressed a hot surge of anger. Some scrap of wisdom kept his mouth shut.

He checked the others. Ashkoliiz seemed to be asleep. DeNardo had cracked his head on the stone. Someone brought blankets from below to wrap the injured. Imago sat on the carillon's platform, waiting in silence until the Tribade doctor appeared. The woman had Biggest Sister at her side.

Even they carried poppies. Somehow he hadn't expected the Tribade to need the flowers.

"Clear them all off," the doctor growled. "Except his worship."

With a glare from Biggest Sister, the Lord Mayor's Own found business inside the tower. Imago beckoned Astaro and Marelle to stay with him.

The doctor flipped back each set of blankets. After she finished examining Bijaz, her last patient, she looked up at Imago. "What in the hells have you done to these people? If I move them, they will die." The doctor shook her head. "I need thick-walled tents, good furnaces within, and a great deal of water.

"Biggest Sister, please send for my large battle bag, and have Willa come with at least two of the Red Sisters." She stopped, thought for a minute. "You realize, your worship, that the return of these people is no more a secret than this morning's sunrise?"

Imago took her point. "Rumors are not our worry now. I'll keep the leeches away."

"You do that," she said harshly. "As you value their lives, get what I need, *now!*"

Back inside the tower, Stockwell had a broadsheet. "See here, sir." His voice trembled as he thrust the paper at Imago.

Imperishable Information, a masthead he hadn't seen before. The headline was new, too. *Lord Mayor Fidelo Declares Amnesty.* No printer's bug indicated where it had been run up. The broadsheets had been shut down since his arrest.

The story was breathless.

It is the right pleasure of Lord Mayor Fidelo, elevated by grace of the Burgs.s, to offer an amnesty to all who supported the Pretender Lockwood in the late unpleasantness, viz. the survivors of the Krewe of Faces, any clerks who served in the Pretender's attempt at governance, Tokharee or dwarffs misguided by their tribal leaders, or others who have stood in unlawful opposition to the Burgs.s and their rightful appointees in the governance of the C. Imperishable and all its citizens, residents, and subjects.

The LM Fidelo further condemns the Pretender for his criminal negligence in summoning the recentmost plague of gigantic insects and their raptors upon the C. Imperishable, and enjoins the felon from further such acts on pain of trial for his life. Neither dwarf nor man, the Pretender is a salacious and venal fellow whose ways with words have misguided the affairs of our Citizens.

It is the opinion of this Editor that the Pretender should be brought to justice for his crimes to date. Should a committee of citizens spontaneously assemble for this purpose, Imperishable Information *would be pleased to donate the rope.*

Glory to the City! Glory to the Lord Mayor Fidelo! Glory to the Burgs.s!

"Well, that was wonderful," Imago said. "I believe I shan't visit the Limerock Palace any time soon."

"There was no mention of First Counselor Wedgeburr," Stockwell offered.

"No matter. This is an effort to incite riot against me. No one outside the Limerock Palace would have the nerve."

A bailiff barged through the door. *No,* Imago corrected himself, *one of the Lord Mayor's Own.* They'd found silk poppies to wear as badges.

"Lord Mayor! There's a steamship come up the river from Port Defiance. They are docking at the Old Lighter Quay."

Imago called for Astaro, then remembered the freerider was up on the roof. "Round up a mount for me, and a guard," he told Stockwell. "I must speak to that captain personally."

The fast steam packet had already tied up when they made the river. A squad of bailiffs was there, several Burgesses in their midst, trapped by a shoving crowd. People thrust money toward the crew in a desperate attempt to garner news of loved ones.

Imago was pleased that the crowd opened a lane for him. He waved to the bailiffs as his little pony picked its way among shouting faces.

A pudgy officer with a walrus moustache waited at the rail with a pistol in each hand. Clearly no one had yet come on or off his ship.

The officer spotted Imago. "Are you the Lord Mayor?"

"Yes!" Imago realized one of the men with the bailiffs had been Fidelo. Thank Dorgau he'd gotten through first. "Is the blockade lifted?"

"I don't know." The officer signaled to someone behind him, then covered his ears. Taking the hint, Imago covered his own just as the steam whistle shrieked like the damned.

In the stunned silence which followed, the officer leaned over the rail to speak quickly. "A naval battle was joined between the corsairs and a fleet of small boats. Captain Fairmond cast off and drove us up the Saltus overspeed. Last we heard was a new set of guns as a third fleet entered the battle."

"Who was fighting?" Imago shouted as the babble around him resumed.

"We don't know!"

Imago nodded and pulled his pony back. The officer began selling tickets for a run back to Port Defiance, at ten times the pre-blockade price. Unguaranteed return fares went for ten times *that*.

Imago nodded to his men, then pointed at the advancing bailiffs. The horsemen bulled through the crowd and into the line of redcoats.

Fallen Arch was with them, looking rather drawn. The rat Fidelo rode alongside, and another man Imago did not know.

"I see you have brought your pretender with you," Imago said.

Fallen Arch nodded, disgust upon his face. Fidelo yelled over the crowd noise: "We are the Right Honorable Lord Mayor."

"Run back to the palace and play with Wedgeburr. He likes to torture Lords Mayor."

Fallen Arch grimaced. "The recent First Counselor is, so to speak, recent. I have that honor once more." Faced with an increasingly hostile crowd, the bailiffs began hustling their charges away.

Wedgeburr's support in the Burgesses must have collapsed, Imago realized. Imago would not have expected the man to survive a shift in power, not with all the trouble he had caused.

BIJAZ

He'd never before been this far from the reaper man. The wheat field was as long as the hills of the Saltus basin. The sky was dull, day-bright but innocent of sun or cloud.

The reaper man walked the far end of the field, scythe rising and falling. Bijaz watched awhile before realizing he saw a pattern. The wheat had been cut to form a giant, rounded hex.

No, a flower.

He saw a flower.

Once again Bijaz felt a desire to speak to the reaper man. But he could not walk—his legs would barely twitch. His arms were wood, his tongue leather. He'd been hung on a pole.

A scarecrow, set to guard this path to power.

He wondered how to get down. If only he had water, his mouth would be moist and he could shout for help. If only he could shout for help, he could be pulled down and drink his fill. His thoughts ran in a tight circle, yielding nothing.

I am a god. I can make light.

A beam leapt from his right hand to flood the day with brightness. Far away, the reaper man stopped his work and turned to look.

I can make fire.

As it had in the mines, a spout of fire leapt forth. The wheat before him caught, and the flames quickly spread until billowing smoke obscured his view of the reaper man.

I can make flowers.

He willed the flames to become bright roses. They did, as smoke crystallized to falling ash.

The reaper man ran with acre-long strides, his scythe across his shoulder as he stepped from hill to hill. Bijaz wondered at his hurry when the first lightning bolt struck behind him.

Thunder tore at his hearing. As it died away, something very large growled. Bijaz tried to look, but the pole trapped him. Instead he twisted his hand so the palm faced behind him and made more light.

Something shrieked. A blow landed which shook his pole, driving splinters into the raw skin of his back.

The reaper man bounded closer. Another roar erupted behind him.

This time Bijaz made fire with his backturned palm.

The answering roar was anguished. The next blow tore through the pole to take him in the head. Blood sluiced down his back.

The reaper man stepped over him, tall as the sky and dark as a thundercloud, to pour down hard rain. Some fell upon Bijaz, washing away his misdeeds. Tongue wetted, he cried for help.

A woman with tight-cropped gray hair and a fierce expression leaned close. "Are you trying to talk to me, old dwarf?"

"Help me," Bijaz whispered. He was hot, and thirsty as the sand sea.

Triumph shone in her eyes as she tipped a flask of water to his lips.

ONESIPHOROUS

They were rioting in the Ivories, the district surrounding the Flag Towers. Onesiphorous limped as quickly as he could over bridges and along balconies, cursing with every step. He found that the ferry at Copperbottom Channel was missing.

He could *see* his destination, but he couldn't get across the water.

The tide was racing, and Onesiphorous was cold already. He would not swim this.

Was there another way? He tried to use the blue jade like a key, as if it would open some ancient, secret door in the rock behind him. Nothing happened, of course.

"*Ssardali,*" hissed a woman. "You hard to catch for little man." She took the jade from his unresisting fingers. "I got boat."

Silver wore a crisp uniform of white duck over knee-high boots. Now he was certain where the fighting steamships had come from.

Onesiphorous followed her to a little launch. Eight uniformed sailors waited at the oars. She barked orders, and they began to pull, coordinated as the legs of a waterbug.

"The Flag Towers," he gasped.

"Yes. Elsewise we no get you out of here." Silver turned the blue jade over in her hand. "Where you find this?"

"Up the coast," he said cautiously. It *had* been the key to get him across, in a manner of speaking. If he'd simply leapt into the current, she might not have caught up to him.

"This buy entire ship. Maybe fleet, if the rock got no flaws." She grinned. "You show me more, I tear up letters of patent."

"All I have, I'm afraid." Onesiphorous slumped. "Have you picked up any survivors out on the water?"

Silver shrugged. "I chasing you, not doing rescue." She returned the jade fragment.

They pulled up at the large stone landing which served as the formal entrance to the Flag Towers. Dead dwarfs were scattered across wide marble steps leading upward.

"By the hells," Onesiphorous hissed. He would *not* have his people killing one another.

"Here." Silver pressed a pepperbox pistol into his hand.

He had no more idea how to use that than the rifle he'd held earlier, but Onesiphorous gripped the weapon tight and raced up the steps. He slipped twice on blood before gaining the top.

A glance back showed Silver following with her sailors. They carried rifles.

Good, thought Onesiphorous. Someone would know what they were doing.

The main hall was empty, except for more bodies. Some still groaned. The furniture had been smashed, and legs taken for clubs. Noise ahead promised a full bore riot in progress.

Onesiphorous raced for the far doors, only to find them barred. Somebody tugged one open from the other side. "Come on, we've al—" The voice stopped when the speaker realized who stood waiting.

Onesiphorous shoved the doors wide and kicked the door warden in the nadgers. He was on a landing above the Harbormaster's receiving room. A high, vaulted ceiling loomed above. An empty throne stood on the opposite landing at the far end of the room. Both landings were lined with brass urns taller than he was.

Dozens of dwarfs and full-men were fighting in the space below. They were killing each other.

Onesiphorous shoved one of the huge urns down the stairs. The clangor distracted most of the combatants. He tried to follow up with a pistol shot to the ceiling, but the trigger was stuck.

Someone sniggered.

A rifle volley from behind him brought down shards of plaster.

That got their attention.

"Hear me," Onesiphorous shouted. "Opener or Boxer, Slashed or Sewn. It doesn't matter who you are. The blockade is broken, the corsairs are banished. If we don't all of us go home to the City Imperishable at once, it will fall!"

"Could be better," Silver whispered.

"Who the hells are you?" called out one of the full-men.

"He's that Slashed bugger," said a dark-skinned dwarf, looking like a boxed Sunwarder.

"I'm a *dwarf*." Onesiphorous' temper was slipping away. "As is every one of you short-arsed buggering little bastards."

He waved the pistol, which went off this time. A chip of gold leaf spalled off the throne at the far end of the room. Wiser heads below ducked.

"You Dorgau-blasted Openers have been listening to full-men. You Boxers are no better. Me, I don't give a thin damn about any one of you dockside bastards." Onesiphorous lowered the pistol. "What I do care about is your children, and their city. I'm going home. This woman's navy is taking me. If any of you want a ride, you're welcome to join us. Otherwise stay here and be hanged with the Harbormaster and his men." He hurled the weapon to the steps, where it bounced and discharged once more.

Everyone down below ducked that time. Onesiphorous turned to see Silver getting to her feet. She and Onesiphorous pushed past each other. He was heading for the entrance as she retrieved her pistol.

"Launches be outside soon," she shouted. "Anyone want to follow him, to come."

Moments later they were back down in the boat. The riot did not seem to have resumed, but no one had followed them to the landing either.

"We are done for," he said mournfully. "My people will not listen to reason."

"My pistol may be done for." Silver turned the weapon over in her hand. "You hard little man."

"We are a people used hard."

"I send launches anyway."

They reached one of the big steamships. Silver scrambled up a rope ladder, leaving Onesiphorous to follow up the tall hull. He hadn't realized how big this ship was.

On board, he found himself alone with four of Silver's sailors. They seemed to want him at the rail, out of everyone's way. He looked back across Port Defiance.

The city was waking up, as it had not done since the corsairs had come. Lights, laughter, boats in the water. Onesiphorous had hoped for justice tonight, but he supposed peace might have to be enough.

When Silver finally returned, he told her, "We must find Jason. I need to take him up the river."

"Who Jason?"

"An ally of mine. He was east of the city in a little sloop. He attacked the corsairs from the landward side."

She nodded. "Yes. He signal when he see us. Admiral think we found out."

So Jason had brought them into the fight. Onesiphorous wondered how he had been able to find the Gronegrii fleet when the corsairs hadn't seen them. "I need to find him and his sister Kalliope. She was with me on the assay boat *Xanthippe D.*"

"Where *Xanthippe D.* now?"

"Lost," he said shortly.

"She come out of water with you?"

"No."

Silver sighed. She spoke quickly to one of the sailors, sending the man off at a run. She turned back to Onesiphorous, saying, "Letters you make me still to be honored by City Imperishable?"

He knew a change of subject when he heard one. "Certainly."

"Then we go up river when tide is right." A smiled flashed. "Your Jason come. We find this Kalliope, she come too." Silver saluted, then departed.

This version of Silver was so different from the ragged fishing girl he first met. She had so much in common with Enero, though they spoke two different languages beneath their Civitas. Onesiphorous wondered what it would be like to live in the young, uncomplicated nations along the Sunward Sea.

He reminded himself that nothing in life was uncomplicated. Especially the politics of cities.

Jason's sloop had been taken in tow behind Silver's ship, *Princeps Olivo*. By daylight the iron-clad steamer seemed impossibly tall and strange, with her raked masts and enormous guns mounted in turrets upon the deck. She was white too, crisp as the linens in a Heliograph Hill restaurant.

The other two steamers shepherded their prizes back south. Negotiation had resulted in the undamaged corsair ship sailing free. Silver seemed pleased, whatever the arrangement had been.

"I want to go down to the sloop," he told her.

Her face set in a hard quirk. "No. Bad on ship. Jason live, let him be."

Onesiphorous was too tired to argue.

The Gronegrii navy had brought several dozen dwarfs aboard as well. The riot had reportedly not resumed, though individual grudges continued to be settled throughout Port Defiance. No one had seen the Harbormaster.

Onesiphorous hoped they'd find a new government soon. He was in no mood to play kingmaker.

Princeps Olivo sailed with the dawn, ghosting into the Saltus channel dead slow until she found her bearings. Onesiphorous stared west into the shadows of Angoulême. People stood there in dories and little flat bottomed boats, and even canoes.

He raised his hand high to them, something between a wave and a salute. Red birds burst from the canopy of the jungle, circling like feathered flame as *Princeps Olivo* picked up steam, heading north.

Silver found him an hour later. "Hello, Oarsman."

"Actually, my name is Onesiphorous."

"Oarsman better name." She laid a hand on his arm. "You know a man name Enero in your city?"

He was surprised. "A Bas Luccian. High officer, working as a mercenary. Lord Mayor Imago would struggle much harder without him. I think he was due to return south this spring."

Silver smiled. "Enero, my *massatro*. Eh... we to be married."

"Betrothed?" Onesiphorous found it delightful that such a warlike, clever woman was destined to marry such a warlike, clever man. "Your children will be beautiful and fierce."

"I glad you know him."

"I'm glad to know you. I will dance at your wedding."

"Of course!" She laughed.

They steamed north between walls of jungled swamp, heading for whatever had set even the queen of Angoulême to worrying. *At least some good will come of this*, Onesiphorous thought. He'd never realized that Enero had a girl waiting at home. He hoped the freerider was still in the City Imperishable.

Imago.

Back at the Rugmaker's Cupola, Stockwell slipped him a note. He didn't recognize the handwriting.

Dwrf awoke, took wtr, slpng now

Imago's heart leapt. "Bijaz?"

Stockwell nodded. "Doctor says leave him alone. If anything happens, she'll send a Sister for you."

"Very well." Within, he exulted. He had not managed to kill the old dwarf. It would be very good to hear what had actually taken place on the Northern Expedition.

Stockwell plucked at Imago's sleeve. "One more thing, sir."

"Yes?"

"The farms to the north? Up around Sourapple Roads?"

"Yes?" This didn't sound good.

"Their people are coming in. Saying there's thunder to the north and west. Riders out that way aren't returning. They're afraid sir, but no one can say what of."

"How do you know?"

Stockwell blushed. "Been listening in the Root Market when I'm out shopping. Saw a lot of those big horses, the ones that pull the plows. They don't usually come in to market. So I sent boys to ask around."

"Well done," said Imago. "I haven't heard so much of this intelligence as I used to. Please do keep me informed."

The clerk bowed, still blushing, then stumbled off.

Imago sighed and climbed the stairs. When he reached his office, he saw that Marelle had covered everything in rough brown paper. She'd blocked his shelves, his desk, his daybed—all but the window. Even the back of the door.

Notes were everywhere.

All his flat surfaces were stacked with books, papers, scrolls, mounded in tides of paper. Pencils, quills, fountain pens, sticks of chalk were scattered about.

It was a mess.

"I am searching for the truth embedded in our history," she told him. "Look here."

A chart was drawn on a paper hanging next to his window, covering the bookshelf behind his desk.

Wasps	*Giant*	*Intramothers*
	Small	*Eater of Forests (above?)*
	Poppies?	
City Imperishable	*Stone dogs*	
Alates	*History*	
The inevitability of change		

"We're missing something," she said.

"We're missing a lot." He took her in his arms a moment. "Bijaz awoke briefly while I was at the docks. Something has happened at Port Defiance. The river blockade may be broken. We await further news."

"Excellent!" She broke away and pointed at her chart. "We need to know more."

"What you've got there doesn't mean much to me now," he admitted.

"Think about this: A farmer grows grain. His cattle eat the stalks and stubble. They shit in their pens. The farmer spreads the manure on his fields to help more grain grow. It's a cycle."

"Like money," Imago said. "Seed money becomes operating cash, which generates profit to repay the seed money with interest."

Marelle giggled. "You should have been a dwarf. That would be obvious to anyone raised in a box."

"Not me. I learned it the hard way."

She continued. "The wasps and the trees are part of something. That word the Alate used, 'intramother.' I found it in the archives, but there's no explanation."

"It means something," he protested. "It must."

"Of course it does." She flipped her grease pencil in her fingers, staring at the sheet. "I've been reading on the life cycle of wasps, on species gigantism, on forest plagues. There's just not enough here."

"There may never be," he told her.

"There's not enough time. And what do the poppies have to do with it anyway?" She snapped her grease pencil.

He eyed the chart. "Don't put them with the wasps. Put them under the City. Those only grow *here*, they're thickest in the Potter's Field, and no one has ever seen them before. They fit the cycle."

"Maybe that makes sense."

He watched her scribble notes awhile longer, wishing mightily to go up on the roof and see to Bijaz. Imago had learned to heed what the Sisters told him. And while he was most afraid of Biggest Sister, the doctor came a very close second.

Reports of wasp attacks began filtering in that afternoon. After Stockwell's first two notes, Imago went downstairs to leave Marelle in peace.

His people had lost the giddy mood which had overtaken them in the wake of the attack on the Winter Grove. Poppies were present in profuse abundance as well—on hats, buttonholes, weapons harnesses, as well as stacked in a big tub by the doors.

Imago wondered what would happen when the blooms ran out.

Astaro and a bailiff named Orrey were in close conference over a map of the City Imperishable. Imago stepped close.

"…three by the Limerock Palace," Orrey said. "And three more around New Hill."

"It is to being too worrisome."

"How many total?" Imago asked.

"Lord Mayor," Orrey replied with a sharp nod. "We don't really know. The swarms are smaller than what was in Terminus Plaza. Lindens and poplars and chestnuts are collapsing. They're taking horses, dogs, people—anything outside without a poppy that doesn't get away fast enough."

"Not to be coming into buildings yet," added Astaro.

"That won't last." Imago looked at the marks on the map, trying to spot a pattern. Could they predict the next assaults? "Doors are wood, and people leave windows open. Buildings will be easy for them."

"What are they to be doing?"

"My fear is that there's a great nest growing somewhere within the City."

"*More* of them?" Orrey seemed incredulous.

An idea occurred to Imago. "I need Saltfingers," the Lord Mayor said.

Waiting for the old dunny diver in Marelle's office, Imago considered the problem of the false Lord Mayor Fidelo. He decided he simply didn't care. If the little buggerer could do more than Imago to repair the life of the City, perhaps he *deserved* to be Lord Mayor.

Saltfingers appeared far sooner than Imago had expected. "Your worship," the old dwarf said, climbing into a wingback chair to huddle like a dog. He wasn't wearing a poppy.

"How is it beneath the stones?"

"Busy." The dwarf shuddered. "There's things down there we ain't seen in lifetimes. I got three dunny divers swear they crossed from Sudgate Number Three to Cork Street Bypass without ever going under the Little Bull or meeting the Old Twins. Which is as likely as my finger passing from one ear to the other from the inside, if you takes my meaning, sir. Not to say them wasps are getting in as well."

"Blow me for a dog," muttered Imago. "I hoped the sewers would shelter our people if things grew worse."

"'S possible," Saltfingers said cautiously. "We can stop a few tunnels. But it would not last, your worship. No food, no clean water. Also, a lot of people go crackers in darkness. If you needed an hour or even a day, I could find the way. Not more."

"There's one other thing." Some words were difficult to say.

"Sir?"

"I may have to seek the Old Gods again."

Saltfingers gave Imago a long look. "Yes?"

The words came out in a rush. "Would you take me to the tombs if needed?"

"And why would your worship want to go down there?" Saltfingers asked softly. "What with all the trouble you personally gone to so's *they* could sleep once more in their comfy stone beds."

"Because I won't let these wasps take my city down to the stones. We deserve more than bloody bones and sawdust."

"Ah." Saltfingers sat in silence a moment. "Just remember this. The present is only a moment long. Then you've got a new moment. History is forever. So think careful on what you want to live with, your worship."

"Thank you," Imago said gravely. That was tripe worthy of a priest, and quite surprising coming from Saltfingers. All men could be prophets in times of need.

BIJAZ

It was dark outside when he awoke.

Again?

The furnace by his bed had died down to coals. Bijaz squinted. It was a Little Moloch. A fine make. He'd owned one himself.

Clarity of thought was a novelty, in distinct contrast to the painful workings of his body. He couldn't move his shoulders, though his wrists flexed. His right hand was bandaged. The rest of him was not so much paralyzed as unstrung.

He'd felt better. But he was still breathing.

Bijaz decided to try out his voice. "Where the hells am I?"

A woman slipped through a tent flap and secured it tight behind her. She was young, with close-cropped pale hair, wearing a dark dress. A Tribade sister, but comfortably round where they tended to resemble old shoe leather. Oddly, she wore a pale-waxy poppy tucked into her collar.

"You are atop the Rugmaker's Cupola," she said. "In a tent where you have been warmed since this morning. You were too injured to be moved."

The memory of the teratornis exploded into Bijaz's head. A spinning vertigo assaulted him. He gripped his cot for fear of falling out. "The world was too far beneath my feet."

"Birds will do that to you." She inspected him critically. "You're lucid, but I'd guess you couldn't stand if your life depended on it. Still, I think Sister Medica plans to move you downstairs tonight. Open air isn't safe."

"The Eater of Forests is here."

"You mean the wasps?" Her eyes narrowed. Probably wondering if he was crazed.

"Yes, the wasps. Both little and big."

"You are correct," she said shortly.

"I need to speak to the Lord Mayor as soon as possible," Bijaz said urgently. "Along with Enero and Kalliope."

"I'll see." She slipped back out the flap.

A few minutes later the sister returned with the Tribade doctor, accompanied by half a dozen men. They were an oddly mixed lot—a bailiff, two Winter Boys, and three civilians. Each wore a pale silk flower as well as a wilted poppy.

"The stairs are more in the nature of a ladder," the doctor said, staring at Bijaz. "We'll have to tip the cot too far."

"I'll use my feet," he growled.

"Go ahead." The doctor rested her fingers on her chin. "I'm ready to see this miracle."

He'd done miracles before. The first problem was getting the blankets off him. After pushing ineffectually for several minutes, Bijaz gave up. "I'm sorry."

"So now you'll believe me?" The doctor's sarcasm could have cut bread.

"Yes," he said. "I will. Just bring me to Imago. Or Enero."

That produced a ripple of nervousness among her helpers.

What are they hiding?

The doctor had the men strap him to the cot with cargo slings over folded pads of silk and cotton. Then they picked his bed up and carried him quickly out of the tent. The night air was cool, but he could hear distant screaming and a high pitched buzz.

"They're here," Bijaz whispered, sliding into vivid recollection of the wasps in the mine shaft.

The men bearing him bunched up at the trap door leading below. "Be quick about it," the doctor hissed.

Two went down the ladder, while the other four tipped him into the hole headfirst. The doctor began to protest, but it was too late.

He felt the bedclothes slide beneath him as the straps snagged. Some slipped, others held. The ceiling of the tower spun by him to the sound of cursing. Then he was flat again.

"Here," the doctor said. They hustled him into a room. He wasn't sure whose office this had been, but most of the furniture had been smashed, then swept into the corner at the wide end of the room, along the outside wall. A canopied bed sat in the center of the space, another Little Moloch heater beside it.

"I am not lying on pink silk beneath a roof of lace."

"You're free to get up and leave at any time." The doctor's tone was nasty. Her helpers unstrapped Bijaz and moved him into the bed. They filed out, some grinning.

"I believe you can expect visitors soon," she told him. "Sister Nurse will be with you to watch for trouble." She reconsidered her words. "My sort of trouble,

I mean. I'd tell you not to strain yourself, but there's no point in me wasting my breath."

Imago bustled in, accompanied by Marelle and a freerider Bijaz vaguely recognized. The freerider also wore the silk flower.

"Hello," Bijaz said simply, wondering where the rest of them were.

Imago grinned. "You look silly. The sweet prince cocooned in silk beyond his mortal estate, but I misremember the lines."

"'Sweet prince,'" Marelle recited, "'sleep your last

"'Cocooned in silk and death's dark mask

"'To slip forth from this mortal fate

"'And find your soul's last estate.'"

Bijaz was baffled. "What are you talking about?"

Marelle shook her head. "Where is your education? Mandorello gives those lines, near the end of *Porcini, Prince of Bas Luccia*. One of the greatest plays by Guillaume of Rock."

"There was little theatre in my growing box," Bijaz said darkly. "You both make me feel the fool." He added, "It is good to be home."

Imago took his hand. "It is good to have you home, old friend." He nodded to Marelle. "She is my chamberlain now. Onesiphorous lies in his grave to the south. Astaro here speaks for the Winter Boys and the Lord Mayor's Own."

"Where is Enero?" Bijaz asked. "And Kalliope?"

Astaro looked away, while Marelle's smile vanished. Bijaz felt his heart plummet.

Imago took that question almost straight on. "Kalliope is in the south with Jason, hoping to salvage something from the fall of Port Defiance. There's news just today of that. Enero was killed at Wedgeburr's orders. Along with many others. These have not been good times."

Bijaz let his breath out in a slow, painful gasp. "The Eater of Forests is here, too, I see."

"Wasps?"

"Yes. Believe me, there were far worse things under the ice up there. Pray they never find their way down the mountains." Though he wasn't so sure about Iistaa. "We were pursued by a demonic fetch before the Alates caused us to be taken away."

Imago sat on the edge of his bed. Marelle stood close. The Lord Mayor's arm slipped around her waist, which told Bijaz much. "We need to know," Imago said, "what became of you."

"Something great and terrible in the history of cities is afoot," Marelle added. "We think this might be what Terminus sought to avoid. What did the Northern Expedition find?"

"And DeNardo," the freerider added. "What of him?"

Bijaz began to talk, telling the story from the beginning so he didn't lose his thread. He recounted the manipulative perfidy of Ashkoliiz, the strange behavior of the Northmen and the bear, the death of the *Slackwater Princess*, and on through the whole sorry business.

ONESIPHOROUS

Surely the pilot of *Princeps Olivo* would have preferred a less rapid pace, but Silver had caught Onesiphorous' urgency. His erstwhile rescuer clearly stood in the highest councils of Bas Gronegrim and its navy.

The sailors kept a respectful distance, while allowing him the freedom of the main deck. The rest of the City dwarfs huddled under a canopy with a water butt and a beer barrel, not permitted to move about.

Onesiphorous found himself time and again at the stern rail, watching the sloop wallow along behind. Something was very wrong. The mast and bowsprit had both fallen away. The deck bulged. Groaning echoed across the water.

He wondered what transformations Jason endured now. Whatever passed for that man's soul must be battered beyond all measure.

Though Onesiphorous had come to find respect and affection for the Angoumois and their shadows, he was glad to be returning home. If only Kalliope had made the journey as well. The likelihood of her surviving the sinking of *Xanthippe D.* seemed less and less with each passing hour.

That afternoon Silver found him staring southward. She handed him a waxed paper packet. A rolled-up flatbread was tucked within. "Eat, Oarsman."

He tugged at it. Salt fish and pickled cabbage lurked inside the bread. Nothing that appealed. "We pay too high a price for our games."

She laughed. "Everybody got games. Fisherman in his hut play stakes against tide and current. Merchant in his shop set himself against bank and supplier and customer. King in his palace gamble empire against glory. You play game, pay best price you can."

"I fear Kalliope is dead," he said slowly. "Jason is become something monstrous. My people tear themselves to pieces, arguing whether raising another generation of dwarf children is a sacred duty or an abomination. I don't have any idea what's become of the City Imperishable. It must still be standing or we'd have seen a flood of refugees come south."

"Blockade gone," she said softly. "You going home. I soon see Enero. Everybody pay price, move on. Some move along soul's path, others keep walking through world."

"You must have strange priests in Bas Gronegrim."

"My house..." Her voice trailed off. "My house we ask our mothers' help. Old mother, older mother, oldest mother. We got bones go back a thousand years. First mother my family come from sea, daughter of Sea King. Legend… eh… truth… eh." She caught his eye with her gaze. "We got silver box. Thousand-year-old-fish fin inside. All crinkle paper like wasp wing. Is real? I got no way to know. Is my first mother? Of course. I believe first mother, she first mother. She teach me, she pay price to come from sea, she move on. Me in world is just her moving on another… eh… generation?"

"Generation," said Onesiphorous. "I can't help but take it more personally."

"Is personal. Only one you, only one lifetime." She squeezed his free hand. "Eat now."

He began chewing at the rolled bread as she walked away. *Princeps Olivo* followed the River Saltus through open country now, Jason's sloop trailing on its tow lines. Low hills rolled from on both banks. Odd patches of growth stood out at the water's edge. Onesiphorous wondered what he saw, until he realized they had been trees.

A force substantial enough to gnaw down full-grown cypress and willows had passed here recently. That gave him pause. Then someone began shouting excitedly up on the bridge deck. A cannon boomed.

Something huge and improbable curved past the stern rail with a buzzing that set his teeth to aching.

A wasp, he realized. Though it was so big…

His imagination failed.

Gunfire rattled from the fore as the City dwarfs began screaming. Onesiphorous heard a splash. Moments later the corpse of the wasp bumped past the stern of *Princeps Olivo*, struck the bow of Jason's sloop, and spun away on the current. Its translucent wings were spread wide as a grain barge. Pale jelly leaked from ruptures in the abdomen.

His gut flopped, threatening to follow the wasp into the River Saltus. What *had* happened to the City Imperishable?

Princeps Olivo gave three short, sharp whistle blasts as she increased her speed yet again. He was not the only one with that question in mind.

Somewhat to Onesiphorous' surprise, they steamed into the night. Even the fast packets usually anchored rather than push on through darkness. The moon was the barest sliver past new, and the stars were bright, but the River Saltus ran black and slick.

Onesiphorous was no expert at river navigation, but he'd spent enough time drinking with clerks to hear numerous tales of how disaster could befall an honest man who was only shaving a few hours for the sake of the delivery bonuses in his contracts.

The River Saltus craved change, it seemed. The channel rarely shifted, but bars constantly built up or washed away. Escaped logs formed snags. Debris entered the river from tributaries.

He wondered about hazards, still alone at the stern rail watching Jason's sloop ride ever lower in the water. The whistle gave a long shriek. Someone bellowed in a Sunward tongue, then in Civitas, "Brace for impact."

Onesiphorous sat down and clung to a stanchion.

A loud bang echoed, which he felt through the deck as much as he heard it. *Princeps Olivo* shuddered. The boilers grumbled loudly, accompanied by a rising screech of steam.

A series of shouted orders arose from further forward, followed by a fusillade of gunfire. The deck rolled as cannons roared.

Moments later a burning raft of debris passed him by. The sound of the boilers stepped down and the ship resumed its course with a short blast of the whistle.

Silver came to him again a few minutes later. "You still not hungry, eh?"

"No." He hadn't bothered to stand up.

"I find you bunk somewhere, you want."

"No." Sleep was only slightly less interesting than food. The sloop trailing them wallowed ever lower. "It's sinking," he said.

"We know. We go fast, get there before all done. No one will board to repair. Ghost boat now, after he kill so many in battle."

"I don't think he's dead yet." Upon reflection, Onesiphorous realized that was a profoundly stupid thing to say about Jason. "Again, I mean."

"Your City Imperishable, *ssardali*. Vile. Like water monitor raised in barrel, eat her children."

"*Ssardali?* What happened to 'everybody pay price'?"

"Everyone still complain about cost. Is to be human, eh?"

"Yes, I suppose." He stared at the water. The last embers of the debris had drifted out of his line of sight. "That racket, a little while ago. Did we run down a snag?"

She chuckled. "Log raft. Gunnery section take target practice on what we hit. Everybody get chance to do some hot work, everybody happy."

It must be nice, Onesiphorous thought, *to carry arms under your city's flag. Fight who you're told, stand down when you're done, and never worry about the consequences.*

Somehow he couldn't square that little fantasy with Enero, who took everything with a deadly, detailed seriousness, yet always seemed amused.

"I believe I'll just sit here," he told Silver. "Thank you."

"As you wish. Maybe fight tomorrow, maybe die tomorrow. Better on good night's sleep."

"Everything is."

She touched his shoulder. "Sleep well."

The night wind cramped his legs. Jason's sloop only depressed him further. Onesiphorous picked himself up, stretched, then went to join the other dwarfs.

Most of them were sleeping under blankets given them by the ship's crew. A few sat talking quietly. The guard was down to one bored-looking sailor next to a table of food.

He wandered over there first. Maybe eating wasn't such a bad idea. The offerings were fish and bread, with bread and fish as an alternative. He tugged a couple of pieces free and went to sit with his fellow dwarfs.

The whispering fell silent at his approach. Six dwarfs, three dwarfesses. In the shadows he couldn't see their faces as anything but pale ovals.

"If it isn't mister high and mighty City dwarf," one finally said. "Come to visit the prisoners?"

"Hardly. I see free dwarfs of the City Imperishable enjoying a ride home at someone else's expense."

"You wander the deck while we are forced to huddle here," a dwarfess told him.

"I wander nowhere," Onesiphorous said. "I have charge of a dying man on the boat in tow. He's too ill to come aboard, and I cannot join him there, so I watch him from the stern rail." Almost true, as far as it went.

"The tree man," another dwarfess said sympathetically. "And you're the one who raised the fleet."

"Both fleets." Bitterness slipped free, though he didn't mean to share it here. "Otherwise you'd still be knifed on the walkways and the corsairs would still be drinking the Harbormaster's wine. Good men and women died to free you." His anger began to boil again. "Then I find dwarfs, *dwarfs*, killing one another in the Flag Towers."

Enough, he told himself. *Let go, or they will not heed you.*

"Collaboration," said the dwarf who'd first challenged him. "And shame. You don't know what it was like."

"I know that I saw people chained to drown for helping me escape. I know that I crawled through the swamps of Angoulême for weeks on weeks to raise a fleet to save you. A good friend died beside me in that battle. On that boat behind us her brother sinks into a fate I wouldn't curse my worst enemy with. While you people fight over the best way to end our race."

"What race?" asked another. "We are a made folk, not born. I am who I am, but my children could walk tall and never know a day's misery."

"All we have to do is let go," the sympathetic dwarfess said.

"And then what?" Tears stung Onesiphorous' eyes. "A thousand years of our history drifts in the wind? Even if the answer is to smash the boxes, that should be decided in peaceful debate. Not by bluecoats breaking down doors and casting children out."

"There have been many wrongs," another told him. "Wrongs built on wrongs as we were pushed out of the City Imperishable, persecuted and taxed and cursed, only to be sent to the Jade Coast—"

"Some of us by you," someone else whispered.

"—where we were treated as freaks and interlopers, wanted only for our money."

"If you'd kept your wits," Onesiphorous said, "in a generation your fortunes would have bought you seats at the Harbormaster's council table. But you were fighting even before the corsairs came."

"Some of us allowed ourselves to be used," said a voice bitterly.

Onesiphorous looked around to see many of the sleepers had awoken. A larger circle had drawn close.

"I have said too much already," he told them. "And perhaps certain wounds will not heal. But we must do this thing together. If not in agreement, at least in amity. If the boxes are to be broken, let us be sure we know what we do and why. If not, let us understand that as well. I am tired of the politics. Let us be dwarfs together."

They argued much farther into the night, in the manner of dwarfs. Onesiphorous finally fell asleep under the food table, next to the snoring sailor.

IMAGO

Dawn brought light to a city under siege. Wasps covered the City Imperishable in great clouds. Messages had stopped coming, as it had become too dangerous to brave the streets even with the poppies.

His skin itched.

Now Imago looked out his window toward the Limerock Palace. The small wasps were gathered in low places like dark, glittering fog. The giants flew higher up, with an occasional struggling figure in their mandibles. People had tried to combat them with fire, and entire blocks now burned out of control. It was a war they had not meant to fight.

Marelle came into his office. "I know more," she said. "But it's not making sense yet."

"Another day or two of this and nothing will matter," Imago told her. "There's not a tree left standing in the City. They've begun to go after wooden structures. What the wasps do not destroy, people have set fire to in their panic."

"The insects burn and die, as well."

"In their numbers, it does not matter." He had to change the subject before he drove himself to despair. "What have you learned?"

She took a deep breath. "The Numbers Men told Bijaz that he is the City's luck. Luck runs both ways. In a sense, it can be said to balance as an account book should. You sent him away—" Marelle held out her hand, forestalling his interruption. "You were not wrong. The Northern Expedition was a great challenge. From what Bijaz has said, none of them would have made it back but for him."

"Fair enough." Imago did not feel very fair at all. Something exploded down by the docks. He watched flames climb as she continued to speak.

"As I was saying, you sent him away. Think of that as a roll of the dice, casting your bet northward. He unleashed something in the North that the Imperator Terminus apparently went to great pains to bind there, very far away from his beloved City Imperishable. The Eater of Forests."

"How is this our luck?" He leaned his head against the window frame. "Unless we are just the fleas on the stone dog that is the City Imperishable. What is a city, without people?"

"Maybe this is the City's luck."

"*How?*" Imago whirled, stomping across what little open floor remained in his office. "I am out of men, out of time, out of ideas. That toad Wedgeburr still sits in the Burgesses plotting my ruin. The City is being killed around me, stripped and burned like a bull carcass at a harvest festival to leave nothing but ash and empty, blackened streets."

She gave him a level look. "We are a long way from defeat."

"Then this is a war," Imago grumbled. "Killing my folk. I do not know who to fight or how, except to waste bullets shooting at wasps."

"We have more than war here," she told him. "We have history. The Alates claim to be part of that. I don't know what they mean, but, think, Imago. Even *I* am history. A librarian who's lived as long as I have? I've spent centuries hiding in alleys and ladling stew from potshop fires just to get by. Yet when the City needed me, here I was. With my archives at the ready all those years in the Footsoldiers' Guild Hall. Is this simple happenstance?"

"You are history," Imago said slowly. "This city saved you, just like it saved Bijaz. Against future need." He jammed his hands into his armpits at a wave of remembered pain. "I know how that works. The City saved me once, too, and made me its own. I have my hard-won expertise." He chased the idea. "So if Bijaz is war, the luck of the blade and bullet, and you are history, the mother of law and justice, then Jason with his greening of sewers and the fir tree amid the Bridge of Chances was just the thing the City needed to fight the Eater of Forests.

"*And I sent him away!*"

He could have cried for sheer frustration. The wrong moves, the guesses, the harassment from the Limerock Palace which distracted him over and over and over. "I sent him away," he said slowly. "Our fertility god, the one who could restore the green and growing things of our City and stand firmly against the intramothers."

"Perhaps," she said. "Or perhaps the wasps don't need to be stood firm against."

He continued to stare out the window. The mix of smoky haze and glittering lines of wasps was almost pretty.

Were they searching for something? Even through the glass of his window, he could hear the buzzing of the billion wings that now controlled his streets.

It was time to go down to the Old Gods. Finish his sacrifice. They were the soul of the City Imperishable.

His scars flared at the thought, so that he stumbled. "I am going to send for Saltfingers. In case you are wrong."

"If you wake them, they will take you," she warned.

They both already knew that. Imago leaned close, kissed the pale dwarfess. "Live more," he said. "Whether or not I come back."

"Imago." Her voice was pleading. "Not yet. Please."

Something else burst into flames outside, close enough for them to hear a whoosh. "I cannot wait." His mind was made up in full. Sometimes the king was a sacrifice, blood in the soil to raise up another generation. "Send a runner after me if the situation improves."

They both knew that was a hollow order. No one would be able to find him in this chaos.

Toiling slowly down the stairs, Imago asked himself why he'd dismissed the Card King's plan to address their problems with another staging of a krewe trial. Here he was setting out to try the same thing twice over.

Perhaps he was just too tired to learn anything new.

The base of the tower was crowded with sweating, bloody men and horses. Women, dwarfs, and children were packed in as well, and the rugmakers had opened their doors to the refugees.

The wasps would be here soon enough.

Imago pushed his way through until he found Stockwell clinging to a little podium and trying to take a headcount.

"I need Saltfingers." Imago shouted to be heard above the racket.

Stockwell shook his head. He leaned close and cupped his hands to Imago's ear. "Long since departed, sir. There's no one to send, unless you wish me to go after him."

"No, no." Where could he find his way down? The sewers were everywhere, but Imago didn't know the entrances except for the few he'd been shown. None of which were in the immediate vicinity of the Rugmaker's Cupola. He nodded to Stockwell and turned back for the stairs, with the intention of finding a quiet place to plan. Four of the Lord Mayor's Own blocked the way, to keep the refugees from flowing upward.

Stockwell plucked hard at his sleeve. "You can go down through the rugmakers' kitchens," he yelled. "Have one of the Tokhari take you. You want the midden, behind the butchery."

Imago marveled at how his nervous, sweating clerk had grown so much. Anything he could think on, to keep his mind away from the Old Gods.

BIJAZ

He was back in the wheat field. This time the reaper man was nowhere to be seen. The wheat was different, though it still followed a strange oneiric logic. Tiny flowers pushing through the golden grains clustered at the head of each stalk. They looked like poppies, waxy and pale, with a dot of blood welling at the base of each petal.

Bijaz walked among the rows, seeing them differently, too. He was taller. The cowl kept flopping over his eyes, so he pushed it aside, only to find he was carrying a scythe.

Something rippled across the flowering grain. People, he realized, tiny dwarfs and full-men side by side, running from him. He stepped after them, legs long as pine trees now, eating the yards and miles as easily as any wind out of the North, reaching to claim the vermin.

Everything was easier now. He felt stronger this morning. The light was inside his skin, much as when the Numbers Men had first changed everything. Bijaz slid from beneath his blanket and stood.

His legs swayed slightly at first, but otherwise he seemed steady. He was naked. Ribs stood out like ladderwork. His limbs were thin and rope-muscled, all the fat leached away. All his hairs were snow white, from the long hanks down his shoulder to the curled wisps on his arms to the thick thatch around his cock.

Bijaz was youthfully strong again. His shoulders ached and his mouth was dry, but otherwise he felt fit. Not the gleaming, wired health the Numbers Men had visited upon him, but something more honest, earned in a thousand miles of trekking and a season spent under the sun.

Going to the window, he pulled back the drape. The City Imperishable burned. Wasps circled overhead, big as ships. There was not a tree in sight.

He was ready to tear the wings off every wasp in the City. He gathered the blanket around him and found his way into the hall.

A great racket rose from below. Bijaz leaned over the rail. A crowd flowed through the base of the Rugmaker's Cupola and into the complex beyond. It was a controlled movement, people helping people.

He flexed his hand, light stabbing from between his fingers, and followed the curve of the balcony to Imago's office.

The Lord Mayor was not within, but Marelle was. She'd surrounded herself with brown paper, written all over in a dozen inks and colors. It was a map, he realized. A map of her mind. Or the mind of the City Imperishable, if there was a difference.

The only open surface was the window, which showed no more hope than his had.

Marelle looked up. "You're back," she exclaimed, then stopped. "Bijaz?"

"Yes." His voice was thick with the timbre of youth. His hand still glowed. A sword would have fit well in his grip. "Where is the Lord Mayor?"

"He has gone…" Her voice trailed off.

Bijaz could see the light within her, too. "Do not worry about what you see, Marelle. Worry about what you are."

"I am a dwarfess," she said. "A woman. A librarian."

He looked around the room, drawing her gaze with him. "You have written out the thoughts of centuries, mistress. You are discovering history's light within yourself."

Holding out his glowing hand, Bijaz stepped toward her. Marelle reached for him, not even noticing the light which began to stream from her own fingertips.

Outside, cannon fire rippled. The reaper man within him noted it, but Bijaz was too close to the Mistress of History to hear the present.

ONESIPHOROUS

They steamed past the winch tower. Fires burned across the skyline. Enormous wasps cruised above the City Imperishable, vultures over a kill. *Princeps Olivo* had been on alert since spotting the rising smoke, but ever more whistles shrilled now as sailors pounded the deck.

Onesiphorous was at the stern rail once more. The sloop was down to the rails now, bulging like a sack of rotten grain. Whips of lithe wood grew out of holes in the hull, winding around the little vessel or trailing in the water.

The blue jade shard within his shirt felt hot and heavy. He tugged it out, wondering if the stone would perform some ancient magick now.

A wasp buzzed close overhead. Onesiphorous looked up to see a screaming human face embedded in its chest. His spine shivered. Warning? Greeting? Or nothing more than the twitch of a dying dog's feet?

Gunfire erupted from an upper deck. The wasp dipped, staggered in the air, then headed toward the west bank to escape its tormentor. Once the insect had gained distance from *Princeps Olivo*, the cannon opened up.

The wasp vanished in a flash of smoke and pale guts.

A cheer rose from the sailors, but that died off as people tried to count those still circling above the City.

This was the purpose of the journey, right here. Jason had come so far, through such torment. They could not fight the wasps except through whatever purpose he carried in his metastasizing heart.

Onesiphorous turned. "Get him ashore!" he shouted. "Get the sloop ashore, now!"

An officer ran toward him, head low, hands covering his neck. "Princess say you need boat to go to shore." His accent was almost too thick to understand. "You go down on boat, eh?"

"Me?" He would rather have cut off his hand than go near whatever Jason had become.

"We put more steam, cut rope, someone take tiller, drive her to shore." The officer grew agitated. "Must go now."

"You couldn't have thought of this before?" Onesiphorous turned to look at the sloop. As *Princeps Olivo* backed water, the smaller boat's towline went slack. It drifted toward the steamer, but turned on the current as well. Water washed over the rails. The little vessel hadn't quite gone down.

"Down the stern ladder," the officer said. "Please. Now."

Onesiphorous leaned over the rail. Rungs were set into the back of the ship. With a long glance at his burning city, he slipped over the rail and climbed.

"Wait for catch," the officer shouted.

Whatever that meant.

He wished Silver had come to see him off, wished that someone had warned him of this. Going near the monster that was Jason was making his guts water.

He was six rungs down, his feet nearly in the river. The water just below him churned from *Princeps Olivo*'s screws. With a short-long blast of the whistle, the steamer backed harder. The sloop, already closing sideways, rushed toward him. Onesiphorous curled his feet up. He was afraid of being crushed between the hulls. Jason's boat slammed into the steamer's stern about two feet below him, buffered by a long, twisting root that bristled with hairs.

Onesiphorous ignored his terror and let go of the rung to drop to the deck. The sloop drifted away from *Princeps Olivo* as he clung to its rail, the river soaking him.

The boat settled from the roll of its impact with the steamer. Onesiphorous scrambled toward the stern. He climbed over a twisting braid of wooden root-ropes. A bristling knot moved as he passed it, opening to a gray eye which blinked.

Jason's eye. The color it had been in life.

He yelped and nearly tumbled into the River Saltus.

The eye blinked again. Onesiphorous scrambled further aft, struggling to get away. He set his grip on something gelid. The sloop shuddered as he jerked his hand away from another eye, now ruptured and oozing clear fluid.

This time his shriek was a yelp. The Gronegrii officer was shouting something from the rail. *Time*, Onesiphorous told himself. *There is no more time.* He scuttled toward the tiller, ignoring what he saw.

The ship's wheel still stood at the sloop's stern. It spun freely as the boat rode on the current. Onesiphorous nearly broke his wrist grabbing for the wheel. He tried again, reaching for a spoke on the upswing and leaning into the turn, trying to stop it with the weight of his body.

The hull protested. Wood groaned as the wheel slammed Onesiphorous shoulder-first into the deck. So close to the wood, he could see hair growing up between the planks. That gave him another shiver.

He fought the wheel back upright and checked his course. *Princeps Olivo* was pulling away from him again as the tow line's slack picked up. They had already passed the Sturgeon Quay. The Old Lighter Quay was burning. Worse, the sloop pointed wrong way round, her bow toward the west bank, her stern dragging. He forced the wheel to starboard, splinters jammed in his bleeding palms.

The sloop wallowed through a turn. Onesiphorous realized that dozens of gray Jason-eyes blinked at him from knots in the twining roots and hair-filled gaps where the planking bulged. The eyes all stared. They all wept, as well.

"I'm sorry, my friend," he said.

The wheel seemed easier then, or maybe what was left of the sloop's keel had come back across their heading. The steamer's whistle wailed a double long blast, then the towline parted with a resounding snap.

He now drifted free. The Old Lighter Quay was definitely on fire. Beyond it was the paved outlet of the Little Bull River, where it spilled into the River Saltus. The next possibility was Miller's Quay, but without a tow, his speed would be slowed too much by current before he could reach it.

Onesiphorous made for the Little Bull. The river had never been meant for navigation—it lost too much elevation between the east wall and the waterfront—but it had a wide channel to minimize the formation of debris dams during floods. The river's mouth would accept his draft for a few feet, at least.

Cannon fire roared again from *Princeps Olivo*. Onesiphorous had no time to look as the sloop slid between the two riprap points marking the exit of the Little Bull into the River Saltus. He ran the boat under the Water Street Bridge. The hull jammed itself beneath the southern span with a horrendous crush of tortured wood. Onesiphorous tumbled backward off the stern. He sank until the surface was a distant green dot and the curtain of bubbles he'd brought with him vanished.

Clutching his shard of blue jade, he tried to kick upward, but he didn't know where or how. Air was leaving him when strong hands grabbed him to drag him deeper down.

IMAGO

He stumbled through the tunnels beneath the City, utterly lost. He'd found his way down from the kitchens well enough. The path had quickly gone wrong after that. Pursuing a distant lantern, Imago had taken an unexpected turn and lost the light. He knew enough to follow the steam pipes, but when they led him toward a deep buzzing, he turned away only to drop into a lacuna of stagnant water.

On he wandered, hearing occasional screams, and once something that sounded like cannon fire.

He should have been able to find his way down here. He'd walked these very tunnels when he'd taken the City into his blood and bone.

Something began dragging at his feet. Imago reached down in the darkness to find himself ankle-deep in parboiled wasps. He recoiled, nearly losing his balance again, then panicking when he realized what he'd fall into.

The dunny divers had passed this way with one of their steam pistols. He'd thought this a terrible journey when he'd done it under Saltfingers' guidance. Venturing alone seemed impossible.

He followed the flow downhill, knowing that would take him toward the Little Bull. If he could find the deeper, older tunnels there, he could pass beneath. Then he'd be near the New Hill.

Somebody shouted close by. Imago stopped and listened. Dead wasps sloshed around his ankles. The deep thrumming resumed.

"They's building something, your worship," Saltfingers whispered, almost in his ear.

Imago leapt. He bit his tongue to keep from shrieking.

The dunny diver tugged his arm. "The quiet man lives longest," he breathed. "Best be coming with me."

The two of them backed by feel around several corners and through a side tunnel before Saltfingers sparked his helmet light to life. For a moment, Imago was taken back to his first underground journey with the crazed old dwarf.

"Don't go that way," Saltfingers told him. "Not if you wants to return." He gave Imago a long look, pink eyes lost in the shadows of his helmet. "Now what would a hard-working Lord Mayor such as yourself be doing down the sewers this fine day? Not seeking the Old Gods again, I hope. You're a man with more sense than Dorgau lent his pizzle, I'm thinking."

"Dorgau can have his damned pickle," Imago said quietly. "This is the end, Saltfingers."

"I know it's not good, your worship. We sees a lot down here beneath the stones, for all that we're deep in darkness. And them bugs have opened up a well we didn't know was there, between the Nannyback Downflow and the Little Elbows."

On our maps, that's solid bedrock."

"Maps lie."

"Or bugs dig good. Which is my kindly old way of saying that we fight for everyone's life down here, your worship." The old dwarf's voice dropped to a growl. "Which is my not-so-kindly old way of saying that you should find your way back up top and fight you some fires, without having me send a man to escort you to your untimely demise."

"I'm the Lord Mayor here," Imago told him. "You work for me. This decision is mine."

"No, your worship. I don't work for you. I works for the City Imperishable, stone, street, and soul. It's bigger and older than you or me, and it will never know us any more than we knows the fleas in our hair, but still I works for it. And so do you. Now, if you're bent on dying young, I'll give you a helmet and directions as a funerary offering. But you're cracked, begging your pardon. And better you mend that broken head than be off sticking it beneath the stone knives of them best left sleeping."

"Then give me my damned helmet," Imago said, "and let me go on."

Saltfingers took his own off and placed it on Imago's head. "Here you go, pup. Follow the Billgate Bypass, take the second stair you find on the left. Mind the old blades down there, still it'll get you under the Little Bull. On the other side it should look familiar." Imago's light full on his face, the dwarf's complexion was fungus pale. "And luck to you, your worship. I thinks you're wrong, but I can still admire your courage."

"Luck to you," Imago said. "Fight well."

Saltfingers' last words echoed after him. "Die well, you."

Bijaz

Clothed in light, they descended the stairs. War clasped History's hand close, lord and lady arriving at the ball. The floor of the Rugmaker's Cupola cleared rapidly.

He felt bright and shining as the shard of the sun. It was within him now, transforming and transformative. History had her own light. The deeper, more subtle tones of law and justice infused her narrative, the opposite of his uncomplicated purity.

They stepped into the street.

A little man blocked their way. Some part of War vaguely recognized him. History slipped away from Marelle, and she said, "Stockwell. What are you doing?"

"Don't." His voice squeaked. "Whatever it is you're doing, don't. You have to go down to the Water Street Bridge."

The light from War's hand became a sword to strike this Stockwell creature down, but Marelle grabbed his arm. She shrieked at the feel of him.

It was enough to wake Bijaz. He pulled the blow, slashing Stockwell's cheek. The clerk staggered back as the poppy in his collar fell loose. It tumbled to the ground. He raised his hand in protest. A giant wasp snatched him up on a buzz of wings as Stockwell wailed Imago's name.

Bijaz hurled light and fire after the wasp. Marelle grabbed at him again as Stockwell tumbled to the pavement.

"The bridge," she said. "Whatever's missing is there. He *knew*."

They scuttled toward the wounded clerk. Marelle set the crushed poppy on his chest. Stockwell just stared, eyes blank with terror.

"Bless you." Bijaz immediately felt foolish.

"B-b-b-ridge," stuttered Stockwell.

Marelle tugged and they hurried on. Cork Street was empty, gaming parlors shuttered. Only slivers of heartwood remained of the trees in the median park. At the Little Bull they turned on the North Pleasaunce, heading for Water Street.

No one was about but them and the billions of wasps circling above. The giants buzzed higher, occasionally visible in gaps amid the glittering streams of their lessers. There was a pattern to the movement. None of the insects disturbed Bijaz or Marelle. They followed in a spiral, drawing their fellows in, until a storm buzzed above the heads of the two.

"What were we?" Bijaz asked.

Her voice was distorted. "The City Imperishable."

Ahead, they could see a ship jammed beneath one of the arches of the Water Street Bridge. A tree rose, swaying as it climbed skyward like a wooden snake from a stone basket. The wasps flowed around it without settling, a turbulence of chitin and rainbow wings reflecting the tree's mad growth.

Coming near, they saw that it bore fruit—great heavy globes which blinked at them, gray eyes shedding tears like rain upon the broken cobbles.

ONESIPHOROUS

He fell from the water onto a matted mass. Boudin released his wrist. Onesiphorous gasped for air, amazed that he could breathe.

The boy was pale, his skin wrinkled, eyes squeezed shut. Whatever glad words Onesiphorous had died in his mouth.

"The fare can be paid, but the journey is hard, ah."

The voice was the swamp-mother's. Onesiphorous looked around the little cave of roots. Eyes blinked from knots and shadows—the brown eyes of the queen of Angoulême.

Boudin sat corpse-still.

"You are everywhere," Onesiphorous said. "And nowhere."

"We are born, we live, we die. It take longer for some than others, ah."

"Am I here because I paid my fare?"

A laugh echoed with the crinkle of growing roots. It stank in here, the reek of life beneath dark water. The smell of Angoulême.

"Sea King, he don't own no rivers. Angoulême, she lie on the border between the river and the sea. So he come to my door like a brother or a bridegroom. He come to your stone City like a beggar from a distant shore."

"So?" Onesiphorous felt hostile. "This is not my place. My City is dying, I should live or die with it."

"Listen, you. Make a treasure of your anger, little City man. Such flame is difficult to find after too many years. But I not your enemy today."

Onesiphorous sat huddled on the roots. "What, then?"

"Do you know me, Oarsman?"

"You are the queen of Angoulême," he said.

"No. I *am* Angoulême."

"The place."

"The city, little City man. I tell you my tale once. Cities never die, they just become something else. What you think those jade veins are? Life of another city, another race and time."

He opened his hand and showed the blue jade.

"That city much older," she told him. "Name is lost, but not idea. Angoulême lies amid it. Port Defiance stands amid Angoulême."

Onesiphorous looked into the blinking brown eyes. "But you were a person once, weren't you?"

"Once. All living things make more things, ah? Intramothers, they come to make more."

"Jason is growing into another of you."

"No!" she shouted. "He grow to himself. He grow to be his city, if you people not burn him or slay the intramothers or otherhow stop him. That fail, your city fail. One lifetime, maybe another. You seen empty cities, ah? That grow, your city grows."

"Like Angoulême?" he asked, then was immediately sorry.

"Angoulême still here," she said quietly. "Now go."

The roots creaked, opening into a dark, root-lined tunnel. With one long look at Boudin, Onesiphorous stepped into the darkness. He didn't say good-bye.

His steps were small as the seconds that count out a man's dying. He walked through the narrow, damp tunnels of a jade mine, across a swaying metal bridge in a city of high canyons, down a lane paved with ice between walls of falling water, through a granite-floored hall lined with paintings of women with the heads of birds, across a gull-haunted, sun-warmed dockside empty of people where fish rotted in their nets. Tall square towers burned, gray-capped men like mushrooms slunk along fungus-slimed walls, metal carts slithered overhead on high wires, a withered white tree bloomed in an empty courtyard. With every footfall, his body stretched and tightened, shorted and lengthened, became heavy as time and light as the soul's breath.

Onesiphorous walked through the idea of City, knowing that if he missed his step, he'd never go home.

Thought was deed. Between that moment and the next, he found himself in an alcove beneath a broken bridge—the Bridge of Chances, he realized, looking up. Overhead, wasps swarmed in a great circling spiral. Out on the River Saltus, cannon boomed.

He had to stop the firing so this change could finish.

Heedless of the circling clouds of wasps, Onesiphorous scrambled up the rusted iron ladder, gained his footing on the South Pleasaunce, and raced toward to the waterfront.

IMAGO

The Lord Mayor of the City Imperishable stumbled along the moss-slimed ledge of a half-familiar tunnel. Dead wasps glittered in the water beside him, and the occasional bat.

He was lost, replaying his own past. There had to be a better answer. One could not call the Old Gods as if they were servants. He didn't care for what they'd do to him, either.

Imago turned a corner to find another dwarf hunched on the ledge. For a moment he thought it was Saltfingers, 'til he realized this dwarf was naked, and very badly used.

He bent down. "Archer?"

"Aye." Nothing showed in the godmonger's eyes except deeper shadows.

Had that been true when Archer visited his cell?

"They have not let you go."

"They will not let me die." Archer tried to smile. "I sold myself to them years ago, Imago. Do not sorrow for me."

"Can you take me to them now?"

"No. You tread the wrong measure here."

"Saltfingers said much the same."

Archer tugged at his beard. "Do not mistake that dwarf. He has no temple nor regalia, but he is as great a priest as any in the City Imperishable."

"I have seen that in him," Imago admitted. "If you do not like my course, how would you have me set myself?"

"Birth is painful. Even the gods cry out. But you must go to the Limerock Palace and stop them."

"The last time I went there, they murdered my train and imprisoned me," he said. "How shall I stop them, and from what?"

"Go, there is no more time." Archer stood and tugged open a door Imago would have passed by without seeing. "You will know."

"Archer," Imago began, but the godmonger had vanished like a blown candle. The door still stood open.

This was the tunnel which had been dug by Prothro and his cohorts to reach the shattered temples buried beneath the New Hill, Imago realized. Now he followed the route of old conspiracy to stop something new.

What, Imago did not know.

He climbed. This had not been made for the flow of water, so it was narrow. Twenty minutes passed before he came to a ladder. Above him was a trap door set within a wooden floor.

Imago set his helmet down, leaving the little carbide lamp flickering, and climbed. He did not like having the tiny flame behind him, but wearing a dunny diver's helmet into the palace was foolish. Cloaked and booted, he might be just another clerk. With the flame still there, he could see his escape route.

Pushing at the trap, Imago found that something above resisted him. He climbed one more rung to set his shoulder to the effort while still clinging to the ladder. He took a deep breath and pressed again.

It opened far enough for him to see that the door was beneath a rug. He shoved harder, then wriggled his way through. A button popped off his shirt, and he took a nasty scrape across his back.

He struggled free of the rug to a blank-walled room where a few electricks burned over an array of tables. Great vats stood on them, each over a little electrick fire. Bottles stood ranked before every vat. A sick sweetness hung in the air.

Imago grabbed a bottle, opened the door and stepped out confidently. Skulking was an admission of guilt, and the bottle would make it seem as if he had an errand.

The room beyond was a garage. The floor was clear except for a large wagon. Several men in gutta-percha aprons and coated boots used a pump to fill a huge tank on the wagon's back. Two more stood atop the tank to check the fittings on a great nozzle like the water cannon from a fire apparatus. A second wagon waited nearby, a steam engine mounted on it.

He sniffed. More of the same smell. They must be working at poison for the wasps. How to stop it?

Imago turned back and nearly ran into a bailiff.

"My pardons," he said, stepping aside.

It was Imre, his arms full of more coated boots.

"You—" the bailiff began loudly. Imago reached up to touch his finger to the big man's lips.

"This way," he hissed.

Imre followed him into the side chamber.

"What are you doing here?" the bailiff growled.

"Stopping a disaster."

"Don't you have people to do that for you?"

"Not today." He had no time for a decent lie, so he tried the improbable truth. "I was seeking the Old Gods when they told me to come here and stop the Burgesses."

"We've a plan to drive off the wasps," Imre said proudly. "Burgess Norwalk conceived it. We will spray them with a chemical caustic to insects that is also flammable. Once they've begun to flee, we will set them afire."

Imago was aghast. "You'll burn the City down!"

"No, it flares and is gone. Like gunpowder."

"What if the spray falls across roofs or people?"

"The City is already dying, sir."

Imago hated being lectured about his own obsessions. "I know. But we need to leave the wasps alone."

"You're cracked," Imre said. "Come with me now and I won't turn my staff against you."

"You haven't got your staff with you. Even if you did, the last time I was here Wedgeburr tried to have me killed by two squads of your fellow bailiffs."

Imre looked pained. "I'm sorry. He was voted out."

"*Voted out?* He murdered bailiffs and a fellow Burgess. Why isn't he hanging from the rafters?"

"Because too many would lose their position. He has files that will ruin others."

"For that you let him go free?" Imago let the disgust into his voice, hamming it up. Once more he was arguing for life, before a very difficult bench of one slightly slow-witted bailiff. "Listen, Imre. They lie here. They lie to you. They lie to me. They lie to the City Imperishable. They lie to themselves. I don't want to overthrow the Burgesses—what comes next might be worse. But I want them to stop making decisions they don't understand. Starting now. The wasps need to be left alone."

"They've killed hundreds. Including two Burgesses."

"You didn't burn Wedgeburr out when he killed a Burgess."

That stopped Imre. He set the boots down on the floor, taking care to arrange them in pairs. "I have an oath, you know."

Imago exulted. He'd won the argument. Imre only needed the rationalization. "Yes," he said, stealing freely from Saltfingers, "and your oath is to the City Imperishable. Not to one set of greedy men or another, but to the stones and soul of this city. They've lied to you every day. I've never lied to you. Who do you trust to best serve the City's interests?"

He might have aimed over the bailiff's head, but it was the best he could do. The only alternative was to bash Imre with the glass beaker, but Imago did not have much faith in that solution.

"What will you do?" Imre asked.

"I think all we need is to spill their tank. After that, this will end soon one way or the other. The wasps are the near the conclusion of their purpose." He wished he were as confident as he sounded.

Imre's brow furrowed. "I thought you said that—"

"Nothing is certain," Imago added smoothly. "Let's go spill their tank."

"No killing," Imre warned.

"I don't even want to hurt anyone," Imago promised him. *Except Wedgeburr.* Together they walked toward the wagon with the tank. The men in the gutta-percha coats were putting away their pumps. A groom harnessed a pair of draft horses into place.

Imago hurried to match the bailiff's stride. One of the coated men strode to meet them. "Stop him," said Imago, and pulled himself up onto the wagon board. A large lever served as a handbrake. He released it. A spring groaned somewhere below him.

"Hey," the groom shouted, as Imre turned to the coated man. Imago slapped the reins and pulled the draft horses to the right, intending to make for the outside doors.

Unfortunately another groom was alert and began rolling them shut. Imago slapped the reins harder and circled toward the back of the garage. A hallway led out, too small for the wagon. He glanced over his shoulder. A pair of men struggled with Imre, while five or six more chased the wagon.

He had seconds at best.

No choice but to spill it, Imago thought. He urged the horses toward the hallway. They were not having it, and began to turn once more.

Imago leaned on the brake. The wagon shuddered, its altered momentum challenging the strength of the horses until the traces snapped.

The horses screamed, one tangled in the harness while the other broke free. Imago tried to jump away from the swaying wagon, but the top-heavy weight of the tank took it sideways and him with it.

He smacked hard into the wall but avoided being crushed. The tank burst, spraying Imago with a flood of stinking wasp killer. Most surged the other way, through the open door into the workroom where he'd come up.

Where there was a trapdoor in the floor, with a lit carbide lamp beneath.

Imago began scrambling backward, mouthing a meaningless jumble of oath, prayer, and terminal panic.

BIJAZ

Someone on the river was firing cannon at the tree. The trunk swayed as great sprays of splinters erupted. The eyes blinked away tears of blood. Circling wasps dove on the wounds, then streamed back toward the river.

"Now what?" Bijaz screamed at Marelle. Whatever he had been, minutes before—War?—was gone. He was once more a frightened, angry dwarf.

She cupped her hands to his ear. "If you are War, and I am History, then he is the blooming spring which feeds the City! Fertility."

Ulliaa's memories leapt unbidden to Bijaz's mind. *This* had been the ice bear's game all along, that the Northmen had followed along with in hopes of controlling. Iistaa had aimed to bring about the death shout of a city.

And the birth cry, perhaps unknowing.

For good or ill, the die was cast. Bijaz tugged at Marelle to follow as he began to run toward the erupting trunk.

Another cannon volley whistled overhead, several shells striking close by to shower them with sap, blood, and splinters. Bijaz climbed up a gnarled knee next to a blinking, weeping eye.

It focused on Marelle as she clambered up beside him. "We are here," he whispered.

The eye blinked again. A steam whistle shrieked out on the river, the noise rising higher and higher. Bijaz realized that whatever ship had been firing must have a ruptured boiler.

The sky lit with a yellow-white glare as an explosion erupted to the south, sound rolling past them like thunder. It had barely died when the shrieking boiler blew. Bijaz turned to see a ship lifting from the water, back broken. Another blast ripped it apart while still in the air.

Gunpowder? he wondered, distracted from the moment. Flaming shards began to fall from two directions.

ONESIPHOROUS

He vaulted up onto the bridge to see two dwarfs clinging to the swaying tree. It had become sky-tall, branches spreading out to cover most of the City, leaves like green hands each the size of a garden. Eyes blinked in their thousand from the ramified, hairy trunk as burning bits fell in a rain of fire.

He scrambled up to the dwarfs. "By the gods!" Onesiphorous shouted when he realized who he was seeing, "You're alive!"

"You're dead," Marelle told him, reaching to swat out a fire in his hair.

Bijaz just smiled, benevolent and divine.

Onesiphorous brandished the blue jade in his fist. It *was* a key. Angoulême had shown him that. He slipped the lump of rock between two of the rippled tendons of Jason's trunk.

The wood parted like flesh, opening a familiar, hairy passage. "Go," Onesiphorous shouted.

Marelle passed within.

Bijaz looked at Onesiphorous a moment, then said, "Every beginning is an end, every end is a beginning." He followed her into darkness. The tunnel snapped shut before Onesiphorous could take his own step forward.

A long, quiet moment stretched, then the City Imperishable shook as if in the grip of an earthquake. The impossibly high tree began to sway. Winged creatures circled it—giant wasps, mountain teratornis, Alates, bats, clouds of the small wasps—all darting in and out of the shivering foliage.

Onesiphorous stumbled back to sit down heavily on the pavement of Water Street. The bridge was gone, swallowed by the massive trunk. A city block to the south was missing as well, while roots extended into the river.

When the tree fell, it came down not like a forest giant, but the way the queen of Angoulême had swallowed herself. The trunk folded like a sleeve being rolled from within, sucking itself into the stones. Most of the fliers were trapped in the clutching branches. Onesiphorous clung to the post of a gas lamp, trying to keep himself from being pulled down as well.

Behind him, the City Imperishable shouted.

There was no other word for it.

Buildings hurled upwards in a silent explosion, people and animals and furnishings and an entire burning forge shooting into the sky. The tree vanished in that moment.

A gossamer bubble rose from the shout, barely more visible than the air around it. Onesiphorous' thoughts slowed to sludge. Within were mists, the ghosts of streets and buildings and bridges, all the cities he'd passed through to return from Angoulême, and none of them. It was the dream of a city, the idea of a city, the ghost of a city.

The egg of a city, he finally realized.

The City Imperishable had given birth. Its progeny would ride the wind, he supposed, until it found a promising riverbend in the river or verdant forest, and settle there to wait for history to begin anew.

The casualties of that birth plummeted to the earth. Onesiphorous rolled into the gutter and tucked himself tight, covering his neck until the shattering stopped.

When he sat up again, an Alate stood beside him.

"History," it said in a strange voice, narrow and thin. "Your gift out of the North, though they sought to slay you in the giving. Your gods have defended their own. Most of you will forget, but the City will remember."

He reached out a hand, intending to offer it his shard of blue jade, but the key was gone. Bijaz or Marelle must have taken it into Jason.

"I think we have fifteen Old Gods now instead of twelve," he told the Alate.

"Be more careful next time." The bird-man leapt into the air.

The sun was out. The wasps were gone, though fires still raged across the City Imperishable. There were dead to be counted.

At least he understood, a little. This was a cycle of life writ across centuries and leagues. He wondered if the whole affair of the Imperator Restored had been an abortive attempt at blossoming.

Trial of Flowers, indeed.

Someone climbed up the rubble of the Water Street Bridge toward him. They'd come out the Little Bull, skin soot-black and burn-pink, tattered clothing soaked with Saltus mud.

"Oarsman," she said. He realized this was Silver. "I am here. Where is Enero?"

IMAGO

He didn't recognize the hand which reached through the stones for him, but he took it. Imago fell down a narrow hole even as his boots were singed.

"You not worth it, ah," said a crabby old woman in a very old dress, "but he love you. He not so bad for a little City man." Then she pushed him again, until he found himself staring up at Saltfingers.

"Changed our mind, did we, your worship?"

Imago noticed that the other dwarf had gotten a new helmet.

"It seems so," he said. "What just happened to me?"

"I'm not one to be speaking overmuch on the business of others, but there's tunnels and then there's *tunnels*, if you takes my meaning."

"No." Imago sat up and rubbed the soot from his face. "Actually, I don't."

"Then that's too bad, I'm supposing. Just remember that all cities are one and you'll be well." Saltfingers cocked his head to the sound of a clanging pipe. "And it appears that some fool has blown a great big hole in the Limerock Palace, as well as tearing up our streets something fierce."

"The wasps—" Imago began.

"What's done is gone. I'd say you played your part, your worship. I'll just have Wet Hernan nip you back over to the Rugmaker's Cupola now. I expect your work is finished here."

"Saltfingers." He tried to frame his next thought. "If you see Archer…"

"That'n's dead and lost to us." Saltfingers' face closed tight as the stones of his underground kingdom. "Let him rest. But if I sees him, I'll give him whatever comfort is mine to offer."

"That's all I can ask," Imago said.

"Go tend to your duties, and I'll tend to mine." Saltfingers gave him a gentle shove. "Now away with you."

IV
HARVEST

IMAGO

"They've found a dead bear, sir."

He looked up from a letter sent by a very angry dwarf in Port Defiance, named Ikaré. "What? Where?"

The new clerk filling in for the injured Stockwell bobbed up and down, excited. "A great huge dead bear, washed up against the wreckage of that Gronegrii ship." He handed Imago an envelope. "These were in his mouth."

"Thank you." Imago had grown accustomed to Stockwell, by the nine brass hells. The man should be back soon enough according to the Tribade doctor.

Imago tore open the envelope. Three bells, fire blackened and deformed, dropped into his hand. He laid them out with the intent to crush them, then swept them into his desk drawer instead.

Onesiphorous was back on the job, but seemed to be suffering from permanent distraction. That pestilential female Sunward naval officer was nursing DeNardo the freerider night and day. She alternated between threats of execution and elevation to Gronegrii lordship against anyone who tried to help her. Biggest Sister continued to think the man would recover.

Worse, the Sunward woman had demanded to open graves at the Potter's Field until she'd found Enero for herself. Only Onesiphorous had been able to talk her out of that. The two of them continued to make long visits to speak with the dirt.

He wished Kalliope would turn up. An excruciatingly polite but well-armed delegation of Tokhari elders had been waiting three days to see him, camped right next door in the Rugmakers' Guild complex. At the same time, he wished Ashkoliiz would vanish. The lynch mob would have numbered in the thousands had Imago freed her to walk down the street. But no one was willing to speak formally against her; or for her, for that matter. DeNardo refused to discuss it, while the last of the Northmen had died in his room, a strangled rat in his hand.

All in all, Imago thought, *business as usual.*

The evening bell rang, deafening him briefly as always. Within moments, the rest of the peal was picked up around the City. He went to the window and looked south.

The Limerock Palace was already being rebuilt. So far as he knew, Wedgeburr was still in there somewhere. Imago had sent a hundred gold obols as death geld to Imre's family. They turned out to be a very surprised mother and pair of sisters in a tiny apartment near Fish Trap Lane, apparently supported on Imre's modest salary.

Meanwhile, dwarfs were coming back up the river from Port Defiance in greater numbers, bringing their money and their heads for business with them. One of Onesiphorous' little distractions was his continuing involvement in a dwarfen colloquium in permanent session at the old Footsoldiers' Guild Hall.

The last miracle was that every shattered stump for miles around had sprouted a tall, strong sapling when the Jason-tree had vanished down into the ground. War, History, and Fertility had infused the City Imperishable, or so Onesiphorous had tried to explain to him. Most people didn't seem to know the difference, which Imago found profoundly disturbing.

A cannon shot echoed faintly through the glass of his window.

Imago cursed. He shouldn't even have turned a thought to war. He stared at the river.

Three big steamships, each with guns out and elevated, appeared around Dragoman Point.

Imago yelled for his clerk, yelled for Onesiphorous, yelled for that dreadful woman naval officer.

He leaned against the window while he waited, wondering with aching heart if he would ever see Marelle again.

"The City is," he whispered. On this day, no one answered.

Night Shade Books Is an Independent Publisher of Quality SF, Fantasy and Horror

ISBN 978-1-59780-097-6, Trade Paperback; $13.95

Six months have passed since the end of the world, leaving a handful of survivors holed up in a Welsh manor with little to do but survive. They've made the best of things, planting food, drinking their way through the cellar's wine and ale, and reminiscing about the way life used to be. But with supplies running thin, everything is about to change...The arrival of a stranger named Michael sheds new light on their circumstances. If the survivors can reach Cornwall, a few days' journey south, they will find a safe haven, called Bar None, quite possibly the last bar on earth.

From Tim Lebbon, author of *Berserk, Dusk, and Dawn* comes *Bar None*, a novel of chilling suspense, apocalyptic beauty, and fine ales.